Death (

This edition first published 2017 by Fahrenheit Press

10 9 8 7 6 5 4 3 2 1

www.Fahrenheit-Press.com

F 4 E

Death Of A Devil

By

Derek Farrell

The Danny Bird Mysteries

Fahrenheit Press

For Veronica Scott.
A strong, proud and brave woman, who I loved, and who loved me.
I wouldn't be here today without her, and neither, I suspect, would
Danny.

And for Helen Cadbury.
Who welcomed me to the fraternity with open arms, a cheeky smile and
an off-colour joke. Her generosity of spirit and of talent will stay with
me ever.

And for Michael Hardman,
Who was always a wonderfully generous host, an oasis of calm, and a
true friend, and who – I hope – will forgive me for moving a gangster
into his home. Miss you, Mr H.

And also, as always, for my father, with all my love.

"Now I know the things I know,
And do the things I do;
And if you do not like me so,
To hell, my love, with you!"
-Dorothy Parker

ONE

Ali gestured across the packed bar. "I'm cutting off Carmen Miranda," she stated, turning her attention to the twin barmen working beside her. "She's shitfaced. If she makes it back to the bar alive, you two are serving her nothing stronger than Ribena."

Dash squinted into the heaving throng. "She looks alright to me," he said, frowning in his attempt to spot whatever it was that his hugely more-experienced manager had seen.

"Dash, she's just pulled one of the apples off her hat and tried to eat it," Ali said, and as the realisation dawned that the apple in question was plastic, Dash's confusion eased.

"Everything alright here?" I asked, shrugging my cape to one side.

Ali turned, smirked, said, "We're managing, thanks, Little Lord Fauntleroy," and – before I could explain that, actually, my costume was Dracula – scuttled off to the other side of the bar to serve the three witches from Macbeth.

"*She knows*," Caz said, coming up behind me. "She knows *exactly* who you are."

My best friend had come dressed as Elsa Lancaster in *The Bride of Frankenstein*, her wig towering a good two feet above her immaculately made-up face. She eyed me up and down once more, reached out to adjust my cape, and smiled, pleased with her work. "It's perfect, my Prince of Darkness. Now, go and mingle."

The Marquess of Queensbury public house had been

under my management for a little less than a year, and tonight we were celebrating with what I'd feared we might optimistically have declared *The First Annual Halloween at The Marq.*

The posters had been up around the neighbourhood for a month, and the website that Dash's twin brother Ray had built for us was a carnival of virtual cobwebs and coffins. But I'd been worried. "Are people really going to dress in costume and come to the pub?" I had wondered aloud, receiving, for my concern, a pitying glance from Caz.

"*It's a gay bar, Daniel.* People have been dressing up to go to *them* since the dawn of time. And it doesn't have to be Halloween either. Relax, sweetest. If you build it – and festoon it in pumpkins, candlewax and fake webbing – they will come."

And they had.

The room was heaving, and I mentally calculated that I might, after all, be able to make enough money tonight to pay Chopper Falzone his entire month's cut.

Chopper was the local gangster. He ran every chop shop, knocking shop and pound shop in the neighbourhood, and virtually every pub too. Although I was technically running this boozer, it was on his say-so, and the cost of his say-so was a defined pay-out every month, regardless of whether I'd made enough to cover it or not.

But tonight, as I ventured out into the crowd to smile and glad-hand the punters, my money worries were – for once – abated.

I passed two young men, one dressed in a cowl and skeleton mask, his scythe propped at the bar, while the other was dragged up as a not entirely unconvincing schoolgirl, a sulky pout in place. It took me a moment to realise: *Death and the Maiden.*

"Well Larry didn't get it," the Maiden was saying, at which point Death heaved a heavy sigh.

"But sweetheart," Death drawled, "Larry's so stupid it's a miracle he can breathe unaided. I mean, he thinks *dog grooming* is when a paedo says he's got puppies in the van."

Moving on through the crowd, I passed a couple of Kardashians, a Frankenstein with scarily-realistic bolts, a gaggle of zombies, another Dracula (not so convincing as mine, I thought, and remained smug until I was several feet from him and realised he was actually a Quentin Crisp) and a tall broad man wearing a leather peaked cap, a leather-studded harness that framed hugely-extended nipples pierced with what looked like a pair of curtain rings, a red leather codpiece, black leather chaps and biker boots that gleamed even in the dim light of the pub.

The odd thing was his companion, who was being dragged on a lead through the crowd.

"I mean, for chrissakes, Colin, what were you thinking?"

Colin, who seemed to be dressed as a rather short and depressed King Kong shrugged his shoulders, and the black fake fur gorilla suit he was wearing jiggled appropriately. "I couldn't really hear you," he explained through his monkey mask. "I mean, I did think it was odd."

"*Odd?*" The leather queen stopped, turned to the hapless Colin and opened and shut his mouth as though he were trying – and failing – to find the words to express his outrage at Colin's stupidity. "Odd? Colin, you're dressed as a fucking monkey. Who comes to a gay bar on Halloween dressed as a fucking monkey?"

"Well it was a bad line, Chris," Colin attempted, once again, to justify his costume choice. "I thought you said, 'Get a Chimp suit.'"

"*Gimp*, Colin. I said, '*Get a Gimp suit.*' Christ almighty," Chris tugged on the lead and led his simian companion towards the bar. "My mother was right. I need a fucking drink."

I watched them go, and at that moment Caz sidled up to me. "They're heeeere," she sing-songed in my ear, much as the unfortunate child in *Poltergeist* had done all those years ago.

Except that poor cursed child had only been announcing

the arrival of ghosts and demons from the nether world, and the opening of the hell mouth.

Caz was announcing worse. Much worse.

TWO

When the local council's health officer – the man designated with the authority to decide which places offering entertainment and especially catering facilities should be allowed to remain open, and which should be closed on account of the fact they're basically salmonella factories – asks if it would be okay if he and some of his 'like-minded' friends visited your establishment on a particular Saturday night to take part in, 'Something we like to do when we get together,' one doesn't really like to say no.

And when the venue in question is a rough gay boozer, one assumes that the public servant is simply trying to rustle up a private booth and a complimentary bottle of prosecco so he and his mates can get mildly drunk before retiring to a Holiday Inn for a night of no-holds-barred health-officer-on-clerical-assistant action.

But no, that wasn't what Mr Tavistock had had in mind at all.

What he'd really wanted was to bring a bunch of his mates round my pub on one of the busiest nights of my year, and look for ghosts.

Ghosts.

The gang were some sort of spirit hunting team. "We're quite well-known in South East Ghost-Hunting circles," Tavistock had said, which had made me wonder just how big the South East Ghost-Hunting circle actually was.

I mean: Was there a whole subculture of spook spotters I'd been unaware of? Were they hanging around like the illuminati in cagoules waiting for the appearance of a wisp of smoke that might signal the arrival of Anne Boleyn? Had I been missing out on something?

I, of course, wanted to tell him that no, it would not, sadly, be possible for he and his spirit-stalking mates to trawl through my gaff in search of the wandering souls of the Kray Twins.

Ali had been happy to go one step further: "Tell him to fuck off. Fucking weirdo. As if we haven't got enough to deal with, without the bloody Ghostbusters crawling all over the sodding place."

Then I'd remembered that the Krays had been active in East, not South, London and that the man in question could visit – and close me down – at any time.

And the same day, the chest freezer in the kitchen – a huge deep box that had been in situ so long that the once white plastic casing had faded to a yellow-beige redolent of the varnish on an old master painting – had started to make a funny noise.

It was like a high-pitched whine at first but, over a couple of hours, the whine had turned into a constant steady clatter, as though something inside was desperately banging to be let out.

"It's a bit Edgar Allen Poe," Caz had noted on arriving to be greeted by the news that the freezer was on the fritz.

"Death rattle," Ali had pontificated, nodding from the other side of the kitchen at the white good in the same way that an ICU visitor might nod sadly at, say, a vague acquaintance with a bad case of Ebola. "That freezer," she intoned sonorously, "is fucked." And so saying, she'd left us to return to her place behind the bar.

I'd taken that moment to inform Caz of Tavistock's request that I provide the venue for his Halloween Spooktacular

"You're turning him down, obviously," Caz had said,

taking two Waterford Crystal champagne flutes from her handbag, setting them on the table and reaching back in to the bag to extract a magnum of Veuve.

"What?" She frowned at my look of disbelief. This, even for Caz, was somewhat extreme. "I won the residents' association raffle."

"Jesus," I shook my head. "Where I grew up, if you won the residents' association raffle, you got a joint of beef."

"Ah, but you didn't live in the Fulham-Chelsea borders," she responded, expertly uncorking the bottle so that only the merest hint of a sigh escaped.

"So," she turned back to me and offered me a glass, "how exactly are you going to tell Gollum to sling his proverbial?"

"Well that's the thing," I said. "I'm not. Not now."

Caz, the glass halfway to her mouth, froze, blinked like someone who's just been told that their Gainsborough painting was actually knocked up in a garage in Dagenham last week, and, having finally processed my answer, swigged the glass down in one.

"Are you out of your mind?" she asked, topping the glass back up.

"No," I sighed, "but I am out of money."

"Ah," a flicker of understanding blazed briefly behind her eyes, "and he's offered to pay. How much?"

My friend was nothing if not focussed. Caz has always had a heart of gold, but – as she once said to me – a heart of gold without the cash to back it up is as much use as a title from the Holy Roman Empire.

Sadly, she was as skint as me most of the time.

"He's not," I answered glumly. "Well, that is, he hasn't offered to."

"So what's the state of your finances got to do with the proposed visit from The Undead Inspectors?"

"That." I nodded at the freezer, which, at that very moment let out a burp and went silent.

Caz and I looked at each other. "Do you," she whispered

in tones which suggested she'd read a few too many Stephen King novels in her day, "think it's dead?"

And, in answer, the freezer clicked and began to make the high-pitched whine again.

"Thing is," I answered, "I've got no money to fix that."

"So?" she asked, topping us both up, dipping into her bag and extracting a selection of Fortnum pâtés and a demi baguette. "Help me out here, Daniel, because you're making about as much sense as the lovely Ali on a bad day. Is it Stockhausen syndrome?"

"Stockholm," I corrected her, thus adding to her confusion.

"You need the money to go to Sweden? Ah," she nodded sagely, "is there a man involved. Only ever since you and the pretty policeman broke up…"

"No," I shook my head, waved aside her offer of a Brussels pâté on baguette, "I'm not going to Sweden. That's the syndrome you were getting at; and there is no man; and Nick and I have not broken up. We're just…" I paused, searching for the right word, and failed, "we're just on a break."

"I see," she said through a spray of crumbs, then she nodded, swallowed her pâté, washed it down with fizz and gave me the gimlet stare that Caz always used on me whenever she felt I wasn't being entirely true with myself. "Not broken up. Just on a break. Seriously, Daniel – what *is* actually occurring with you and Nick?"

"Nothing," I answered her, as the freezer began moaning like a warped Enya record on the wrong speed. "We're good," I said, "we talk from time to time, we might go for a drink next week, or the week after."

"Lord," Caz drawled, "you're basically a middle-aged straight couple. Only duller. Life, Daniel, is passing. I mean, you do know that, right?"

I sighed. "Yes, Caroline, I do know that."

"So how do you feel about him?"

"Feel?" I was puzzled.

"Yes, feel. I know I've spent my life repressing all my feelings, but that doesn't mean I am completely unaware of them. Or of how important they are to the lower orders. So: How. Do. You. Feel. About. Him?"

I shrugged. "I really don't know."

"Not good enough," she answered. "Not at all good enough. When you think of him, what's the first thing you think of?"

"His smile," I said instantly. "It's just – when he smiles it's like his whole body smiles. Like he finds all the joy in the world at that exact moment, and just amplifies it."

"Oh dear," Caz hoisted the bottle and filled our two glasses to the brim. "You've got it bad, haven't you?"

"It's—" I searched for the word.

"If you say 'complicated,' I shall brain you, Mr Bird," Caz said.

"Difficult," I settled. "Nick's married."

"It's a marriage of convenience," she replied. "One he entered for genuinely altruistic reasons."

"It's a sham marriage to a woman who would – otherwise – be an illegal immigrant. And he's a copper. The whole thing is a mess, and one that could lose him his job – and get him charged with breaking the law – if it gets discovered. And, as if that weren't enough, the immigration mob are now sniffing around them looking for a crack in the story."

"So he keeps the façade going a little longer, and then – when everything's sorted and wifey can safely move on, on her own – they get a nice clean divorce, and he moves you in."

I shook my head ruefully. "Caz, if I take that approach, I get to be a guilty secret in the background – someone to be shamefully shuffled in and out of back doors. And I don't think I can do that."

"Oh sweetest," she refilled our glasses, toasting me, "you're only a guilty secret if he – or you – feels guilt. Otherwise, you're doing what people the whole world over do every day. People with less idealism but more pragmatism than you – you're living your life; making the best of an imperfect situation. There's no guilt, no shame in that. And I'll tell you one other thing, Mr Nick Fisher – the pretty policeman, whose smile lights up his whole body and makes you – even in the remembering – light up, *loves* you, Mr Bird. Don't let idealism stop you loving him back."

I stared at her open-mouthed. "When did you get so good at reading me?" I asked.

Caz smiled at me like a mother smiling at a slightly slow child. "Sweetest, you're basically *The Ladybird book of Lovelorn Gay Best Friends*. I just try most of the time to avoid pointing out what a shambles you are emotionally. Glasshouses and all that, innit," she said, making 'innit' sound like something Shakespearean, before winking at me and pecking me on the cheek.

The room was suddenly rent with a loud banging again as though Lenora herself was trying to bust her way out of her coffin, and Caz let out a small shriek, splashed a little champagne on her blouse, shot the freezer a filthy look (the waste of good champagne being about the only sin Caz could simply not accept), and, as she dabbed at the spot on her Westwood, jerked her head at the offending item of kitchen furniture.

"So what has this got to do with you letting Tavistock and his pals in here?"

"Because," I said, "if Tavistock comes here unannounced, on – say – an official visit, and finds out my chest freezer is on the fritz, I will be shut down. Inability to chill prepared foods, or to keep frozen ingredients at a safe and consistent temperature. No more 'Kitchen at The Marq.'"

"Ah." The light dawned. "Whereas if we invite him in, we can more easily manage where he goes and what he sees."

"Exactly," I said. "So long as he doesn't sense the spirits of the dearly departed in that bloody thing."

"Okay," Caz nodded, satisfied now that I'd explained my rationale, "so, how many of them are there, and how do we keep them out of hearing range of that thing?"

"That," I said slathering pâté on a chunk of bread, "is something I have yet to figure out."

THREE

I followed Caz's eyes across the bar, past a frighteningly detailed attempt at a Creature from the Black Lagoon, a couple of bearded nuns wearing miniskirts and enough doctors and nurses of every description to staff an A&E on a Friday night (though I doubted whether the Hippocratic Oath encouraged the physicals that some of them were delivering).

Standing in the doorway, looking for all the world like a selection of Victorian spinsters who'd been set down in Bedlam on Bang-your-neighbour-Friday, were Mr Tavistock and – I assumed – his band of ghost hunters.

"Mr Tavistock!" I pushed my way through the crowd, a smile of what I hoped looked like welcoming plastered on my mug, and reached out my hand to shake his, which caused him to recoil as though I'd held a live asp out to him.

Then I realised I was in costume, and I assumed he'd not recognised me.

"It's me," I slipped my plastic fangs out and smiled directly into his face as what can only be described as a collection of voles in macintoshes of various shades of beige huddled behind him in varying degrees of catatonia.

"I know who it is, Mr Bird," he answered, peering into my face with eyes made almost comically mole-like by the thick lenses of his huge horn-rimmed glasses, "but I'm puzzled as to what on earth is going on here!"

I, too, was puzzled; but by his obvious confusion. "It's Hallowe'en," I explained, waving a hand which got entangled in a passing mummy's shroud, and had a pissed-up Ramesses II telling me to, 'Watch where you're waving your fucking hands, you moron,' before he fell over and had to be hauled to his feet and becalmed by two passing male nurses and a woman who seemed to be dressed as a cello.

"I am fully aware," Tavistock said through clenched teeth, "of the date. I thought we were to have the pub for a psychic investigation."

And then it dawned on me: Tavistock and his mates thought I was actually going to shut the place, and leave it entirely at their disposal.

"Well, you see," I explained, "this is a really big night in the trade. I'm sure we can do a bit of investigating in some of the less public areas," I finished lamely as he continued to stare at me like a furious mole. "Why don't you come through to my flat and we can talk."

I ushered them into the pub, the two women and one man behind Tavistock behaving the way Caz would if, for example, I waved her into the middle of the opening day of the January sales. At Primark.

Speaking of which, halfway across the pub, as I attempted to simultaneously herd the pack of increasingly concerned loons and clear a way through my increasingly inebriated punters, Caz caught up with us, attempted to greet Tavistock, was met with the same look of horror, and, taking her cue from me, suggested we go upstairs to the flat.

By this time, we were behind the bar.

"The flat?" Tavistock asked. "Surely the kitchen would be better. Kitchens are a great place to listen for knockings from beyond the ether."

Caz looked at me. I shook my head. Ali sidled up, sniggered at the phrase, 'knockings from beyond the ether,' and asked the assembled what they were having.

"A difficult time breathing," said the other man in the group – a man with a body so impossibly obese and legs so stick-thin that I wondered if he was actually wearing a fat suit.

"All the better reason," Caz announced, leaping on the emphysematic wheezing of the red-faced man with a shock of unruly dark hair, "to go upstairs. It's warmer in the flat. Give you all time to settle down and collect yourselves."

"She does have a point, Thomas," a tall, stick-thin woman – her blonde hair hanging in limp greasy curtains either side of a long pale face – said, casting a concerned eye towards the other side of the bar, as though the regulars might, at any minute, chorus, as one, *Braaaaaains*, and lurch at her.

Tavistock shrugged his acquiescence, but Ali – sensing four possible sales slipping through her fingers, tried again, putting her most genial smile on and forgetting, again, the fact that both Caz and I had told her that smiles worked best when they reached the eyes too.

We're here to help you have a great time, her curved lips said, while her squinted eyes chorused, *buy a drink you miserable fucks*.

"Tea," Tavistock finally announced, as though giving instructions to a Victorian parlourmaid.

Ali's smile faltered, burst into flames and went down quicker than the Hindenburg when the two women asked not only for tea but – in the case of the mousy woman with the moustache and the big ears – specified, "Earl Grey, no milk, but lemon if you have it."

Not even the decision by the obese midget staring raptly up at the ceiling that he'd have a half of lager helped and – as I led the group out of the bar and towards the stairs up to the flat – I could distinctly hear Ali banging cups on the bar and loudly commenting on how she'd clearly not realised this was, "A fucking Lyons corner house."

Between us, Caz and I herded the five up the stairs and into the tiny space which served as my sitting room. A sofa, a couple of club armchairs, a small TV and a coffee table, I realised a little too late, filled the space so completely that there was barely room for us all to squeeze in, and the enclosed space seemed to make the fat man's wheezing more pronounced, so that it sounded like we were in a TARDIS taking off.

Tavistock peered suspiciously around the room and made noises that suggested it was far too small. In order to distract him from the reintroduction of his proposal that we all retire to the kitchen Caz attempted to relieve him of his overcoat and scarf.

Which, since he didn't really want to be relieved of them, ended up as less of a courtesy and more of a close-to-violent mugging that concluded with her triumphantly dragging the gabardine mac from his still flapping arms as he screeched from the rope burn inflicted by her whipping the scarf off his neck at speed.

The others squawked their outrage but, when Caz turned her attention to the fat man, saying, "Here, let me take your coat," he – and the rest of them – literally flung the garments at her, assuming, I suspect, that handing them over voluntarily was less likely to result in injury or death.

As Caz tottered under the weight of four heavy overcoats, assorted scarves and a bobble hat, the door slowly creaked open, and the squat solid figure of Ali appeared, backlit by the landing light, a tray in her hands.

"Here's your teas," she grumbled, advancing into the room so that Caz – half hidden by the coats – had to step to one side, shoving one of the women from the group, with a squawk, onto the sofa.

Ali dumped the tray on the coffee table and Caz tottered out of the room to deposit, I supposed, the coats in my bedroom.

"Right," Ali said, her displeasure at having to dole out non-alcoholic drinks to the assembly, writ large in the tone she adopted, "who wanted the tea, strong, one sugar?"

"That'll be me," said the tall blonde, stepping forward.

"Mr Bird," Tavistock said, deciding to use this opportunity to get the announcements out of the way, "this is Miss Jones."

"Charmed," Miss Jones smarmed, attempting to reach a hand out to me while holding her tea and flicking her hair out of her eyes.

"Oi! Watchit!" Ali hollered. "You're spilling tea all over the Afghan."

Miss Jones winced, blushed, muttered her apologies and took the seat out of which the short moustachioed brunette had just climbed.

"I'm the Earl Grey, no milk," the brunette piped up, in an accent too posh for her plastic shoes.

"Hold your horses, milady," Ali barked back, "I'm getting to you." She handed the half a lager to the no-longer-wheezing fat bloke, handed Tavistock his mug, barking, "Tea. Just tea. Like you asked," before turning back to the brunette, her mousy bob, mousy features and a small cats-bum mouth all offset by ears that an African elephant would have been envious of.

"'Ere ya go, jugs," Ali announced, handing a cup of Earl Grey over to the woman, who smiled acceptance, before realising what she'd just been called, and frowned furiously as she tried to decipher the insult.

"Mr Bird," Tavistock tried again, this is Miss Baker," he indicated Earl Grey woman, who smiled at me, sipped her tea, stared downwards at the front of her blouse, and frowned deeply.

"Cheryl Baker," she expanded her name, sticking a thumb in her mouth before withdrawing it covered in saliva and attempting to scrape at a stain over her left breast. "But obviously not the real Cheryl Baker," she clarified, leaving me wondering if she was, in fact, some Cheryl Baker-shaped figment of my imagination.

"Well obviously," Caz murmured in my ear, as, relieved of her coat pile, she sidled back into the room and up behind me.

"Oh dear," Cheryl Baker finally sighed, "I'm afraid, Mr Tavistock, that you've got your special sauce all over my blouse."

Caz choked, the blonde giant gasped and the fat man snorted. Ali made the sort of noise you might expect from a bulimic at a breakfast buffet – part gag, part sob.

"To be clear," Tavistock jumped straight in, "we went to McDonald's before we came here, and when I bit into my Big Mac, it squirted condiment at Miss Baker."

"We do meals here, you know," Ali shot back, squinting daggers at Tavistock, who stared her down, nodded and confirmed that he was well aware of the fact.

"Yes," he dryly responded, "and I've inspected the kitchens where they're prepared, remember?"

Ali shut up.

"Anyway, where were we?" Tavistock turned his attention back to me. "Miss Jones, you've already met."

"Anna," the blonde expanded.

"And Miss Baker."

Cheryl did not look up from her left bosom, which, lying under a silk blouse in a colour that, somewhere on a pantone chart, was labelled 'Sadness,' was now jiggling round like an epileptic puppy, testament to the absence of a bra and her determination to rub the remains of Tavistock's burger sauce out of the fabric.

"This," Tavistock gestured at the fat bloke, who had already downed the half a lager, belched and put the glass back on the tray, "is Horace."

"Just Horace," the fat bloke explained.

"Horace," Tavistock beamed with pride, "is a medium."

"Looks like a three-XL to me," Ali snarked, reaching a hand out to collect Anna Jones' empty tea cup with the sort of smile that one assumes a table maid in the know might have delivered to the Tsarina on the last morning at Ekaterinburg.

"Miss Baker," Tavistock indicated the mousy woman with the big ears, "isn't really here."

"I'm not really here," said the mousy Miss Baker, slightly shaking her head, confirming Tavistock's statement, and denying the evidence of my own eyes, "Which is to say, I'm here, but only so I can absorb Horace."

Eyeing up the difference in their bulks, I assumed Cheryl had absorption capabilities close to those technologically marvellous sponges they sell on the telly at four in the morning, but I chose to pass no comment.

Ali, however, chose to pass wind, cough discretely, collect the rest of the empties and waddle out of the room.

"Energy, I mean," Cheryl said, as though these three words would clarify her previous statement. "The psychic energy generated by Horace when he's in a trance can build up quite sharply, and, well, I'm here to relieve him of that excess."

I really didn't need the mental picture of Horace being relieved of his excess energy by Cheryl Baker in my head, so I turned in desperation to Caz, who had a look of pure bewilderment but, having been trained by the finest Swiss finishing schools that money could buy, was always adept at moving on from uncomfortable silences.

She raised an eyebrow at me, and at exactly the same time, Horace started humming like an obese Buddhist on a day retreat.

"Shall we get started?" Caz asked breezily.

FOUR

"Where exactly was she found?" Cheryl asked in a stage whisper, her eyes shining brightly as she surveyed the empty room.

"Silence!" Tavistock hissed, gesturing at Horace, who was standing in the middle of the room, his eyes closed, his body rocking backwards and forwards as the humming increased in volume.

Cheryl turned her questioning eyes to me and I indicated, with a glance towards the corner of the room, where we'd discovered the lifeless body of Lyra Day, the disco diva I'd once hired to perform at the pub.

Lyra's murder had been something of a cause célèbre at the time, and clearly it had fired up Cheryl's imagination. She followed my eyes, and frowned, as though trying to summon the spectre of the strangled chanteuse to appear.

Anna Jones, standing to one side with a large camera, snapped off a set of shots. Cheryl, as though competing with Anna for usefulness, held up what looked like a hair straightener that was connected, via a long snaking wire, to a box which was attached to a belt around her waist, and pointed the device towards the corner in question.

"Darling, if Lyra turns up, I'm off," Caz murmured in my ear. "She was a bitch in life; can you imagine what she'll be like now she's realised that there are better singers where she's gone."

"Where d'you think she's gone?" I murmured back, keeping my eyes on Tavistock, who was, in turn, keeping his fixed on the rocking blimp, whose brow was bathed in sweat.

"Basingstoke, for all I care," Caz responded. "But you can be sure that – up or down – she will not be the biggest celebrity in the place. If she pops up here, you and I are done for."

Horace opened his eyes. The humming stopped.

The group, as one, leaned forward.

"Brandy," he croaked.

A series of perplexed glances were exchanged.

"Brandy," Horace croaked again.

Once more the threesome looked at each other, as though there was an obvious meaning they were missing. Finally, Caz tutted loudly, stepped forward and held out a hip flask.

"It's Armagnac," she said, as Horace took the flask from her and slugged greedily at it.

Sated, he returned Caz's offering, and she retook her place behind me, all the better to whisper in my shell-like, "Empty," she said. "The only spirits this one's likely to contact tonight are the ones that are eighty per cent proof."

"I sense death," Horace spoke at last. "In this room."

I looked at Caz. She looked at me. We both looked at the group, who were looking at Horace with the sort of jaw-dropped awe that suggested group amnesia.

"Well, yes, we know," Caz said aloud. "That's hardly news. It was in all the nationals, the local paper, the news, and on *The One Show* on the anniversary."

Eight eyes turned to us.

"If you're going to mock," Tavistock said coldly, "I'll have to ask you to leave."

"No," Horace held a hand up to stop him, whilst eyeing Caz in a way that suggested he was either sizing up how long she'd take to cook, or – more likely – debating whether she had any more booze secreted about her person. "It's a valid point. But I'm not sensing that death. Not the one that was in the papers."

"This is a man. Two men. I see two men and – wait – two women. A blonde and a brunette."

"Brilliant," Caz muttered, "he's now seeing ABBA getting offed in your pub. That'll bump up the takings. 'Come see where Frida fell. Examine the spot where Bjorn and Benny were bumped off.'"

"What about the blonde?" I muttered.

"Oh blondes always sell tickets," she answered, indicating her *Bride of Frankenstein* wig, "just by being present."

"One of the men is dead," Horace went on. "He's lying on a bed over there," his finger went to the wall opposite the fire breast. "And the other three are arguing over something. They're wearing…" his eyes squinted as though he were looking closer at something that was clearly visible. I found myself peering at the thin air he was squinting at, as though I, too, would see whatever he was imagining. "They're wearing Victorian clothing. Top hats, canes and bulky overcoats."

"What," Caz asked, "even the women?"

Tavistock shot her a warning glare.

"No," Horace clarified, "just the men."

"But I thought you said one of them was dead in a bed," Caz said. "Why would he still be wearing his hat and coat?"

Horace looked at her and licked his lips, "I don't know," he answered tetchily, "maybe he feels the cold."

"Mr Bird," Tavistock shot, as Cheryl stepped forward to absorb some of the sweat and psychic energy from Horace's brow, "perhaps we would be better conducting this review on our own."

I suddenly had a vision of the gang – unchaperoned – walking straight into the kitchen as the freezer went into full drum 'n' bass, and blanched.

"No, really, Mr Tavistock," I stammered, "we're sorry. This is all very new for us, and, well, we'll be quiet," I promised.

"And respectful," he pressed.

"And respectful," I agreed.

He glanced at the assembled; at Anna, taking photographs of the empty corner; at Cheryl, who had tucked the wand device under her left armpit and was now using both hands and a tea towel to mop sweat from Horace; Horace who was now breathing deeply and rolling his eyes back like someone in a Georgette Heyer approaching 'fulfilment,' then back at Caz and I, nodding curtly.

"Okay," he said, "but one more unnecessary comment and you will leave."

"I'm on a higher plane," Horace suddenly cried out, before throwing his hands up in the air, staggering backwards and forwards, then slamming his arms downwards while doubling his body over at the waist.

I frowned, puzzled as to where I'd seen the movement previously, and it was a moment before I realised he was clearly channelling Tina Turner doing *Proud Mary*, but by that stage he'd straightened up, opened his eyes and was staring sightlessly into the middle of the room.

"Lumme," he said in a voice several octaves higher than he'd previously used, "looks like George is a goner."

"He's channelling the spirits," Cheryl explained to me in a whisper which still earned her a vexed stare from Anna.

I looked at Caz, who rolled her eyes and swigged from the hip flask, before realising it was empty and shooting daggers at Horace.

"It's the typhoid what did it, I suppose. Though it might have been the sulphur at the match factory or the pneumonia what he had last year."

I kept staring, expecting the huge figure in the middle of the room to burst into a chorus of *As long as 'e needs me*, mash it up with a medley of *Oom pa pa*, a couple of lines from *Waiting at the church* and perhaps a reading from the death of little Nell, but no; despite the fact that this was clearly a load of old rope, he kept on wittering on about George, who – from the list of ailments being wheeled out – sounded like a medical marvel.

At length, and completely unprompted, the spirit Horace was channelling suddenly announced: "My name is Victoria Clarke and I live in this pub with my husband George. I don't know what I shall do when George is gorne. I suppose I shall 'ave to go live with my son Edward in Worthing."

Caz poked me in the ribs, and I turned to look at her. Her face was set in an angry stare. "That's word for word the first Google entry for the history of this place," she hissed. "He's not channelling a dead landlady, he's channelling the bloody internet."

This, to be honest, was hardly news to me; the entire performance had been so obvious as to make me wonder at the sanity of the other three, who stood rapt, listening, noting, sound recording and photographing the event.

And then, as quickly as it had started, Horace repeated the *Proud Mary* dance, opened his eyes and looked at us. "Was… was that okay?" he asked, and I wanted to lamp the fat fraud.

"Wonderful, Horace, absolutely wonderful." Tavistock was in raptures. "Is there anything else in this room?"

Horace shook his head. "I think that's it for here," he said, overlooking the fact that a victim of a violent crime had not bothered popping in for a chat, or to recite her *Wikipedia* entry.

"Where should we try next?" Cheryl asked, her eyes shining with excitement.

"She really needs to get out more," Caz whispered in my ear before, a glint of mischief in her own eyes, calling out, "what about the cellar?"

"The cellar?" Anna Jones frowned. "Why the cellar?"

"Well," Caz said, "it's a dark place, lots of history. I bet people died down there all the time, back in the day."

Horace looked unconvinced, but Caz sealed the deal by saying, "And it's where we keep the stock, so there'll be brandy if – you know – we need to revive old Horace here."

"The cellar," Horace suddenly announced, one hand held

out to the ether, the other on his ear, as though he were listening to a running commentary from the beyond via a cheap, badly-fitting hearing aid. "Sounds promising. I'm getting some vibrations that suggest the lower part of the building might be fruitful."

And so we left the room, trooped along the landing and down the stairs to the ground floor, where Caz swiftly killed off Tavistock's suggestion that we might, perhaps, examine the rooms on this floor first by pointing out that the noise from the packed house, much of which was coming from roaring drunks, singing along to a selection of four to the floor 80s dance tunes and stomping their costumed arses all over the place, might put Horace off his stroke.

"I don't think Horace has a stroke, per se," Tavistock responded, blinking at her in a way that suggested he was trying to decide whether she was taking the piss or not.

"Well I'm sure he'll find it easier to contact the other side in the quiet and dark of the cellar. Won't you, Mr – um – Horace?" she countered, but the old lush, lured by the suggestion that there might be unprotected bottles of brandy below, was already forging ahead towards the doorway to the cellar.

FIVE

We stopped at the top of the stairs and Tavistock peered dubiously down into the darkness below.

"It's a bit dark," he said.

"Well it's a cellar," Caz answered, unhooking the industrial torch that we always kept on a hook just inside the door, "they're not usually lit up like Oxford Street."

To be honest, Tavistock was sort of right: The electrics in The Marq weren't up to much, and the single dim bulb in the cellar provided not much more than a pool of thin illumination around the bottom of the stairs.

Another light on the apex of the L-shaped space provided another pool of light but, beyond the two circles, the space was pretty much in darkness.

A third light used to sit between the two, and a fourth around the corner in the short leg of the L; but the fourth light hadn't worked as long as I'd been at The Marq, and the third hadn't worked since someone had attempted to burn the pub down the previous summer.

Caz and Ali, after each replacing the bulb, had decided that the fire brigade – who, despite the fire being out by the time they'd arrived, had doused the hallway with several gallons of water 'just to be safe' – had probably flooded and shorted the electrics.

"You're lucky the bloody ceiling hasn't caved in," Ali had said. "I mean, this place is made out of bloody cardboard.

Water damage? They could 'ave washed the bloody pub away. You should sue."

"Ali," I'd pointed out, "they were trying to save the pub. I don't think you get to sue the fire brigade cos they put a fire out."

She'd shaken her head at me, as though I were some tragically backward child she'd been lumbered with. "Where there's blame, Danny, there's a claim."

And, that pronouncement made, she'd handed me a bag of batteries. "You better get another torch, mate. Cos the water damage down there," she sucked her teeth and shook her head, "takes months to show, but you'll flick that switch one night and either short half of London or fry yourself like the Boston Strangler."

I didn't think the Boston Strangler was electrocuted but I'd run out of energy to argue with Ali.

And right now, I was running out of the energy to deal with Tavistock and the Ghostbusters, who had started bickering about roles and responsibilities.

"Well I should hold the torch," Cheryl Baker was insisting, "because I'll be in front."

"Why will you be in front?" Anna Jones demanded, looking at Tavistock to reinforce her umbrage.

"Because I've got the recording devices," Cheryl answered, a touch of the smartarse schoolgirl evident in her response. "Therefore I'll go in front, otherwise all I'll record are your big feet stomping all over the place."

"Well how," Anna snapped back triumphantly, "are you going to hold both?"

"Because I can clip this," Cheryl brandished the wand, "to my lapel," and clipped the wand to her lapel as though to prove the fact.

"Ladies," Tavistock said, "I think it makes little difference. Anna, why don't you come with me? Miss Baker can go in front with the torch and Horace, as Horace will then be able to pick up vibrations first, then you and I can take up the rear, as it were."

Anna looked somewhat pleased with the suggestion, while Baker, who had fought to be up front with the torch, suddenly looked as though she'd been set up and was not remotely happy about the fact.

"What about us?" Caz piped up, and Tavistock and Anna turned frowns on us.

"Oh," Tavistock said, "I suppose that means you're coming downstairs with us?"

"Wouldn't miss it for the world," Caz answered, smiling.

Tavistock squinted suspiciously, and Anna shot daggers at us. "Very well, Miss—"

"Lady," Caz corrected him. "I'm Lady Holloway," and she smiled again as the two continued to shoot filthy looks at her.

Tavistock bowed, "Your ladyship," he murmured. "Well if you're coming, then I must, once again, insist that you are silent and courteous at all times."

Caz favoured him with the look she normally kept for shop assistants who queried why she was returning something from last year's collections without a receipt, and said simply, "Mr Bird and I shall be the silent embodiment of courtesy. Shan't we, Daniel."

"Absolutely," I murmured, peering somewhat dubiously into the darkness below as, in the distance, the DJ put on Dead or Alive's *You spin me round* and the house went mental.

"Shall we proceed?" Horace asked.

We lined up as arranged, Cheryl flicked the switch on the torch and we slowly, with a worrying degree of creaking – most of it coming from the stairs as they strained under Horace's bulk, but some of it definitely coming from Horace himself – made our way down into the cellar.

Caz had, of course, lied: There were no cases of vintage brandy down here. The Marq ran on bare minimum stock levels and, apart from the beer barrels stacked against the wall behind the stairs, the space was basically filled with junk that had made its way down here over the years.

Cheryl came to the bottom of the stairs, and stopped, the

torch shining ahead into the darkness until Horace, unable to stop his bulk which was barrelling forward, slammed into her back, jolting her forward and making the torch beam jiggle upwards to the ceiling, then down to the concrete floor, before Cheryl managed to steady it and step forward, allowing the rest of us to gather in a semi-circle just outside the circle of light cast by the overhead bulb at the end of the stairs.

Above us, I could actually hear the floorboards creaking, as the weight and noise of two hundred people stomping to a disco beat and yelling song lyrics, drinks orders and chat-up lines, reverberated along the joists.

Cheryl shone the torch around, showing the brick walls, with recessed alcoves dotted at regular instances along them.

Beer barrels were stacked in two of these.

The third contained a life-sized cardboard cut-out of Bruce Forsythe, which had put the shits up me when I'd first stumbled upon it one day whilst accepting a delivery of the hooky lager which my nephews had set me up with. Tonight, however, and considering the spook patrol were supposedly here to be shocked and disturbed by unexpected events, not one of them blinked. It was as though they were used to having their torch cross the dead-eyed perma-grinning face of Bruce Forsythe on an almost tedious basis.

"What do we do now?" Anna asked, snuggling a little too close to Tavistock for them to maintain the 'we're only friends' façade.

Horace stepped forward to the edge of the circle of light, closed his eyes, and began breathing deeply in through his nostrils and out again via his mouth.

This meant that the constant wheeze we'd experienced on his arrival was now replaced by a thin, high-pitched whistle followed by a long, laborious wheeze.

"He keeps doing that," I whispered in Caz's ear, "he'll attract dogs before he attracts ghosts."

Horace walked forward, out of the circle, his slowly shuffling gait and deep breathing managing – despite the din from above – to echo around the space. He vanished into the darkness and I began, once again, to hear the low moaning sound that he'd been using to suggest he was going into a trance.

This continued for several seconds, until it was abruptly cancelled out by an almighty crash, a shriek of, "Shittin' hell," from Horace and a cry from Tavistock, who rushed forward.

Cheryl, a stream of orders being barked at her by Anna Jones, swivelled the torch wildly as Horace continued to issue oaths and epithets that I thought unlikely to have come from the ghost of Victoria Clarke, late of this parish.

It wasn't until he growled, "What cocksucker left that there," that I stiffened and, as Caz mused aloud, whether, perhaps, anyone thought he might be suffering satanic possession, Cheryl found Horace sprawled on top of a partially dismantled petrol lawn mower.

"Oh, my 'ead," he moaned as Cheryl struggled to haul his unfeasibly large bulk upright. "I nearly lost me prospects."

The cross-bar on the handle of the lawn mower had rusted away and as a result a couple of rusty spikes were all that remained, pointing upwards at an odd angle. One of these had somehow ended up, as he tripped and – one assumes – flew through the air, shoved up Horace's right trouser leg, stopping just short of skewering his crotch.

Tavistock and I rushed around him – me apologising profusely about the random bit of garden kit lying around in my cellar – and managed, with Cheryl mopping his brow and shushing him like a worried mother, to pull Horace to his feet.

"Bird!" Tavistock turned furiously on me. "What the hell is that doing here?"

"I'm so sorry," I attempted to explain. "It was dumped in the lane outside and I didn't want to leave it there. It was a trip hazard," I finished lamely.

"We are, for once," Tavistock stated coldly, "in agreement on something. Are you okay Horace? Should we call this a night?"

Horace looked around at us. "A night? But you haven't had your full session yet. We agreed a full hour."

"Well," Tavistock sounded doubtful, "after a fall like that, perhaps you might want to rest."

"Nonsense," Horace hauled himself upright, winced, looked around for Caz and asked, "Lady Caroline, you wouldn't happen to have any more of that Armagnac, would you? Medicinally, of course."

And Caz, from somewhere about her person, produced another hip flask and, wordlessly, handed it over.

"How many of those," I asked, "are you carrying? And where the hell are they?"

"Daniel," she looked at me and smirked, "I'm shocked that you'd even ask. A lady is always prepared for all eventualities. And a gentleman never asks her where she keeps her stash."

"Firstly," I answered, "that's not a lady; it's a boy scout."

"And secondly?"

"And secondly, what gave you the idea that I was a gentleman?" I wiggled my eyebrows like Groucho Marx and only a gentle cough from Horace as he downed the contents of the second hip flask brought my attention back to the now rather bedraggled group.

Horace, having handed back the empty, went into his routine and we all slowly – and, this time, carefully – made our way along the length of the cellar, stopping at various spots for Horace to 'feel the veil,' and moan a bit before picking up various signals then losing them again.

"Honestly," Caz muttered as we turned the corner into the short leg of the L-shaped cellar, "he's not so much a medium as a faulty transistor radio."

"Perhaps he only picks up medium wave," I joked back as Horace suddenly stopped dead in the middle of the pitch-dark space and went into his *Proud Mary* again.

Cheryl shone the torch on him, and his hands waved in front of his face as his eyes watered in the glare.

"Not in his face," Tavistock chastised her, swiping the torch off to the right so that it illuminated a stretch of plastered wall, a large dark crack snaking from the ceiling down through it.

Horace opened his mouth and, before he could speak, the room above was filled with the opening bars of Michael Jackson's *Thriller* and the crowd, once again, roared its approval and began jumping up and down, sending small showers of dust and plaster onto the now only partially-lit medium.

"Death is here," he whispered. "Horrible death. Its smell lingers."

"That might just be the drains," Caz said, "I'm fairly sure they run under here."

"Out!" Tavistock barked, pointing back the way we'd come.

"Sorry," Caz mouthed, but made no attempt to leave.

Tavistock glared at her, as we all moved to stand in a semi-circle around the by now profusely sweating Horace. I wasn't sure about the smell of death, but I could definitely detect the scent of Armagnac as it seeped out of the man's pores.

"Death," he whispered, and the rocking back and forth began in earnest.

Within seconds I realised we were all mirroring his movements, as he continued to moan.

"We are on burial grounds," he hissed. "A sea of death. A wall of souls."

I glanced at Caz, whose face showed the same level of interest I felt; this was different. He wasn't summoning up anyone specific, just generalities about death and so on, but it felt a little more disturbing for that.

He cocked his head to one side. "Who's that?" he asked as, from above, Vincent Price advised him that the midnight hour was almost here.

"You!" Horace suddenly boomed out, his arm flying up and his right index finger pointing directly at me, "I see you, and a hammer."

I shook my head. Poor Horace had been on Google again.

Caz, annoyed now at how easily she, herself, had fallen for the pantomime we'd just watched, sighed deeply, exclaimed, "Oh really!" and was silenced only by a sudden loud cracking noise.

"That doesn't look right," said Cheryl, as she turned towards the wall, her torch beam showing the crack she'd highlighted earlier widening as we watched, and spreading out and downwards at an alarming rate.

And as we watched, whilst from above us Michael Jackson sang, accompanied by a cast of pissed up tuneless party-goers, something from within the wall began to push forward, to press the wall itself outwards, a shape appearing through the crack as it widened.

And, like a thing from *Lovecraft,* it wasn't until the shape materialised itself into a skull, desiccated skin stretched tightly across the cheekbones, the teeth grinning the rictus smile of death, that anyone said, or did, anything, and by that stage, it was too late.

The body lurched forward, Cheryl began to scream hysterically, the crowd upstairs – at the song's end – burst into crazed applause and stamping, the torch was dropped, plunging us all into darkness, and, above Cheryl's howls, I distinctly heard the mono-titled Horace exclaim, "Fuck me, I never saw that coming."

SIX

The phone call came at 7:00 a.m. the next morning.

Being that it was a Sunday and the police and forensics had only left about two hours previously, the place was quiet as the grave.

This, as soon as I thought it, made me shiver.

It had been a grave. But for how long? And why?

The police were fairly sure that what we were looking at was not some Victorian cadaver. Mine own eyes – thanks to the presence, on said corpse, of an Oasis t-shirt – confirmed the fact.

So, some time from the 90s onwards, then. But why?

We'd been ushered out of the room as soon as the first rozzers had arrived and shone a torch at what was now half-in and half-out of the wall; but, in the few seconds I had before I was evicted, I saw a large dark mark on the back of the head.

I was upstairs in the rapidly emptying bar by the time I realised it was a hole.

Downstairs, bricked up behind one of the alcoves in the cellar of my pub, a man – I was assuming it was a man, though in truth I hadn't had time to check – someone, who had been shot in the head some time after the early 90s had laid waiting for twenty years.

First opinion was that a combination of water damage from the fire upstairs, vibrations over time (culminating, quite possibly, in the double-whammy of *Dead or Alive* and

Michael Jackson) and a basically botched job on the bricking up, had resulted in the false wall weakening, the body dislodging and the unpleasant surprise that had put an end to Mr Tavistock and Co.'s spiritual safari.

Why it had been put there seemed obvious: Someone had been forced to brick the body up because they had blown a sizeable hole in the back of its head. But that meant there were still a lot of unanswered questions: Who was the body? Who had put it there? When had it been hidden?

But who – who the killer was, who the victim was – and why they had been shot and dumped here were still ringing around my head, even as the phone kept on ringing.

I didn't want to answer it; it would be journalists, or some thrill-seekers looking to pop round and, 'See where it happened,' but the ringing wouldn't stop.

Eventually, angry, I yanked the receiver up and, before I could say a word, a voice I knew – a gruff, gravelly voice with a slight accent and a barely suppressed fury – said: "The car is outside. Get in it. Now," and hung up.

Shit!

I put the phone down, raced over to the window, twitched a curtain and looked down on a shiny black BMW idling outside the pub.

I let the curtain drop and looked around the room like a hunted animal.

Shit!

The man who'd been on the end of the phone was the real owner of The Marq. He was a gangster who owned every chop shop, knocking shop, dodgy bookies, bar and racket between Borough and Peckham, and he did not sound happy.

Chopper Falzone had never done time, despite being the recognised Top Man in Southwark, but the nearest he'd ever come was when the bodies of two of his business competitors had been discovered partially dismembered in a lockup he may – or may not – have been renting from a man with the charming sobriquet of Johnny 'One Thumb'

Malone.

On the day the jury had unanimously found in his favour, Chopper's mugshot had appeared on the front of *The Sun* alongside the headline, 'Innocent?'

That question mark spoke volumes.

If he could chop his opposition into little pieces, was it wrong to wonder whether he might, just possibly, have shot one of them in the head and buried them in the basement of The Marq?

And if he'd done that, was it wrong to assume that he might be a bit pissed off with the moron who allowed a selection of municipal employees to go pouncing around in his gangster graveyard, disturbing the evidence he'd so obviously assumed was long concealed?

I looked desperately around the room. I could make a run for it, obviously, but to where: Knowing Chopper, he had people waiting at the back door to prevent just such an eventuality.

The phone rang again.

I stared at it, my panic rising.

It kept ringing. I picked it up.

"You're not in the car yet," he said, managing to imbue those six words, that one statement, with a universe of menace.

"I'm just on my way," I lied, looking furiously around the room to see if there were any weapons I could smuggle in, then deciding that I had little that would be of much use against a man who could shoot another man in the face and brick him up alive in a basement.

Okay, I had no evidence that the deceased had been shot in the face, or, indeed, that he'd been anything less than as dead as a Spice Girl's solo career before he was walled up, but I was now at the point of panic, where it was a sure thing that Chopper had butchered the man, and I was next in line for the old bang-bang and brick send-off.

"I was getting my coat," I finally lied lamely.

"Well now you've got it," he answered, and hung up, the

ending of the sentence unnecessary.

I grabbed my jacket from the sofa, and, shoving my keys in my pocket (whilst hoping I'd be returning in a state to be able to use them) made my way downstairs, through the empty bar and let myself out, locking the door behind me.

The car, from this angle, was a highly-polished black Bentley, the windows themselves tinted darkly so that there was no way to see who was inside.

I opened the rear door, peered into the empty back seat and slipped into the car.

"Sorry," I explained to the impassive driver, who had neither acknowledged my presence, nor, in fact, shown the slightest evidence that he, himself, wasn't actually stone dead, "I was looking for my jacket. I can never find it. Are you the same?"

His eyes flicked to the rear-view mirror, caught mine and the car slowly and smoothly moved away from the kerb.

"Oops," I giggled nervously, "nearly forgot to put my safety-belt on."

Yeah, I thought, cos you really don't wanna injure yourself in a road traffic accident before Chopper gets the chance to injure you in a real-life hatchet horror.

Driver, again, did not respond, and I realised that – what with the racing heart and the nervous chatter – I was clearly on the edge of hysteria.

It'll be delayed shock, I reasoned. I mean, it's not every day you find a dead body in your basement.

Then I looked at the back of the man in front of me, his smart tailored black suit, the peaked cap perched solidly on his head, the neatly cut dark hair, the sharp freshly-pressed white shirt and, although it took me a few moments to realise it, the missing ear.

My driver had one ear which was present, correct and visibly observable. It didn't stick out like Cheryl's had last night, but it was definitely there.

However, where the left ear should have been was a mashed-up set of scaring suggesting he'd come a cropper with something – or someone – which had tried to ensure he'd never need to shell out for a surround-sound telly again, and I realised that it wasn't, possibly, delayed shock, so much as very present and real shock, with just a soupçon of terror.

The car continued on in silence.

Eventually, we pulled up outside a business premises I knew well. One, in fact, that had struck fear in the hearts of anyone who'd grown up in this neck of the woods ever since Chopper had made it his headquarters.

He'd had a new sign put up, which now actually allocated ownership to him – a fact which had to show an ego of an entirely different scale.

CHOPPERS' POUND SHOP, it said, and though I really wanted to mention to Van Gogh that the apostrophe was in the wrong place, I figured I was in enough shit without trying to correct a psycho's grammar.

He waited, and I waited, and at the very minute where I began to realise with mounting horror that he might be completely mute, he said, "Unless you want to fuck him off more than he already is, I'd get in there now."

SEVEN

I pushed the shop door open, setting off a jangling bell, and stepped into the store. Chopper had done it up since I'd last been there: The overhead lighting no longer had the yellow tinge of a jaundiced alcoholic, the floor tiles didn't seem to be as chipped as they had been on my previous visit, and the stock – though it was still a random collection of the shiny and the shitty – seemed to be arranged a little more carefully, the tat less haphazardly shoved on shelves.

I glanced to my left. There was nobody behind the tills. A stack of remaindered James Patterson paperbacks and a pricing gun lay abandoned on the counter top.

Behind me, there was a click and the door locked electronically.

"Hello," I called. "Anyone there?"

Silence.

I knew that there was an office at the back of the shop.

And I knew that this was where Chopper had been known to take recalcitrants when they needed either softening up or chastising (hence the irony in the name of the shop: Many a victim had received a pounding in the pound shop), so I was somewhat reluctant to walk merrily in there.

I called again, and waited. Nothing.

Then, as if from heaven, there was a loud click, an ear-splitting scream of feedback, and Chopper's voice came over the tannoy.

"I'm in the back, fuckwit."

The tannoy clicked off again.

There was nothing for it. I took a deep breath and wended my way down the household aisle, past rows of generic bleach, 'Spring fresh' scented candles (in autumn) and a full set of gardening implements including gloves, secateurs and shovels, and it wasn't until I was at the end of the aisle that it dawned on me that I'd just passed enough product to allow Chopper to kill me, cut me up, clean the scene of the crime, bury me and have the whole place smelling like spring flowers without even needing to leave the shop.

In front of me, the door to the office was ajar.

I stepped into what looked like a security room, a small bank of screens displaying various views of the shop outside. An elderly man, his white hair creating a corona through which the light from some of the screens filtered, was scrutinising the images of the empty shop.

"You took your time," he said without looking up.

"Sorry," I began, then stopped as he held a hand up, swivelling in the chair to face me.

"What is the world coming to, Danny?" he asked, gesturing beyond me to the shelves of cheap product outside. "This shop, which – let's be honest – started off as a hobby; somewhere I could keep busy in my retirement," he went on, smirking slightly at the word *retirement*, "has ended up very *very* profitable.

"People like a bargain, you see, Danny."

I nodded, though I had no idea what this was all about, or where it was going.

"And you know what follows the bargain hunters?" he asked and I panicked, thinking I was actually expected to know. "Fucking thieves," the man who'd knocked off every warehouse between Luton and Gatwick snarled. "Light-fingered fucks who haven't got the balls or the brains to pop up west and help themselves to something nice from Selfridges. Turn up here and pinch six-for-a-fiver stir-fry sauces off the fucking shelves."

"That's a good price," I said, making a mental note to check the stir-fry sauces on the way out. If I was still walking.

He squinted at me. "You taking the piss, Danny?"

"No," I shook my head. "God, no, Ch—, Mr Falzone. I think I pay more at the cash and carry."

"Right." Chopper nodded, still looking at me as though he were unsure of whether to believe me or not.

"So here I sit," he waved vaguely at the surveillance room, "in an office checking out the security cameras. In a fucking pound shop. What's happening to the world?" he asked again. "There's no class. No fucking loyalty. And then there's no fucking brains. Who was he?"

I realised that he'd segued from a general complaint about the state of the world and that the last question had been directed at me personally.

"Who was he?" I asked, realising, as I did so, that Chopper was referring to the corpse.

"Well I'm assuming it was a he," he said. "Haven't had confirmation of that yet. So: Who was he?"

I flapped my gums, as the realisation that Chopper Falzone seemed to think I'd killed the body in the cellar sank in.

"You mean you don't know?"

"Danny, if I knew, I wouldn't be wasting my – or your – time asking you, now would I? Now: Who. Was. He?"

My jaw dropped. "I—, I don't know, Mr Falzone. I've no idea."

"Danny," he said, flicking off the monitors and turning his full attention on me, "I've got used to you offing the punters. I know," he held his hand up to silence my protest, "innocent as charged. Who isn't? I mean, Danny, overseeing a fucking charnel house with gin is one thing, but now you're disinterring the fucking corpses. It's a pub, mate, not Rillington Place. So, what the actual fuck have you been doing in my pub?"

"It was nothing to do with me," I stammered. "I swear."

He paused. "So you didn't off him?"

I shook my head violently.

Chopper harrumphed, paused a moment, considering, then smiled at me in much the same way that Mack the Knife might have smiled at Lotte Lenya, or Little Jenny or whoever the fuck was waiting for the blade to slip between their ribs.

"I didn't think you did. I said to my missus – he's a good boy, that Danny. Y'know, for a pufta. No offence," he added, knowing full well that what he'd just said was offensive.

I chose not to take offence and told him as much.

"C'mon," he said, standing up, "walk with me."

He put his arm on my shoulder and guided me back out into the shop. I relaxed a little; figuring he was hardly likely to get out the brass knuckles by the plastic croquet kits and Jenga sets made of what I was fairly sure was protected wood.

We strolled up the aisles in silence, until he let out a deep sigh.

"So if you didn't do him," he said, "who did?"

"I thought," I said before I'd had a moment to think and then, realising what I was about to say, I froze.

"You thought what?" He stopped, turning a gimlet eye on me.

"I thought," I scrabbled around for anything, "that you might have had an idea?"

"Me?" he asked, startlingly believable incredulity settling over his face, "a simple shopkeeper? Why would I know who killed some poor bastard and shoved him in your cellar?"

The ownership did not slip my attention. Chopper reminded me every month that I was running The Marq only through his good graces, and that the monthly 'rent' had to be paid. And suddenly, with the arrival of the desiccated bloke behind the wall, it was *my* cellar in, I assumed, *my* pub.

"Well," I vamped, hoping against hope to get away here without insulting Chopper too much, "you know so many people, and so many of them – I guess – die. Of natural causes," I hastened to add.

"Natural causes?"

"Yes," I began gabbling, "you know: Colds, flu, old age."

"Did this one look like he died of old age, Danny?"

I shook my head in the negative.

"No," he said definitively. "And do you know how we know this Danny?" Chopper asked rhetorically, and, his voice rising alarmingly in volume, answered himself, "because he was buried in the basement of my fucking pub!"

And now it's *his* again, I thought, though – as usual – I said nothing.

"You hear anything, Dan, you bring it to me."

"Hear anything?" I squawked.

"Don't worry," he said, bringing his temper back under control, "the rozzers find anything, I'll know it before their bosses do but you've got a knack, boy, for finding stuff out, and I want the motherfucker who had," and again his temper snapped and he roared, "the audacity – *the fucking audacity* – to do someone and stash 'em in my fucking pub without even having the courtesy to ask me. D'you like biscuits?" he suddenly asked, the switch flipping back to genial old coot.

"Biscuits?" I was puzzled.

"Yeah," he said, "biscuits? What? Is there a fucking echo in here? Y'know: Bourbon fingers, Jammy Dodgers, Garibaldis."

"Yes," I gasped, my poor addled brain trying to figure out where this was going.

"What's your favourite?"

"My favourite biscuit?" I closed my eyes, tried to calm the panic that was building and wondered why the fact that a human being had been murdered and secreted below my bedroom was worrying me less than the fact that I had to pick and declare a favourite baked good.

"Gipsy creams," he offered, twinkly-eyed and jovial.

"Choc-chip flapjacks?"

"Custard creams," I finally shouted, more to make him stop reciting biscuit names than because there was any truth in the statement.

He stopped, looked me up and down. "Yeah, I figured."

And then Chopper Falzone leaned towards me, right in to me, his eyes locking with mine, and the first thought that went through my mind was; shit, he's going to kiss me, followed by; or head-butt me.

But he did neither. Instead, he reached over my shoulder and snatched two packets of custard creams off the shelf behind me, proffering them to me like he was one of the Magi and I was a virgin mother.

"They're a few weeks past the sell-by," he advised, "but they'll still go nice with a cuppa. Now here's the thing, Danny, you get wind of the motherfucker who did this, you let me know."

"And what will you do?" I asked, not wanting, really, to know the answer to the question.

"Me?" he chuckled. "I'll cut their fucking legs off and put them through a mincing machine. Here, take some Bourbon fingers with them. You got my number."

EIGHT

"I think Caz suspects," I said, leaning my head back on Nick's chest.

"Suspects?" Nick reached around me and lifted a slice of pizza from the box that lay open on the floral bedspread. The clash between the tomato and cheese topping and the almost fluorescent giant peonies was eye-watering.

"This," I nudged him playfully. "Us. Here."

"Oh," he responded through a mouthful of margarita. "You mean you still haven't told her?"

"Well," I twisted around, grabbing a slice of the pizza and sitting up on the bed so that I was facing him, "I was going to. At first. Only I was afraid she'd get all judgemental."

"Caz," Nick intoned, taking another bite of his slice, "does not strike me as the judgemental type."

"I know," I said, feeling a little crestfallen, "but maybe I was."

He reached out and stroked my face fondly. "Now that," Nick smiled, "isn't an entirely unfair statement. What was it? The lies? The secret wife? The deceit? Or the fact that you'd doomed yourself to a lifetime spent in cheap hotels?"

"I don't mind lies," I bristled, and, at Nick's gentle chuckle, I blushed, realising he had managed to not only find all my buttons, but play them like a green-eyed, full-lipped Liberace.

"Okay," I admitted, "maybe I do prefer truth. But, really,

how much better would the world be if people only told the truth? I nearly lost you last year because you didn't tell me the truth about Arianne."

"Two things there," Nick smiled back, "firstly you never came close to losing me. But I came quite close to losing you because of what happened. And secondly, for a man who loves truth so much, you're letting your best friend think that we're not still together. Which is coming dangerously close to an outright lie."

"It's complicated," I said at last.

"It usually is," Nick smiled fondly, "with you."

"I should have told her, right at the start. But I didn't, and now it feels really uncomfortable."

Nick took another bite of the pizza, swallowed it and said, "Well baby, this is going to go on for at least another three years, so you should probably bite the bullet and tell her. Soon."

The three years was a reminder of just what I'd signed up for. Nick had, last year, been sent on a police trip to Albania. Some villain had been tracked there and the Met had wanted to negotiate with the local cops to get him back.

Only, while he was there, Nick had come across a young woman who had been sold as a slave to one of the local villains, and who was being slowly tortured and starved to death.

No matter what Nick did, the local rozzers, unwilling to risk the wrath of the local gangsters, simply wouldn't help the woman; whose name he had discovered was Arianne. And so, Nick – my Nick, who was snuggling me now on a hotel bedspread, but who had never been out at work – had, in desperation as his time to return neared, explained the situation to Arianne and suggested they get married.

Arianne knew the whole story; she knew this was a way of getting her away from Tirana to a place of safety. She knew there was no romance or sexual interest there. And she knew, instinctively, she had since told me, that she was dealing with the first – the only – truly honourable man that she had ever met.

So she and Nick had embarked on a sham marriage so that Nick could return to England with her.

This was, of course, a criminal offence.

Not, admittedly, one as serious as, say, shooting someone in the head and burying them in the cellar of my pub, but one which would, if discovered, result in criminal charges and dismissal from The Job – the one job that Nick had dreamed of his whole life.

The couple needed to stay married for three years and, during that period, they would be monitored, investigated and interviewed at random, and so any suggestion that Nick was not really married to Arianne, but was, instead, bumping – as some are wont to say – uglies with me, would have ruined Nick and had Arianne sent back to almost certain death.

So, here we were, sneaking around, checking into small hotels, paying cash, grabbing our time together when we could and lying to my best friend.

"Talking of biting the bullet," I said, desperate to change the subject, "any news on my cellar-based friend?"

Nick frowned. "You know I can't tell you anything about an ongoing case."

"Obviously," I said, "but if you were to say anything to me, what would it be?"

He laughed and shook his head despairingly at me. "Well, the first thing I'd do would be to ask whether you're actually, like, making a thing of this corpses-in-the-pub, thing? I mean, are you going to rebrand or something? Y'know, like, 'Come to the Marq. You might never leave,' sort of thing?"

"Not funny, Nick," I said recalling Chopper's use of similar phrasing today. "Someone was murdered and that body has been sitting under me for – I mean, Lord knows how long."

"Forensics reckon at least eighteen to twenty years. Based on the speed of decay and the Oasis at Donnington t-shirt," he said, telling me something I hadn't known.

47

"Jesus," I shook my head, "so he was down there all the time I was with Robert, and long before I took over the pub. I'm assuming it was a he…"

Nick chuckled again. "Yes, Danny, it *was* a man. And no, Danny, we have no idea yet who he was. Fingerprints aren't particularly easy to retrieve after that long behind your partition wall, though they've got some partials and are putting them through the computer."

"Did you find the gun with him?"

He shook his head. "No. No sign of the gun, but the main suspect wasn't known for throwing away guns unless he had to."

"Main suspect?" I frowned. How could they have a suspect already?

"Oh come on, Danny," Nick actually laughed this time. "Your boss Chopper. It's his pub and this looks very like a gangland job. Clean, quick and then safely disposed of."

My frown deepened. I was certain that my last chat with Chopper had not been theatre on his part, but wary of letting Nick know that I had too much contact with a man he considered public enemy number one. "But why would Chopper leave the body here? Where he had to know it would be traced back to him?"

"Cos he didn't think it would ever be discovered," Nick answered.

"But he…" I sighed. Maybe Chopper *was* playing me.

"He what, Danny?"

"Nothing."

"Danny," Nick's voice was suddenly stern, his green eyes staring with concern into mine. "You're staying away from him, right?"

"Away from him?" I suddenly felt like a 50s housewife being ordered by the husband not to use that brilliantined butcher on the high street. "Nick, he owns the pub. I'm not popping round for tea and biscuits," I added, glancing guiltily at the carrier bag full of custard creams on the bedside table, "but it's not like I get to completely ignore the man."

"I know." Nick sighed and pulled me closer to him, his back pressed against the cheap headboard, mine against his chest, the two of us spooning in a half-sitting pose, and he pressed his lips to the top of my head. "I love you," he said, and my heart lightened.

"I know," I said. "I'm just sorry that life is always so bloody complicated."

"Complicated?" He laughed. "Mortgages and shift patterns are complicated, Danny. What we have is beyond complicated. It's," he searched for the word, and finally settled on, "byzantine."

I chuckled. "I know," I answered. "And by the way," I said, my voice catching in my throat, "I love you too."

I coughed to clear my throat, "Listen," I said, forcing myself back to business, "I know how unprofessional this is, but I'd really like to know as soon as they put a name to that body."

"Unprofessional? Danny – that would be illegal. And why do you want to know the name?"

"Firstly, I'm pretty sure it can't be illegal. They do it all the time on the telly – calling their sources at the *New York Times* and telling them that they've found Jimmy Hoffa under the car park in Queens."

"Yeah, well this is the Met Police," he answered dryly, "not *Law and Order Southwark*, and the last time anyone from my lot spoke to the papers – *New York Times* down to the *Borough and Bankside Bugle* – there was a sacking and an internal investigation that made a lot of people uncomfortable for a very long time."

"Well, an internal investigation will do that," I answered, trying – and failing – to lighten the mood. "Listen, he was down in my cellar for twenty years. I think the least I'm entitled to know is who he is. That's all I'm asking."

He sighed deeply and kissed the top of my head again, reaching across to grab a bottle of beer from the bedside table. "I'm not promising anything," he said, and I thought that that single phrase could have been the motto for my entire romantic life.

But right now, as he swigged the beer and handed the bottle to me, as the TV in the corner continued to flash coloured drama at us, as the heat from him mixed with the heat of me, and the twelve-inch pizza shrank slice by slice, I didn't need promises.

Now, I felt certain, was good enough.

NINE

A sudden gust of wind caught me as I turned off Fulham Road on to Caz's street, and the carrier bags in my hands were yanked as though the Gods themselves were trying to prevent my delivery.

The deal with Nick and I was that we would meet every few days, have some time together, and then head back to our respective homes in the wee hours of the morning, which was, frankly, playing havoc with my sleep patterns and, so, having arrived into The Marq at four in the morning, having Caz telephone me at not much after 9:00 a.m. on a Sunday hadn't been the most pleasant of experiences.

I'd sat up in bed, my mobile jangling away, and, as I'd lifted it, I'd thoughtlessly lifted a packet of biscuits from the carrier bag beside it, my sleep-deprived brain clearly demanding cheap sugar and hydrogenated fats.

"What are you doing?" Caz, without preamble, had asked.

"Good morning to you, too," I answered, tearing open the custard creams and pulling one out.

"Yes," she sounded distracted, "morning. Hope you're well. Have a nice day. All that stuff. What are you doing?"

I bit into the biscuit. It was soft.

"I'm eating a stale biscuit," I said through a mouthful of crumbs.

"Quaint," she deadpanned, "and guaranteed not to add to

your already expanding hips."

"Cow," I muttered through a mouthful of crumbs. "What's up?" I asked, taking another bite and deciding that – despite the slight mustiness – the custard creams weren't too bad.

"Can you come around?" She asked.

"Now?" It was Sunday, we were promising a roast this lunchtime, and I could imagine Ali's face if I swanned out into the bar and announced I was going out.

"Well, as soon as you've finished your biscuits, obviously," she responded, somewhat testily. "How many have you got?"

I dragged the bag towards me. "Two – no – three packs."

"Dear Lord. Are carbs the new *No carbs*?"

"They were a gift," I said shamefacedly.

"Well you need to get better dates, sweetheart. A man who gives you stale biscuits on a first night will give you chlamydia by Christmas."

"I hope not," I said, my throat going dry. "They're from Chopper."

Caz was silent for a moment, then: "Neatly-jointed corpse Chopper? The one that had those three Russian gangsters hacked to bits?"

"Allegedly."

"Allegedly if you're his lawyer," she said.

"Which I'm not."

Caz snorted. "Clearly; I'll bet his legal rep gets paid a lot more than a bag of broken biscuits. Anyway, I can't wait for you to finish three packets of biscuits so you'll just have to bring them with you. And stop on the way, would you, and pick up some Vermouth. And some lemons. What time do you think you'll get here?"

"Caz, I do have a pub to run, you know?"

There was a moment of silence as she audibly swigged something from a glass which clinked against the phone, then: "Daniel, you have staff that run the pub. Your role is to direct and inspire, and right now I bet they'd be more inspired by knowing their leader is helping me rather than licking his wounds and a selection of rancid baked goods in the kitchen."

"I'm in bed," I admitted shamefacedly.

"Lord," she sighed theatrically, "how the other half live. Listen," she finished, "this is a Stage One Red Alert. I really need you, Danny."

I straightened in my seat. "What's up?"

"Look," she said, "I know you have enough drama in your life, and I really wouldn't ask if it was at all avoidable, but I need you. Can you come over? Now. And wear something smart and good shoes. The Sweeney's."

I checked my watch. "What on earth is going on?" I asked.

"Prissy's in town," she finally said, "and demanding an audience."

"Jesus," I gasped, then realised I needed to remain calm for my best friend and released my breath. "This will be fine," I said. "What time does she want to see you?"

"Us, dear heart. It's me plus you that's requested, at The Savoy at six this evening."

"Caz, it's just gone nine. What do you need me for this early?"

"Because," she announced, "I'm out of Vermouth and lemons. Oh, and you may as well bring another bottle of gin. Just to be safe."

"I thought Prissy didn't drink."

"She doesn't. The martinis are for us before we go. See you in twenty minutes. And thanks. I'll leave the door open."

I'd called her back, of course, and negotiated a happy (for Ali and me) medium whereby I'd finish prepping the Sunday roast, leave it to be served by Ali and the twins, then grab the necessary liquid refreshments and make my way to Fulham.

Which was where I found myself, now, at just after midday, the sudden leaf-filled gusts abating as I was buzzed into Caz's apartment block and made my way up to the second floor.

"Angel," Caz said, offering an absent-minded air kiss as she relieved me of my carrier bags.

"What's happening?" I asked.

"Prissy's staying at The Savoy," she answered, telling me no more than I already knew, "and she wants to meet me and my lovely friend; the one – as she says – who runs that charming pub."

"Okay," I slipped off my coat, noticing her nodding approvingly as she appraised the dark brown brogues, slim dark-blue jeans and super-soft flannel shirt that she'd bought me for Christmas the previous year.

"Except she's never been to The Marq," I answered.

"Clearly," Caz answered, plucking absently at the shirt and adjusting the hang, "but to Prissy and her ilk, every pub is charming or interesting. She's the sort of person who would look at a TB ward and describe it as 'Characterful.'"

"So what's she want, do you think?"

"Well I doubt she'll want to ask you for decorating tips. Not if she ever *sees* the inside of your charming pub."

She ushered me through to her galley kitchen and I stood aside as she busied herself baptising some olives in a cocktail jug. "But you can be assured, my sweet, she will want something. That woman has never so much as smiled at someone without having an ulterior motive."

"Perhaps she wants to rent the pub," I said trying not to think of what had happened last time I tried to pitch The Marq as a destination for poshos.

"If she does, I strongly recommend you decline the booking. She's never exited a room without leaving the sound of sobbing behind her. Mind you," Caz mused, straining two gin martinis into tumblers and handing one to me, "on consideration – and recognising how regularly your patrons are bumped off – perhaps we should actively encourage her to come. What news of last night's desiccated arrival? And why on earth were you biscuit shopping with the Maltese Machete?" she asked, referring to Chopper by the sobriquet *The Daily Express* had conferred on him

I filled Caz in on the summons to the pound shop, the realisation that he seemed as blindsided as we were by the dead man, and finished up by mentioning the fact that our crumbly pal had come with extra ventilation.

"Chopper knew he'd been shot?" Caz asked.

"Well," I blushed. Busted. "Not exactly."

"Out with it," she drained her glass, refilled it from the pitcher and waved the jug in my direction, frowning when I declined.

"I spoke to Nick."

"Ah," she smiled. Caz was rather fond of Nick, which was odd as she tended to react towards anyone who upset me in much the same way as Mary Queen of Scots would towards anyone knocking on her door trying to sell *The Watchtower*.

"And how," Caz asked, sipping her martini, grimacing, uncorking the gin bottle and pouring a slug of gin straight in on top of the cocktail ("Too much ice," she muttered before returning to me), "yes how is the pretty policeman doing?"

"Still married," I said glumly.

"And still gayer," she said, "than Christmas on Christopher Street. So there's always hope."

"Caz, he married a woman. And forgot to tell me."

"Firstly, dear, he didn't forget, he deliberately chose not to tell you. And secondly, he did so for all the right reasons. The problem with The Gays these days – and you know, dear heart, how dearly I love you – is that you've all become so bloody decent.

"He's a decent man who married a woman so he could get her out of terrible abuse in Albania, and you're a decent man who doesn't think sham marriages – let alone sham marriages which your intended keeps from you – are acceptable events."

"Intended?" I snorted. "Thank you Emily Bronte." Then, by way of changing the subject, I said, "Talking of *intended* how's your latest boyfriend?"

Now Caz went uncharacteristically quiet, finally

muttering, "Ludo and I are no more."

I was shocked. Caz hadn't mentioned the ending of the affair.

"Well it's not something you announce, really," she said. "He went on that rugby tour of Europe. His wife decided to fly out to Heidelberg to surprise him."

"Wait," I said, "Ludo was married?"

"Darling," Caz sighed, sipped her martini, fished out an olive and popped it into her mouth, "the man – when his papa finally pops his proverbials – will be worth millions. Of course he's married. All the best millionaires and heirs are these days. Though his wife deciding to pop over to Heidelberg was nearly the end of the marriage."

"What happened?" I asked, accepting a top-up.

"Well, imagine her surprise, on arriving, to find dear old Ludovico in bed with a hooker."

"Oh shit," I gasped, the cocktail suspended halfway to my mouth.

"Worse," she said, "the fly half was hiding in the wardrobe. I mean, who even knew the Germans played rugby?"

"Wait," I put my glass down, "you went out with Ludo for how long? Six weeks? And in that time, you turned him gay?" I couldn't help myself – the accumulated stress of the past twenty-four hours came out in hysterical laughing.

Caz shot daggers at me. "Bisexual darling. Like all aristos. And he needed little prompting from me."

"So why do you think Prissy wants to see me?"

"Sweetest, if I had the remotest inkling of how her bitter little mind worked, I'd be able to answer that question. But sadly, I have not, and so I can't. But meet you – and I – she desires, so we'd better finish these sharpish and get ourselves to The Savoy."

TEN

A light drizzle, borne on a gust of chilly autumnal wind followed us into The Savoy as, behind us, the revolving door continued its turn, each rotation slowing it marginally.

Caz paused in the lobby; glancing around at the huge fireplace, a warming fire blazing away in the grate; at the richly upholstered sofas dotted around; the portraits placed as though someone had just casually flung some family memorabilia on the walls; and sighed contentedly.

"Never underestimate the restorative power of a five-star hotel, Mr Bird," she said, locking eyes with a passing octogenarian, his brilliantined hair glistening in the soft light as his thick cashmere coat floated along behind him.

"Hello!" I had to snap my fingers in front of her eyes before the naked flirtation was ended and her gaze reluctantly returned to me. "We're not here for you go sugar-daddy hunting," I reminded her.

"God," Caz groaned, "why did you have to remind me?" She shook herself, straightened her back, acquiring a tall hauteur that she rarely wore these days, threw back her head and stalked – with me scuttling beside her – across the lobby, down a small flight of stairs and – turning to the left – entered an opulent cloakroom where her serviceable but slightly worn Givenchy raincoat was soon placed on a hanger next to my Debenhams overcoat (the latter receiving noticeably less care than the former at the hands of the cloakroom attendant). The coats safely stashed, a small compact having been used to check hair and make-up were in place, we exited and headed straight into the foyer.

"So," I said, trying to catch up on Caz's family tree, "I thought you had two brothers."

"I do," she said, "Gamble and Tarquin."

"And they called you Caroline," I said, wondering whether they'd run out of pretension by the time they got to her.

"Well Gamble's real name is Robert. Everyone else calls him Bobby or Bobbers, but when we were children, he loved nothing more than a round of Baccarat or Roulette, so his nickname sort of stuck."

"When I was a kid we had Monopoly and Cluedo," I observed, as we entered the palm court.

The space was light and airy; a huge glass dome filling the room with what little light was available this late in the day, and wall sconces, table lamps and peripherally dotted chandeliers filling the gap so that the space seemed almost to sparkle lightly.

The centre of the room was filled with a large ornate gazebo, a gatekeeper by a small lectern positioned in the entrance. Within the gazebo, small round tables – each one covered in pristine white linen and set with sparkling silverware and bone china crockery – hosted small parties, and, in the corner, a grand piano issued notes which managed to resemble a jazz standard whilst – as if by magic – managing to strip the melody of anything that could be either spirited, distasteful or recognisably jazz.

Caz walked straight up to the uniformed woman and announced that we were joining Baroness Holloway for tea.

The gatekeeper made a show of inspecting the book before her.

"Don't bother checking," Caz advised her. "I know she's here, I can smell the sulphur."

The woman blushed, muttered something completely noncommittal and ushered us across the room to a table in the corner where a small dark woman – her hair in a chignon so high it resembled a beehive – sat perusing a small hardback book, a pot of tea before her.

"Your ladyship," the waitress said, managing to include a discrete cough in the sentence.

The beehive came up, a pair of surprisingly bright plastic reading glasses were slipped from the end of a long aquiline nose, dropped into a handbag sitting open at the petite woman's feet and a hand waved to silence and dismiss the flunky.

"You're late," Caz's sister-in-law said to her as another waiter arrived, pulled a chair back and ushered a tight-lipped Caroline into it.

I seated myself. The watery blue eyes were turned on me. "And you're not waiting to be asked," she said in a voice which – if it had finished with a whinny and the tossing of a mane – couldn't have been more horsey.

"I was busy elsewhere and he was never taught that one should wait for a Baroness to ask you to sit," Caz said stonily. "What do you want?"

The watery eyes tore themselves away from inspecting me as though I were some sort of exotic flower and turned themselves to the waiter who had finished seating Caz, and stood, now, waiting silently.

"More tea, Benjamin," the Baroness said, "and perhaps some coffee for the lady. Strong coffee. She looks like she needs it. And bring some more pastries."

I blushed, as Benjamin murmured, "Certainly my Lady," bowed and bustled off to fetch as requested.

"Really, Caroline," the tone changed to one of concern, but one heavily influenced by the late and (in many quarters) unlamented Margaret Thatcher – equal parts sadness, concern and unspoken judgement, "it's so lovely to see you. But did you have to consume the crate of gin before lunch?"

Caz glowered. "What I do, Priscilla, where I do it and who I do it with is none of your concern." She looked around her, spotted a waiter, raised a finger to summon him

59

over, and said, "Two large gin martinis, please. Stirred. With olives. And as dry as you can make 'em without delivering neat gin."

The waiter nodded, made to move away, and Caz stopped him with a hand on his arm before turning to me as Benjamin arrived with the earlier order. "D'you want a drink?" she asked me and, glancing at the purse-lipped woman on the other side of the table, I considered declining, before realising that to do so would be to abandon my best friend, and requested, as there was already coffee on the table, a large Calvados.

Caz glared at Benjamin as he placed a coffee cup and saucer before her. "Unless you want a scene of epic proportions, Benjamin, I would consider – very seriously – your next move."

Benjamin, the coffee pot poised to begin pouring, froze, a panic sweat breaking out on his forehead, his gaze immediately going to the coiffured gorgon on the other side of the table.

"I'd love some coffee," I said brightly, sliding the cup and saucer across the table in front of me.

The pursed mouth broke, favoured me with a tiny smile – displaying, before the pink painted lips closed firmly, a set of teeth so small they might have belonged to a Yorkshire terrier – and Benjamin filled my cup. Priscilla accepted a refill of her tea and raised the cup to her mouth, waiting until she had sipped, swallowed and put the cup back almost silently into her saucer before speaking again.

"Caroline, I really don't understand why we always have to be so uncomfortable with each other," she said, as the two martinis and the Calvados hit the linen.

Caz favoured the waiter with an apologetic smile, murmured her thanks, raised one of the glasses to her lips and swallowed most of the contents in one before putting the glass down and responding to the other woman.

"Because," she said, "when we were at school, you persuaded an entire year of girls to ignore me. For an entire year. You had me blackballed from every club, group or gang I tried to join, and you put out the rumour that I was illegitimate.

"To add insult to injury, you then managed to hook my idiot brother, deflower him, bully him into marrying you and then had the audacity to behave to me as though we had never even met."

The woman opposite sipped her tea, put the teacup, once again, silently, into the saucer and said, "We all do stupid things when we're children. And, my dear, I would never have suggested – openly or via rumour – that you were illegitimate. Although I may have suggested that your mother wasn't much better than she should be."

Caz drained what was left in the glass, held it above her head and yelled, "Another martini," so loudly that the distant sounds of a neutered *Ain't nobody's business if I do* were disrupted by a series of bum notes, and a woman three tables away gasped (though whether at the raised voice, the demand for grain alcohol, or the flat keys, it was hard to tell).

Caz addressed the woman opposite her in a voice so quiet now that it was almost a whisper. "You married into my family, Priscilla, and I can do nothing about that. But if you mention her one more time, I will personally come around to your side of the table and rip that ridiculous periwig from your scalp strand by strand. Now: I will ask this only three times, so for the second time: What. Do. You. Want?"

The two women stared at each other in undisguised loathing, each of them completely ignoring me while I reached across, picked up my calvados, sniffed, sipped and finally said, "If you'd like to book a room and a selection of duelling implements, I'm sure that The Savoy can arrange it. Just call me when you're done," I finished, addressing the last line to Caz and watching as each of the women snapped back to the present.

"Bobbers has done something brainless," Priscilla finally said, a look of supreme discomfort – at, perhaps, the fact that she was having to discuss this with Bobbers' sister – crossing her face.

"Stupider than marrying you?" Caz shot back.

"Caroline," Prissy responded, the Thatcher tone creeping back in, "I know you're not a fan of mine."

"In the way that, say, a mongoose isn't a fan of a cobra. Or penicillin of syphilis," she sighed. "Who's he been shagging now?"

"Caroline," Prissy fixed my friend with another angry glare, "your brother's made some, shall we say, marital errors in the past, but they are all – as I say – very far, and very firmly in the past."

Caroline laughed, lifted her martini and sipped from it. "Mistakes? They were cries for help from a drowning man." This last addressed to me.

"Now," she put the glass back down, "for the third time—"

"He's ruined the entire family," Priscilla, Baroness Holloway said in the same tone that, I imagine, she might have said, say, *he's served the Burgundy with the foie gras*, "while I was having my hair done."

I eyed the cut and blow-dry opposite me and decided that, yes, the rich truly were a different race.

Caz jerked upright. "Explain."

"Bobbers wanted to look big, so he did a deal. Something to do with some oil rights that the Fifth Earl had acquired in Kyrgyzstan or Uzbekistan or some bloody Stan. Thing is, he thought he was doing a genuine decent deal."

"Except?"

"It was sanctions busting."

"Sanctions busting?" Caz asked, in the way she might, for example, intone the phrase, *Primark sale rack*.

"It's illegal to trade with some people, or countries," I offered, "regardless of how much money you might make from them."

"Yes, Daniel," Caz turned eyes that were blazing angrily on me, "I am familiar with the phrase, and that to willingly and knowingly enter into trade with those people or countries would be sanctions busting."

"Which," Prissy finished, "leads to prison sentences, financial implications and reputational disaster."

"Just what did you have done at the hairdresser?" Caz demanded.

"I was in Monaco."

"You had one job, Prissy. Stop Bobbers from doing anything stupid. So what, exactly, has happened?"

"He's been shaked."

"Shaken?"

"*Shaked.*"

"Shook?"

"Are we doing verb declensions all afternoon?" I asked.

"Define *shaked*?" Caz demanded.

"Some idiot who dresses up as a member of Saudi royalty," Prissy explained. "Not, obviously, the one who went to prison for it, some other con man in a keffiyeh has recorded Bobby's misdemeanour," she said, reducing Bobbers' contravening of international sanctions to the status of a parking ticket. "Has recorded him, and is threatening to send the recordings to the police and to the papers. But, for a fee, he's willing to forget any of it ever happened."

"Which is a good thing," Caz said, downing her second martini as the third one arrived, and growling, "keep 'em coming, sweetheart," to the bemused waiter.

"So how much does Sheikh Shakedown want to wipe the tapes and develop amnesia?"

"Two million pounds."

Caz downed the third martini, reached into her bag, pulled out a bottle of gin, filled the empty glass to the brim, downed that, all without glancing in my direction, and looked Prissy full in the face.

"How much is Bobbers worth?" she asked.

"Between what he got from your grandfather, and what he's likely to inherit, far more than that," Prissy answered, "but none of it is lying around cash."

Caz frowned deeply. "What does Bobbers say about this?"

"Your brother," Prissy answered, her face setting angrily, "knows nothing of our conversation. He's not – as you know – a strong man at the best of times."

Caz snorted humourlessly. "So what does he think you're doing here?" she asked.

"I'm looking for a painting for the chapel," Prissy responded, as I might, for example, say, *I'd like a nice print for the guest bedroom.*

"There's a sale of late Renaissance religious work at Frankleby's – all anaemic saints and gym-toned Christs writhing in ecstasy. He thinks I'm rifling through the school of Veronese. And I want it kept that way," she commanded, eyes blazing. "This *situation* has left him knocked for six. I don't want him upset or disturbed any further."

"I should imagine he'll be somewhat disturbed if he goes to prison for the rest of his life," Caz murmured.

Prissy rolled her eyes. "Which is why we need to figure out a way to make this situation go away," she said, pouring another cup of Darjeeling.

"So let me get this straight," I said, "you want us to go see this man. What's his name, by the way?"

"Balthazar Lowe," she answered, splashing a drop of milk into the cup and stirring it briskly. "Vile little man, calls himself an intelligence broker, lives in a huge house near Regent's Park."

"Okay, you want us to see Lowe, and – what? Pay him off?"

She sipped from the cup and before Prissy could speak, Caz had butted in. "If paying him off was the plan, Daniel, I suspect neither you nor I would have been invited to tea this evening."

"As I say," Prissy said, carefully replacing the bone china teacup in the saucer, "we simply don't have enough cash at hand to pay him off even if we wanted to. Which we don't."

Her eyes blazed. "This family," she announced, channelling her inner Thatcher again, "does not negotiate with blackmailers."

"Just with oligarchs and sanctioned terrorists," Caz responded, staring absent-mindedly into an empty martini glass.

"It was business," Prissy hissed. "And I should imagine that someone with," she paused, searching for the right words, "your moral compass would be highly unlikely to cast the first stone."

Caz didn't even flinch. Her eyes rose from their contemplation of the glassware and blazed, briefly, with fury. "And yet, here you sit, opposite someone with my moral compass. So," she sat up straight, and stared solidly across the table at Prissy, "what do you want me to do?"

"Go to this man – this Balthazar Lowe – and figure out how to close this down."

Caz frowned. "How? In what way?"

Prissy looked at her, smirked, looked at me pointedly, and said, "Caroline, we have the internet even up north. We know what you and your," at this she jerked her head at me, "friend have been up to."

"What exactly does that mean?" Caz firmed up against the gorgon.

"We've seen how you two have been making names for yourselves for sorting out problems that other people have trouble sorting out."

"You've made us sound like the A-Team," I protested, receiving, for my stab at ice-breaking humour, a warning stare from Caz.

"So if you're not going to pay him off," Caz pressed, "what do you want us to do? Threaten him? Murder him? Break into his house and tie him up until he hands back the tapes?"

Prissy shrugged, "What you do, Caroline, is up to you but you can be certain of one point – if you do nothing," she said, leaning forward slightly, "Bobbers goes to prison, what's left of the family cash goes to lawyers' fees, and your dear old daddy goes to his grave knowing that the family name is disgraced."

ELEVEN

Caz was halfway towards Waterloo Bridge, marching in front of an aggressively-honking Nissan as she sailed across the road before I caught up with her.

"Calm down," I entreated as she stomped aggressively up the Aldwych. "What's up?"

"Up?" She stopped dead, pausing only long enough to fling her Pucci patterned scarf over her shoulder. "Have you suffered a blow to the head?"

"You're not skint," I said, shivering as an arctic gust swept down from Kingsway and made me wish I'd been wise enough – as Caz had been – to swipe a bit of decent schmutter from the last fashion mag job we'd both had. "I know your grandma left you money."

We stood on the pavement as, behind Caz, the Sunday matinee crowd from the new Duran Duran Jukebox Musical *Planet Earth* (a show with a plot so Byzantine that one reviewer had titled their demolition 'Is there something I should know?') oozed out of a theatre, and – with the look of a coliseum mob on whom the Christians had been set – milled about absently.

Caz tilted her head back, breathed through her nostrils, refocussed her somewhat bleary eyes on me and said, "Funds. She left me funds, Danny. Money is something one never needs to talk of or think about. Funds are what one acquires then watches slowly but inexorably drain away."

I laughed dryly. "Okay, but you're not exactly skint, so what's the problem?"

She slumped her shoulders, set her face and stared upwards at the impressive frontages of the buildings around us. The whipping wind made her eyes tear up. "Really? After everything, we're having this conversation?"

"No," I looked around desperately. "We're not having this conversation but," I looked around absently, "are we looking for a taxi or what?"

"No," she said definitively, "we are not looking for a taxi."

"So—" I said, but, before I could say another word she interrupted me.

"We are going somewhere I can throw up a pint of gin – The Waldorf has nice restrooms – and then we are going somewhere quiet to talk. Because talk, Mr Bird, we must."

*

"People have been trying to demolish this building forever," Caz looked around her at the rather plain interior, the checkerboard flooring reflecting dully in the mixed moon- and street-light.

"But it's still here."

She regarded the empty, moonlit church, the blue-orange light from outside leaking into the space and shivered slightly, wrapping her arms around herself.

We'd made our way – after Caz had dealt with the immediate effects of a martini overdose – to a small church which seemed to sit in the middle of a traffic island in the middle of Aldwych, and, as I'd stood outside wondering why we were huddling in the doorway of an architectural anomaly, Caz had dug into her capacious handbag and extracted a set of keys.

"Perk of the trade," she'd said, explaining nothing as she slid, firstly, a couple of slim modern keys into their matching padlocks, then a larger, more aged key into a hole in the door.

And thus, we'd found ourselves sitting in the apse of St Clement Dane, alone, listening to the whoosh of passing traffic and watching the slashing upper-deck lights of buses as they passed, unseeing beyond the high, dim leaded windows.

"But it's still here," she finished.

I waited, silently, wondering what, exactly was the issue between Caz and Prissy. After a while, she spoke again.

"My mother used to take me here. When I was younger. Before she left. Later, of course – after she'd packed her bags and left us – they said she'd been meeting her lover here. She was, as they said," Caz inhaled deeply through her nose, her back straightening, "no better than she should have been. Except her father flew multiple air raids. On Dresden, on places that – even today – can't be talked of. He was a soldier and a gentleman, and she was his daughter. And I'm hers."

She sighed, then cracked and pushed a stray hair from her eyes as she coughed briskly.

"And – for her and for me – money is not the point."

"So, what," I essayed, "is the problem?"

"That woman," she glanced over her shoulder, towards the doors we'd come through. "That attitude."

I waited, glancing around in the gloom, as random faces from gilt-framed portraits were suddenly illuminated by passing buses, glared at me, then vanished.

"My family have done what needed to be done. Because it had to be done and because it was the right thing to be done. We're very much aware of our privilege. And of our origins. And we are not traitors or sanctions breakers. We're better than this."

"The Russians," I prompted.

She nodded. "Bobbers is not – despite all you may have heard – a moron. Mind you, he's not exactly a genius either. I find it highly unlikely that he's managed to find, hook, catch and reel in a sanctioned oligarch, do it all on his own and then get caught on tape discussing the deal."

"So what do you think happened?"

"Prissy," she spat the word. "Prissy loves money, she loves power – or, at least, she loves people thinking she has power. Over them. My bet – if I had any ready cash to place a wager with – would be that Prissy found the Russians, introduced Bobbers to them and then made the fatal mistake of assuming that the deal was done, thus she could take her eye off the ball. With disastrous results."

It made sense.

"So what are we going to do?" I asked.

"*We*?" She turned to face me. "*We* are going to do nothing my dear. This isn't your problem, though she tried to make it so."

"I'm your friend," I insisted, "and friends help each other out."

Caz shook her head. "It infuriates me that that woman has managed to manoeuvre this so well. To get me to bring you along, knowing that you'd feel obliged. To drop Bobbers into the mess, so that she knew I'd feel obliged. To throw my daddy at me, and make it my job to fix the mess her greed undoubtedly got us in to. And she gets to go back to shopping for frocks while the mess is sorted. I hate her so much."

I sat in silence as another bus – the light from its top deck illuminating the church, showing our breath coming from us in clouds – whooshed past on the street outside, then: "Hatred notwithstanding," I said at length, "what are we going to do?"

Caz smiled sadly. "You'd really help?"

I put an arm around her, felt her bristle slightly, then relax and lean against me. "I have to help," I said. "It's what friends do. It's what you have done for me so many times before."

"But I'm never there," she said. "Any time you need help I'm missing, on holiday with some man or off gallivanting somewhere."

"You're there when it counts. So I'm here."

"When it counts," she slurred, the gin – or the emotion – finally hitting her.

"So what are we going to do?" I pressed.

Caz sat up straight, rifled through her capacious handbag and pulled out her mobile phone. "We're going to call a cab. Then, I'm going to head home and consume several litres of water, a sachet of Dioralyte, a fistful of paracetamol. Then, we're going to sleep and tomorrow – after all that – we'll figure out what's to happen next."

She smiled at me in the moonlight, her eyes twinkling with what was either tears or gin weep, stroked my cheek gently and then hit dial on her phone.

"Thank you," she whispered as the phone at the other end began to ring.

TWELVE

"Is this gonna take long?" Ali asked, dropping her not inconsiderable bulk into a kitchen chair which groaned almost as loudly as the chest freezer on the opposite side of the room. "Only, I've got a pub full of punters out there, and that part-timer you got to help me wouldn't know the difference between an IPA and an IUD."

I looked around the table. Ray and Dash sat on one side, Caz at the head, Ali facing the boys and me at the other head of the table.

"Look," I started, cleared my throat, then starting again, "I know that this latest, um…" I searched for the right word.

"Disaster?" Ali offered.

"Debacle," Caz proposed, a gently mocking smile playing around her lips.

The twins looked at each other, and – as one – suggested, "Horror story."

"I was going to say *situation*," I stared at them all, "though *disaster* is probably a fair stab," I nodded a grudging acknowledgement at Ali, before turning to the boys. "*Horror story*, however, seems really over the top."

"You've been 'Serving sausage rolls and ploughman's lunches in a room feet away from where a decomposing corpse lay rotting,'" Dash said, quoting from that morning's *Daily Mail*.

"'The Marquess of Queensbury puts the 'Pub' in 'Bad

Publicity',"' Ray added, having flicked through *The Sun*.

"Right," I said, "I'm banning those rags. Both of them. Immediately. Possession will be a sackable offence from here on in."

"Oh sweetest," Caz said, "even *The Guardian* suggested this might be the most murderous boozer in Britain. Though, of course, they misspelled *murderous*. Look, the thing is—" she said, but was interrupted by Ali.

"The thing is," she said, "like I always say – every time – there is no such thing as bad publicity. We are rammed out there, so unless you want Flighty Fiona giving away free pints, I really need to get back to the bar sharpish."

"Okay," I looked around the assembled. "Does anyone," and here I fixed my headiest stare on Ali, "have any idea who the stiff was?"

"Oh Gawd," Dash moaned, "he's off again."

"Why you looking at me like that?" Ali bristled, a deep red blush suffusing her from the neck to the hairline of her crew-cut head.

"Because you've been around here the longest," I said, turning to Dash, "and what does, 'He's off again,' mean?"

"Danny, mate," Ray said, "we love you. Really, we do, but this whole Jessica Fletcher thing has got to stop. Let the five-oh do their job. Get back to the ploughman's."

"So just cos I've been here longer than ten minutes, you think I've been burying stiffs in the cellar?" Ali's umbrage dialled up a notch.

"No, Ali," I protested, before turning back to Ray. "*Jessica Fletcher*? She's a little old lady. Couldn't I have been Sam Spade?"

Dash sniggered. "You can claim to be six foot three on the internet," he said, "but that don't make you Jack Reacher."

I shook my head exasperatedly, "What does that even mean?" I asked.

At which point Caz slapped the table with her open palm. "Focus, people!" she called.

"Look, Ali," I turned back to my bar manager, who was now silently fuming, in the manner of a double-denim-clad Krakatoa, and tried to diffuse the tension. "I was not for a second suggesting you had anything to do with the body; only that you might remember something – some event, some person – that might have put them down there."

"Have you been on drugs for the past year?" Ali asked, the first tremors evident. "The pub is owned by Chopper Falzone. *Chopper fucking Falzone.* And you're asking me if I have any idea who would have planted a stiff in the cellar?"

"Fair point," I held my hands up in obeisance. "Except I don't think Chopper did this. It doesn't fit what we know of his MO for starters. And you two can stop sniggering," I added, pointing at the twins.

"Sorry," they removed the smirks from their mugs, before Dash added, "but MO is so not a Jessica Fletcher word. You just put that in to look hard, didn't you?"

"Oh, grow up," I groaned.

"So, Ali, do you have any idea who might have been planted downstairs? Or any idea who might have done it? I mean, twenty years ago, was Chopper the force he is today? Were there other, I don't know, faces on the scene?"

"Faces?" Dash rolled his eyes and pulled his phone out of his jeans pocket, tapping at it.

"Bit Guy Ritchie," Caz said, a single raised eyebrow suggesting I might be going a little deep-end on the gangster parlance.

"Boys," I turned to the ASBO twins, "can you do some digging? Check out the history of this place. Any specific mentions of this pub in papers, court cases, any suggestion that there might have been another gangster who could have been – I don't know – muscling in on Chopper's territory."

"Can't you ask the pretty policeman?" Ray asked, and received my most venomous glare

"No."

"Why not?" he persevered.

"Cos he's got a wife, and Danny here is still coming to

terms with people who appear to be one thing and turn out to be something else," Caz announced.

"And Ali," I pleaded, glad of the opportunity to move the discussion on from Nick and Arianne, "if you do think of anything, can you let me know."

Her eyes blazed. "I won't think of anything," she said, "cos I don't know nothing. Now," she stood from her seat, "you need anything else? Or should I get back before Flighty Fiona starts handing out free shots to the neighbourhood drunks?"

She bustled out of the room, and I looked around the table. "Is it me or did she seem a bit too eager to get away?" I asked.

"She's just worried about the bar," Ray said.

"Plus," Caz said quietly, "of all of us, she was probably the only one anywhere near the place twenty years ago."

"Jesus," I shook my head. "How long has Ali been working here?"

The trio looked at each other as though attempting to silently calculate the woman's tenure. "Since God was a small boy," Caz decided.

"But that doesn't mean she had anything to do with…" Ray whistled and pointed downwards as the freezer recommenced it's banging.

"I know," I said and sent the boys back to the bar before Ali could complain about being deliberately short-handed.

"So what happens next?" Caz asked as they trudged back to work.

"I really don't know. I guess I wait for Nick to call again, and see what I can get out of him."

"Or you could call him first."

"Or I could call him first," I agreed. "But we have the other issue to deal with as well," I said pulling my chair around so it was next to hers. "So how do you propose we handle that?"

"Easy," she said, "we go and see this Balthazar Lowe, blackmailer to the stars."

"You think that's wise?" I asked. "This early in the game?"

"Oh we've already lost some time. I'll bet that Prissy spent days trying to figure out how to make him go away or intimidate him or simply ignore him out of existence before she realised she had to do something."

"And the something was calling us."

"Exactly. And now that we *have* been called, I propose to take the skirmish – if not the battle – to Mr Lowe, rather than waste any more time trying to figure out a strategy."

"So – what? We just go knock on his door?"

"Or we call the number he gave Prissy, tell him we've been authorised to negotiate and make an appointment to see him tomorrow at his office," she said, reaching for her phone.

As Caz dialled the number, I headed out of the kitchen towards the bar and stopped just outside of the door.

The long hallway that lead to the bar was, as usual, filled with boxes of crisps, cases of booze and the usual detritus that really should have been in the cellar if anyone could be bothered to continually go up and down to that dark dank space (and if it hadn't already been filled with slowly decomposing bodies, my overactive – and over dramatic – mind pointed out).

And at the end of the hallway, huddled down as though trying to hide and peering through the beaded curtain that lead to the bar proper, was Ali.

I cleared my throat and she jumped, staggering backwards and landing flat on her back a few feet from me.

I ran to help her up, enduring her most outraged glare and a furious – but whispered – entreaty that I keep my voice down.

As I helped her to her feet, I realised that Ali – the woman who had faced down drunks, gangsters and deranged drag queens – was shaking and visibly upset.

"What's up?" I asked, trying to keep my voice light.

She tore her eyes from the curtain at the end of the hall –

the low autumn light making it impossible to see anything beyond it – and stared wildly into mine.

"That man outside, the one who's just walked in. Can you get him out? Please." she entreated me, her eyes filling up with tears.

"What's going on, Ali?" I asked, and she shushed me.

"Get rid of him. Don't let him know I'm here," she begged.

I nodded. "Wait here," I said.

I made my way down the hallway, entering the bar just in time to hear Dash say, "Yeah she was here a minute ago. Danny? You seen Ali?"

"Ali who?" I asked, shooting daggers at Dash.

"Ali—" he broke off, finally getting my point.

I turned to the man on the other side of the bar, who was regarding the two of us with a faintly-amused turn of the lips.

"She here?" he asked.

Despite the fact it was November, he had a tan (which did look like it had been applied with a brush) and a check flannel shirt which was open at least two buttons deeper than was strictly necessary, displaying a matt of silvery hair at odds with the vibrant 'beach blond' barnet atop his head. Basically, if he'd been going for '80s Sybaritic chic,' he'd hit the jackpot. Only his face – leathery and 'lived in' like a derelict squat – rang a bum note.

I shook my head. "No. We used to have an Ali work here, but she quit."

"She quit?" he asked, the smirk accompanied now by an upturned eyebrow. "Only, I'm fairly sure I saw her standing…" he waved his hand up and down in my direction. I noticed that the back of his hand had a tattoo – a crude devil, the shape still visible, all sneering grin and spiky horns with a tail that snaked up inside his leather jacket, "right where you're stood now."

I shook my head. "She's not here," I said, noticing – as the low autumnal sunlight caught it – a gold chain with an ankh charm nestling in his chest hair.

"Not any more," he said, the smile dying as a cold look came into his eyes.

We stared each other out for a few moments until eventually the other man grinned, nodding as though at a private joke. "Well," he said, turning to go, "if she does pop in – y'know, for her redundancy money, or whatever," and here his voice rose in volume, "can you let her know that Jimmy was asking after her and Carlton? Give her my best, won't you." And so saying, he nodded at Dash and allowed his eyes to stray slowly and pointedly towards the beaded curtain through which Ali had fled, before turning his gaze back to mine, winking and leaving.

THIRTEEN

Balthazar Lowe's offices were in a large Georgian Square in Marylebone and were showing, on Google, as the home of: The Children's Protection Fund.

"Maybe he's a genuine charity," I mused to Caz as the taxi crawled its way down Marylebone Road.

"Or maybe," she answered, applying another layer of bright scarlet lipstick, "he's smart enough to know that anyone who receives large amounts of cash from frightened people needs to have something other than *International Extortionist* on his letterhead. Whatever," she decided, "setting up Bobbers and then demanding money by menace is hardly the act of a Mother Theresa. Okay, you're clear on how we're going to play this, right?"

I nodded. After Ali's visitor had left the day before, I'd spent a considerable period of time trying to get her to talk to me, but she'd closed up like a broad-shouldered, crew-cut clam and would not be drawn on who the man had been, only that, if he ever came in here again, none of us was to give him her whereabouts or even mention her name.

Eventually, I'd headed back into the kitchen, where Caz had been hunched over her iPad, a small leather-bound notebook open beside her as she made notes for the battle campaign on Balthazar Lowe.

"We don't have the money," I recited, as in the front of the taxi my dad gesticulated at a cyclist who had just cut in front of him and demanded to know what sort of death wish the individual in question actually had, "but we're trying to get it. We need to have a little more time."

"How much more time?" she asked.

"A month. Maybe six weeks."

"And what's happening in the meantime?"

"We need to see the evidence. All of it."

"Why?"

"Really?" I frowned at her. "So we can see where he keeps it all – safe in the office, offsite, wherever."

"But we're not going to tell him that," Caz prompted.

"No," I shook my head, "of course not. We're going to tell him that we need to be sure there is sufficient evidence to justify the money he's demanding."

"Good," she patted me on the thigh, slid her lipstick back into her purse and peered out the window. "We're there." Caz turned and winked at me. "Showtime."

The taxi pulled up outside a three-storey Georgian town house, three steps leading from the pavement to an ominous black doorway with a huge concrete urn filled with some sort of evergreen plant sitting to the left of the door.

Two large unshuttered windows sat, one either side of the doorway, though there was no sign of any life beyond them. The wind had stripped the trees in the square and packs of rustling brown leaves were being blown across the pavement.

A discrete brass plaque to the right of the doorway, positioned over a single bell press and polished so definitively that our reflections – distorted and haunted – stared back at us from underneath the words: The Children's Protection Fund. 'We are children of the world.'

"There you go," Caz nodded at the plate. "If you ever needed proof that the whole thing was a sham."

I frowned at the plaque, puzzled by her reference.

"He's quoting the bloody Bee Gees," she tutted, pressing her finger firmly on the bell press. "Hardly Mother Theresa."

A woman's voice – tinny and adenoidal – came through a

speaker discretely concealed behind the evergreen plant and, as she spoke, an almost imperceptible movement just above my eyeline drew my attention upwards where a small black security camera had swung into motion and was now pointed at us.

"Hello?" the woman's voice said.

"Oh, hello," Caz spoke in her most cut-glass RP. "It's Lady Caroline Holloway and Mr Daniel Bird to see Mr Lowe."

"Oh." The adenoidal robotic voice seemed puzzled. "Wait a moment, please," it said, and there was a click, then silence.

The door remained firmly barred against us.

Caz stared pointedly up at the camera and was just lifting a finger to press the button one more time when the locks clicked and the door swung slowly open.

A tall, almost skeletally-thin woman stood before us, her salt and pepper hair swept into a meringue-like confection atop a head which looked like its brothers might have modelled for Easter Island.

At the end of her long, pointed nose a pair of almost comically-harsh horn-rimmed spectacles perched. She peered down the proboscic slope, through the lenses and, having registered that we were, in fact, still standing on her doorstep, smiled a smile so broad as to be almost deranged.

"My Lady," she said, displaying a set of teeth which – like Britain's transport infrastructure – were stained, crooked and fucked beyond repair. They didn't need a dentist; they needed demolition.

She switched off the gurn and stepped to one side, ushering us into the building. "How kind of you to come. Mr Lowe awaits you in his office."

We stepped into the hallway.

Ahead and to our right a set of stairs lead upwards. To our left another hallway lead, I assumed, to what would have been the parlour and the kitchen. To the left and right were doors into other rooms, and the one on the right was partly open showing what looked like a reception desk within.

On the walls, wherever there was a bit of empty space, framed portraits of photogenic children looking wistful were displayed.

She introduced herself as Miss Morgan and, having taken our coats, waved us towards the stairs.

"Mr Lowe is on the first floor. If you would take a seat, he'll be with you shortly. Would you care for some tea or coffee?"

Caz gave her a look of pure outrage and I declined on both our behalves.

"A million pounds," Caz muttered as we trudged slowly up the stairs, "and he's offering tea? You know, Danny, if there's one thing worse than an extortionist, it's a cheap extortionist."

We reached the top of the stairs and, on the landing, were met with a selection of large sofas dotted around a selection of low-level coffee tables.

On the tables, brochures featuring more tragically photogenic young 'uns were piled. Even I had to admit that The Children's Protection Fund were laying it on a bit thick.

We sat and Caz picked up one of the brochures. I watched her pretend to flick aimlessly through it as her eyes darted around the bland space.

"Anything of interest?" I murmured.

Her eyes dropped to the pages before her and she pursed her lips. "Malawi, Namibia, villagers in India, and more ill-placed apostrophes than a butcher's convention," she concluded as, from behind us, a man's voice rang out.

"Miss Holloway."

I stood and turned.

Balthazar Lowe – for I assumed it was he – was, well, not to put too fine a point on it, Balthazar Lowe was *fine*.

He stood about six foot two, his shoulders broad and his waist trim. His hair was jet-black, and styled into a seemingly casual quiff that I reckon took weekly – if not daily – barbering to maintain. He was tanned, but in the way of someone who spends their time in executive lounges rather than in the style of Ali's visitor, who looked like he spent his time in back lounges.

Lowe's eyes were almost turquoise-blue, almond-shaped, and – along with his chiselled jaw and high cheekbones – lent him the air of a Mongol overlord, if Mongol overlords did catwalk modelling.

He wore a pale-blue shirt, open at the neck, a pair of slim-fitting black jeans, and a pair of black suede loafers. At his wrist, a single silver bangle gleamed. There was no sign of a watch, or of a wedding ring.

Caz stood slowly to her feet, turned as if in slow motion to face him and held a hand out to him. "Lady Holloway," she said coldly, "is the actual title."

At this, Lowe's lips curled slightly. He nodded, took her hand, bowed and kissed it gently. "As you wish," he said, seeming to register me for the first time. "And this is...?"

"This is my associate Mr Bird," Caz said, and I stepped forward offering my hand, which he gripped solidly.

"Good to meet you," he said, somewhat dismissively, before turning back to Caz. "I thought we agreed you alone?"

"Mr Bird goes where I go," Caz deadpanned. "Shall we get started?"

Lowe stared her down for a moment, then nodded curtly. "Shall we?" He gestured behind him

Caz, in high dudgeon, swept past him and headed towards the open door of what I assumed was his office. Lowe watched her pass him, a small sardonic smile on his lips, glanced briefly at me then gestured for me to follow her. "After you, Mr Bird," he said.

The office we entered was high-ceilinged, light, thanks to well-placed halogen spots, and furnished in an odd selection of styles. In one corner of the room hulked a huge dark wooden desk, leather-topped and looking like something that generals and industrialists would once have sat behind. Behind the desk was a tall metal filing cabinet.

The windows looked out on the square, the little park in the middle already crowded in shadows as the sun began to move westwards.

Lowe directed us not to the mahogany desk, but to a pale wood round table on the opposite side of the room, three chairs gathered democratically around it.

"Tea?" he said, sitting himself at a chair. "Coffee?"

"No thanks," Caz, managing to make a polite decline sound like a giant 'fuck you,' answered for both of us.

"Well, then," he placed his hands palm-down on the table and spread his fingers, "how may I help you?"

"Mr Lowe," Caz addressed him, "I am lead to understand that you have some evidence that places my brother in a difficult situation."

Lowe smiled, "It places him in prison, Lady Caroline. If it ever gets out."

Caz stared him down. "My sister-in-law," she said at length, "tells me that you played her some recordings of Bobby down the phone."

"That's true," Lowe said, turning, now, to me, "are you sure I can't get you some tea?"

"No," I shook my head, adding, "thanks," as an afterthought.

"I wonder if you could tell us, Mr Lowe, just how these recordings came into your possession?"

"Well it's rather simple, Lady Caroline," Lowe seemed to be enjoying this game, his smile broadening a he recalled his scam. "I dressed up as a representative of a certain Middle Eastern government, had some associates wire me for sound, approached your brother and proposed buying from him the lease to an oil well which he holds in Central Asia."

"Interesting," Caz murmured. "Do go on."

"There was a considerable amount of money on offer for the rights and your brother seemed very interested in the proposition, suggesting, at length, that we settle the funds via the Luxembourg branch of a St Petersburg corporation which he has an interest in, as a way of avoiding taxes on the sums payable."

Caz nodded, a look that said she was absorbing all of these facts on her face but a twinkle in her eye that told me she'd already made her mind up. "And this St Petersburg corporation…" she prompted.

"Is half-owned by one Oleg Nikolayevich. Who is explicitly named on the list of both European- and US-sanctioned individuals, with whom it is illegal to trade," Lowe finished, shaking his head and tutting as though disappointed by the situation.

"And my brother suggested this transaction himself?" Caz asked.

"Suggested it and enthusiastically lobbied for it," Lowe answered.

Caz looked around the room. "I'd like to see the evidence, Mr Lowe," she said.

"You can hear it," he answered, "any time you'd like. Just let me have a telephone number and I will have the tapes – as much of them as you can bear – played to you."

"But I'd like to see it," she pressed.

Lowe frowned. "It's a sound file, Lady Caroline. An mp3. There are no physical items to show you."

Now it was Caz's turn to frown.

"But I stress," Lowe said, "as I stressed to your sister-in-law that, unless a sizeable donation is made to The Children's Protection Fund, the relevant sound files could well end up in the hands of the British, European and American authorities. And that wouldn't go very well for your poor brother."

He paused to let this sink in, then turned to me. "You're very quiet, Mr Bird," he said, "don't you have anything to add to the conversation?"

"I'm just here to make sure she doesn't leave fingerprints when she garrottes you."

Lowe chuckled. "Oh, bigger beasts than Lady Caroline have tried worse," he murmured in response.

Caz looked around the room.

"Tell me, Mr Lowe, what do you do here?" she asked.

"Do?" Lowe seemed puzzled for a moment, then recovered his equilibrium and waved a hand airily at the space around him. "I run The Children's Protection Fund. We support programs to help support, protect and develop the lives of young people in the developing world."

"And I'm guessing that this *supporting*," she said, lending the word a pointed tone, "brings you into contact with many intelligent people."

"We're lucky enough to deal with many experts in their fields."

"And then you met Robert. Or Bobbers, as we who've known him his whole life call him."

"I fail to see—" Lowe began, but was cut off by Caz.

"My brother, Mr Lowe, is – not to put too fine a point on it – an imbecile. Really. He wears loafers and boots because he can't tie a decent knot in his laces. His businesses – the family businesses – are run by other people precisely because Bobbers and those around him know that he's a knife so dull he couldn't cut water. In fact, his principal employment in business is exactly to be a charming sweet figurehead. To entertain visiting Americans or Sheiks.

"Because he's good at that, Mr Lowe. He's sweet, loyal and loving, but he struggles with the plot twists in *Peppa bloody Pig*. So I find it hard – not to say impossible – to believe that this simple man, on his own and with no prompting from anyone, concocted a sanctions-busting, tax-evading complicated corporate dodge the likes of which you're describing."

Lowe tilted his head, the smirk widening. "And yet," he said, snapping his fingers.

From hidden speakers in the corners of the room, a voice – posh, reedy and slurring slightly as though speaking after the consumption of a few bottles of champagne – issued, "So we'll funnel the money through the Blackgold accounts in Luxembourg. Ever been to Luxembourg? Dull, but great chocolate. But dull. What?" he asked as another voice muttered something. "Oh, yes, we'll settle to Luxembourg – no tax then, you see, cos they'll send it straight off to some Johnnies in The Caymans. Dull there too. Why is it always really bally dull where rich old farts send all their money? Oh, I don't mind if I do," he slurred, and I could almost see him holding his glass out for a top-up.

Lowe snapped his fingers and the tape stopped. His face, now, had a different look to the amiable and slightly-bemused one he'd worn in the face of Caz's hostility for the past few minutes. Now, his almond eyes, high cheekbones and the smile on his face gave him a wolfish air.

"Terms, I believe, have been explained already. So what I'd really like to know, *Lady* Caroline, is why you've wasted my time and yours by coming here."

Caz stood up. "I came," she said, "because I like to look in the faces of the people who are attempting to extort money from my family before I tell them to go to hell."

"Oh I've been to hell, Caroline," he said, dropping the honorific. "I've been there and I've seen the faces of the children and women there. And I've seen the tax-dodging internationalists who swan in and out and try their damnedest not to see the people who can never leave the place."

"And tell me," Caz snapped back, "did you get the Cartier Bangle at duty free *before* flying in to hell, or on your way back out?"

Lowe shrugged. "Three million. I prefer cash, bullion, stones, or bearer securities. In ten days."

"I was told the figure was two million," Caz squawked.

"It was," Lowe said, standing too, "But that was before today. Now, I believe Miss Morgan has your coats. We won't meet again. Unless you're bringing the funds."

And so saying, he crossed to his desk, unlocked a drawer, withdrew a small laptop, opened it and began typing on the keyboard.

"Do show yourselves out. It was pleasant meeting you Mr Bird," he said without looking up.

FOURTEEN

Down on the pavement, Caz dived into her handbag, extracted her phone and jabbed furiously at it.

"Bastard!" she spat.

"What are we going to do?" I asked, assuming that she'd have a plan.

"Crucify Prissy," she said, her eyes blazing as she lifted the phone to her ear.

"It's me," she said into the phone. "Are you still in town? Where? Well don't leave… No. You stay exactly where you are… What's happening? Oh," she said, "nothing much. I've just met your Mr Lowe. Yes," she nodded, "I thought you might."

And hanging up, she turned to me, eyes still blazing.

"D'you think your brother was drunk?" I asked.

"Drunk or doped," she answered, stalking towards Baker Street. "Either way, that toad," she gestured back towards the building we'd just left, "set him up, recorded him and now has us over a barrel."

"Okay," I said, feeling less than optimistic, "so what do we do next?"

"Taxi," she shouted, waving at a passing cab, which pulled up to the pavement.

I clambered into the back as she leant down and gave the driver our destination before joining me in the rear.

I frowned. "Why are we going to Bond Street?" I asked.

"Because that's where my bitch of a sister-in-law is," Caz

said through gritted teeth.

At that point, my mobile phone rang. I reached into the pocket of my coat and pulled it out, frowning at the caller ID on the screen.

"Nick," I tried to make my voice light and breezy, though I suspect it came out more slightly manic. "What's up?"

"Why did you visit Chopper Falzone the day after a dead body was discovered in the basement of your pub?" he asked, with no preamble whatsoever.

"Oh, good afternoon to you, too," I said sourly. "I'm fine. How are you?"

"Danny," he said sternly, "this isn't a joke. I have a murder investigation on my hands and pictures of you going to see Falzone. What's going on?"

"So it was definitely murder, then?"

"Well, unless he managed to shoot himself twice in the back of the head by accident. Stop changing the subject."

"Chopper called me in," I answered, seeing no point in hiding the facts. "Said he wanted to speak to me. But wait," I added, suddenly realising what Nick had said, "how have you got photos? Have you been having me followed?"

"No, Danny; we've been watching Falzone."

"Watching him? What the hell is this? *The Untouchables*?"

"Danny, we've been here before. He's a crook. A gangster. A mobster. We watch him, and we especially watch him when something like this happens on what he likes to think of as his patch. So why were you called in?"

I debated telling Nick to mind his own business then realised that it probably was his business. "He wanted to know if I had anything to do with the body," I answered, as, beside me, Caz pulled her phone from her handbag and began furiously jabbing at the screen again.

"So, you're telling me that he's claiming he had no hand in this?" Nick said, the disbelief ringing loud and clear down the phone.

"That's the sense I got," I said. "He was furious – not cos there'd been a dead body in the basement of his pub but because he hadn't put it there."

"But that doesn't make sense," Nick said. "I mean, if he didn't put it there, then who did?"

"Who exactly. But, to be honest, it sort of does make sense," I said. "I mean, you've been telling me for ages what a big-time serious gangster Chopper is."

"He *is* a big-time serious gangster, Danny. That's not just my opinion, you know; it's a known fact."

"Whatever," I waved his protestations aside. "But if he's so good at gangsterism, why would he leave the body somewhere that would link right back to him. Do we have any idea who it was, by the way?"

"I'm not at liberty to divulge that information," Nick deadpanned.

"Which means you still don't know," I clarified, just in case he thought I was impressed by his cloak and dagger impersonation.

"Like I said, it's hard to get fingerprints off a mummy," he muttered. "We're on dental records now, so fingers crossed. But meantime Danny – and I mean this – please don't get involved. This is a genuinely nasty case, baby. Anyone who could do this would be dangerous to tangle with."

The taxi turned on to Bond Street. "Got to go, Nick. Busy, busy. I'll call again," and – as he continued to plead slash berate me about the risks and dangers of poking my nose into criminal cases – I ended the call and dropped my phone into my pocket, turning to Caz as a single, triumphant, "Ha!" escaped her lips.

"Got you!" she shouted, dropping her own phone into her handbag, and directing her attention to the driver. "Anywhere here will do, thank you," she called, as the taxi pulled up alongside the front door to Frankleby's Auction House.

Caz turned to me. "Darling, I'm short of cash, would you mind paying the man?"

I settled up and followed Caz – calmer now, and stalking

like a runway model down the red carpet that the auction house had actually rolled out on the street, as though their clientele could hardly be expected to ever actually set shoe leather on pavement – into the lobby of Frankleby's, past a bemused security guard, a couple of seemingly unphased receptionists and a professional greeter with a clipboard who was waved aside as Caz announced herself and, glancing at me, added, "Plus one."

"I have a name, you know," I reminded her somewhat testily.

"Of course you do, sweetness," she responded, stepping into a lift and pressing a button, "but it's not one that's likely to get you into this place unimpeded. Right," she pulled out a small silver compact, checked her make-up, adjusted her boobs so her cleavage was fully front and centre, added a touch of lippy to her bottom lip, clipped the compact shut, recapped the lipstick, dropped both back into the handbag and turned to me.

"I thought we were visiting Prissy," I said, willing myself not to stare at the cleavage.

"We are," she answered, "and I want to look my best when I look that lying bitch in the eyes and tell her I'm on to her game."

The lift pinged, the doors opened, and we stepped into what felt like an art gallery; with recessed spots diffusing gentle light onto a space hung with paintings, some bare canvasses, some wooden panels thick with old oils and lacquer, some huge gilt frames with dimly-lit crucifixion scenes buried within armies of wooden cherubim and cornucopias.

Caz stalked her way through the armies of doe-eyed virgins and pale, twisted messiahs, seeking, single-mindedly, Prissy; who was discovered, at length, standing in front of a vast nativity scene, the night sky – thick with stars – dwarfing the tiny stable and the figures within it.

"I wouldn't bother viewing those," Caz snarled, grabbing Prissy's arm so tightly the other woman – her permanent

---

91

bouffant in almost exactly the same position it had been in the day before – winced and attempted to pull herself away.

"Caroline," she cried, her tone a mixture of outrage and upset, "you're hurting me!"

"You can't afford it," Caz said by way of response. "Rather, you won't be able to afford it if you're to pay Lowe what he's owed."

Prissy stopped struggling and turned to Caz. "Pay him?" she asked, her brow – or the bit of it that wasn't pumped full of Botox – furrowing in confusion. "You mean you couldn't fix it?"

"Oh I *could* fix it," Caz snapped back, her eyes glittering with what, to me, looked like a mixture of fury and enjoyment. "I know exactly what I'd need to do to resolve this without Bobbers having to pay a penny. But I'm not going to."

"You're...?" Prissy's face fell. "You'd abandon your brother to the wolves?" she asked, the more-in-sorrow-than-anger tone dialled firmly to eleven.

Caz laughed, yanking Prissy down onto a bench in front of an ascension scene filled with more heavenly hosts than the average telethon, and turned to face her.

"Prissy, Bobbers fed himself to the wolves the day he met you. What I want to know from you is just how you managed to set him up."

"Me?" Prissy bristled. "Set him up? Caroline, you may find this hard to believe, based on the gadabout way you've leapt from relationship to relationship your whole life," (this last said while she watched me to be sure I was hearing it), "but some of us are dedicated to our spouses. I love Bobbers, and for you to suggest that I would..."

The words died on her lips as Caz held her phone up in front of Prissy's face. I angled to get a good look at it. It showed a nightclub scene, mirrored walls, a red-velvet-lined booth, a bunch of men in black tie sitting around a table covered in empty champagne bottles and glasses.

"You don't have any social media accounts, do you

Prissy?" Caz asked, tapping the picture so as to enlarge one part of the frame. "Bit too nouveau for you, I suppose. But not all of your friends are as careful as you are."

Caz glanced over her shoulder. "This," she said, addressing herself to me, "is the feed of one Henrietta 'Hank' Mallowan. Hank is not one of the brightest sparks in the box. Is she, Prissy? But what Hank is, is extremely well connected.

"She loves a party, and she hosted this one in the summer. It was a benefit for The Children's Defence Fund. A charity cocktail party and disco night at Bijouxs.

"Lowe was there, of course, but look who else was present."

Caz tapped a nail twice against the picture and the shot zoomed in to show the mirrored wall behind the men.

"Now, who could that be?" Caz asked innocently as her finger pointed at a fuzzy figure, the features a little vague but the towering hairdo clearly visible.

"That's Prissy," I said, receiving for my comment a furious glare from the pinched little face beneath the hair helmet.

"That's *Lady Priscilla* to you," she snarled.

"So you had met Lowe as early as the summer," Caz said to her accusatorily.

"This had nothing to do with me," Prissy answered, ignoring the topic completely and attempting to refocus on her own innocence.

"So why lie?" Caz demanded.

"Lie?" Prissy struggled. "When did I lie?"

Caz shook her head despairingly. "A lie of omission. You never mentioned that you were already familiar with Balthazar Lowe and his larcenous charity scheme."

Prissy slumped. "Because I knew that – if I told the truth – you'd be less likely to help us," she admitted.

"And not because you're in league with Lowe?"

"League?"

"You get the mark, set him up, hand him over to Lowe

and split the proceeds?'

"Caroline, this isn't *Paper Moon*, you know." Prissy sighed heavily. "Okay, I'll admit, I was rather smitten with Balthazar – Mr Lowe. I was struck by his dedication to his charity. But I had no idea he was a crook. None at all."

Caz considered this. "So what happened?" she finally asked as the cherubim and Nephilim gazed down on the scene. "I suppose that, somewhere that night, you had a few drinks too many and couldn't help yourself blurting out about the oil wells in Kyrgyzstan. Probably complained about how the sanctions were making it so hard to get at the money they'd generate. And Mr Lowe saw his blackmail opportunity.

"No wonder you didn't want Bobbers bothered with this. Does he even know that he's being blackmailed?"

Prissy, shamefacedly, shook her head.

Caz pointedly raised an eyebrow and stared pointedly at Prissy, "I'm still not entirely convinced that the whole thing wasn't cooked up by you and him."

"I swear—" Prissy began her protestations again but Caz, having dropped her phone back into her handbag, held up a hand to shut her up and off.

"Can it, Prissy," she said bluntly. "You need to know this – I don't like you. You're a snob, a bully, and you have terrible taste in clothes. And as for that disaster atop your head, well I've been on to the Red Cross and they're considering sending aid. But – despite the fact he's also an idiot – I love my baby brother.

"So, if you ever do another thing to put him in jeopardy; if you ever lie to him – or to me – about your actions, I will provide Bobbers – and The Earl – with a full and detailed account of this debacle."

"I'm sorry, Caroline," Prissy said, her lower lip trembling.

"No," Caz shook her head, "you're not. You don't think enough of me to be sorry, Prissy. You're sorry you got caught, that's all. And that's fine. Danny and I will sort this, and in return you will do one thing for me."

"Name it," Prissy whispered.

"You will ensure I am *never* invited to your home for Christmas ever again. Your cook's efforts are almost as awful as your hairdresser's and, quite frankly, your cellar is more fearful than poor old Danny's here.

"Also," she said, "we're going to need some expenses." Caz glanced around the gallery, taking in more suffering, pain, ecstasy-through-pain and transfiguration than most dancefloors at midnight. "You can send twenty thousand to my account. Bobbers has the details."

"But how are you going to sort this?" Prissy whispered as Caz stood, towering over her.

"We have our ways," Caz said. "Now go home. And for Christ's sake, Prissy, buy something a bit more cheerful for the chapel. There's been enough misery in that house."

So saying, Caz turned and, if she'd had a cape, would, I'm positive, have swished it, before smiling at me and stalking from the gallery.

"That was amazing," I whispered as she pressed the button for the lift.

"I know," she smiled gently back at me as the lift doors opened.

We stepped into the box and the doors closed soundlessly. "So," I turned to her as the lift began to move, "how are we going to sort this Lowe situation?"

Which was when she stopped smiling. "I have absolutely no idea," she said, "but sort it we will, because I'm telling you this Danny, I will not spend another Christmas with that bloody woman."

FIFTEEN

"So what do you think?" Caz looked hopefully across the table at the twins, who looked back at her with a mixture of incredulity and concern.

"I'm outraged," Ray said.

"Outraged," Dash echoed, before glancing at his brother and repeating the phrase as a question.

"That she'd think," Ray started explaining to Dash, before turning to Caz and addressing his remarks to her, "that *you'd* think that we might even know anyone who could do that. I mean, we're not a couple of crooks, you know."

"We're not?" Dash asked, before picking up on his brother's tone. "We're not!" he restated emphatically.

"I never said you were crooks," Caz protested.

"You just said we were bound to know a few," Ray answered.

"I didn't *say* you were bound to know a few," Caz protested. "I merely inferred you might. And that I might be willing to pay them a sum to perform a certain act."

"What? Like juggling?" Dash suddenly ejaculated, causing everyone to pause and stare at him in confusion.

"Sorry," he muttered sheepishly. "Comedians are good too."

"Dash," his brother shook his head, "leave this to me. We might know a few geezers," he said, turning to Caz as his tone moved from umbrage to sales pitch, "but they don't come cheap."

"Geezers?" Caz said, looking at me in a way that suggested she was concerned she might have just had a stroke; could hear words but no longer had any idea what they meant.

"Geezers," I repeated, wincing as the freezer in the corner of the kitchen began a high-pitched series of squeaks, wails and shrieks that made it sound as though I'd entombed Mariah Carey in the Zanussi.

In return, I got a blank stare and a tilted head.

"Faces," Dash called out, ignoring Ray's instruction to leave this to him. "Villains, doers, factors."

"Crooks," Ray clarified, adding to Caz's experience of the criminal thesaurus. "You want us to get a bunch of crooks to burgle this geezer's office, pinch the offending and torch it."

Caz looked at me in the way I imagine Jane, surrounded by silverbacks all grunting their outrage, might glance at Tarzan. "Yes," she said uncertainly, then, gaining confidence from my glance, she straightened up. "That's basically it."

"Well I'm still outraged," said Ray.

"Yes," I muttered dryly. "I think we've gathered that."

"And what," Caz asked, dipping into her handbag and coming out with, firstly, her purse; and secondly, a bottle of Jägermeister, "would it take to assuage your outrage?"

She dipped back into the capacious Gladstone and extracted four shot glasses. I stared at her in open-mouthed wonderment.

"It's not us you need to sewage," Dash explained as, from her frosty tomb, Mariah went into the last half of *Emotions*, "it's Fat Larry and his band."

At this, Caz and I – old enough to spot the reference, but reluctant to admit being old enough to do so – started, stared at each other and, as Mariah was suddenly throttled by the return of the scratching thumping sound, turned back to the ASBO twins.

"And just who," Caz enquired in an approximation of Priscilla, "is Fat Larry?"

"And his band?" I asked.

"They do weddings," Ray stated baldly.

"And burglaries," Dash blurted. "Usually before they pop round to do the first dance."

"And often on properties owned by the happy couple," Ray, shooting daggers at his brother, admitted, before sighing. "Okay, look – if you need someone to do a bit of second- or third-level entry, alarm work and a clean exit, then Lazarus is the one you need."

"Rises like the dead," Dash intoned as though reciting a brand slogan.

"Wait," Caz said, filling all four shot glasses, handing them round, downing hers before the rest of us had even reached for ours, refilling and slamming it, "who's this Lazarus? I thought we were discussing Rotund Laurence."

"Caz," Ray fixed her with his most sympathetic look; the one he usually used for his brother, "if you were christened Lazarus Fahey, would you start a wedding band as Big-Boned Lazarus or Fat Larry?"

Caz refilled the glasses. "Understood," she nodded, slamming another measure of the aniseed liquor, "but why does he rise like the dead?"

"Cos," Ray explained, "the PoPo never find a ladder, a scaffolding, or so much as a rope. He just sort of levitates."

Caz looked at me.

I looked back.

"So can you get him?" she asked.

"Well," Ray slammed his shot, paused, inhaled deeply through his nose as though to steady himself, "I'm still frankly outraged that you'd even ask us to arrange a burglary."

"Yeah," Dash – already smashed – nodded in agreement, "we ain't never arranged buggery."

"Oi!" Ray slapped Dash firmly across the chest, glanced meaningfully at me and grimaced an apology, "he hasn't eaten today. Ali's got us on a Christmas diet. No food and press-ups every hour."

"Bigger tits make bigger tips," Dash – completely

oblivious to any offence he might have inadvertently caused – parroted Ali's slogan.

Caz shook her head at me. "I repeat," she addressed Ray, "how much, and how soon?"

"Oi!" Ali's voice echoed above the scratching thumping of the freezer, startling us all and causing Dash to splash Jägermeister on the table. "Are you two gonna be getting behind that bar any time soon? Only Fiona's had new gels and can't use the fucking till. Or the optics."

I turned to the door where my bar manager stood, squat, broad and clearly agitated.

"Or the fucking pumps, to be honest. But since you," this last addressed to me, "thought she was – what was it? – 'a good soul,' I've a barmaid what can't maid a bar and a couple of barmen who're sitting in here getting shitfaced while their public awaits outside. So, any chance of a hand this century?"

The boys, as one, leapt to their feet and shuffled towards their boss as Caz stared helplessly after them.

At the door, Ray paused and looked back. "We'll call him," he said, "tonight. Then his people will call yours. It'll happen," he said, pulling his t-shirt over his head as Ali handed him a bottle of baby oil.

And then they were gone, leaving Caz topping up her shot glass and mine and exclaiming, "But I don't have people, Danny."

"It's okay," I explained, sliding the cough syrup away from her, "the boys'll sort it out."

Caz eyed the bottle and her own empty glass and suddenly slumped, the stresses of the past day evident in her face. "Daniel, I think I might need a lie down."

"My bedroom's upstairs," I said, though I knew she was well aware of its location.

"Would it be awfully rude of me…" she began, before I waved the rest of the sentence aside, helped her from her seat and took her up the stairs to my bedroom.

"I'm awfully sorry," she murmured, as I slipped her

Manolos off, "I can't imagine what's come over me. It must have been a bad oyster."

"Caz," I said, as her head hit the pillow and I lifted her feet up onto the bed, "you've not had any oysters today."

I was about to mention that – as far as I'd seen – she'd had nothing more than two lattes and a third of a bottle of Jägermeister, and faced-down the biggest bully she'd ever known and a blackmailer intent on downing her family; but she started snoring gently so I decided to let her sleep without the lecture, lay the throw over her and, softly closing the door, tiptoed from the room.

It was the tiptoeing that lead to what happened next.

I mean, there was no reason why I couldn't have just tramped down the stairs and back into my bar. Except, I'd started slinking so I continued and, as I reached the bottom of the stairs and headed towards the rumble of the crowd in the bar and the thumping music sound-tracking them, I passed the parlour, noticed the door – which was usually closed – was half ajar, and heard lowered voices coming from within.

I inched forward, sensing, suddenly, that what was happening inside was not a casual chat.

"You find 'em," a voice, gravelly yet familiar, snarled. "You find 'em, and you bring 'em to me, or I'll find you. And Carlton. And then—"

I inched closer to the door, peeking through the gap.

Inside, the bleached-blond thug from yesterday had Ali – rock solid, immutable Ali – held up against the wall, a single hand around her throat, the other hand raised, ready to strike her if she moved.

I kicked the door open.

"What's going on?" I asked.

The thug flinched, tightened his grip on Ali's throat a moment, released her, turned towards me and then smiled, the smile growing into a wider grin.

"Oh," he said, "it's you." He glanced back, briefly, at Ali, who was gasping breath back in, glowering at him and running a hand across her neck.

"I said, what's going on?" I repeated.

"Just having a word," he said, gesturing behind him at Ali.

"Well you've had it," I said, twisting to see Ali, who was glowering at the back of his head. "Ali, you alright?"

"I'm fine," she muttered.

"Hey," he held his hands up, a smile breaking out on his face, "she's fine."

"I didn't ask you," I answered. "How'd you get in here?"

"Me?" he asked, clearly delaying. "Ali asked me back here for a chat. Didn't you Ali," he turned and smiled wolfishly at her.

Ali stared back, the fury in her eyes floating over something else.

"I'll call you," she said, her voice catching at the end.

"Yeah," the bleached blond smiled and reached out a hand to stroke her face; Ali doing her best, and failing, not to flinch at his touch, "you do that."

"You've had your word," I snarled. "Now, take your hands off my bar manager and get the fuck out of my pub."

He paused, slowly removed his hand from Ali and turned to me, the look on his face suggesting he was surprised I was actually still here.

"You wanna watch that potty mouth," he said, the smile dying. "Chat like that'll land a boy in trouble."

"You're barred," I said, staring him down. "Get the fuck out of my pub and don't ever come back."

He snorted. "Else?" he asked, stepping towards me.

I'd dealt with bullies before, had the threat of physical violence hovering over me. I knew better than to shrink from him but it still took all my will to stand firm, such was the pure malevolence seeping from him.

I kept my voice calm, though I felt anything but inside. "Else you'll have more than me and a woman to deal with," I said, stepping to one side and opening the door wide.

"That so?" he asked, deliberately moving as close as he

could without touching me as he headed towards the door. "Well," he paused, his face inches from mine, his eyes glittering menacingly, "I'll bear that in mind."

And so saying, he left the room.

I pushed the door closed and turned to Ali.

"What the fuck is going on?" I demanded.

"Not now Danny," she collapsed onto an overstuffed sofa. "You got a brandy or something?"

I walked over to the sideboard and, opening one of the doors, located a bottle of Remy and a tumbler, splashed some of the golden liquid into the glass and handed it to her.

"Thanks." Ali accepted it and swallowed half the brandy in one mouthful.

I waited. Ali stared intently at the rug before the sofa and mouthed the rest of the brandy.

The silence stretched out, sound-tracked – distantly – by the muted rumble of the crowd in the bar and the steady drumbeat of an old swing beat record on the jukebox.

"I'm waiting," I said.

"I don't wanna talk about it," she said at length.

"Ali, we can't just not talk about this. What the fuck is going on?"

"You still got the spare room upstairs?" she suddenly asked.

I frowned. "Yeah," I stammered eventually. "But what's that got to do with this?"

"Any chance my cousin could stay for a few days?" The pause before the word 'cousin' – not much more than a split second – was long enough to tell me that whoever she was asking for was not a cousin.

"Your cousin?" I asked pointedly.

"Yeah," she said defiantly.

"Wait," I said, gesturing at the door, "that wasn't your cousin, was it?"

"Don't be so fucking stupid," she snapped. "As if I'd want that toerag anywhere near me."

"Okay," I said, "but why's your cousin need somewhere

to stay? Doesn't he have his own place?"

"He's been," she paused, "away. For a bit. Not sorted out his own place yet."

"Away," I asked, "or *away* away?"

"What d'you mean?" she bristled.

"I mean," I answered, "has he been overseas or in *the nick*?"

"No," Ali answered, turning a furious glare on me, "he has not been in the fucking nick. He just needs somewhere to stay. So, can he stay for a few days, Danny, or not?"

"What's his name?" I asked, letting her know from the tone of my voice that I believed not a single word of the story I was being told.

"Carlton."

I knew something was up but if Ali needed a room for her 'cousin,' then I wasn't going to make a thing of it. "Sure," I said, "how long's he going to need it for?"

"A few days," she said. "He's going away soon."

"I thought he'd just come back from somewhere?"

"And now," she said, the tension in her body – now I'd agreed that Carlton could stay – draining away, "he's going away again. For a long time." She stood.

"Ali," I held my hands out, almost beseeching her to hold on, "who was that man? What does he want? And what the hell is going on?"

"It's complicated, Danny. I'm sorry you had to see that, but it won't happen again."

"*You* don't need to apologise," I said, "*he* was throttling *you*."

"It's alright, Dan," she said, "I'll sort it."

"Let me help," I pleaded and, in return, I got a deep and long sigh.

"I wish you could." She crossed the room, opened the door and was just about to leave when she glanced back at me. "Thanks, Danny," she said.

And was gone.

SIXTEEN

Carlton, when he turned up several hours later, was a tall, rangy mixed-race guy, about, I'd say, nineteen years of age. His hair was cut tight at the sides and styled in a pompadour at the front. His eyes – a mossy green with flecks of brown through them – peeked out shyly from behind a pair of heavy-framed spectacles.

He removed the baseball cap that had been perched on the back of his head and, holding it in one hand, held out the other.

"Hey," he said quietly, "I'm—"

"Carlton," Ali jumped in, finishing his sentence for him. "My cousin. Who's gonna stay for a bit. Carlton, this is Danny."

I shook his hand. "It's good to meet you," I said. "Any cousin of Ali's," I said, pausing before the word 'cousin' just long enough to make it clear that I didn't believe the statement for a second, "is welcome here. I've put *Carlton*," I said to Ali, "in the guest room."

"C'mon you," Ali smiled at the blushing Carlton, who stooped to snatch an overstuffed duffle bag from the floor, "I'll show you upstairs. Thanks again," she added, nodding stiffly at me and leading the boy from the bar.

"And why, pray tell," Caz murmured, sidling up beside me, "isn't cousin Carlton being offered the empty spot in your bedroom?"

I shook my head. "You, my friend, are incorrigible."

"Well if he's not your type," she responded, "do I have permission to engage in manoeuvres?"

I smiled at a punter on the other side of the bar, asked what I could get him and began pouring his pint.

"Like you need to ask permission," I said to Caz as her phone began buzzing discretely.

"This is she," Caz said, answering the phone. Raising an eyebrow, she moved away to the rear of the bar, paused, turned back to me and mouthed 'Fat Larry.'

I moved closer, heard a tinny voice at the end of the line, watched Caz frown, saw her nod in – I thought – agreement and heard her say, "That sounds... acceptable. And you'll revert to me with findings? Good," she nodded again, "I look forward to hearing from you."

She rang off. "Well," she said after a moment's silence, "*alea est iacta*. Let's just hope Fat Larry can bring the Balthazar Lowe situation to a satisfactory end."

"So what exactly is he going to do?" I asked, receiving a withering glance in response.

"Daniel, does one ask a magician what exactly they're going to do; how exactly they're going to amaze and astound you? No, one doesn't. And so – for the same reason – I have no idea what, exactly, our levitating friend is going to do or how he's going to do it. I simply hope he will do it promptly, efficiently and successfully."

"Everything alright here?" I turned to find Ali eyeing the two of us suspiciously from the doorway.

I smiled. Wider than I should have, perhaps. "All fine, Ali. Absolutely tip top. Why? What makes you even need to ask?"

"Danny," she fixed me with her sternest glare, "I'm not a total fucking idiot. You've just let me move a strange boy into your guest bedroom and avoid answering questions about the shit that's been happening round here for the past few days, and you just actually used the phrase tip-top. Something's going on."

"Ali," Caz stepped forward, ushering me towards the bar

where another punter was waiting to be served, "not everything that happens revolves around you."

I missed Ali's response, as the customer on the other side of the bar delivered a drinks order that seemed modelled on The Gettysburg Address and, by the time I looked up, Ali had begun serving another. Ray and Dash were doling out bowls of the turkey chilli or minestrone that were the lunchtime specials as Caz made her way through the crowd delivering pecks on the cheek and greetings to regulars.

The lunchtime rush went on until almost 3:00 p.m. and we were down to a couple of regulars sipping their pints over copies of the *Racing Post* – Ali wiping tables and Dash refilling the fridges, his brother in the kitchen filling the dishwasher – when the door was flung open and the bleached blond from the day before stormed in.

"You're barred," I said as he stood just inside the bar, glaring around.

"Where are they?" he growled at Ali, who looked up spotted him and blanched.

"Jimmy," she said, "I ain't got them, and I don't know who has."

I came out from behind the bar and moved towards him.

"You lying bitch," he said, moving menacingly towards her, "you haven't even looked. I know what you've been doing."

I stepped in front of him, deliberately invading his personal space and blocking his view of Ali. "I said you're barred," I repeated, keeping my voice low and steady, locking eyes with his.

"You think I don't know what you been up to?" he demanded, ignoring me and twisting as though to move around me.

I stuck my right foot out, slamming my right arm bolt out a second later so that, as the foot tripped him, he fell forward, my forearm whacked into his throat, momentarily choking him before curling around his neck as I stepped to the side and behind him so that I now had him in a choke hold.

The blond – muscular and, now I was close up to him, fitter than I'd expected – twisted, pushed himself suddenly upright, slightly unbalancing me, and turned, the head-butt he'd been attempting to deliver going slightly awry as he still managed to slam the crown of his head into my chin with such force that my head was jolted backwards and I momentarily lost my grip on him.

A moment was all he needed. He twisted again and was free. And this time, when I refocussed on him, he was holding a long and very threatening knife out in front of him, and grinning wolfishly.

"I've heard about you," he said to me. "I'd get back behind your bar if I was you and mind my own business, boy."

"You're not me," I said as Ali, hefting an empty beer bottle from one of the tables, edged her way towards him.

"Don't even try it, sweetheart," the man, his leathery face twisting into a dismissive scowl, snarled, without even looking her way. He jerked the knife, gesturing with his free hand that she should come and stand with her back to the bar in front of him.

Ali hesitated, eyed the door and put the beer bottle down, as he said, "You been busy spiriting people away, ain't you Ali. So busy. Too busy to do a bit of business for me. Cos you've never really been that bright, have you, doll? Never really known when your bread's buttered. But that's alright, cos we're here now, ain't we? Now, why don't you go get Carlton and we can have a nice little chat?"

The mention of Carlton seemed to work like an electric shock on Ali, who suddenly let out a shriek and, snatching up a drip tray from the bar, swung it at him, the arc of spilled beer making a thin amber rainbow in the air as – seemingly in slow motion – the leather face twisted to one side and collapsed in surprise as said drip tray collided with the side of his head.

Almost simultaneously, his other hand shot out and he

lunged forward, grabbing Ali by the throat, eliciting a strangled squawk from her as he yanked her forward, the knife coming up before her terrified eyes, his own eyes – enraged now – staring into hers.

"You silly—" he said, but got no further before Ray – summoned, no doubt, by his brother – smashed the previously considered beer bottle down on his head.

The blond grunted, released Ali, who fell to the floor choking and gasping as the man flailed; one hand on his head, the other waving the blade blindly around as random profanities poured from him.

Dash, his presence now exposed, crouched low, his hands out before him defensively as the blond that Ali had referred to as Jimmy focussed, his lip curling in a sneer. "I'm gonna cut you like a fucking steak," he said, as he stood and began moving slowly towards Dash.

Dash stood slightly more erect. "You don't want to do this grandad," he said slowly. "Why don't you just take your little wetter, pack your little bags and fuck off back to wherever you came from."

He got no further as, with a bellow of rage, Jimmy charged at him.

Dash reached behind him, pulling a tea towel from the back pocket of his jeans and stepping quickly to one side, before flicking the towel out and down, watching as it wrapped itself around the blade of the knife.

Then – as Jimmy's momentum kept him moving forward – Dash yanked the tea towel straight up and, with a flash and a heavy thud as it hit the floor, the blade flew from the man's hand.

But Jimmy hadn't completely passed Dash and now – both hands being empty of weapons – he flung his arms around the boy, gripping him in a bear hug that dragged them both across the room and body-slammed Dash against the floor, Jimmy on top of him.

Dash squirmed, but Jimmy had his hands around the younger man's throat.

I ran over and threw myself bodily at the older man's shoulders, hearing a grunt as the sheer weight of my body dislodged him. I felt a stab of pain as somehow, in the dislodging, we became twisted so that this time I landed on my back, the older man now sitting on my chest, his eyes gleaming as his hand pulled back and descended, ready to slam straight into my face.

I twisted my head, heard a loud crack – followed by the sound of splintering – but felt no pain and when I opened my eyes, Jimmy's eyes were no more gleaming, but glazed.

For a moment, time went into slow motion and then he toppled, slowly, to one side, disclosing cousin Carlton, the remains of a bar stool still gripped in his hands as Jimmy finally collapsed to the floor, shook his head and – still disorientated, but slowly recovering his faculties – rolled onto his belly and crawled to all fours.

"Quick," I gasped, staggering to my feet, "get him out of here."

As one, Carlton, Dash, Ray and I dragged the already struggling Jimmy to his feet and bundled him towards the door.

"Ali," he growled, then finding strength from somewhere he twisted from Ray's grasp as his voice rose, "Ali. I want them stones. I wanna know who did this."

Carlton punched the man squarely in the kidneys, eliciting a howl as Jimmy doubled over, allowing Ray to regain his grasp. Still struggling and throwing wild punches, Jimmy was brought to the doorway of the pub and forced out onto the pavement.

"And don't come back," I growled at him as the doors were slammed and bolted shut.

He hammered on the door, bellowing at Ali that, "This ain't over, girl. You hear me?"

"Get the fuck away from here," Dash shouted, "or you'll know real pain."

The voice on the other side of the door was silent a moment, then a chilling cackle issued forth. "Pain? Boy, you don't know shit from pain. I been robbed, and I want what's mine."

When this brought a puzzled silence from us, the cackle was repeated along with another, half-hearted, bang on the door and a cry of, "Little piggies, little piggies, let me in."

And then all, apart from the tinny jukebox in the corner which had been playing all along, went silent.

"I think he's gone," Ray whispered.

The two regulars went back to their *Racing Posts*.

I turned to Ali, who was ashen-faced and staring in terror at the bolted door. "What have you done?" she said, her voice coming out in a horrified whisper.

"Ali," I said, crossing to her, "I think it's time you explained just what the hell is going on here. You two," I called to the two regulars, "can you keep an eye on the place?"

"And don't touch them optics," Ali, always the consummate bar manager, snapped as her shoulders slumped; and she allowed Caz to put an arm around her shoulders, slip a large brandy into her hand and lead her out of the bar and back towards the pub kitchen.

SEVENTEEN

Ali, her hands still shaking, sat at the kitchen table and lifted the brandy to her lips. The rest of us sat expectantly around the table staring alternatively at her and at each other in puzzlement.

She heaved a deep sigh and nodded as though she'd come to a decision. "This," she gestured at the young man opposite her, "is Carlton. He's my son. I'm sorry we lied – about who and what he was – but I needed to hide him, and I was panicking a bit." She smiled sheepishly.

"Just a bit," I said quietly. "We'd sort of guessed he wasn't your cousin. But who were you hiding him from?"

"Who d'you think? That," she jerked her chin towards the bar beyond, "that *thing*," she gasped back a sob, "is my husband, Jimmy Carter."

"Your husband!" Dash gasped. "I didn't know you were married."

"To be honest," said Ali, "neither did I until a couple of days ago. I hadn't seen or heard from him for over fifteen years. I'd been told – ages ago, by someone who knew someone – that he'd been topped in Tenerife. Some fight that got out of hand."

"I was glad to hear he was gone – whatever happened to make him that way. Then last week, he turned back up."

"Why?" I asked. "After all this time?"

"Cos of your body," Ali answered, jerking a thumb

downward to indicate she was referring to the corpse in the cellar and not my own figure, desirable as I might like to think it. "He reckons he knows who it was. Said he'd done a job with some geezers and they ended up coming back here."

"Here?" I was puzzled. "Why here?"

"Cos the place was closed for a refurb."

"Christ," Caz muttered. "When was this? 1890?"

"There'd been a flood. The central heating pipes had burst and they had to close the place for a week or so to patch it up, so this gang knew it would be empty at night. And they had a key." At this point, she choked back a sob.

"Which I assume," I said, "Jimmy stole from you."

Ali nodded. "I'm guessing so. There was some job in Hatton Garden. They'd tunnelled into some diamond merchants and got away with a shitload of uncut jewels. The gang split as soon as they left the Garden and arranged to meet back here but, when they turned up, the ringleader – the guy who had all the stones – was nowhere to be seen. And they all assumed that he'd done a runner and dropped them in it."

"And then, ten years later," I muttered, "the papers report that a body has been uncovered in the cellar."

Ali nodded. "Jimmy's convinced it's the gang leader – that one of the others did him in, stashed the body and took all the stones for themselves."

"So what's he want you to do about it?" Carlton asked.

His mum reached out a hand towards him but the young man stayed on the other side of the room, his arms crossed defensively across his chest.

"Jimmy's been away – wherever the fuck he was – for ten years. He's lost touch with half the gang. But I've been here. So he wants me to round them up. Find out where they are and get his stones back."

"Well that's not happening," Dash said. "you're never going to see that scumbag again."

"You don't understand," Ali choked back another sob,

"we have to help him. We've got to find these stones or he'll…" she trailed off, stopped dead and stared at the tabletop, her whole body trembling.

"Or he'll what, Ali?" I pressed.

"Or he'll kill us all," she finally said, looking up as tears rolled down her face. "He murdered my sister and he…" her body was suddenly racked by sobs, so that Carlton finally came around and put his arms around his mum.

"Shush," he whispered, "we'll take care of it, Mum. He won't hurt you. I promise."

"Oh God," Ali sobbed, the words coming in a rush. "I'm so sorry, Carlton. I'm so sorry. He murdered my sister and he murdered your dad. And I should have told you years ago, but I thought he was dead and what would have been the point? Only now he's back, and I don't know what I'm going to do."

Now Carlton, his face transformed from a look of concern to one of horror, uncoiled his arms from around her and stepped back, almost staggering. "He did what?"

"I left him," Ali sobbed. "I walked away from Jimmy cos I met Arif – your dad. And for the first time in my life, I felt like I was…" Ali swallowed down more sobs, breathed deeply and slowly tried to quiet the emotional overload that was obvious on her face. "For the first time in my life, I felt like a person. Not a thing. Not a possession. Not just Jimmy's bird.

"But with Jimmy and his gang, if you were their bird, you were their bird for life. You didn't leave. They might throw you to one side if some tart turned up but even then you weren't allowed to even look at another man.

"Then I left Jimmy. I walked. And he came after me. Even when I was with Arif – even when I was pregnant with you and after you'd been born – he'd turn up at the flat, carry on like nothing had changed. 'You're on loan,' I remember him saying. 'You'll never not be mine and right now I'll allow this performance to go on. But you're mine.'"

Carlton's face changed again – anger showing now, and,

as I glanced around the table, evident on the faces of every one of us.

"I was so afraid to say anything. There was a girl once, and she dumped one of the gang. Chucked him cos she'd had enough of his bullshit. And the bloke she dumped threw acid in her face, blinded her in one eye. They used to laugh about it, call her *The Phantom of the Opera*. After that, I was so frightened and I couldn't tell your dad, Carlton, or anyone, cos I was so afraid of what would happen if I did. And then – though I knew nothing about it at the time – they did that robbery, and it all tuned to shit, and I guess Jimmy must have felt slighted – I mean, one of his best mates fucks him over, vanishes into the night with his money. He started turning up, saying he wanted me back."

"What happened?" I asked, realizing as I did so that I'd been holding my breath.

"I—" she started, choked again, swigged the rest of the brandy – which Caz immediately refilled – and, taking another gasping breath, began again.

"I was out with some friends one night and my sister was babysitting Carlton. There was a fire. Janice managed to throw Carlton out of the bedroom window, but they were too small for her to fit through and whoever had set the fire had blocked the front door so she couldn't get out. She died. Of smoke inhalation. When I went to identify her, they'd cleaned the soot off her face. She hadn't been burned. The fire hadn't touched her. She was so pretty."

Ali broke down and, through great gulping sobs, continued the story. "Carlton was in hospital for a while. It looked like he wouldn't make it." she sobbed and Caz, her face pinched in worry, wrapped her arms around Ali and shushed her. "You nearly died," Ali swallowed hard and reached out to Carlton who stood staring at her in shock.

"And my dad?" Carlton asked through gritted teeth.

Ali reached out to him, grabbing at his hand which he pulled away from her.

"What happened to my dad?" Carlton demanded once

more.

"Your dad was killed – the same night – by a hit and run driver."

"That's what you always said," the young man responded, his voice flat.

"And it's true. And it's all anyone's ever been able to say or to prove. But I knew. I always knew who the driver was."

"Him."

Ali nodded. "I never heard from him again. I thought, at first, that he wanted to kill you and me with the fire. Then I realised he'd actually meant to kill Janice and you."

"So all that was left was for him to kill Arif and I'd be left completely alone. That's what he'd wanted. Like Anita – not to kill me, but to leave me alone and with a reminder every single day of my life of what it cost to defy him. He wanted me alive and everyone I loved dead."

"Can I have some of that?" Carlton nodded at the brandy and Caz, fetching a handful of glasses from the cupboard, poured him a large shot, before dumping a shot into a glass for herself, for Dash, for Ray and for me.

Caz downed her shot in one slug and looked around the room. "So what do we do now?" she asked.

Carlton swigged his brandy in one mouthful, winced and put the glass down on the table. "Well I don't know what you lot are going to do, but I'm going to find that fucker and kill him."

Ali cried out, beseeching him to do nothing. "He'll kill you Carlton."

But the boy had already fled the room.

Ali, her whole body collapsing in paroxysms of grief, cried after him.

"Don't worry," Dash downed his drink, "I'll sort it." He paused, put a hand on Ali's shoulder, looking longingly at her – and if I'd been unaware of the fact before now, I was finally unavoidably faced with the fact that my nephew was in love with this irascible, mercurial woman – and, without another glance at the rest of us, he too fled the room.

EIGHTEEN

"Any news?" Caz asked the next morning, as she sat on a stool at one end of the bar and nodded her head at Ali who was back behind the bar.

"Nothing," I shook my head. "Carlton hasn't been home. He hasn't phoned her, and she's been phoning him every hour since she got in this morning."

As I spoke, Ali – who'd finally insisted on being taxied home by my dad late the previous night in case Carlton had gone there – pulled her mobile from the pocket of her jeans, glanced at it, sighed and shoved it back into her jeans before ambling over to serve the next punter.

"And what about Dash?" Caz asked, accepting a gin and tonic from me.

"I got a call from Ray about an hour ago. He's home. They're due in shortly."

As I spoke, the door of the bar opened and Carlton, minus the jacket he'd had when he'd left the previous afternoon, with his shirt torn and the hems of his trousers matted in crusted filth, stepped in. Ali, still serving the customer, glanced up, let out a shriek, shoved the round she'd produced so far across the bar, saying, "It's on the house. Just fuck off and enjoy 'em," and ran around from her side of the bar to throw her arms around the boy, expressions of concern and – when she spotted the huge purple bruise around his right eye – outrage pouring from her.

"The prodigal returns," Caz said quietly.

"I'm just glad he *has* returned," I said. "Having heard some of what we heard about Jimmy Carter last night, I was worried."

"You think he'd have harmed the boy?" she asked.

"I think," I said, "nothing would be out of the realms of possibility. Can you keep an eye on the bar for a minute?"

Caz nodded, slipping from her stool and heading around behind the bar, as I crossed to Ali and Carlton and suggested we head back to the kitchen.

Carlton looked sheepishly at Ali and me; his good eye expressing a degree of sorrow, his bruised eye almost useless. "I'm sorry about last night, Mum. I needed to get away, but I shouldn't have just walked out on you. And I shouldn't have left you," he turned to me, "to be the one looking after my mum. That's my job."

Ali, tears now streaming down her face, shushed him and we headed back to the kitchen where I put the kettle on and, as I made three mugs of tea, Ali hammered the boy with questions:

"What happened to you? Where did you go? Did you find Jimmy? Did he do this to you and, if he didn't, who did?" (This last referring to the facial bruising.)

Carlton, having expressed his apologies, clammed up somewhat.

"I ran out," he said, "hoping to catch him. What I would have done, I don't really know. I mean, would I have killed him then and there in the street?"

He paused, lost for a moment in his thoughts. "Doesn't matter anyways, cos he'd gone by the time I got out on the street."

"So where'd you go?" Ali asked again as I slid a mug of tea in front of each of them, poured some of Chopper's custard creams onto a plate and plonked myself at the table.

"Around. My head was," he waved a hand in the air as though trying to conjure the words up, and finally settled on, "fucked. Mum, why didn't you ever tell me? I never even got to know my dad cos that bastard murdered him. And all this time I thought it was a hit and run."

Ali opened her mouth to speak and he shook his head, silencing her. "I used to look at people in cars – cab drivers, old blokes, women drivers – I'd look at them and think, 'Was it you? Did you kill my dad? Did you leave him lying in the gutter and drive off cos you were too pissed, or stoned, or scared to call for a fucking ambulance?' And then I'd get angry, and I'd see them smiling or singing along to something on the radio and I'd think, 'How can you do that? How can you run him over like a dog and leave him to die, and now you're laughing at a joke or singing along *to Robbie fucking Williams?*'

"Except, they didn't, did they? *He* did. *He* murdered my dad cos – in a way – cos of me."

"No!" Ali grabbed for his hand, held it and stared beseechingly into his face. "You mustn't think that. You must never for a second think that you had anything to do with this."

"But I do," he pulled, with some difficulty, his hand from her grip. "Cos if it wasn't for me – if you and my dad had just been together – then it might have been easier for you to go back to Jimmy. He might have got you back."

"I'd have died first," Ali, gravel in her voice, spat. "Carlton, I loved your dad. He was the first man who ever made me happy. And he gave me you, and every time I look at you, I see him, and I am happy to have known him. And you – you've never given me a moment's trouble."

Carlton laughed mirthlessly. "I'd never have dared give you a moment's trouble."

Ali reached out and stroked his face, causing him, as her hand floated over bruised skin, to wince.

"What happened to you?" she asked again. "Who did this to you?"

"I don't know," he finally sighed. "I didn't know what to do. I wanted to kill him. Then I was angry at myself for not killing him when I had the chance – when he was on the floor in there. Then I was angry at you for not telling me all these years and finally I was angry at myself again, for being angry at you.

"And all this time, I'd been going from pub to pub, in a wider circle, figuring that he'd have to go in somewhere to get cleaned up, and I might find him if I asked around. Except the pubs got rougher and rougher as I got angrier and angrier.

"And as I got angrier and angrier, I got more and more drunk. Then I was in a pub down by the river and some bloke took exception to me, and the next thing I know punches are being thrown."

Ali launched into another round of heartfelt apologies, threats against the life of whichever 'Lowlife scumbag' had done this to her boy and promises that she'd deal with Jimmy.

Carlton – at this last point – shook his head. "No, Mum. It's gone past the time for you – or me – to deal with Jimmy. This is police business."

He looked at me for support, and I agreed with him. "The guy's out of control, Ali. You've got murder, threats, arson, maiming and burglary. I don't think this is something that any of us can handle. Let the professionals deal with it."

Ali shook her head. "They'll wag a finger at him. Nothing ever sticks to him. He's like the devil."

"Ali," I beseeched her, "he's a nasty, brutish thug who's blighted your life. And this time he's gone too far. We can talk to the police. I bet – if he was involved in that robbery – they're looking for him," I said. "That would be a start."

But Ali shook her head. "Nobody ever knew who did that job," she said. "I only knew cos he turned up here and started demanding I get the bastard who took his share of the proceeds."

"He's not the devil, Ali," I insisted, but she just shook her head like a woman defeated.

Carlton sipped his tea and stared at her over the rim of

the mug. "Mum," he said, at length, causing her to look up at him, her red-rimmed eyes softening just for seeing his face, "I know this much. He's never going to hurt you again. I promise."

And putting down his mug, he lifted her right hand in both of his, brought it to his lips – swollen and split – and kissed it gently.

"Never," he said again, with a fire in his eyes.

NINETEEN

The ASBO twins arrived for their evening shift at about 5:00 p.m. and I immediately noted that Dash, like Carlton, had a bruised face and scraped knuckles.

"I fell over," he said flatly when I asked about the source of his injuries.

"Repeatedly, by the looks of it," Caz said, wincing as she inspected the damage. "I'm not sure how pleasing our regulars'll find the view for the next few days," she opined, "but we could always do a pugilistic theme night. Have you got any boxing gloves?" she asked me in the same tone she might have asked, say, a fashion stylist whether they had a pink Chanel suit in their Jackie Kennedy dress-up box.

"Oh yeah, sure," I muttered, "I keep them next to my shin pads and hockey mask."

"Don't be sarcastic, dear," Caz shot back, "it ages you. And talking of age and beauty," she said, turning her attention back to Dash, "*you*, my boy, should give that broken-hearted little woman over there," she nodded towards where Ali was skulking on the other side of the bar, as though she had no right to be involved in our conversation with Dash and Ray, "a hug and tell her how you feel."

Dash blushed to his roots. "I dunno what you're on about," he muttered, looking blindly around the bar.

"Mate," Ray clapped him on the shoulder, eliciting a

wince of pain, "there are people in comas on the other side of the planet who know what she means."

Dash settled his eyes on Ali, who glanced at him, smiled and went back to studiously polishing a glass that was in danger of being worn back, by the sheer power of her effort, to smears and sand.

"I'm not her type," Dash said sadly.

"How do you know if you never say how you feel?" Caz asked.

"Because she likes Jimmy fucking Carter," Dash announced, a sudden flash of fury in his voice.

"Idiot," Caz punched him gently in the shoulder, getting another wince. "She's afraid of Jimmy Carter. She loathes the man. I think, once upon a time, she might have endured him. But I don't think she has ever liked him. But you know what I think she does like? Kindness."

Dash blushed. "She's too old for me," he muttered.

"Says the rest of the world," Caz answered.

"Says you," he shot back.

"I mentioned age and beauty, it's true," she answered, "because they are simple facts. Not because I think either of them – her age or the fact that her beauty is less obvious than yours – a reason for the two of you to carry on this ludicrous pretence of disinterest for a second longer. Now, you can at least ask her how she's doing. If she wants a cup of tea or – I don't know – what do working class people like you two drink? A milk stout or something?" and so saying, she gave him a gentle shove and watched till, his blush suffusing even the back of his neck, Dash walked, like a man approaching the gallows, towards Ali.

Then turning her gaze towards me, Caz raised a perfectly-plucked eyebrow and pursed her lips. "And what, Mr Bird, is the source of that smirk?" she demanded.

"You," I said straight out. "Since when did you start turning into Clare Rayner?"

"Watch it," she smiled, "or I'll start advising you on your own romantic situation. That pretty policeman's not going to sit around waiting for you to get some sense and bury your misplaced pride forever, you know."

"I know," I smiled back at her, "which is why he's coming around here this evening."

"At your invite?" she asked eagerly.

"At my invite," I nodded, "to talk."

"Well," Caz smiled happily, "all's well with the world. God's back in his heaven and you, my boy, can get back into that kitchen and drag out the decent gin, because the stuff you've been feeding me lately has clearly had something wrong with it. How else to explain this," she moued disgustedly, as though experiencing a repulsive aftertaste, "*empathy* I've taken to feeling."

From behind her, Ray coughed discretely. "Not entirely sure that all's well with the world," he said gravely.

"What news from the Rialto?" Caz asked, turning to him.

"Our fat mate called me this morning," he said, beckoning us towards a quiet corner. "His friends visited your friend in the early hours of the morning. They found the venue somewhat short of pickings."

Caz, an expression of puzzlement on her face, stared blankly from Ray to me and back.

"In short, the mission," Ray continued, "whilst accomplished, accomplished very little."

"Wait," Caz held a hand up, addressing me rather than Ray, "are you also hearing a string of words which make absolutely no sense whatsoever?"

"He's talking in euphemisms," I said.

"Well thank God for that, I thought he was talking in tongues. Why," she asked, addressing herself, now, to Ray, "aren't you talking in English? Plain. Simple. English."

"Because," the unbruised twin replied, "I'm discussing illegal activity."

"With the two people who instigated said activity."

Ray frowned, processed her words and nodded. "Fair point," he acknowledged.

"So, they broke in," Caz prompted, and Ray nodded.

"And there was nothing there," he finished.

"Nothing?" Caz frowned again, her confusion resurging. "Explain." She held a hand up to stop him as he opened his mouth. "In plain English."

"Well, when they gained access," Ray began.

"And you will note," Caz added, "I have still not asked how, exactly, this was effected."

"It was effected," Ray deadpanned, "via the use of a euphemism. And a crowbar."

"Charming. So they gained access," Caz prompted.

"And there was nothing there."

"Yes," Caz snapped, her impatience beginning to show, "we've already had that line. It makes it sound like the entire building had evaporated."

"Oh, no," Ray assured her, "the building was there. There was chairs and pictures and coffee tables with magazines on them, an' all that shit. But there was nothing anyone might possibly want to pinch. No laptops, no desktops, just a bunch of generic furniture and an empty filing cabinet. Nothing."

"But I don't understand," Caz frowned. "Where's he keeping the evidence if there's nothing there?"

Ray smiled at her. "And we're back to age and beauty," he said, receiving, for his words a squint of warning from Caz.

"Explain," she said.

"Nobody, these days, needs to keep physical artefacts with them ever. Books, CDs, files of blackmail ammunition. It's all in the cloud."

"And we're back to euphemisms," Caz answered, before frowning again.

"Look," Ray explained, "I'm guessing from your confusion that you're of an age that assumes everything has to be physical, but the beauty of Lowe's data management approach – if I'm right – is that he can go anywhere, be anywhere, travel in just his boxers if he needs to, and still have access to the dirt he's collected on his victims."

Caz smiled fondly at Ray. "I've always liked you, Raymond. You're pretty, and smart. But not too smart. But this latest news – and your clear admiration for the loathsome Mr Lowe – are causing me, right now, to reconsider my admiration."

"No, hear me out," he interrupted. "Lowe's smart. He's got to know that sooner or later one of his blackmail victims will call his bluff, decide that they don't care about whatever damage his evidence does to them and call the cops. Then, he'll be raided and filing cabinets full of photos and tapes and – I don't know – spunk-stained dresses, whatever, would not only cook his goose, but also wipe out most of his stock in trade.

"So my guess is that as soon as he's got his victims on the hook, the evidence is converted to data, uploaded to the cloud and burned. Now, he can play the tapes of your brother's conversation any time he wants by accessing the recordings from a private – and presumably anonymous – account in the cloud and just streaming them."

"A sort of Black Spotify," I said, and received a despairing look from Caz.

"You had to, didn't you?" she asked, before returning to Ray. "So what are we going to do?"

Ray shrugged. "Not entirely sure, but I've got a mate."

He stopped talking mid-sentence, his gaze fixing over Caz's shoulder, the blood draining from his face and, on turning around, I discovered the source of his sudden attack of nerves.

The pub door had opened and into the bar had stepped two uniformed PCs.

Then into the pub stepped Detective Constable Nick Fisher.

I smiled, remembered we weren't supposed to be friendly to each other, reshaped my face to a flat impassivity and stepped forward, making eye contact with him momentarily before he tore his gaze from me, directed it at the far side of the bar and, turning his back on me, walked over to Ali.

I crossed the room as he reached the bar and introduced himself to Ali who sniffed, straightened her spine, stared him straight in the face and advised him that she not only knew who he was, but that, "We've met before."

Nick froze, at just the moment I arrived next to him.

"Everything okay?" I asked, feigning a bright and breezy tone as dread crept up my legs.

"Not really," Nick responded, glancing from me to Ali and back. "Is there somewhere private we could talk?"

"The kitchen," I said, as Ali – dropping a slice of lemon into a G & T, handing the drink to a customer and, with a nod, indicating that Dash should complete the order and accept payment – walked, wiping her hands on her t-shirt, towards the gap at the back of the bar.

"What's going on?" I asked Nick as the two of us, his uniformed back-up in attendance, followed her.

Nick, his jaw set tightly, glanced sideways at me. "My least favourite part of the job," he said, "is what's going on."

We made our way to the kitchen where Ali stood, her back to the industrial cooker, her arms crossed defensively, her face fixed in the angry scowl that I'd come to recognise as her habitual defence against both authority and disappointment.

"What's going on?" she echoed my query.

"Mrs Carter," Nick began and, before he could get another word out, the kitchen door flew open, slammed against his straight-backed, impassive-faced cohorts, throwing them forward until their outstretched arms stopped their journey against the kitchen table.

All eyes turned to the kitchen doorway where Dash and Carlton, looking like a couple of Conor McGregor tribute acts, stood half in and half out, a mixture of emotions playing across each of their faces.

The two stepped into the room, offering guilty apologies to the two constables, looking at Ali, me and Nick and, as one, echoing – as if it had become some sort of popular refrain – the words, "What's going on?"

Nick glanced nervously from the two newcomers to me, to Ali, licked his lips and, seeming to decide that diving in was better than delaying the moment, said, "I'm sorry, Mrs Carter, to be the bearer of this news but I have to advise you that the River Patrol pulled a man's body from the Thames today and that, further to the inspection of various documents on said body, we have reason to believe that the body belongs to your husband James Carter.

"I am therefore," he continued, as Ali gasped, unfolded her arms and staggered backwards, her arse catching the switch on the cooker and filling the kitchen with the smell of gas and the sound of a flint ignitor failing to catch, "asking you to accompany my colleagues and I to a facility at which you will be asked to confirm the identity of the deceased."

Ali, caught in the gas-scented, click-filled moment, stared at the assembled in confusion, her hand clapped squarely across her heart, before saying, "Oh thank Christ; I thought you were here about my telly licence…"

TWENTY

"Are you okay?" I asked Ali, and realised as I asked the question how stupid it was.

She barked a wordless positive and stared at the wall opposite her.

The wall was one of four, relaxingly painted in a calm beige with a hint of green; as though we were suspended in a nutmeg-scented, crème fraiche spinach puree, which formed the room in which we sat, mostly mute and totally alone.

I coughed, unnecessarily, and looked fully at her.

"You sure?" I asked.

Ali stared silently at the wall for a minute or so then turned her gaze fully on me. "You reckon they wire this room?" she asked.

I flapped my gums like an Alzheimic Tory Lord presented with an openly homosexual male and repeated the word wire, but with a question mark after it.

"Record," Ali said. "Listen in. Earwig. Like, if I said right now, 'I killed the bastard,' would they hear it?"

"I don't know," I admitted, correcting it to, "I'm not sure. I doubt it," I finished, half-heartedly, adding, "I mean – if they did, what would be the point? How admissible would anything they recorded in this room be?"

"True," she nodded, staring absently at the anaemic wall opposite us before fixing her gaze on the figures observing us from the window opposite.

"Feels like I'm on the conveyor belt on *The Generation Game*," she said bitterly. "Remember? A trip to Paris, a cuddly toy, a far-from-grieving widow."

She chuckled dryly, then, looking down, she added: "I'm glad he's fucking dead. And I hope he died in pain. And alone."

I followed her gaze down to the slab we were stood beside and to the body laid out on it.

The functionaries had offered her the choice of observing the body in person, or – like a patron at the cinema considering the latest Tarantino flick with the hope that it will prove to be better than one expects – from behind a window, following the slow opening of curtains.

Ali had chosen the in-person, face – as it were – to face approach.

And so we were both standing over the very lonely and very dead figure of Jimmy Carter. I stared at Ali as a single tear rolled over her lower eyelid, down her cheek and dropped sloppily off her chin. She glanced downwards at the body before us and then blinked, shrugging aside the trail so that none of its brothers might follow it, and turned directly to me.

"Well unless he's got a previously unknown tribute act, I'd say that's him. What d'you reckon?"

The body was almost glowing with a blueness that seemed to seep from within and that was darkest around the lips and up to the roots of the hair. Even the hair, so suspiciously blond in life, seemed to have a miasma of blue-green floating over it, as though the spirit of Jimmy Carter – a nasty, angry spirit, I had no doubt – was still floating protectively over the ruined hairdo.

"That's him," I said. "What do you want to do?"

"Throw a fucking party," she said, then catching my eye, frowned. "What do you think I *should* do?"

"You've options," I said quietly, casting an eye around the room. "Say it looks like him but you've not seen him for years, admit it's him and you've seen him lately, or say you have no idea who it is."

She stared at me for a moment and then chuckled dryly. "Jesus, you've a crooked mind," she muttered.

"Too much time working at The Marq," I admitted.

"He's dead," she said, glancing down at the body, naked to the waist, and back up at me.

I looked down at the cadaver – surprised at how brightly the chest hairs still glinted, how lively the shadows around the arm pits still seemed – then glanced back at her.

"Good decision."

Ali crossed the room, pressed a discretely-hidden button, and a moment later a door opened and she – with me following – left the cold room.

Nick looked at her, his question unnecessary, but, "That's him," Ali said flatly, to close any doubt down.

"You're sure?" Nick asked. "Only the only ID on him is an out of date Tesco Clubcard, so we have no photo ID."

Ali adopted the pose I'd seen her take when faced with a punter suggesting her double vodkas were anything less than a full double, and nodded solidly.

"I'm sure," she said.

Nick frowned. "When did you last see your husband?" he queried.

Ali stared Nick straight in the face with the attitude of someone expecting the gas man to believe that the meter hadn't been tampered with in her lifetime and said, "Twenty years ago, when the bastard walked out on me."

"Really?" Nick asked. "And yet you're sure it's him now, after two decades out of your sight?"

"Love," Ali fixed him, once again, with her most basilisk-like stare, "my abiding memory of that man is flat on his back drunk. Add a few years, it's still him."

"Definitely?" Nick asked, and Ali nodded solidly.

"As sure as I'm standing here," she said.

Nick met her gaze and then nodded to one of the functionaries, who tapped a few times on a tablet in her hands and then walked briskly off.

"What happened?" Ali finally asked, jerking her head towards the room we'd just left.

"We can't really say," Nick answered; nodding in what I assumed was his default 'dealing with widows' mode, "other than that he obviously drowned."

"Well I didn't think he dozed off in the fucking bath."

Nick shook his head. "Look, there's a bloody great lump on the back of his head. Looks like someone lamped him solidly with a rock-solid great weight. Some bruises on his chest and back, looks like he was pushed and held under – an oar, perhaps, something like that."

Ali and I looked surreptitiously at each other. I couldn't know what she was thinking, but I knew I was recalling the struggle at The Marq and wondering whether the lump had been acquired then.

"So could that bang on the back of the head have killed him?" I asked, feeling like Perry Mason.

"No, Danny," Nick said, giving me the sort of look I imagined he'd give to someone who'd just asked if, maybe, an absence of positive reviews had killed the musical *Martin Guerre*, "but I doubt it helped."

Ali sighed theatrically, "Maybe," she said, digging for an explanation, "he just fell into the river, only he'd had a fight with someone earlier?"

"No," Nick said, "the marks we've found clearly suggest he was pushed in and held under till he drowned. I'm sorry if this upsets you," he added, and was met by a withering look from Ali.

"I was married to the bastard," she snapped. "the only thing that could upset me right now would be if you said he was faking it in there."

Nick paused, blinked, and nodded. "Make no mistake, Mrs Carter, this definitely looks like murder."

"Well thank fuck for that," Ali announced, squaring up, "only I'd hate to think he turned up after twenty years and accidentally toppled into the fucking Thames."

Nick squinted. "*Turned up*? I thought you said you hadn't

seen him since he left you?"

"I hadn't," she shot back, "but he's clearly turned up in there."

Nick nodded, not entirely satisfied with her answer. "Well this was no accident. I'm glad we can allay your fears," he said, ushering us out of the room.

It was half an hour later, as our taxi slowly made its way back towards The Marq, that Ali turned towards me.

"What if Carlton caught up with him?" she asked

"Carlton?" I asked, confused.

"Or Dash," she added. "They both had bruises like they'd been in a fight."

"I'd noticed," I responded dryly.

"Jesus, Dan – what if one of them killed him?"

"They didn't. Did they?"

"There's more," she announced, staring at the water below her. "The body, in the cellar."

My blood ran cold.

"I think I know who it is. Jimmy used to hang around with a pretty rough gang. But there was one guy who vanished. Billy the Brick."

"French, was he?" I asked, wondering whether perhaps Edouard Du Briquet had come over with the conqueror.

"No, you fuckwit. He was a brickie by trade and a nasty piece of work by preference. He was as nasty as Jimmy, only smarter."

She stared out at the water as the taxi crawled along the embankment. "He vanished. I remember it vaguely. I wasn't really paying much attention to anything going on with that lot at the time, cos I was too busy trying to get away from Jimmy, but I remember the shit hitting the fan when Billy Bryant vanished. And now I think about it, it's obvious that part of that vexation was cos certain people thought he'd done a runner with them stones."

"Until," I murmured, as we turned off the main road towards The Marq, "he turned up in my cellar."

Our taxi had clearly taken the scenic route because, as we

pulled up outside The Marq, a couple of police cars were sitting outside the pub.

Ali got out as I paid the driver and we walked into the bar to be met by Nick's boss, Detective Inspector Frank Reid.

"Evening Danny," Reid sneered. "Long time no see."

"What's going on?" I asked, glancing around the room.

Three uniformed officers were on the opposite side of the room, surrounding the gangly figure of Carlton. As I watched, they moved, positioning him in front and surrounding him, his hands clearly cuffed behind his back.

"Carlton?" Ali stepped forward, and one of the officers held his hand up to fend her off.

"Someone called us," Reid announced and I eyeballed the regulars wondering which of them could have been the caller.

"Apparently," he continued, his voice a sing-song mockery of innocent surprise, "young Carlton here assaulted Mr Carter – *the late Mr Carter* – yesterday in this very bar, and was seen following him when he left this pub. Nice joint you're running, Mr Bird." He motioned to the uniforms to carry on taking Carlton out of the pub at which Ali, looking from Carlton to me and back, stepped in front of the boy.

"He didn't do it," she cried.

"Well, we'll see what he has to say about that down at the station, shall we?" Reid sneered.

"You don't need to take him to the station," Ali insisted, as one of the uniforms attempted politely but firmly to move her to one side, "cos I did it."

Everyone paused, turned and looked, first at each other, and then at Ali.

"Did what?" Reid snarled, his beady eyes looking piggier than ever.

"I drowned him." Ali outstared him, turned her glance to me and looked back at Reid. Not once did she let her gaze fall on Carlton.

"He called me. Last night. Told me he was going to hurt me and Carlton. So I arranged to meet him, down by the river. And I drowned him."

"Why'd you do it?" Reid asked; his eyes dancing from Carlton, whose horrified gaze was fixed on his mother; to Ali herself.

"He was Jimmy Carter," Ali said. "Wouldn't you?"

TWENTY-ONE

"Mum," Carlton called out, "don't do this. Please."

"Shut it, Carlton," Ali snapped back, her eyes never leaving Reid's face, "I'm not gonna see you suffer for something I did." At this, she tore her eyes from Reid and looked at Carlton, "For something I should have done a long time ago."

"Right," Reid gestured to the uniforms, "take 'em both."

"What?" Ali whipped back on him. "But he did nothing. I killed Jimmy. It was me that drowned him."

"So you say," Reid answered as one of the uniforms moved from Carlton towards Ali, "but Carlton here's just confessed to the same crime and, until I get to the bottom of it, I'm taking you both in."

"He said that to protect me, you fuckwit," Ali shouted, as the uniform stepped behind her and attempted to jerk her hands behind her back. Ali squirmed out of his reach and Reid chuckled.

"Changed your mind, Ali?" he sneered.

"He's fucking innocent," she snarled back. "And you know it."

The uniform paused, seemingly uncertain whether to cuff a woman who was now having a conversation with his boss, or not.

"Mum, please," Carlton begged. "Don't get involved."

"And yet he's confessed," Reid shot back.

"Maybe," he mused, "you both did it. Together. Carlton here, tells me that you recently told him that your husband had killed Carlton's dear old dad. Maybe the two of you decided to take revenge on Jimmy when he showed up here. Why did he show up anyway? Anything to do with that body that disinterred itself recently?"

"Carlton had nothing to do with this," Ali shot back. "Nothing. Now stop being a complete twat and let him go."

Dash stepped across to Ali but was held back by a glare from the uniform behind her. "Ali," he said, reaching out a hand to her, "don't do this. Please."

Ali smiled at him. "I have to," she said. "You wouldn't understand, but I have to."

Carlton, again, beseeched his mother to stop the argument and, as his pleas rang around the pub, and Reid laughed at both mother and son, I sidled up to Nick. "You know this is all wrong," I whispered. "There's no way either of these two killed him. He terrified them both."

"And yet," he said coldly, "an hour ago you and Ali were, apparently telling DC Fisher how *you'd* never met the man and *she'd* not seen him in two decades."

"Okay," I admitted, "we lied. But only cos we were…" I scrabbled to explain myself, "surprised to find him stretched out on a slab."

"Not as surprised as I'll bet he was," Reid shot back. "Right," he shouted, appearing to have had enough fun for the night, "take them," he barked at the prevaricating constables.

Ali and Carlton were then cuffed, dragged out to one of the waiting police cars, packed into them and driven away.

"See," a by-standing punter said to another as Caz and I, leaving the twins behind to man the bar, followed the parade, "I told you it was worth coming here on a Wednesday night. Better than the telly, it is."

TWENTY-TWO

It was the early hours of the next morning when Caz and I returned to The Marq.

Dash, his eyes lighting up when we trudged through the door, slumped when he realised we were unaccompanied.

"What's happened?" he asked tensely. "Where's Ali?"

"They're holding them both," I muttered darkly, "for questioning."

"Shit," Dash gasped, his face paling.

"Sweetie," Caz patted him on the shoulder as she headed to the kitchen, relieving the bar of a bottle of Captain Morgan en route, "it's Southwark nick, not The Lubyanka. They'll be fine."

"Danny," Dash scuttled after us, his brother switching off the lights and checking that the door was firmly bolted, following, "you've got to do something. She didn't do it. She couldn't have."

"I know," I said, dropping into an alarmingly creaky kitchen chair "Or at least, I think I know. But Dash, someone killed him."

Ray put the kettle on while Dash and Caz also dropped into chairs around the table.

"What are we gonna do?" Dash groaned. "What am I gonna do?"

"You're gonna drink rum-spiked coffee," Caz said, "calm down and think."

"Wait," I held a hand up as Caz passed the bottle over to Ray, "when you say she couldn't have, how do you know she couldn't have?"

In the background, Ray got busy with mugs and a jar of Nescafe and, at the table, Dash suddenly became somewhat abashed.

"Because she's a good woman," he said. "She couldn't kill anyone."

"Are you certain of that?" I fixed him with my steeliest glare and watched as the blush crept from his neck to the roots of his hair. "Only, how well can we really know anyone?"

"Thank you, Soren Kierkegaard," Caz muttered, as a huge mug of steaming black liquid was placed in front of me.

"Dash?" I pressed.

Ray presented a mug to Caz, put one down in front of his twin and then sat himself at the table. As one, he and Caz lifted and swigged from their mugs, Ray wincing and Caz reaching for the rum to top hers up.

Dash stared into his mug as though the steam might, at any moment, transform into an answer to the question he still hadn't answered.

"How can you be certain she didn't kill him?" I asked.

"Because I killed him," Dash blurted out, tears springing to his eyes.

"Fuck!" Ray whispered.

"Indeed," Caz responded.

"Explain," I said simply and nodded at his mug as I, in turn, took a deep gulp of the almost coffee-flavoured hot rum.

"She was here," Dash said, having sipped from his own mug, "until she left."

"This much," I noted, "is indisputable," and received, for my comment, a kick in the shins from Caz. "And what happened then?"

"I followed her," Dash said. "When I left here I rambled around for a while, until I realised I'd lost Jimmy and wouldn't find him. Then I realised that he would probably come back for Ali. He kept coming back to her. Frightening her. And I didn't know if she'd have anyone there, in case he came back. Or if he went to her house and stayed there, waiting for her. So I came back here and waited for her to leave, then I followed her home and waited there to see if he showed up."

"So to get this straight," I demanded, "how long have you been stalking my barmaid?"

Dash glared angrily at me. "She's a *bar manager*," he said, and I had to nod.

"Fair point," I said, "but doesn't really address the main point. Dash, stalking people is illegal. And creepy."

"And unnecessary, I'd hazard, in this case," Caz noted. "She really likes you, Dash."

Dash blushed. "I've never followed her anywhere before. I promise. But I knew that this time I had to keep an eye on her. To keep her safe."

"Yeah," I nodded. "Still creepy."

"You fucking muppet," his brother muttered. "She could have brained you."

"I didn't know what else to do." Dash turned tear-filled eyes on us.

"And besides," Caz added, "moral opinions on dear dumb Dash's stalking behaviour aside, he has just confessed to murdering Jimmy Carter."

Which did, sort of, add some perspective.

At which point Caz topped everyone's mugs up, turned to Dash and said, "Do continue."

"I followed her home," Dash said, miserably, "and waited outside. All night. And she didn't leave the house."

"But why did she go home?" I mused. "I mean, she had a place here. She could stay safely here all night if she wanted."

Caz sipped from her mug and shook her head. "Carlton had a place here. That was all about keeping the boy away – and safe – from Jimmy. But as soon as Jimmy saw the boy, that plan was a bust."

"So, what? She deliberately went home to lead Jimmy away from here?"

Caz shrugged. "Mothers have done worse to protect their kids," she murmured quietly.

"Jimmy turned up," Dash said quietly, "'bout one in the morning. Drunk. He was banging on the door, asking her to let him in and then demanding she open up. I…" he gulped, swigged again from the mug, looked up and around the table at all of us, "I was scared. I didn't know what to do, but Ali never opened the door, never switched on a light. She must have been sat in darkness. Listening to him.

"Eventually, he said, 'fuck you. I got somewhere to be. Someone who gives a fuck about me,' and he turned to go. And that's when he saw me."

"Fuck," Ray whispered again, and, once again, Caz nodded.

"Indeed. Top-up anyone?"

I glanced at her. She did not appear to be taking this as seriously as the rest of us.

"Jimmy came over and started having a go at me. Calling me her bodyguard, her pet. He was taking the piss out of me. Out of Ali. So I swung a punch at him."

"Bravo," Caz said. "And that," she nodded at the bruises on his face, "is what, I assume, you received in return?"

"He was a better fighter than me," Dash explained, "but I got lucky. Landed one punch that knocked him out. He hit the deck – I think he cracked his head – and I managed to get away to the opposite side of the road.

"Then I ran away. I left him, lying in the gutter."

At which point, I began to see why Caz had not been taking this quite as seriously as she might have.

"But Dash," I said, "Jimmy wasn't killed by a blow to the head. He was drowned."

"And unless you're vastly overpaying your genial bar manager," Caz murmured, "I had wondered how a fracas at her house could lead to her husband floating down the Thames. I mean, riverside accommodation is not exactly the standard for bar staff."

Dash looked from one of us to the other, a flame of hope sparking up in his eyes, only to die as he considered what he'd done. "But the knock on the head," he said. "It must have thrown him off balance. Maybe he staggered down to the river and then fell in."

I sipped from my mug, noticed it was empty and, nodding at Caz, received a large slug of neat rum into it.

"If he fell in because of the blow to the head," Dash went on, "then it was my fault. I killed him."

I shook my head. "The person who held Jimmy Carter under the water killed him," I said, and Dash frowned.

"Held him under?"

I nodded. "I've seen the body. He didn't fall in and drift off, so to speak. Someone actually held him under."

"But that doesn't make sense," Dash frowned.

"And it also doesn't give Ali the alibi you thought she had," I noted. "You ran off leaving Jimmy there, outside her house."

"But she couldn't have," Dash insisted. "She couldn't have," he whispered, as though trying to convince himself as much as us.

"Carlton could have come home," Ray said morosely.

"All we know," I said as his brother's head dropped further, "is that you didn't kill Jimmy Carter."

"So," Caz said, as though announcing we might do a day-trip tomorrow to the coast, "all we have to do is find out who did, get Ali and Carlton out of the Chateau D'If and reunite Dash with his amour, and all will be well."

"She doesn't even know I exist," Dash moaned onto the table.

"No. Well, there is that," Caz considered, before brightening up. "How are you with explosives? We could always blast them out."

Three pairs of eyes stared at her in puzzled shock. Caz smiled dryly.

"Or not. Which means, back to plan A. Who do you

think killed Jimmy Carter?" She nodded at Ray.

"You got a phone book?" he asked and, in response to her quizzical glance, expanded: "It could have been anyone in that. Or a shitload of people not in it. Like Ali said, it was Jimmy Carter. I can't think of anyone who wouldn't have wanted to kill him."

I filled them in on the conversation that Ali and I had had.

"So, what? You think it's one of this gang?" Dash asked.

"Well someone bumped off our man downstairs," I explained, "and made away with what's been described as a shitload of stones. Jimmy was looking for that person – it's what he was harassing Ali about. What if he started sniffing around and discovered the double-crosser?"

"So we're looking for an ex-crook with a vast fortune and no obvious source of wealth," Caz answered. "Can't be many of those around."

"I know," I said, then brightened up. "But we're actually looking for one who also stayed local. If they pissed off to the Costa, they wouldn't have been around for Jimmy to bother. Which means Jimmy would still be alive."

Caz frowned and then nodded her agreement. "So how do we find them?" she asked. "I mean, who are they? Who was in the gang?"

"Billy the Brick, Charlie Chatham (aka 'Charlie Chisel'), Jimmy Carter, Johnny Ho, 'Tiny' Tim Boyle and Al Halliwell," Ray announced from his side of the table, gaining amazed looks from all of us.

"Google," he waved his phone, "is your friend. ITV3 did a documentary a couple of years ago – *Danny Dyers' Dodgy Dudes*."

"A companion piece, one assumes, to *Letitia Dean's Murderous Molls*," Caz returned as Ray, unperturbed, continued.

"One of the episodes was completely about what was called the Old Kent Road Massive – the OKRM. It's on YouTube," he finished, tapping the screen on his phone as the smoky tones of Mr Dyer echoed around the – for once – silent kitchen, "*There's not an inch of London ain't got a gang running it. But for a while in the nineties, there was one gang that ruled 'em all south of the river. They 'ad tasty geezers from Balham to Brixton brickin' it. Then it all went wrong. This (*dramatic pause*) is the story of the Old Kent Road Massive.*"

I glanced at Caz, who returned my glance, raised an eyebrow and, as one, we pulled our chairs closer to the tiny screen.

TWENTY-THREE

Charlie "Chisel" Chatham may well, at one time, have been part of a gang that ruled the rougher parts of South London, but some time in the past two decades he'd moved a little further out, and considerably further up in his fortunes.

A carpet of dead brown leaves crunched underfoot as Caz and I stood opposite his house, a large white-fronted Georgian mansion. On the drive, a scarlet vintage Ferrari sat next to a huge, tank-like four-by-four.

Caz shivered, pulling her coat tighter around her. "Can you hear that?"

From somewhere in the distance a mass of voices was singing *Sweet Chariot*.

"It's the rugby ground," I said. "Carrying on the wind." Caz visibly relaxed.

"I thought, for a minute…" she murmured vaguely. "Well, you know, what with the spiritualist and so on…"

I shook my head. "You thought you were hearing a chorus of heavenly voices," I finished for her and received a raised eyebrow in response.

"Are we going in?" she asked, gesturing across the road. I remained standing where I was.

"How are we playing this?" I asked and received, for my query, a shrug.

"Same as always, I suppose," Caz said. "The way a swallow gets to Africa. We're winging it."

"I was afraid of that. So we're going to walk up to the door of a notorious gangster, ask him if he murdered one of his partners twenty years ago and then enquire whether he's been feeling a bit murder-y lately."

"That's about it," Caz nodded, shivering again as a gust of wind wafted down the road.

"Well," I said, "I suppose – if we are going to go – that we should do so soon."

"Yes," Caz agreed, "before hypothermia sets in."

"Or we get arrested," I said, and jerked my head across the road. "The upstairs curtains in the house next to our friend Chisel Charlie have twitched three times while we've been stood here. I reckon it won't be long till the Neighbourhood Watch are on to the local rozzers. C'mon," I set off, Caz behind me, "we might as well get it over with."

The curtains in the house to the left of the one we were aiming for stopped twitching. Now, they were pulled firmly back and an elderly gentleman, his hair closely cropped, stood staring at us with an air of quiet aggression, as though he was saying, I know you, and I know what you're here for.

We crossed the pavement and slid between the Ferrari, polished and gleaming even in the grey morning light, and the Range Rover, the sides and back crusted with dried mud, and made our way up a set of stairs to the front door, where I rang the doorbell.

"Whatever it is, we don't want it," said a young man's voice. "Either that, or we've already got two." I looked around, confused, then realised the voice had come from below me.

At the bottom of the stairs, having come from what I could now see was a basement entrance to the house, stood a creature from mythology.

Even from this elevated position, I could see that he was tall. His hair, cut short at the sides and back, was a mass of dark luxuriant curls on top, over a face that looked like it might have been carved from marble in antiquity, the head sat atop shoulders that were broad and muscular and – like all of him – deeply tanned.

The last I could tell because he was wearing nothing but a tight black singlet with a blue X on the chest, a pair of grey Lycra shorts so tight I could see his pulse, and a pair of fluorescent orange trainers.

Over his shoulder was a kitbag, also black, and he shifted this as we descended the steps towards him.

"Hi," I said breezily, extending a hand, which he studiously ignored, his gaze remaining fixed on Caz's face.

"We're looking for Mr Chatham," Caz said, equally breezy, and receiving in response a sneer, a raised eyebrow and a delicate pink tongue, which flicked out and licked briefly at his lower lip.

"Oh are we?" he mimicked. "Well, like I say, whatever it is, he won't want it."

"But I might want something from him," Caz responded.

"Whatever you want from the old man," the youth responded, shifting the weight of the kit bag once again, "I reckon I could let you have it. Twice as long – and twice as hard."

"Yes," Caz's voice had dropped to something more sultry now, "I'll bet you could. But all my friend and I want, right now, is a chat."

The young man turned his back on us, waved the car key in his hand at the red Ferrari, and the vehicle clunked, the lights flashing wildly as the central locking disengaged.

"That's a Mondial, isn't it?" I asked, and received his interest.

"Damn straight," he said. "You know this model?"

"It's a classic," I answered. "Made between – what? – eighty and ninety?"

"Ninety-three," he corrected me, and I bowed to his superior knowledge.

"Cream leather or black?" I asked, aware, as I did so, that Caz was staring at me with raised eyebrows.

"Black," he said, checking to make sure that Caz was still paying attention. "Tight and shiny."

"Nice," I nodded, as Caz sighed deeply, muttered something about kindergarten and stared pointedly across the roof of the car towards the street beyond. "You got the ABS too?" I queried

"Got the lot, mate. And less than five hundred on the clock."

"Looks pristine," I said, reaching out to touch the bonnet.

"It's been garaged for years. No," he swiped my hand roughly away from the car, "the only thing that gets to touch this pussy magnet is polishing cloths and," he stared pointedly at Caz, "pussy."

"And pigeon shit," she observed, nodding to an almost imperceptible dark dot on the roof.

The youth swore, opened the door, put his kit bag into the car, whipped a polishing cloth from the dashboard and, spitting on it, began to buff up the roof of the car.

"Fucking shit-rats," he spat, casting a murderous glare skywards.

"So," Caz asked once again, "is your dad home?"

"What d'you want?" he demanded, his true colours – now he'd been made to feel small by the mere presence of a speck of dirt – coming out.

"Well I wanted – with my friend here – to have that chat with him before we went all the way back home."

The brat clambered into the car, the electric window wound its way down and he sneered at Caz again, having clearly decided that belittling her was more important than continuing his auto-bonding with me. "Well just so you know, he's a lot less gentle than I am. Slag!"

And so saying, he turned the key in the ignition, the deep rumbling bass of the Ferrari engine kicking in and drowning out any verbal response Caz might make.

The window wound itself back up, he reversed out of the drive, straightened up on the road beyond and, holding a middle finger directly upwards, whooshed off in a squeal of tyres.

"What a charmer," I said dryly.

"And since when," she asked as we both turned back to the house, "have you been a – what do they call them? – carhead?"

"Petrolhead," I corrected her, "and I'm not really, but my sister Val is. She could recite the specs of every high-performance car before she could do her twelve times table, and used to make me help her practice them. I guess something must have rubbed off. Shall we try this way?" I nodded at the basement door, which was down three small steps and lead to what would clearly, once upon a time, have been a tradesman's entrance.

A single bell-press was embedded in the doorframe and I applied pressure to it, hearing an electronic tone coming from the other side of the door.

"What'd you forget now?" The door was opened by a bear of a man, his salt and pepper curls, barrel chest and the aquiline nose attesting to his parentage of the Ferrari Brat.

He stopped in the doorway, frowned, clenched his jaw and puffed out his chest further.

"What d'you want?"

"Mr Chatham?"

"Who's asking?"

"Lady Caroline Holloway," Caz beamed at him, stepped in front of me and held her hand out, "and this is Mr Bird."

Chatham hesitated, squinted suspiciously and went to close the door. "Whatever it is," he said, echoing the boy's words, "I don't want any."

"Hatton Garden," Caz said, quoting the dates and places we'd arrived at via Google the night before, "August tenth, 1996."

He paused, an angry flush darkening his face. "The fuck you say?" he demanded.

"It was a Saturday," Caz said. "But I'm sure you remember that."

"Listen," he hissed, moving to close the door, "I don't know who the fuck you two are, or what you want, but you have thirty seconds to get off my property."

"Or what?" I asked, as Caz stepped to one side.

"Perhaps he'll call the police," Caz said.

"Unlikely," I answered her, watching as Chatham's eyes squinted suspiciously, "cos if he does that, he'll have to admit what he was doing that weekend."

"We're done here," he said, moving to close the door.

"Seen Jimmy Carter lately?" I asked and, once again, the door paused.

"Carter? That fucking wastrel? What the fuck are you going on about?" He looked from one of us to the other, frowned and then opened wide the door, stepping to one side. "Ten minutes," he said, as we stepped across the threshold.

The basement of the house showed no sign of its former utilitarian purpose. There was a large modern granite-topped island with a six-ring hob in the nearest corner of the room, a vast stainless-steel extractor fan over it.

On the far side of the room, an extension had turned the space into a comfortable family room, with vast leather sofas arranged in a semi-circle before a cinema-sized flat screen affixed to the wall.

Chatham gestured at three tall barstools and closed the door behind us. We climbed onto the stools, and he went to the other side of the island.

"Now," he growled, "what are you going on about?"

I glanced at Caz, wondering, once again, where exactly to begin. "We know about the stones," I said and watched as his face set impassively, only a flaring of the nostrils betraying his emotions.

"I dunno what you mean," he deadpanned, though a nerve in his left jaw twitched suddenly.

"I think you do," I answered, glancing around the space. "Nice place you got here. Roomy." I slid off the stool and walked over to the collection of sofas. On the wall behind them was a series of framed prints and photos surrounding a larger black and white one of Chatham and the boy from outside.

"Your son?" I asked, gesturing at the shot.

"Alex," he nodded, crossing the room and holding an arm out as though to usher me back to the stools. "Now, I've given you time, mate, only, you've not really used it very wisely. So, unless you can tell me exactly what you're doing here, the door is that way."

"We know about the job you did on those diamond merchants in Hatton Garden," I said.

"Yeah," he said, "well I'm hearing words, but I have no sodding idea what any of them mean."

"Okay," I said and headed back to the island to resume my seat, "let's get theoretical, okay? Suppose there was a gang of mates. Let's call them – I don't know – the Old Kent Road Massive."

"Because a 'gang of mates' isn't enough," Caz murmured. "Everyone, nowadays, needs to think they're in a Scorsese. I'm sorry," she responded to my raised eyebrow, "do go on."

"Well," I resumed, nodding at Chatham, "this gang of mates. This gang of crooks—"

"*Theoretical* gang of crooks," he said flatly, his interest clearly piqued.

"*Theoretical*," I acceded, "decides to rob a jeweller in Hatton Garden. One that has a vault full of uncut, unpolished diamonds. Virtually untraceable."

"Now that's where you're wrong," Chatham said. "There's a register of them – size, shape, carats, distinctive colouration etc. Every jeweller would log their stones that way precisely as a way of having something to show the rozzers if they were stolen."

"*Theoretically* stolen," I corrected him. "So, not untraceable, then?"

"Not easily traceable," he said, "and not impossible to make them untraceable – polish, recut, set then unset them. But that takes time, money and contacts that the Old Kent Road Massive – in your story – wouldn't have had."

"And yet," I said, someone pinched all the stones from

under the noses of the gang. And here you are, sitting in a – by my guess – one-point-five-million-pound mansion. With a vintage Ferrari outside."

Chatham threw his head back and a bellow of a laugh ripped from him. "You think I pinched the stones?" His shoulders jogged with mirth and tears sprang to his eyes. Then, as suddenly as the hysterics had begun, they ended.

He planted both hands palm down on the granite and stared across the hob at me, all good humour gone from his face. "Mate, that was worth the entry fee. But you're done now."

"Everyone thought Billy the Brick took 'em and did a runner," I said. "My guess is that the gang has spent the past twenty years waiting for Mr William Bryant to resurface so they could put him six feet under."

"Except," Caz joined in, "he was already six-ish feet under."

Chatham frowned, his two huge dark brows pulling together. "Explain," he said simply.

"Check the papers," I said, "or the BBC website."

"Oh," Caz brightened up, "did we make the BBC?"

"We did," I said, sharing her pride at the achievement.

"Local or national?"

"Local," I answered and watched as her excitement flickered.

"Ah well," she said, "national next time."

"We can only hope. See, the thing is, Charlie – may I call you Charlie?" Charlie said nothing, his frown now fighting with a look of bubbling outrage. "Charlie, I run a pub. In Southwark. And not long ago, someone found what was left of your mate – sorry, your *theoretical* mate – Billy Bryant.

"He'd been there since someone put a couple of bullets in him back in 1996. So he couldn't have been the one to run off with the stones. And here, as I say, you are, sitting in a hugely expensive mansion."

"Motherfucker," Chatham snarled, but not at me. "Whichever of those bastards did this, I'll tear them apart.

151

Wait," he snapped out of whatever vengeance-filled reverie he'd been in and refocussed on Caz and me, "you think I did it?"

I gestured around the room. "It's a nice place. Didn't come cheap."

"Fuck me," he tilted his head back and roared with laughter, this time so hard that the extractor fan above his head vibrated along with him.

"Ah, mate," he said, when the laughter had died down and only a few chuckles remained, "I made all of this legitimately. But nice try. You ever need a job, you should get in touch with the Inland Revenue. They've been trying that shit on me for years."

"Legit?" I looked around.

"My nickname," Chatham said, "used to be Charlie Chisel."

"What? Like…" I mimed sniffing a line of blow and the Greek opposite shook his head.

"No, you stupid fucker, like…" and he mimed picking up a hammer and chisel and smashing away at a chunk of marble.

"I'm demolition. If you want it taking down, then I'm the one you call. Or called. I got bought out by one of the big multinationals about seven, eight years ago. Business was good already, but they paid me enough to never need to work again."

I glanced at Caz, who glanced back, purse-lipped. "We can check that, you know," I said.

"I know," he answered, staring angrily at me. "Wait, you thought I'd nicked the stones and then murdered Billy the Brick? Jesus," he shook his head. "But what's Jimmy Carter got to do with this?"

"Ah yes," I vamped, glad to be back on solid ground. "Have you seen Mr Carter lately?"

"Mate, I ain't seen any of that lot for," he blew out his cheeks, "years."

"Jimmy's dead," I said, watching his reaction, which was

disappointingly bland.

"So?" he asked. "People die. 'Specially people like Jimmy. He was never exactly the most stable of geezers, if you know what I mean."

"Well he seems to have met someone even less stable," Caz murmured.

"He drowned," I said.

"Pissed?" Chatham asked, dragging a stool around and climbing into it. "Fell in?"

"Deliberately drowned, Charlie," I answered. "Held under until he stopped breathing."

His frown deepened. "Jimmy was the sort to piss people off, pick fights."

"He told someone – someone we trust – that he was looking for the stones, or at least for the person who nicked them."

"I don't blame him," Chatham said, forgetting that he'd previously denied all knowledge of the stones or the robbery. "They were worth a fortune."

"Except, of course," I explained, "if he found whoever had the stones, he found a murderer."

"Cos whoever took them has to have offed The Brick," Chatham said, realisation dawning.

"Exactly. So, Jimmy never came here?"

Charlie seemed, now, to be off in a distant place, and it took him a moment to come back from his reverie, replay my question and shake his head. "I've been away – it was Alex's birthday. We went to St Lucia." He shook his head again. "He's eighteen – I bought him that bloody sports car. He wanted to go on some boozed-up party weekend to Ibiza with the lads from his club, but I wanted to spend a few days with him first. Time flies, you know? I realised that when my wife died. You don't get back the lost days. So I made him come with me. We just got back a couple of days ago."

"So any idea who Jimmy might have seen?"

He'd dropped, at the mention of his dead wife, back into the reverie and once again he had to consciously snap himself out of it.

"Hmmm? Oh… Fuck knows. Like I say, it's been ages since I saw any of that lot."

"Right. You said." I thought for a moment. "Could you tell us about them?"

"In what way?"

"Well, we know next to nothing about the Old Kent Road Massive, but it looks like one of them killed Billy Bryant, and twenty years later did Jimmy Carter. If we knew who they were, we might at least have some idea of where we're looking."

"Fair point," he nodded. "Mind standing up?"

We slid off the stools and he moved around the island to stand before us gesturing that we should raise our hands skywards before he patted each of us down.

Finally, satisfied that neither of us was wearing a wire, he nodded at the sofas across the room.

"Why don't we sit down?" he said. "D'you guys want a drink?"

"How bizarre," Caz replied, "I normally get the seat and the drink before I'm felt up. A brandy would be much appreciated. Daniel?"

I ordered a beer and, drinks served, seats taken, Chatham tilted his glass of Glen Fiddich to us and sipped from it.

"Fact is, folks, I got nothing to lose by talking to you. All of this was years ago, and I never did no murder. I was just the lift-and-shift man on a couple of jobs," he said with a smirk that suggested he might not be telling the entire truth.

"So who was?" I asked him. "Who were the members of the Old Kent Road Massive? And where are they now?"

"Where are they now, indeed," he mused, sipping again from his glass. "The leader – if you could call that rabble leadable – was Billy Bryant, he was the brains. He was known as Billy the Brick on account of he was a brickie."

"How prosaic," Caz murmured.

"Worked for his father-in-law, 'Tight-arse-Gruber.' 'orrible bastard, he was."

"Quite," Caz purred, "but unless he was one of the Old Kent Road Massive, he's somewhat out of scope, I'd suggest."

"Fair point," Chatham acceded. "So who else? Lemme see. There was me, obviously – lift and shift. Jimmy Carter, who you've met – muscle. A fucking psycho."

"Johnny Ho was known as 'Bang-Bang,' cos it was his job to get hold of any weapons needed to ensure the job went off well. Tiny Tim Boyle was, besides being a fat fucker, in charge of fireworks – explosives," he clarified.

"Sometimes you needed them to get into a safe, but the Hatton Garden job was a doddle, cos the jewellers had an automated state of the art internet-linked security system, and Billy had this mate – Gary the Ghost – who had some 'in' with the BT exchange who was supposed to be monitoring the alarm.

"So instead of blowing the safe, they literally switched off the alarm and the fucking thing swung open. I mean, there was more to it than that, obviously."

"Obviously," I said.

"Only in them days, we didn't know anything about the internet or hacking or any of that shit, so basically it was described to me as 'Pull the plug, open sesame.'" He swigged his scotch again, the reflective glaze coming back into his eyes. "Mind you, it was a bit of a tight squeeze getting through the tunnel into the vault, so it's just as well they didn't need that fat fuck and his dynamite. He was the size of a house, old Tim, and he was always on a diet. One of them diets where you eat every fucking thing you can get your hands on."

"So tell me a little bit more about the job," I prompted, as much because I wanted to know as because I wanted to move on from the gourmand preferences of Tiny Tim Boyle.

"Billy saw the jewellers first. He was doing a job for Gruber. Some sort of shop refit two doors down from the place. He realised he could get in via the cellars, but it would've been Tiny Tim who had to blow the safe without making it sound like we had the last night of the fucking proms going on under the street. Then Billy found out about the security set-up. Made it an even sweeter proposition."

"How'd he find out about the security system?" I asked, and Chatham chuckled dryly.

"Inside man. Sort of," he said. "Al Halliwell had a cousin who had this bird what worked in the shop. She was flapping her gums at some kid's christening or something and, next thing we know, Tiny Tim is coming along to blow through the wall to the building, but not to get into the safe."

"So who was Al Halliwell to you all?" I asked.

"Driver," Charlie said. "Though, to be honest, he was as mental as Jimmy, so could have been put on violence. But for some reason, Billy always wanted Al kept away from the action, safely in the front seat of a fast motor."

"And Jimmy hasn't been round here lately?"

"Jimmy?" Chatham shook his head. "Nah, mate. I told you, he could have been camped out on the drive for the past fortnight and I wouldn't have known."

"I suspect your neighbours would have noticed him," I said and another chuckle was issued.

"You seen the major, then?" be asked. "Yeah, Neighbourhood Watch. Nosy old bastard, but you need that type these days. World is full of fucking crooks, innit."

I glanced around the basement space, the back a wall of glass that allowed what was left of the day's light to fill this warm, designed space and wondered how much of this was really coming from honest graft. "So what happened after the robbery?" I asked.

"Happened? Not sure what you mean."

"You've got in," I prompted, "you've got the stones, and you've got out. What happens next?"

"Oh," he nodded, grasping the point. "Same as always," he said. "You split up. Including Al Halliwell, there was five people – Billy, Jimmy, Johnny Al and me – in or close to the vault of the jewellers."

"What about this – what's his name? – Gary the Ghost?"

I asked, and Chatham shook his head.

"Hardly ever dealt with him," he said. "He was someone Billy brought in, mostly for this one. My sense was that he was a con man. His job was to get the power off from some switching station in fuck-knows-where."

"Okay," I nodded, "so, five people. Why split up?"

"Five people," Chatham corrected me, "and a shitload of snide rocks. You ever seen *The Massive*?" he asked. "Five huge sweaty blokes all squeezed into a Ford Fiesta?"

"Sounds like your idea of heaven," Caz murmured to me, draining her brandy.

"We'd have stuck out like a sore thumb," he said. "Even if nobody knew what we'd been doing, they'd remember us. And a few days later, when the news of a robbery gets out, they'd be going 'Oi, remember them five big blokes what was hanging around that day? I wonder if we should call the filth up about that.' And the next thing you know, you're being lifted from your bed at ungodly o'clock. Nah," he shook his head, "first rule – split up.

"Second rule – split the gang and then split the cash. Or the stones, in this case. But you never split it till you're all together."

I was confused, and said so.

Chatham exhaled deeply, like I was some annoying, slightly backwards child he'd been lumbered with. "One of you has all the money. Soon as you're away from the scene, the five of you split and go in totally opposite directions. You criss-cross the city, take cabs, cars, buses, tubes. Make sure you're not being followed. And you are all, really, heading back to a pre-arranged place – hours, maybe even days after the job's done. At which point, you get to see how much you've got, and you do the split. Then, you all vanish into the night, and don't so much as speak to each other until long after the air's cleared.

"We arranged to get together two days later to split. Billy took the stones and that was the last we ever saw of him. Or them."

"So where was the split supposed to be?" I asked, already suspecting I knew the answer.

"Some shitty boozer in Southwark," Chatham said. "I always thought something was wrong. Billy was a two-timing bastard at the best of times and he wasn't averse to a bit of rough stuff neither, if he thought he was being crossed. But he was loyal. To us, at least. Always felt a bit odd that he'd just do a runner on us."

"And did none of you look for him?" Caz asked.

Chatham puffed out his cheeks, running a hand through his thick hair.

"Mate, we tore the fucking place apart looking for him. Nobody – not even his missus – ever heard from him again. Thing was, we couldn't make too much noise – or mess – in the search, cos you see the pigs had no fucking idea who had done the job, and making a racket about one missing villain might have attracted attention to us and – more importantly – to our whereabouts on the day in question."

"So who do you still keep in touch with?" I asked.

"None of 'em," he shook his head. "Lost touch, see, with all the old crowd. Ain't got time for all that these days. Still see Billy's missus from time to time. Well her dad's in the same business I was, really. He puts 'em up. I knock 'em down. He's still a mean old fucker, mind."

TWENTY-FOUR

I kissed Nick's cheek and picked up my shoulder bag.

"Wasp?" he grunted, shifting under the duvet, the eye that wasn't pressed into the pillow half-opening as he squirmed towards consciousness.

I stood staring down at him, this beautiful man in the half-light cast from the open bathroom door behind me.

"I'm gonna go," I whispered, wondering, like that nun in *The Sound of Music* (twice as long as, and fewer jokes than, the entire Second World War, by the way) just what I'd done in a past life to deserve this much joy in this. "It's late."

"'S early," he grunted, propping himself up on his elbow and squinting at the bedside clock, which displayed three o'clock. "Stay," he reached out a hand to me, and I smiled, shaking my head.

"I've stuff to do tomorrow morning," I said, "and it's better if I'm home when people start arriving. Otherwise they'll start asking questions."

"You're no fun anymore," he grinned, yanking me towards him and planting a smacker on my lips.

My determination flickered. "Yeah," I laughed gently, "well you're too much fun. And I have work to do."

He sat back, flicked on the bedside light and stared into my eyes. "You are being careful, aren't you, Danny? This body thing and now Jimmy Carter. It's heavy shit. This looks like gangland stuff."

I stroked his cheek. "I'm being careful," I said, leaning in to plant a smacker on him. "I always bring Caz with me, so any funny stuff and I can set her on the offender."

"Ah, the famous finishing school Rottweiler," he smiled. "See you tomorrow night?"

I thought for a moment, mentally running through some ideas in my head. "Probably," I nodded.

"Probably? You going off me already?"

"Yes," I said, then, realising the potential misunderstanding, corrected myself, "I mean, *yes* to seeing you. And no to going off you. I've got some stuff on, so hopefully tomorrow night. Can I let you know later?"

He tilted his head – a gentle curling of the lips making him look, in the soft, angled light, like a cherub; a cherub with five o'clock shadow – and regarded me in silence for a moment. "I still love you," he said, and my heart cracked from the sudden surge of joy.

"Me too," I said, becoming all brusque efficiency; standing up and patting him gently on the shoulder like a best mate. "Now go back to sleep. I'll call you."

And, as he switched out his bedside light and burrowed himself back into the duvet, I picked up my rucksack and, switching out the bathroom light, left the hotel room.

The dingy hallway was empty; the one faulty bulb at the end of the corridor flickering as always, and the lift arrived with a *bing* that sounded – in the stillness of three in the morning – like a dinner gong being dropped down a flight of stairs.

I stepped in and, through the descent and my crossing of the lobby, my heart was still playing the sort of string-filled mush that used to soundtrack stupid melodramas in black and white.

He'd said, 'I love you,' and since those words had come forth from Nick, he'd kept on saying them. And I loved him, but those two facts – sitting together so tenderly – also frightened me.

Just frightened, not terrified, though I was fairly sure that if it went on for much longer I'd start to be terrified, start to expect the break – when it came – to be even harder.

These thoughts were still going through my mind when the revolving door deposited me on the street and the car pulled, brakes screeching, to a halt in front of me.

The passenger window was down and, by bending slightly, I could see that the driver – the same one who'd taken me to Chopper before – was sitting in his peaked cap and shiny suit, staring impassively ahead.

"Get in," he said, his voice carrying in the still and silent morning air. "He wants to see you. Now."

I stood shocked on the pavement. A fine but persistent drizzle began to fall, the sort that soaks you in seconds, and still I stood, dripping and gaping at the car before me.

"How?" I managed to ask from my stupor.

"No one's got any secrets from Chopper," he answered. "You getting in? Only, you're getting wetter the longer you stand there."

I staggered over to the car, opened the rear door and dropped myself into the seat. The driver checked me out in the rear-view mirror, his eyes locking with mine for a second before he changed gear and, the central locking clicking in with a threatening *THUNK*, we moved down the empty and now soaked street.

We didn't make eye contact again, nor did he answer any of my questions as we drove through the West End, an eerie place at this time of the morning, the rain – sheeting now – turning the view from the car – of shopfronts still lit up, traffic lights and occasional headlights of other vehicles using the road – into a dark Monet; all streaked light and impressionistic shapes.

I peered out the window and frowned. We weren't heading to the pound shop.

"Where are we going?" I asked and, when no answer was forthcoming, I tried again. "Look, I don't know what's going on here, but it's got to be a simple misunderstanding. I mean, you've picked me up before. Chopper probably just wants to talk to me about The Marq or something."

Yeah, right, I thought. At three o'clock in the morning.

And then I was angry. "Does Chopper ever actually come to visit people," I asked the back of the goon's head, "or does he always expect you to go fetch them?"

"That's *Mr Falzone* to you," he snapped back, without either taking his eyes off the road or addressing my question.

Outside the car, the familiar landmarks whizzed by. We crossed Piccadilly, the glaring lights still flaming away; advertising products nobody could really need to a square devoid of consumers. The tiny figure of Eros, dwarfed by the greed and the hammering rain, still balancing on one leg and trying to fire his arrows of love up Piccadilly, through which we now drove.

Somewhere off Marble Arch we turned right, drove down a street which seemed, for being so close to the glitz of the streets we'd just left, grimier and the car pulled up outside what looked like a nightclub, the front in darkness but the red velvet rope still pulled across the doorway, hovering over a somewhat bedraggled red carpet.

The rear door of the car was suddenly opened by another suited goon, this one – despite the fact that it was three thirty in the morning, pitch dark and pissing down with rain – having augmented his shaven head, sharkskin suit and standard-issue earpiece with a pair of aviator sunglasses.

"Out," he barked, and I obediently scooted across the back seat and out of the car.

"Up," he nodded at my arms, and I raised them as he patted me down, snatched the rucksack from me, peered into it, threw it back to me and pointed at the door.

I walked into the club, the goon sticking to me like Lycra on a fat bloke, and noted, en passant, that the sign outside named the venue as 'BARishnikov.' Still, I thought, if I was going to be murdered, at least I'd be offed in a venue with a tacky pun in its name.

Inside, I could hear the steady thud of dance music coming from somewhere under our feet. The entire lobby was lined with mirrors, the ceiling tiled in some reflective material, our reflections bouncing back so many times that it became difficult to see where anything – a cash desk, a men's room, a torture chamber – might be located.

But my goon knew exactly where he was going and directed me to a door on the far side of the room, which, in turn, lead to a steep and narrow flight of stairs upwards.

At the top of the stairs, a small landing led to two doors and the suited heavy, still wearing his shades, knocked on the one on the left, and waited.

A moment passed before the door was opened by Chopper himself, wearing what looked like tuxedo trousers, a white dress shirt with the sleeves rolled up and a somewhat stressed look, his normally pristine hair spiking at odd angles.

"Ah, Danny," he smiled, though the smile didn't reach his eyes. "Good of you to join us."

Us? I thought, wondering who else was in the room and scanning Chopper's shirtfront for signs of blood spatters or other gore.

"Cyril," Chopper focussed over my shoulder, the smile dying, "you can lock up now, then pop back up here and wait outside."

The thug nodded, turned to go and was stopped by Chopper's voice. "Oh, and Cyril – lose the fucking shades. You're not Jason Statham, lad."

Cyril, blushing furiously, ripped the glasses from his face, mumbled his apologies and skittered down the stairs. Chopper, shaking his head like some bemused paterfamilias, opened the door wider and ushered me inside.

"Like I say – thanks for coming, Danny."

"How did you know," I asked and, before I could finish the question, he answered it.

"Where you were? Danny," he chuckled, "I like to know where people are. Especially when they're hanging round with shitbags like Charlie Chatham. You want an espresso? Here," he added, before I could say another word, "take this," and he handed me a stack of papers – letters, magazines, bills, bank statements – and nodded at an industrial-scale shredder on the opposite side of the room.

"Do me a favour," he said, gesturing that I should start feeding the paperwork through the blades, "shred that. Every last fucking page. No espresso?"

I shook my head.

"Well I'm gonna have one. Want a latte? It can do them too." He gestured at a Nespresso machine on the desk.

"I'm alright," I said, "but I still don't understand. You've been following me?"

"Go," he said, smiling at me as though I were his favourite grandson and pointing at the shredder.

I began, as though in a trance, to feed the paperwork through the machine and, between the noise of the blades and the gnashing of the coffee machine, it was a few minutes before I could actually hear what Chopper was saying.

"Anyways, it's not like I was the only one following you. Cyril had to deal with some other fucker who was trailing you last night. Any idea who that might be?"

I shook my head. "Look, Chopper – I mean," I caught myself, but too late, "Mr Falzone."

He chuckled. "Y'know, that nickname always makes me laugh. I think I've held a meat cleaver exactly once in my life. No," he shook his head, sipped from his coffee, and his little ice blue eyes glittered like a cobra as he watched me feed a bank statement into the machine, "I've handled shooters, Bowie knives, one time a Black & Decker drill – cheap shit; buy Bosch if you want the job done without the fucking engine burning out – and a couple of chainsaws. If I was to get rid of someone these days, I'd use a wood chipper. Or a fucking shredder. And yet, has anyone ever called me 'Shredder'? But you use one meat cleaver…"

I gulped, tearing my eyes from his stare and looking down at the blades of the shredder.

"So," he said, "you gonna tell me what's going on?"

"It's complicated," I said. "Nick's married, only—"

"Not with the fucking rozzer," he barked. "I can imagine

what's going on there and frankly it's not a picture I want in my head. I mean what's going on with Charlie fucking Chatham. That bastard's no good and when people who know me start hanging round with people like him, Danny, my teeth start itching."

"I needed to talk to him," I said.

"Well I didn't think you were measuring him up for fucking curtains. Talk to him about what?"

I stopped pushing paper into the jaws of the shredder and the machine went quiet. "It's complicated," I said and he drained his espresso, neatly replacing the cup into a matching tiny saucer on the desk.

"Yeah," he growled, "you said that. How about you simplify it for me?"

So I told him.

About the body in the cellar and how it had turned out to be Billy the Brick, how Jimmy Carter had then crawled out of the woodwork and started menacing Ali and Carlton, only to be murdered himself. And finally, how the whole mess seemed to lead back to the Hatton Garden job.

"Wallachs," he said when I'd finished.

"No," I insisted, "it's all true."

"No, you dappy fucker, I said Wallachs, not bollocks. It's the name of the jeweller. They got away with over five mill in uncut stones. Rumour I heard was they was too traceable – laser markings, chemical analysis on file, all that shit – but even at a deep discount for cash, they'd still have been worth a couple of mill easy. So," he said, the statement filled with menace, "you're looking for the stones."

We were sat, now, by the desk, in two swivel chairs facing each other. All the better, I feared, for Chopper to plunge a Bowie knife squarely into my chest if I displeased him.

"I'm looking," I said, looking squarely into his face, "for whoever killed Jimmy Carter."

"And yet two people have already confessed."

"Cos they're stupidly trying to cover for each other," I said. "They didn't do it."

He laughed. "Ah, Danny. You ain't been around much, have you? You'd be surprised what people'll do out of fear. Or for love. Look at you and your pretty policeman – creeping round in the dead of night to shitty hotels."

"Ali's not a murderer," I said definitively. "And nor is her son."

"So, you find the killer, the trail'll lead you back to them stones," he observed flatly.

I wasn't so sure about that fact or about where this conversation was going. "Maybe," I said uncertainly.

"It will," he nodded, considered for a moment, then added, "so you're looking for the remains of the Old Kent Road Massive, right?"

I nodded. He stood up, crossed to the coffee machine and began making another espresso. "My missus would have kittens," he said, nodding at the plume of coffee-scented steam issuing from the nozzle. "Says too much of this stuff is what's fucking up my blood pressure. But I'm gonna need it tonight. Everything in this room has to be shredded before five thirty."

"Why?" I asked, regretting the question even as I asked it. "What happens at five thirty?"

"A fire breaks out," he said, lifting the cup from the machine and placing it gingerly onto the saucer. "Not long after downstairs kicks out. Don't worry," he chuckled at my face, "you'll be long gone. So, Chatham sounds like he had a whole lot of nothing much for you."

I nodded, "I got one address – Billy's wife. But she was never part of the gang by the sound of things. Still, she might have some contact details for some of the others."

Chopper nodded. "Yeah, she was alright. Married some nob eventually, if I remember right. Minted but not through any hot stones. That it?"

"For now," I said.

"Well I know where you'll find Johnny Ho," he said dryly, and I perked up. "Fertilizing the rose bushes at Enfield crematorium. He popped his clogs about ten years ago."

I slumped, but Chopper's eyes suddenly regained the mongoose glint. "Funny thing, though. Johnny Ho had one restaurant in Dalston – The Silver Bowl, The Golden Shower, some shit like that – and then fifteen years ago he started expanding rapidly. Most assumed it was Mrs Ho's doing but what if… Nah," Chopper shook his head, "who'd take a fortune and invest it in a bunch of bloody noodle bars?"

"But what if he did?" I asked. "Who'd be around to take offence at Jimmy's questions?"

"You ever met Lilly Ho?" Chopper asked with a smile. "Makes Myra Hindley look like Mother Hubbard. Nasty cow, and just the sort who'd deal firmly with anything she saw as an inconvenience."

I considered what he was telling me. "You think she's worth seeing?"

Chopper threw his hands in the air. "What do I know from seeing?" he asked in mock humility. "I'm a retired Maltese shopkeeper with three kids, two grandkids, a wife who's thankfully in Fuengirola for the week and an apocalyptic conflagration to sort out in the next forty minutes. You're the sleuth."

"I'm a barman," I said flatly.

He reached out and patted my cheek playfully, "You're a barman with smarts, Danny."

"Not smart enough to spot your men following me around," I answered, and he smiled.

"Yeah, well, now that I know what you're up to, they won't be following you any more. Unless you need them to."

"I don't."

"Fair enough. So, you gonna take a look at the widow Ho next?"

"Maybe," I said. "But if you could get me contacts for any of the living members of the gang that'd be useful."

Chopper drained the cup and bowed to me. "I live to serve," he murmured, placing the cup back in the saucer. "Now go. If you get a wiggle on, you might be able to get the night bus before this place goes up."

I stood to go, biting back the request to maybe have his goons run me home: I figured they'd be needed for whatever was afoot at the BARishnikov.

"Oh, and Danny," he called as I had my hand on the door knob.

I stopped, turned back to face him.

"You find them stones – or any suggestion where they are – let me know, yeah? A favour for a favour," he said, the mongoose twinkle back in his eyes.

TWENTY-FIVE

"And you're taking this straight to the police, of course," Caz said.

I remained silent, my hands busily slashing away with a kitchen knife as I peeled a sack-load of onions and ran each one through a food processor, turning them into billions of translucent slivers.

"Daniel," Caz crossed to me and stood in front of me, attempting to lock my gaze, "put down the knife, and tell me that you did not agree to play hunt-the-diamonds for the bloody mafia."

"Chopper's not in the mafia," I said, placing the knife on the side. "At least: I don't *think* he is."

"Daniel, it makes little difference if he's in the bloody Rotarians. He kills people. For profit, and possibly for fun. And," she said as I opened my mouth to respond, "if you dare say he only kills his own kind, I swear I will pick that knife up and use it."

I closed my mouth. For a moment.

"I need to find the murderer," I said. "It's the only way to get Ali free."

"And what about Carlton?" she asked.

"Ah," I wiped my hands on my apron, sniffing away the onion tears running down my face, "I've been thinking about that. Boys!" I shouted into the hallway, summoning the twins, who arrived in seconds. They were differentiated

169

today by the fact that Dash was wearing a blue button-down while Ray had chosen a white version of the exact same shirt.

"What's up?" they chorused from the doorway.

"I've been thinking about Carlton," I said. "We're in agreement that he didn't do it," I said, to nods from the other three, "so I'm guessing his original story – the pub crawl and pub brawl – is true."

Ray and Dash pulled up two chairs by the table. "Makes sense," Dash said.

"I mean, why would he lie about that?" Ray added.

"Oh I don't know," Caz answered, "maybe because he was unsure how, 'I spent the night drowning the man who murdered my father,' would play."

"Are you with us or Reid?" I asked dryly.

"Depends who 'us' is," she said, referencing back to Chopper.

"You're right," I said, "Reid is going to be focussing his attention on getting one of the two of them nailed for the murder, and my guess is that Ali went to bed alone after you left Dash, which means she has no alibi for half the night.

"But if Carlton is telling the truth, he'll have an alibi that we can serve up to Reid. It might not be watertight, but it'll be a start."

"And how do we prove that alibi?" Ray asked.

"The old-fashioned way, I said, and all three looked at each other. "You two," I pointed at the twins, "start asking questions from pub to pub. Get a map. Draw a circle. Someone will have seen him. Certainly, the pub where he had this punch up will have seen and remembered him – and probably have it on CCTV.

"From that one, work backwards or forwards. If we can prove he spent the night in a series of pubs, it reduces the opportunity for him to have drowned Jimmy."

"Okay," Ray said, "so when do you want us to start this? Only, Danny, we're a bit light on bar staff at the moment, so going house to house in every pub in the area is going to be difficult with only the part-time barmaid left here."

"I'll give Maureen at The Walrus and Sealing Wax a call and see if she can lend us a couple of casuals. Would that work?"

They nodded.

"And any other thoughts on the – um – other situation?" I asked, casting a glance at Caz.

Ray nodded. "Like we said, he's got it in the cloud somewhere."

"I miss the good old days," Caz groaned, "when the only things in clouds were silver linings and acid rain."

"Well if he's got the stuff encrypted and stored in the cloud, there'll be a key – or at least a trail starter – on whatever computer he used to play the recordings to you the day you were there."

"Right," I said, "I know I'm really old, cos I'm hearing words, but they make no sense to me at all."

Dash nodded, pulled his chair forward and said, "It's like this, Danny…" then stopped, looked at his brother and gestured for the smarter half of the partnership to take over.

"If he's got it encrypted in the cloud, it's gonna be near impossible to find – let alone steal – the files. It's like someone steals a book, fills it full of all your worst secrets, then takes it to the world's biggest library and hides it on a shelf somewhere. There's millions of other books in this library."

"Billions," Dash chipped in, nodding vigorously.

"Billions," Ray said. "So even though you know it's in the library, you've got no chance of finding it. But if you could find it, if you could get to the book, you would still have trouble pinching the book and getting it out of the library without being discovered."

"So we're screwed," I said, but was waved aside by Caz.

"There's something coming," she said, smiling fondly at Ray. "I know there's something coming, but I just don't know what yet. Go on."

"Well," Ray said, "what if you hid just inside the library door and waited for your blackmailer to come into the

---

171

library? You know where he's going – where all blackmailers go. He's going to gloat over the book. So you hide, and you follow him, and you see where the book is. And after he's put it back on the shelf – remember, you still can't pinch it, cos you'll never get it out of the library, but – after he's lead you to it, and gone home, you torch the book. Burn it to ashes. Now, neither of you has the book."

I sat in silence, mental pictures of Chopper shredding bank statements and discussing conflagrations running through my head.

"Yes," I said at last, "but what if you accidentally set fire to the whole shelf and burn the library down to the ground?"

Dash grinned, rolling his eyes. "Dan, mate, the library doesn't exist. Or, to be precise, the library is the whole internet. You can't burn it down. But you can burn one of the books in it."

"You mean like deleting a file?" I asked, and his eyes lit up.

"Exactly," he smiled, the look of pride on his face matching, I imagined, the one that Cheryl Cole's singing teacher might have had when her pupil first sang an entire chorus without the aid of auto tune.

"Okay," I said, "so the book is a file and the library is the internet. What's the following all about?"

"Well everything you do on a computer leaves a record of some sort. It's there, even if you delete your history and your cookies. Most computer salesmen will deny it, but there are government bodies who have forced this tech in, so they say."

Caz slumped. "And would the 'they' who say this be the same ones who buy tin-foil hats and don't use oyster cards in case the government spots them going to Wembley Park?" she asked.

Ray laughed. "No, really, Caz, it's kosher. A trace of everything you do on a computer is there forever. All you need to do is get on to the actual computer, find the trace and follow the trail through the library to the book."

"Okay," I said, "can we stop now with the euphemisms? I get it. So we can really do this?"

"Danny, we can set the Sky Box to record from Venezuela. Telling a server to delete some files isn't that hard. Provided you can find the server. And crack the access controls. And find the files. And not trigger any alerts."

"There had to be a snag," Caz moaned.

"But you can do that, right?" I asked.

"No," Ray shook his head. "There is a slight difference between setting the Sky Box and hacking a commercial-grade server." He brightened up, "But I might know a man who can…"

TWENTY-SIX

Lilly Ho had, from what we could gather, over twenty Chinese restaurants in her empire, ranging from corner takeaways to glittering haute cuisine places like Jade Palace, which was located on a side street in Knightsbridge, not far from Harrods and Harvey Nicks.

As we walked through the restaurant door, it closed silently and firmly behind us, the tightness of the fit sealing the outside world where it belonged and replacing the traffic noises and diesel fumes with a low buzz of chatter and a scent, in the lobby at least, of jasmine and magnolia, issuing forth from candles the size of my head, which burned either side of a life-sized terracotta warrior.

The young woman behind the reception desk – more of a reception plinth, really – smiled openly at us, her perfectly-tailored Armani trouser suit and immaculate make-up making it seem that we had walked into an exclusive boutique rather than a restaurant.

"Good afternoon," she said, her accent more Beaulieu than Beijing, "welcome to Jade Palace. My name is Aileen. How may I help?"

Caz stepped forward and, in matching cut-glass tones, informed the receptionist that we were here to see Mrs Ho.

Aileen frowned.

Aileen fiddled with an iPad on the plinth in front of her, tapping it and swiping, and for a moment I considered whether she was maybe playing Candy Crush and hoping we'd get the message and absent ourselves but, at length she looked up, the frown deepening.

"I have no appointments booked in for Mrs Ho today," she announced. "Perhaps you're a day early?"

"Oh we don't have an appointment," Caz smiled sweetly. "But it's rather important we meet with Mrs Ho. It's, you could say, a matter of life and death. In that someone is dead and someone else is facing life for their murder."

Aileen did not like that. She re-tapped the screen, began typing something into it, frowned again and looked back up at us.

"I'm really very sorry," she said, banishing the frown and replacing it with the happy-to-help rictus grin she'd clearly been trained to default to, "but Mrs Ho is a very busy woman. I'm afraid she couldn't possibly see you without an appointment. Perhaps if you could email her with your concerns?"

Behind us, the door opened and another couple arrived. Aileen glanced over our shoulders, dismissing us already, boosted the smile back up to eleven and went into her script.

"Welcome to Jade Palace. My name is Aileen. How may I help you?"

The male half of the newly-arrived couple looked uncertainly at us, as though unsure whether he would be offending us by shoving us to one side and announcing his name and the fact that he had a reservation.

"Oh don't mind us." Caz waved him on, "We're just waiting for the owner to come out." She tapped the side of her ever-present handbag. "We've brought the results of some stool samples. Turns out the whole party wasn't suffering from gastroenteritis. It *was* Norovirus after all."

Aileen blanched, pressed a button, waved on the new arrivals – each now looking somewhat uncertain about their upcoming gastronomic adventure – and turned to us, the smile completely banished, the accent becoming more council estate than country estate, a fury blazing in her eyes.

"Fuck off," she hissed, "or I'll call the law on you both."

"Go ahead," I said.

"Don't think I won't," she answered, fishing in a drawer in the plinth and extracting an iPhone which she brandished as though it were a Colt 45.

"Look," I said, "all we need is a few minutes with Mrs Ho."

"And I've told you," she snapped back, "you've got more chance of getting a few minutes with Princess Di and Marilyn Monroe. Now fuck. Off."

"Tell her," I said, "it's about her late husband, the Old Kent Road Massive and the somewhat sensitive issue of murder."

"Look," Aileen acquired the air of someone whose job was on the line, leaning in to us so that we had to lean in to her and thus drop our voices, "she won't see you. She never sees anyone."

"Thank you, Aileen," said a voice behind us. "I'll take it from here."

We turned.

Behind us, having come through a hidden door behind the terracotta warrior, was a small woman, her chubby figure encased in a shiny black tracksuit, a silver dragon embroidered across her left shoulder and down her front across her right breast, the forked tongue pointing towards the silver Nike high-tops on her feet.

Her round, inquisitive face was topped by a sleek black bob, and her eyes peered out from behind a wire-framed pair of spectacles, the lenses of which were at least two inches thick.

Mrs Ho jerked her head at the door she'd come through and once we'd all walked through, left the lobby and she'd closed the door behind us, she turned to us.

"What's this all about?" she demanded. "And who the hell are you two *gau fahn*?"

I held out my hand. "I'm Danny Bird, Mrs Ho and this," I gestured at Caz, "is Lady Caroline Holloway." I stuck my hand back out and Lilly Ho regarded it with the same level of disdain I suspect she'd display if someone held a still steaming turd out in offering.

"That supposed to impress me?" she demanded, nodding at Caz. "*Lady* Holloway. Only we've had our share of the gentry in here and let me tell you, they're mostly a bunch of fuckwit inbreds."

I glanced at Caz, who had plastered her Princess Alexandra face on – the one I liked to imagine she'd do if she was on a royal visit to open a home for the dangerously insane and had just come face to face with one of the inmates.

Lilly, having waited three or four beats for a response, turned back to me. "See what I mean. Right – I know who you are, but you still haven't said what you want."

"We wanted to talk to you about the Old Kent Road Massive," I said, and she sighed theatrically.

"Yeah," she said, "I gathered that from your little performance out there. Fuck it, I ain't got time for this. Come on." She waved us down the poorly-lit, narrow corridor we were standing in and, displaying a huge and glitzy Rolex on her wrist, shoved aside a swing door at the end of the hallway and lead us into a nightmarish scene.

We were standing in the kitchen of Jade Palace, and if outside had been all tranquillity and jasmine scented luxury, here was chaos, heat and the smell of overused fat.

The kitchen was state of the art, if the art you were looking to be state of was the recreation of a battle kitchen during the Crimean War.

"Willy," she barked at one cowering functionary, "get them fucking lobsters out to table six and go easy with the garnish, alright. Where's my fucking shark's fin soups?"

"Here, Madame Ho," one of the cooks answered, plating up four bowls of steaming broth.

She turned to us. "You couldn't come after the lunch service?"

"We couldn't be certain of finding you here outside of

the lunch service," I answered, and she inclined her head as though acknowledging a simple fact.

"So, the Old Kent Road Massive. Why you asking questions about that lot? I haven't heard them mentioned for years."

"But your husband was one of the gang?" I prompted.

"Gang?" She cackled. "It was more a bunch of silly boys playing games, drinking, waving their willies around, that sort of thing."

"*That sort of thing?*" I eyeballed her, and she eyeballed me back.

"Spot of mah-jong, game of darts, the odd armed robbery," she shrugged at length. "Everyone's got to have a hobby. Anyway, it's irrelevant now. Johnny's dead."

"I'm sorry," I bowed my head. "How did he die?"

"Battered prawn," she said, tears springing to her eyes.

I blinked. She poked a finger behind the lenses and wiped the tears clear of her eyes.

"Silly bastard choked cos he put two deep fried prawns in his gob at once without takin' the head off one of them. Choked to death on a prawn head. It's hardly a heroic end, is it? I mean, why can't people just be happy with what they've got?" She rattled her Rolex and shook her head despondently before turning to bark in loud and threatening-sounding Cantonese at the young man standing at a six-ring hob, all rings blazing as he played the pans like a virtuoso. The only English phrases I recognised in her diatribe were "More rice," "less chicken," and, "you fucking halfwit."

At length, she returned her attention to me and, shaking her head sadly, said, "Greed is a terrible thing, isn't it?"

"Quite. So, do you know where any of the members of your husband's, um, mah-jong circle might be these days?"

She repeated the question as though translating it in her head, blew out her cheeks so that her head resembled, even more, a beach ball with glasses on and shook a negative reply. "No idea, love. Sorry. I haven't had dealings with any of that lot in an age. But why would you be looking for them?"

I hesitated a moment and, before I could decide what to say, Caz had jumped in.

"Because," she said, "it looks like someone in your husband's old circle has decided to reduce the diameter somewhat."

Lilly cast a disdainful eye on Caz before turning to me. "Does she always talk like a fucking fortune cookie?"

"Someone's murdered at least two of the old gang," I announced, choosing to leave out the fact that there'd been a twenty-year gap between the two killings, "and we'd like to find the remaining members so we can – hopefully – prevent any more deaths, and find out who did the first two killings."

"Well why didn't you say that?" she asked, shooting more evils at Caz. "So, who's dead?"

I told her – the mention of Billy Bryant raising little more than an eyebrow but the name Jimmy Carter causing both eyebrows to shoot skywards. "Interesting," she said, "and you say that the filth have Carter's missus for the job?"

"She didn't do it," I said.

"Course she didn't," Lilly stated absent-mindedly, "but it's interesting that you turn up asking me if I know the whereabouts of the rest of The Massive. Cos you're the second person in as many weeks to come round asking."

"And the first was?"

"Jimmy, of course," she said. "Oh yes, he came sniffing round here like some cut-price Goodfella. Making out he had something important to discuss with Johnny. Acted all sorry to hear the news when I told him Johnny'd been dead for years. I told him to sling his hook."

A thought occurred to me: "Did he tell you where he was going next?"

"Nah," she shook her head, "but I'll tell you where he should have been going – a decent barber."

"Any idea where he was living?" I asked. "I mean, if he'd been away for years then Jimmy had to have somewhere he was staying."

She shook her head again. "To be honest, I had no time for that bleached-blond fuckwit when Ho was alive, so I'd even less time for him when he came back from whatever rock he'd been under. The whole lot of 'em were a bunch of useless alley cats but woe betide any of their women who even looked at a bloke. I made it clear to Ho that if he ever so much as raised an eyebrow at me I'd have his knackers off with a cleaver. Unlike that silly cow who was married to Jimmy. She couldn't stand up to a butterfly."

I glanced at Caz. This was not the Ali we'd come to know.

"Christ knows why. That fucking ludicrous barnet. He thought it looked all *Club Tropicana*, only it was more Saga Holidays. I know men like him, and they tend to be more familiar with a knuckleduster than an iron. They need a woman who'll not take their shit. Anything else," she shook her head in disgust, "is weak.

"Weak," she repeated, definitively.

TWENTY-SEVEN

"This," Ray announced proudly, "is Phoenix."

In front of me stood a short, overweight teenager, his unbuttoned plaid shirt and dirty-looking jeans too big for him but the *Buffy* t-shirt visible under the shirt, contrastingly, stretching tight over a nascent pot belly.

"Alright," he said, nodding at me and running a hand – the nails grubby and badly bitten – through greasy hair. A stripe of dark fluff ran down each cheek, gathering under his chin in something resembling a beard, only one constructed of duckling down.

I smiled, holding a hand out to the wunderkind. "Well, Mr – um – Phoenix, it's a pleasure to meet you."

"No." Phoenix shook his head, recoiled from my extended hand. "You haven't met me. I haven't met you. Have you told him?" he asked, pointing at me and addressing Ray.

"Well," Ray smiled the smile that I knew always prefaced a 'difficult' conversation, "you see, Danny—"

"Oh, man," Phoenix threw his hands in the air. "I thought you told him."

"I'm telling him now, Walter."

"Jesus, dude. No names."

"Sorry. Phoenix. I'm telling him now, okay?"

Ray turned to me. "The thing is, Danny, Phoenix here is a wanted man."

"Well, as I always say," murmured Caz, simultaneously fluttering her lashes at Phoenix and downing her second martini of the night, "it's nice to be wanted."

"No, Caz," Ray insisted. "Really wanted. Interpol, the Feds, MI5, they're all after him."

"And he's sitting in my kitchen," I said.

"So what have you done?" Caz enquired.

"I hacked Tesco," the young man said, looking somewhat downcast, "and gave myself a billion Clubcard points."

"But in order to get into Tesco," Ray expanded, "he accidentally went via a Black Ops NSA server and may have accidentally deleted a raft of top-secret surveillance files."

"I'm good at deleting," he admitted, somewhat shamefacedly.

"Well," I nodded at the kitchen table, "we're ready to get deleting any time you are."

Phoenix looked back at Dash. "He knows about the, er, arrangement?" he asked.

"Arrangement?" I frowned at Dash. "What arrangement?"

"It's five hundred up front," Dash said, nodding at Caz. "We've already discussed it."

"And I take no responsibility for the results – or lack of results – of what follows. It's not an exact science."

"Wait," I stayed Caz, who had already dived into her handbag. "What d'you mean, 'It's not an exact science'? Even baking a cake is an exact science today. What's this if not scientific?"

"I mean," Phoenix said, pocketing a fat envelope which Caz handed to him, "once we're in there, there's no knowing what security they've got in place."

This, I did not like the look of. "Security?"

Phoenix slipped a messenger bag off his shoulder and dropped into a kitchen chair. "They sometimes put watchdogs that cut off the connection. Or blast code that exterminates your router. Speaking of which," he added as he pulled a battered laptop from his bag, followed by a

---

length of cable, "what's your Wi-Fi password?"

"Wi-Fi?" I glanced at Dash and Caz.

"Yeah," Phoenix placed the laptop on the table, handed one end of the cable to Dash and plugged the other end of it into the computer, "you know, the thing that sends the internet through the air to your laptop – Wi-Fi."

"I know," I said in my best Johnny Gielgud, "what Wi-Fi is. I just don't know what the password is."

Phoenix rolled his eyes and issued the most exasperated sigh I'd ever heard. "Dude," he gestured at Dash, "I thought you said this was all cool."

"It's *knobber*. Only the 'o' is a zero," Ray announced, plugging the cable straight into the mains as I sputtered and demanded to know who had set up my Wi-Fi password.

Phoenix dived back into this bag and extracted a can of Red Bull, then another and, unzipping a pocket on the front of the bag, two more cans of the high-caffeine, sugary drink, followed by two Mars Bars.

"So I suppose a cocktail is unnecessary," Caz breezed.

"Missus," Phoenix said, a look of shock on his face.

"Miss," Caz corrected him.

"I'm sixteen. I can't legally drink. And I wouldn't want you to lose your licence."

"Oh it's not my licence," Caz replied, then frowned. "Do I look like a pub landlady? Danny?"

I waved her aside. "Sixteen?" I asked.

"Next birthday," Phoenix clarified, his eyes never leaving the screen as he hammered away at the keyboard.

"Jesus," I looked at Ray, who shrugged.

Caz, meanwhile, was grumbling away about how someone could raise the legality of a cosmopolitan, yet be happily hacking the CIA from their back bedroom.

"Problem?" Phoenix asked, raising his eyes briefly from the screen.

"Only that I guess your mum will want you home at a decent time," I said. "I mean, it is a school night."

"Dude," he stared at me, blinked slowly and cracked

open a can of Red Bull, downing at least half the contents in one huge gulp, "chill. This'll be a piece of cake. Be home before *News at Ten* is over. You got any crisps handy?"

I shuffled off to get some crisps, indicating, by a twitch of my head, that Ray should follow me.

"Where the hell did you find him?" I whispered when we were out of sight.

"Walter's a legend," Ray said.

"And what's with the Phoenix shit?"

Ray rifled through a box of crisps, extracting two packets of salt & vinegar, one cheese & onion and a ready salted. "He's an internationally-renowned hacker and activist. Phoenix is all about rising from the ashes of the past, reforming yourself and the society around you through destruction and rebirth. Walter's, well," he handed me the two bags of salt & vinegar, "not. Is it?"

"Any news on the other thing?" I asked as we walked back down the hallway.

"Nothing so far," Ray admitted. "Dash is out right now canvassing the local pubs. We've got the picture of Carlton but nothing much has sparked so far. Couple of pubs recognised him but couldn't say whether it was from that night or some other night he'd been in."

"Well keep looking," I said. "Someone will recognise him, and it's only going to take one to start the chain off. So this guy is good?"

"The best," Ray said, patting my shoulder. "Relax. You're in safe hands."

"Jesus," I sighed, feeling older than Methuselah, "let's do this."

Phoenix held a finger up for silence, tapped a few more keys and said, "Prawn cocktail," which caused Ray to gasp, charge back out to the hallway and return with three packs of the required flavour of crisps. He tore one of them open and placed it on the table before the boy, who shovelled a handful of crisps into his mouth, chewed twice, washed them down with another giant swig from the Red Bull can and looked up at us.

"Already half done," he announced.

"That was quick."

"Well I had the address, and earlier I figured out the service provider, server locator and router he was using. So right now, I'm basically in his internet gateway." He tapped a few more keys and sat back. "Yeah, this is definitely him. He's got some interesting security."

At that moment, my phone rang.

"Yeah," I said, answering it and stepping out of the kitchen and into the hallway.

"You alone?" It was Chopper.

I glanced over my shoulder. Phoenix was still tapping away at his laptop, Ray peering over his shoulder, while Caz attempted to look nonchalant, but had her eyes fixed on the boy's hands.

"I'm alone," I confirmed.

"So how'd it go with the widow Ho?" he asked.

I frowned. Chopper was too interested in this situation. It was unlike him to do much more than tell me to 'Sort it' – whatever 'it' was – and his sudden keenness bothered me.

"Yeah," I said, "not much there."

He snorted. "Yeah, I figured she'd keep things close to her chest. I did some digging and the money for them restaurants came from an uncle of hers back in Hong Kong. I don't think Ho had anything to do with pinching the stones."

And then it hit me. "Listen, Mr Falzone," I said, interrupting him, "you know you said you were having me followed?"

"Not any more, Danny. Not now we've got an agreement."

"Agreement? What agreement?"

"The stones. You find 'em, you call me. We'll split them eighty twenty."

"Eighty twenty?"

"Alright, seventy-five twenty-five. I'm gonna be the one

having to find somewhere to flog 'em."

"Yeah, how long have you been following me?" I asked.

There was a silence at the end of the line, then Chopper said, "A few days. But we're good now."

"So before Jimmy was killed," I said.

"Yeah. Since the other stiff turned up in the cellar. What of it?"

I was aware that I was now skating on very thin ice, but I was already pissed off and this was the final straw.

"You knew, didn't you? You knew who the body was. And you knew about the jewellery heist. You knew right from the beginning."

The silence was there again. "I tend to keep an ear to the ground, Danny, and in my game it helps to have a very long memory. I didn't know anything. But I had my suspicions."

"I'm going to ask you again," I said, and from the other end of the line his voice came back.

"And I'm gonna answer you again."

"Did you kill the body in the cellar? Did you murder Billy Bryant?"

"Dan, if I'd offed him, d'you think I'd be looking for them stones now? I didn't know he was there but from the descriptions, the time frame, the fact that it was well-known that Billy had done a runner with them stones – Christ, the rest of the gang tore half of London up looking for him and them stones back in the day – I figured it was a good bet."

"So you had me followed."

"I like to know where the people who work for me are. Especially when they're as resourceful as you."

"I don't work for you," I said through gritted teeth.

He chuckled. "Ah Danny, everyone works for me. One way or another. Listen," he said, getting back down to business, "I found another name for you. No joy with this Gary the Ghost. Nobody I've spoken to knows who he was, but are you still looking for Tiny Tim?"

I said that I was.

"You got a pen and paper?"

"Hang on," I switched the phone to speaker, shoved it under my chin, pulled a receipt from my back pocket and a stub of pencil from behind my ear. "Go on," I said.

He gave me an address. "Don't go alone," he chuckled, "don't go too close to the bars, and for fuck's sake don't bring donuts or feed him after midnight."

"What?" I asked but, chuckling, he rang off, leaving me staring at the paper in my hand, as the phone slipped from under my chin and dropped, clattering to the floor.

I picked it up, shoved it and the receipt back in my pocket, and re-entered the kitchen.

Now, Phoenix was bent further over the keyboard, Caz was out of her chair and was peering over his left shoulder, while Ray was peering over his right.

"How are we doing?" I asked, as Phoenix grunted, Caz and Ray both shushing me worriedly.

"Got ya, you fucker," Phoenix smiled wolfishly, and hammered away at the keyboard.

"What's going on?" I sidled up to Caz and whispered the question.

"We've had some," she glanced at Ray, essayed, "issues," received a nod of agreement from him and pulled me gently away from the table.

"So he's found the server – the gateway – whatever it was that he needed to find to start the trace to wherever Lowe's parked the files. Only there's a lot more security and encryption on everything than he usually sees. Phoenix reckons it's like Lowe was expecting us."

"Really?" I aped surprise. "Cos I can't imagine why anyone who blackmails people to the tune of millions on a regular basis wouldn't think they might need a little more security on their computer. So what's Phoenix doing?"

"He's trying to shut down the security protocols," she answered, making me smile.

"For a second there, you actually sounded like you had a clue what you were talking about," I said.

She smirked. "Osmosis, my friend."

Suddenly, behind us, the mood changed.

"Fuck!" Phoenix screamed, hammering on the keyboard like a thing possessed.

"What's up?" I rushed back to his side.

"He's got a guard dog," Phoenix snapped, tapping furiously at the keys.

"A guard dog?" I looked quizzically at Caz, who returned my confusion and eyeballed the three empty Red Bull cans on the table.

"And is this a bad thing?" she enquired.

"Course it's a bad thing," he snapped back, pausing to read something on the screen, mutter under his breath and start tapping again.□□ □□□ □□□ □□□□□□□□□□□□□□□□□□□□□□□□□□□□□□□□□□□□

"Because?" I asked.

"I haven't got time for this," he bit back, typing a three-letter code and hitting return a dozen or more times. "Wait," he held a hand up, "it might be asleep."

His shoulders relaxed.

"So, to be clear," I said, tentatively feeling my way back into the conversation, "we're not talking about a real guard dog, are we?"

Phoenix frowned, half-turned himself in the chair and looked at me as though I were deranged. "Are you on fucking drugs?"

"No," I protested, and before I could get any further, Ray interrupted.

"They're old, mate. Tell 'em in plain language."

"Old?" Caz and I chorused in outrage, but before we could further expand on our feelings around the ageist insult, Phoenix rolled his eyes, wheezed like a consumptive at their last, rattled one of the Red Bull cans, swigged the dregs from it and turned to face us.

"Most people put security on their machines, yeah?"

Caz and I eyeballed each other, both of us, I was sure, aware that any wrong move could have us labelled, next time, as geriatrics and nodded.

"Yeah," we agreed.

"Well, most people just want the security to stop a burglar. If the padlock stops you getting in, it's done its job. And if it doesn't, it's failed, and you're in and all their stuff is yours."

"You sound like you've done a spot of breaking and entering before," Caz opined, but Phoenix roundly ignored her.

"This guy," he said, gesturing at the laptop, "went one step further. He's put a piece of code in place after the standard security, so that – even if you get past that – you've got problems."

"Problems?" I didn't like the sound of this.

"What do guard dogs usually do?" he asked, trying – and failing – to keep the irritation out of his voice.

"Bite you?" I guessed, and Phoenix nodded, a glint in his eyes.

"Security keeps you out. A guard dog sees to it that – even if you get in – you get bitten. Or worse."

"Worse?" Caz asked, and we exchanged a look.

"And to be clear," I said, "still not talking about a real guard dog."

"Bitten," Ray said, from the other side of Phoenix, "means the program will latch on to you. Find out who you are. Follow you back along whatever road you took to get here and start deleting your data."

I swallowed hard. "And worse."

"If you get mauled, it isn't just your data that gets trashed. They can take your data first – passwords, credit cards, the lot. Publish them on the web. And then fry the hardware – routers, laptop, phones. All of it."

"So what do we do?" Caz asked.

"Well the guard dog software is still sleeping," Phoenix said. "It might mean we haven't triggered whatever protocols activate it."

"Okay," I said cautiously.

And waited.

At length, Phoenix cracked his knuckles, turned back to the laptop and gingerly tapped a couple of keys. "Okay," he said, "we might have something. I can see a server he's been visiting more regularly than many of the others." He typed a few more commands and silence descended.

"What's he doing now?" Caz interrupted the silence in a stage whisper and received, for her efforts, an angry glare from Phoenix. "Ooh," Caz said, pointing at the laptop screen, "why's it doing that?"

Phoenix turned back to the screen, all the blood draining from his face.

"Oh fuck," he said.

On the screen, our faces – Ray, Caz, me and Phoenix – were clearly visible.

"Terribly lit," Caz murmured as it dawned on me that the laptop camera had been turned on.

"Fuck," Phoenix whispered in what sounded like terror, as the screen froze, blinked, the sound of a shutter issued clearly from the laptop and the camera switched off, returning us to the screen that Phoenix had been entering commands to.

"Fuck!" he shouted, louder this time, as he slammed the lid of the laptop closed. "Where's your router?" he screamed, yanking every cable out of the laptop and hurling it – like a ticking time bomb – across the table.

"Router?" I looked at Caz, who looked at me, and it was Ray, already running, who called out from the hallway "Bar! It's in the bar!"

We three went charging after him, with Phoenix getting there before Caz and me and ripping the router off the shelf it was on, before yanking all cables from the back of the device.

"What's going on?" I asked.

"It wasn't asleep," he almost sobbed. "The bastard had

something that looked dormant and used the time I was faffing around with you two to wriggle its way back here."

"So less of a guard dog, more of a guard worm, then?" Caz asked, and Phoenix turned on her.

"He's got your fucking face," he said, the colour – along with a look of complete disdain for all of us – returning to his face.

"If you're lucky, that's all he's got. But I have no idea how long he was in the router, in my laptop, in your system. Right," Phoenix suddenly charged back down the hallway, into the kitchen and began stuffing everything – laptop, cables, even the empty Red Bull cans – into his messenger bag.

"I'm outta here," he said, slinging the bag over his shoulder.

"Wait," Caz pleaded. "Is that it? I mean, is there nothing else you can do?"

"Missus—" Phoenix paused in the door.

"Miss," Caz corrected him for the second time.

"I don't know who you've crossed or what they want. But whoever they are, and whatever it is, I'd give it to them. Cos you're messing with the big boys now. That," he pointed at the now bare table, "was unlike anything I've ever seen before."

Phoenix shook his head, opined, "You're all fucked," turned and almost ran from the pub.

The three of us remained staring at each other in open-mouth astonishment.

"What. Just. Happened?" I asked after a few minutes.

"I'm not sure," Caz answered.

"But whatever it was," Ray expanded, "I don't think this thing is over yet. Cos now, your Mr Lowe has photographic proof we've been trying to break into his system."

"He's right," I said, nodding at the doorway that Phoenix had lately stood in. "We're fucked."

191

"So how did you spring this?" I asked, pressing the intercom on the stuccoed pillar outside Tim Boyle's Highgate home, eyeballing, as I did so, the inset plate reading, 'Gethsemane Gardens.'

"Oh, you know," Caz said vaguely, "I did what a lady always does when she needs something from a man."

"Odd," I said as the rattling gargle of the intercom continued to ring, "I don't recall you having any virtue left to promise."

"Ah ha ha," she deadpanned, eyeballing the box of delicacies I had acquired from Fortnum's that morning.

"Hello," a voice – tinny, but still managing to contain every line Uriah Heep ever spoke – issued from the intercom.

"It's," I glanced at Caz, who gestured at me, "Mr Danny Bird, to see Mr Boyle."

There was a moment's silence, during which a dark car bearing the livery of a private protection company drove past slowly and meaningfully behind us.

"Come straight up the driveway," the voice said, "turn right at the gatekeeper's cottage and left at the lake. I'll be waiting for you."

There was a click, a buzz and the gates swung open. I glanced at Caz. "I suspect he thinks we're approaching on wheels."

"Which will make our approach on foot all the more off-putting," she answered.

I stepped past the gates, onto a tree-lined drive, Caz behind me. "And off-putting, I suspect, is exactly what you want to be at times like this," she said.

She had a point, and I nodded my agreement. "So, if not by the offering of favours," I asked, "gow did you get us in here?"

"By appealing to his vanity," she said simply. "You boys – no matter who you are and how you got there – all love the chance to remind another boy who you are and how you got where you are."

"True," I admitted. "So, who is he, how did he get here?" I gestured at the trees as we approached a redbrick building that I assumed was the gatekeeper's cottage. "And more importantly, who, for the purposes of today, am I?"

"*He*," Caz announced, again eyeballing the box of sweeties which I was holding rigidly at the end of a butler-like arm, "is SE Man."

She announced this as though it should, truly, mean something to me. "Semen?" I frowned. "He made all this from porn?"

"SE Man," she repeated, looking at me with the obvious expectation that what she was saying would suddenly mean something to me.

I stopped. "Caz, you can repeat that phrase as many times as you want but, at this point, and – I suspect – until you explain yourself, it's not gonna mean anything to me."

Caz shook her head. "Well thank God at least one of us reads the tabloids," she said. "SE Man was an unnamed man from South East London. Hence the 'SE'."

"What? Like Piltdown Man?" I essayed, and she nodded cautiously.

"Yes, dear," Caz said, as though talking to an elderly relative who had woken up and asked if that nice Mr Mosely was prime minister yet, "just like Piltdown Man. If he'd been the largest individual winner of the lottery in London. Ever.

In history."

I stopped. "Tiny Tim won the lottery?"

Caz nodded, eyeing the Fortnum's box as it wobbled precariously on my extended arm.

My shoulder ached.

"An absolute fortune," she explained. "And he ticked the 'No Publicity' box, which meant he was referred to by the tabloids as SE Man for about a year until he dumped his girlfriend at the time, and she went to the papers crying about what a miser he was and how she'd been binned despite all her loyalty."

"So now everyone knows who he is and how he got here," I said, and Caz nodded.

"Mind you," she pointed out, "it also makes it rather unlikely that any of this came from a vault in Hatton Garden."

"He could still be our man, though," I pointed out. "I mean, he could have offed Billy the Brick, grabbed the jewels and then realised that – thanks to fate and the lottery – it had all been unnecessary."

Caz moued. "Valid point," she admitted, "which is why I decided that you – in your guise as a reporter for the *Ham & High* might be interested in talking to Mr Boyle about his, um, achievements."

"Achievements?" We'd hit the lake – not exactly Windermere, but not far off it. "Jesus. He could drown a battalion in that," I said, stopping dead.

"And leave them there," Caz pointed out.

Now, it was my turn to moue, dissatisfied at her point. "But I'm still not letting him off the hook."

We turned towards the house – a large pile that looked like Palladio had, perhaps, gone to work for Barratt Homes.

"And what, exactly, apart from picking a few random numbers, are Mr Boyle's achievements?"

We began mounting the steps to the ludicrously-overbearing Neo-Georgian door, the fanlight above it filled with stained glass that seemed to depict a series of brown discs and a few fish shapes.

"Well," Caz admitted, finally, as I lifted the door knocker – a heavy brass item shaped like an emaciated man caught mid-Macarena – and slammed it down, "he does a lot for charity."

And, at that moment, the door swung open.

Standing in front of us – liveried like he'd just stepped out of Downton Abbey – was a butler, only one who'd clearly, at some point in the past, doubled as an all-in wrestler. He was colossal, his bulk filling the entire door, his shiny bald pate towering almost seven feet above us. Both his knuckles were blackened and bruised, as though he'd been punching oak trees for the past hour and a tattoo of a tear drop seemed to be trying – and singularly failing – to disguise a scar that ran from the edge of his right eye down to the top of his lip.

He looked down at us like some ancient God inspecting the goings-on of mere mortals, and the corners of his lips curled in what was either a smile, a barely-disguised growl or trapped wind.

And then he spoke. "You must be Mr Bird," he said in that Uriah Heep voice, all sibilants and grovelling, and, as I was getting used to the clash between his physical presence and his voice, he stepped to one side and from somewhere under his right arm appeared the purpose of our visit.

Tiny Tim Boyle had been his nickname because, at one stage, he had tipped twenty-five stone. In the interim, he had obviously cleaned up, gone straight, eschewed carbs and become, quite clearly, Hampstead's most successful ever weight watcher.

Mind you, having all the money in the world hadn't failed to deal with one of the most alarming lazy eyes I'd ever encountered. Tiny Tim had a small, sharp, angular face that looked like one of Da Vinci's studies of Renaissance low-lives, but with a nose – broken several times in his past life – and a pair of what my mum would call 'blew eyes' (as in: one blew east and one blew west) that managed to peer, almost, at us and at the giant butler, simultaneously and thus transformed the Da Vinci study into a Picasso painting brought to life.

He stared, with one eye, at the proffered fancies as though they were crème-anglaise-stuffed dead babies. "How kind," he murmured, in a tone that suggested what he really wanted to say was: Are you taking the piss? then handed the lot to the giant. "Green, perhaps you can put these to some use…"

"Thank you, sir." The mammoth, his neck straining the collar of his shirt like a blowsy girl's front testing a kid's t-shirt, reached out and relieved him of the box, as though it were radioactive material, murmuring something about how, "Mrs Green will put them to use," before he in turn dropped the box unceremoniously onto a side table.

I hesitated, feeling the moment was entirely lost, and was then rescued by the woman who had walked me into this situation.

"How lovely," Caz said, in her best Margaret Thatcher, smiling graciously at the goateed, stringy-necked figure that stood before us, his off-white t-shirt hanging loosely over shoulders sculpted, obviously, by a ruthless trainer and hanging down past an ascetic belly, razor sharp hips, a pair of jeans so skinny they made Karen Carpenter's last frock look like an Etam sale rack item, and a pair of knobbly-toed feet encased – I shit you not – in sandals.

Basically, if it had been a week or two earlier, I'd have assumed Tiny Tim was dressing up as Hipster Jesus for Halloween.

Green stepped forward and relieved me of my coat with a lack of genteelness that suggested he wasn't entirely used to people willingly handing their belongings over to him.

"My," Caz gasped, as the Brobdingnagian yanked her tartan cape from her, "what a charming home you have."

The triple-height ceiling towered above us and suspended from it, looming over the entrance hall like original sin over a Catholic school sleepover, was a nine-foot-long wooden crucifix, with a carved wooden Jesus writhing in agony thereon.

Whoever said, 'There's no such thing as too much,' had clearly made acquaintance with Tiny Tim's interior decorator. Although his person spoke of ascetics and abstention, every inch of the walls in the hallway was covered in icons, religious paintings, framed bible tracts and – encased in a rosewood frame and hung over the door to what looked like an ultra-modern kitchen – a life-sized reproduction (I assumed) of the Turin Shroud.

"That's kind of you to say," Boyle smiled, ushering us onwards as the giant shuffled off towards the kitchen. "Tell me," he murmured at Caz, "have you been saved?"

"Many times," Caz deadpanned, "many, many times."

Her response clearly confused the man, which gave us enough time to get into what can only be described as a drawing room slash medieval cathedral.

Here, again, every available inch of space was covered in religious tat, as though Boyle's discovery of Christianity weren't enough in itself and had to be accompanied by the acquisition and display of the entirety of Christianity and all it entailed.

A silver platter in the corner held, rather than the head of Saint John, a tall shiny coffee pot and three cups.

"Coffee?" he asked, gesturing at the pot and then at the sofa, which was covered in cushions embroidered either with religious scenes or tapestried quotes from the New Testament.

Caz murmured a yes for both of us and settled herself gingerly between a woman taken in adultery and Lazarus larking about having been turned into the undead by his Lord and Saviour.

I dropped myself beside her, trying not to notice what was on the cushions around me, failing, and noticing that one said, 'Love thy fellow man,' which made me suspect that I may – once or twice – have taken the instruction more literally than Tiny Tim or Saint Paul would have expected.

"Now," he said, his voice gentle, "what can I do for you?"

I smiled, reassuringly, I hoped and prepared to jump right in.

"We wanted to talk to you," Caz said before I could get a word in, "about your work in the community, and to ask how you felt about the need for individuals to provide services and support that – some might argue – should be coming from central government and the tax payer."

I stared at her in shock – What. The fuck? I then smiled at Boyle. "Exactly," I said.

"Did you have any specific work in mind?" he asked, his coffee, I noticed, sitting untouched by his side as he sipped a glass of water in which a slice of lemon bobbed listlessly.

"Oh all of it," I vamped.

"All of it?" His cheeks puffed out. "Well, as everyone now knows, I won the lottery some years ago. And it changed my life. Before then, I wasn't a very nice person. And, to be honest, even after then, I wasn't a very nice person."

He sipped his water. "I ran with a hard crowd. One that didn't really care about anything but pleasure and possessions, and that didn't care about anyone other than our own selves. Truth was whatever we wanted it to be. Loyalty was whatever was expedient. Women," he nodded at Caz as he said this, "were nothing but possessions."

"You said you were still unsaved after the win," I said, wishing Caz had warned me that I was supposed to be a reporter so that I could have brought a notebook or something, and then deciding that – if challenged – I'd claim to be an impressionistic reporter and say I'd got the gist of the conversation.

Tiny Tim nodded. And sighed.

And sipped his water.

And stared, with his watery eyes, out of the high sash windows of his vast Neo-Georgian mansion.

And sighed again.

And as Ron Moody began singing, 'I'm reviewing the situation,' in my head, he nodded again. "There was a girl, once," he said, "who disrespected one of my gang. She was scarred for life. Acid."

His eyes turned to face me, fixed me hard, and he said, "I had a girl, when I won the money. I saw it as my way out. Of the life I'd been in."

He half-laughed. "I'd been terrified and horrified for most of my life, and suddenly I had all the money I'd need to get away. And I did. Only I brought my girl with me and decided that she was too much of a reminder.

"So, to put it bluntly, I dumped her. Harshly."

He flicked his eyes away from mine to Caz then around the room as the light outside began to dim and a set of spotlights came on, causing eerie shadows to shift across the high ceiling.

"I might as well have thrown acid in her face," he said.

I glanced at Caz. Something more than running to the *Daily Mail* had happened, I figured. "What happened?" I asked.

"She went running to the *Daily Mail*," he answered, then, as I relaxed in the knowledge that the kiss 'n' tell had been the extent of it, he added, "then – two months later – she was found face down in the Serpentine."

The shadows shifted.

"She drowned?" I said.

"Or was drowned," Caz offered.

"Either way," Tim Boyle nodded, "I realised that thinking money would take you away from the past was pointless. Using the money to try to make people less likely to do the things I'd been doing – hurting the way I'd been hurting – was the only way I'd ever escape from it all."

"So you became a philanthropist?" I essayed, and he nodded.

"And before you were a philanthropist," Caz asked, "what were you?"

"You know what I was," he said, fixing her with his jelly-blue gaze as a number of lamps in the room flicked on, highlighting various agonised Christs, "I was a sinner."

"And a crook," I prompted.

"Guilty," he nodded.

"So has any of your past come visiting you lately?" I dived in, and his eyes narrowed.

"Meaning what?"

"Meaning has any of your past come visiting lately," I repeated.

"I try not to spend too much time with the unsaved," he said, in the way a minor royal might say 'The great unwashed.'

"But if, say, Jimmy Carter turned up," I said, as he coughed loudly and the door behind us opened, the bulk of Mr Green blocking out what little light came from the hallway beyond.

"So that's what this is about," he said. "Well, Mr Bird, I gave up lying years ago. Because, you see, when you're rich, you don't need to lie. Truth is, Jimmy came round here a week or so ago, banging on about some job that people may – or may not – have been involved in many years ago."

"So lying's off the menu," I commented, realising that the jig was up, "but prevaricating's acceptable?"

"I'm not prevaricating," he said. "There's just nothing to say. Only other person from that time that I've had any dealings with lately was Billy's girl Eve. She came here a while ago, said she was down on her luck and needed cash.

"She told some story about having to sell off her belongings – even stuff she'd kept from the old days – all to pay debts. Wanted to know if I wanted to buy any souvenirs."

"Souvenirs?" Caz asked.

"I got the distinct feeling she was trying a little bit of blackmail – though whether emotional or real, it's hard to say. Whichever it was, I wasn't playing. I know I was never a saint, but I don't think she could have anything on me that my lawyers nowadays couldn't cut through."

"So what happened?"

"I wrote a cheque. Took her address, in case anything came up, and Green here sent her on her way."

"Do you still have that address?" I asked.

Tim exhaled slowly and noisily – as though he had taken on all the ennui in the world – and gestured listlessly at the hulking Green, who threw our coats at us and jerked his head in a way that suggested that, if we didn't stand, put them on and make our way towards the exit, he'd personally crush us to atoms.

"But regarding Jimmy," Tim added as we were lead from the room, "I have nothing to say beyond this. He turned up here, I heard him out – I didn't want to get messed up in whatever craziness he was getting in to – and he left. As," he glanced at his enormous manservant, "you are about to."

And, with only a pause to get an address in Wimbledon written down on a notepad in the hallway, we were led from the house.

TWENTY-NINE

"Right, it's just here," said Dash, gesturing at the screen.

I leant forward, peering at the grainy images on the flickering monitor. "What am I looking at?"

"Him," Dash pointed out a tall skinny bloke in a shell suit and a trucker cap. "He goes for a dip. Just… About… Now."

I saw the man, as a clearly inebriated Carlton leaned over the bar trying to attract the attention of a busy barmaid, dip his thumb and forefinger partially into the back pocket of the boy's jeans and begin to extract his wallet.

At which point, despite being shitfaced, Carlton clearly turned around – a look of high umbrage on his face – and had words with the beanpole.

"Lowlife scumbag, that bloke," Rodger Reese said over my shoulder.

Reese was a pub landlord straight out of central casting: Shaven head, tight black t-shirt stretched across a chest like a barge, biceps big as my head and hands like boiled hams. On first glance, he was not the sort of person you'd want to spend time with, let alone pay for the privilege of hanging with.

But first glances can be deceiving, and Rodge, his missus Barb and the crew at his pub The Monmouth, were an open, friendly, welcoming bunch… who happened to run a pub on the edges of one of the dodgiest areas of South London.

"Like cockroaches, them lot are," Rodge muttered as, on screen, the pickpocket put his hands up in what looked like a placatory gesture. "As fast as we clear 'em out one door, they're coming in the other. This is where it kicks off."

On screen, another shell suit had, unseen by Carlton, come up behind the lad while he continued to remonstrate with the thief. The new shell suit was squat – fat rather than muscle, I figured – but was in possession of a beer bottle and an angry look.

On the very edge of the screen, Rodge – his giant torso clad in an open-necked short-sleeved shirt – appeared and began to pour white wine into a glass for a waiting customer.

And then, with no obvious provocation, the short, fat shell suit necked the contents of his Corona, flipped the bottle in his hand and smashed it over Carlton's head.

Or rather, attempted to smash it, for either Carlton had a harder head than usual, the bottle was of thicker glass than normal, or the shell suit's arm strength was lacking; and, instead of smashing on Carlton's head in ancient bar-brawl style, the bottle bounced back, startling the fat shell suit and causing Carlton to stagger slightly and to half turn towards whatever it was that had just smashed into his skull.

Then, all hell broke loose.

The skinny one, sensing, I suppose, that the gig was up, jerked to his left as though to escape. He was quick but not quick enough, as Carlton clearly caught the movement out of the corner of his eye, swivelled, his arm coming up and smashed his fist full on into skinny shell suit's face.

Skinny's head flipped back, an arc of dark liquid – visible even on the grainy monitor – spewing from his nose and, as he reached the apex of the arc, his hands flying up towards the source of his pain, Carlton brought his knee up full force into the would-be pickpocket's groin.

Behind me, Rodge *oofed*. "Gets me every time," he muttered.

Fat shell suit – who'd stood in seeming shock while his mate was punched and kneed – now seemed to decide it was time for action, but he'd delayed too late. Carlton was on him, grabbing him so hard by the neck of his shell suit that the fabric ripped, causing the fat one to half-stagger backwards and the tall Carlton's intended side-on punch to become a glancing blow.

Skinny, recovering some of his awareness and doubtless furious at having been bested by the young man, now reached out, grabbed a handful of Carlton's hair, yanking his head back and slamming his fist into the young man's lower back.

"Kidneys," Dash muttered unnecessarily.

Fat bloke snatched a pint glass from the bar, emptied the contents on the floor and eyed up Carlton's exposed throat.

But, again, he waited a second too long and Carlton's right leg swung up, extended – the foot pointing straight up – and was slammed straight between the fat man's legs, causing him to drop the pint glass and double over.

"Well at least neither of 'em'll be spawning any time soon," Rodge growled.

On screen, Carlton snapped his head forward – leaving Skinny shell suit holding a handful of hair – grabbed the fat one by the collar and the top of his tracksuit bottoms and swung him around, using him as a battering ram straight into the gut of his mate.

All of this had taken seconds and it was at this point that Rodger Reese and three bouncers suddenly piled in to the scene, fists flailing and arms flying out to the sides as they herded the three brawlers up and shoved them towards the door.

"Sorry about this," Rodge said. "Looking back at the footage, I can clearly see your mate was the innocent party here but I got a pub to run and, in cases like this, all I can do is get the brawl away from my punters."

The threesome was shoved from shot, the camera stayed where it was, showing an empty corner of the pub, a beer bottle and empty pint glass discarded on the carpeted floor; and, in a few moments, a barmaid came into shot, picked both up, placed them on the bar and rambled back out of shot.

Another few moments passed and fresh customers colonised the vacant bar space, the figures of Rodge and one of the bouncers were seen crossing the shot and heading back to their places behind the bar, Rodge talking animatedly on his mobile, and normality resumed.

"I was calling the cop shop," Rodge explained. "I'm not having that shit going on in my pub and kicking them out doesn't always end the punch up, so I wanted the pros here to handle the outcome. I'm not having a death on my conscience," he explained.

I nodded my understanding. "Okay," I said, "so we have Carlton in a pub brawl at – what time is this, Dash?"

"A quarter to ten," Dash answered, checking the date and timestamp on the top of the screen.

"Which is some time before Jimmy turned up outside Ali's house, so we know he's still alive at this stage. Shame we don't know where Carlton went from here."

Dash smiled and tilted his head at me. "Would I have called you over here to see a pub brawl if it didn't get better?"

My pulse sped up. "What else you got?"

"Rodger," Dash said, nodding at our host, "has had some trouble in the past with dealers setting up shop outside the pub."

"This is a great area," Rodge rumbled, "people are decent, they care about each other. They have to – most of the people up the road think they're all low-lifes, so if they don't take care of each other, who will? But not everyone in this neighbourhood is so decent. The scumbags would turn the whole thing into a crack warzone if they had their way."

"So," Dash continued, tapping on the keyboard of the laptop that was controlling the monitor, "he set up a camera outside the pub."

As he spoke, the scene switched from the now normal bar to a shot of the street outside, the angle suggesting that the camera was mounted high in the eaves of the pub. A moment passed and then Carlton staggered into shot, pursued by the shell suits.

Fat shell suit threw an approximation of a kung fu kick, catching the boy in the small of the back and hurling him forward so that he fell onto the ground, his face banging into the concrete.

Carlton was climbing back onto his knees when Skinny ran around, pulled back his foot and prepared to launch a kick straight into the face. Only he was delayed by something that happened off-screen, his head twisting slightly as something – a beer can or a bottle? – flew across screen.

He turned as Carlton continued to stagger upwards and, even on the flickering screen, it was possible to see the sneer that appeared on his face, as a woman – her short skirt exposing what looked like miles of shapely legs ending in six-inch stilettos, her upper body encased in a shaggy fun-fur jacket – walked calmly into frame.

Carlton got to his feet and, still dazed, fled from the shot as the two shell suits squared up to the newcomer, their sneers developing into triumphant grins as they exchanged glances and began moving apart as though to encircle her in a pincer movement.

But the newcomer wasn't allowing their plan to fall into place so easily. Words were exchanged –how I wished the feed had sound as well as visual – and she stepped back, her hands coming up in a placatory gesture as she retreated slightly so that they had to widen their pincer even further, which – in hindsight, I believed this was a deliberate action on her part – widened the space between the two thugs.

Skinny's mouth moved and the woman's head, her glossy dark bob shining in the light from the pub windows, turned slightly towards him, at which point fat pounced, barrelling towards her.

This, I suspect he realised almost immediately, was a mistake.

In an instant, the woman's hands came down, her body

twisted at the hips towards fatso and he – partly masked now by her fun-fur covered back – seemed to stop dead and jerk backwards before falling to the ground.

Skinny, who had also been in flight towards the woman, paused; she turned her head towards him and, as his friend lay writing in agony on the ground, he stared in horror into her face, the horror suddenly being replaced by a mask of disgust. He mouthed some words at her, hawked a wad of phlegm up and spat it full in her face; then, turning on his heels, he fled into the night.

The woman, wiping her face with the sleeve of her jacket, looked down on the still shaking figure, said something to it and then walked off screen.

A few minutes passed, during which fat shell suit rolled onto his belly, pulled himself to all fours, managed to regain an upright position – the shadow on the front of his nylon trews showing that at some point in the altercation he had pissed himself – looked around as though in search of his mate and slouched off out of frame.

"Jesus," I wondered aloud, "how does so much stupid make it to adulthood?"

Rodge chuckled. "I'm watching out for these two. They cross my door again, I've got a few of the boys'll make sure they don't come back."

"Right," I said, "so this helps fix Carlton's whereabouts up till – what time is it now, Dash?"

"Hold off," Dash held up his hand, "there's more." He gestured at the screen, and I returned my attention to the relatively static shot of the pavement outside the pub.

A few more minutes passed and then the figure of the woman re-entered the frame, one arm under Carlton's armpits as she propped him up.

They paused outside the pub, and she seemed to be talking to him, though his head hung down and the fight seemed to have flown from him.

He said something to her and she nodded, her face still hidden from us, before hoisting him up from his slumped position and, straightening her back, leading him from shot.

"That's it," Dash said, turning to me. "He goes off with the woman, and I can't find any more traces of him on any of the pub cameras round here."

"So if he didn't go on drinking," I surmised, "he went home with her."

"Or, if not home with her, *somewhere* with her."

"Which means she might be his alibi. Good work, Dash. Now, all we have to do is find her."

"Well that's easy," Rodge said from behind me, and Dash and I turned towards him. "Well, it's Tara, innit," he said, as though Tara was someone that Dash and I simply had to know.

I looked at Dash.

He looked at me.

"Tara?" we both asked.

"She's a regular. Sort of," Rodge explained. "I think one of the barmaids might have her address, if you want it."

"That," I said, smiling at Rodge, "would be most appreciated."

THIRTY

I pressed the doorbell and stepped down from the step onto the brick paved drive, Caz – shivering slightly in a short, belted mac – standing beside me.

"Lord," she moaned, "it wasn't supposed to get this cold this quickly."

I cast a jaundiced eye over her ensemble. "That thing's built for style rather than comfort, as my mother would say," I noted dryly.

"It's vintage Givenchy," she said, turning her head to glance at the monolithic motor car filling the entire driveway. "And speaking of comfort over style…"

My eyes travelled over the hulking Range Rover, its metallic green paintwork just visible under the crusted muck spattered all over it.

The front door opened, framing a middle-aged woman of middling height, wearing a selection from the Boden catalogue – a pair of pillar-box red patent pumps, midnight-blue stretch jeans, a billowy top with artfully applied paint splatters and a selection of chunky beads strung around her neck. Her hair was done in an ash-blonde bob that looked as though it had been warned – on pain of death – not to, quite literally, move a hair.

"The ad said you should call to arrange a viewing," she said, in a Home Counties accent, all nasal entitlement with a medium-sized dollop of droit de seigneur on top.

"I'm sorry," I said, switching my best little-boy-lost smile on and stepping forward, my hand extended, "you must be Mrs Stewart."

Eve Stewart recoiled slightly, before bristling, stiffening her back and staring down her nose at me.

"And who might you be?" she asked, channelling her best Dame Maggie.

"Lady Caroline Holloway." Caz pushed past me and extended her hand. "And this is Mr Bird."

Eve Stewart's eyes widened, and she glanced at the hand as though unsure whether to shake it, kiss it or use it to steady herself as she attempted a deep curtsey.

In the end, she sniffed, turned her back on us and said, "Well you can come in, but it's as good as sold already to be honest."

I glanced at Caz, who waved me on through the front door.

The hallway was almost bare, save for a couple of bland watercolours on the wall and a side table on which an empty vase sat.

"You can make a counter offer if you like," Mrs Stewart said as she continued to sail on down the length of the hall. "I've got all the stuff in here, if you want to take a look."

We followed her into a basic suburban kitchen – plain-fronted cupboards and melamine worktops, with a view out onto a small but tidy garden made somewhat unwelcoming by the grey skies and generally unkempt state of the lawn.

In the corner of the room sat a small oval table and four chairs.

"I'm asking fifteen for it," Eve Stewart said, waving distractedly at a pile of paperwork on the tabletop, "but it's worth at least twenty-five. Would you like some tea?" she asked, as though finally remembering her manners.

"Not for me," Caz responded immediately, barely managing to suppress a shudder.

"I'll have one," I said jauntily, "if you're having one yourself."

"I'm not," Mrs Stewart answered flatly.

My jauntiness dispersed. "In which case," I said, "I suppose I'm not either."

"It needs a clean," she said, gesturing again at the paperwork, "and I'm sorry about that. I'll ensure it's fully valeted before sale, but I had to use it at the weekend and it got rather muddy."

"Ah," the light dawned, "the car."

"Well of course the car," she frowned. "What did you think I was talking about?"

"I'll be honest," I answered, "I didn't really know."

She frowned. "Who are you, again?" she asked me, and I repeated my name. "And, if you haven't come about the car, why are you here?"

"We're here about your husband," I said, and she rolled her eyes.

"Take a look around you, love," she said, suddenly dropping the Lady Muck act. "This place is rented. The car's up for sale. The house – my beautiful house with eight bedrooms, seven en suites, a heated indoor swimming pool and a four-car garage – is up for sale and most of the proceeds will go to the bloody building society. I get to go and walk around it nowadays but as soon as the market picks up it'll all be gone.

"So whatever he owes you, you're just going to have to get in the queue. Even my boy's had to sell his car to pay his college fees this year."

This last one – as though being unable to pay school fees was the final indignity – caused her to choke back a sob. "So you know where the door is," she said, pointing back along the hallway.

"You're still paying off his debt?" I asked, wondering what debts Billy the Brick could have left behind if they were still causing grief two decades after his demise.

Eve Stewart looked at me like I was simple. "Well of course I am," she said. "That bastard left me in so much shit I'll probably be paying his debts off till the day I die."

She clicked the switch on the kettle, indicating that she

might, after all, be having that cup of tea, and took two mugs from one of the cupboards above her head.

"I've never had much luck with men," she sighed.

"I'm confused," I said as she poured boiling water over two tea bags, scooped each of them out and into the sink, and handed me a cup, nodding to a milk jug and sugar bowl on the table. "Billy's not been around for twenty years. How are his debts still causing grief now?"

Eve Stewart paused in the act of adding milk to her cup, and looked at me in confusion. "What's Billy got to do with this?" she asked.

"Well we were talking about your husband," I said as Caz removed a penny from her purse and let it deliberately drop from the fingers of her left hand into the open palm of her right.

"Yes, she nodded, Frank. Frank Stewart. He died two months ago, and that was when I discovered he'd been bankrupt for years and robbing from his business and anyone else who was stupid enough to lend him money. I've had everyone from pensioners to bailiffs turning up at this door, and half of them threatening menaces if they don't get what's owed to them."

The penny dropped. "Hence why you're selling everything off."

"Is he always this bright?" she sarcastically enquired of Caz.

"Only on every second day of the week," my best friend responded.

"And anyways," Eve said, "Billy?" She shook her head, "Billy was never my husband." She snorted humourlessly. "Marriage wasn't exactly Billy's thing. Listen," she suddenly perked up, frowning, "how'd you find me? Only, I haven't exactly publicised this address."

"Tim Boyle told us where you were," I admitted, and her lip curled in disgust.

"That prick. I went to that holier-than-thou bastard when I realised what a mess Frank had gotten us in to. D'you know what he said to me?"

I didn't, but before I could admit this fact, Eve answered her own rhetorical question. "'I'll pray for you.' Like prayers ever put bread on the fucking table."

I looked around the room. There was a loaf of bread on the worktop. This was hardly on the doorstep of the workhouse.

Eve Stewart, I guessed, had lost more than a husband when Frank Stewart popped his clogs. She'd lost a house, a lifestyle and a sense of perspective.

"They were all bastards, that lot. Either tight or violent, and Tiny Tim was both when he wanted to be."

"And what was Billy?" Caz asked quietly.

"Billy?" She sipped from her mug. "Billy and his mob, they liked to call you their missus, make it clear to you and to everyone that they owned you, that you were untouchable and shouldn't even think of looking at another man. But actually make a commitment themselves?" she shook her head. "Frank was the best thing that ever happened to me," she said, her eyes taking on a faraway look. "I suppose I should have known it was too good to last."

She sipped her tea again, came back to the present and turned to me. "I often wonder where he is now," she said.

"Frank?" I frowned, figuring that he was, surely, in one of only two places. I was wrong.

"*Frank*?" She repeated the name incredulously, shooting Caz the 'is he for real?' look once again, and shook her head once more. "Frank's in Putney Vale," she said. "I wonder what Billy's up to. Where he's got himself to."

I glanced at Caz, who glanced back at me with a look that can only be described as confused.

"That's a two-parter," I said, "but, and not wishing to shock you too much, the answer to the first question is – not much."

Caz pushed herself away from the worktop she'd been leaning against. "The thing is, Mrs Stewart," she said, approaching the woman, readying, I assumed, to catch her should she fall into a dead faint, "Billy's dead."

"Dead?" Eve Stewart frowned. "What d'you mean? Billy did a runner. Everyone knows that."

"It's complicated," I said, "but basically it looks like someone shot him and bricked him up in the cellar of a pub in Southwark."

"Well, the Southwark-Borough borders," Caz corrected me on my geography.

"They did what?" Eve dropped into one of the kitchen chairs. "Why?"

"We don't know," I said, "though I'd hazard – because they wanted him dead and undiscovered."

"And what's it got to do with you two?" she asked, suddenly turning her beady eye on us. "You're not police, are you? Only you never showed me a badge."

"We're not police," I said, a glance at Caz making me wonder if Eve Stewart had had many rozzers in vintage Givenchy turning up at her door.

"So what's it got to do with you?" she demanded again.

"It was *his* pub," Caz explained, gesturing at me.

Eve Stewart shook her head, the faraway look coming back into her eyes. "I thought he'd just done a runner," she said. "Billy was always up to no good. When he never came home, I thought he'd just bitten off more than he could chew and had had to go on the lamb."

She turned her face to me. "So what exactly happened?"

"Truth is nobody really knows yet. We can't even prove it's him right now, but Jimmy Carter— "

She flushed at the mention of the name. "What the fuck's Jimmy Carter got to do with any of this?" she demanded, the cup of tea being unceremoniously dumped on the table beside the now forgotten Land Rover paperwork.

"Yeah," I paused, unsure how, exactly, to tackle that question.

"Jimmy's also dead," Caz explained. "Only more recently."

"Someone drowned Jimmy in the river," I explained

patiently, as Eve's head turned from Caz to me, her eyes growing larger with each statement.

"And what does any of this have to do with me?" she finally asked.

"I'm not entirely sure that it has anything to do with you, to be honest," I said. "Except that we're trying to track down the members of the Old Kent Road Massive."

"The Massive?" She chuckled. "Do I look like I've had any dealings with those scumbags lately? I married a respectable businessman. He was going to go into politics. Until he died," she finished lamely, and I couldn't help silently reflecting that his death had disclosed the fact that he wasn't anywhere near as respectable a businessman as she'd assumed him to be.

"There was a diamond robbery," I explained, "about twenty years ago. The thieves got away with a fortune and none of the stones have ever been recovered. The current thought is that the robbery went well but then one of the gang double-crossed the rest.

"We know where Jimmy Carter, Johnny Ho, Tiny Tim and Charlie Chisel are. And Billy is obviously accounted for, but we're still missing Al Halliwell and some character called Gary the Ghost, about who nobody seems to know much at all, and who we've not been able to find.

"Billy had the stones, and was due to hide them until such time as the heat had died down. Only we think one of the gang killed him, hid the body behind a fake wall in the pub and made off with the diamonds."

She looked at me incredulously. "They bricked him up?"

I nodded.

"Jesus, how much time did they have to do that? Half the pub would surely have heard the noise."

"It's a good point," I answered, "but the pub was closed for a refurb, which means everything they needed – well, bricks and mortar – were all probably sat in the cellar beside them. And they killed him on a Friday night, so they would have had all weekend to hide the body."

She frowned. "But why wouldn't whoever killed him have just dragged the body out of the pub – I dunno, rolled up in some raggy carpet or something – and dumped it in the river?"

"Also a good question," Caz nodded, "except while the inside of the pub was likely to be relatively quiet and undisturbed, the streets around The Marq, twenty years ago, weren't exactly dead, especially at weekends."

I nodded. "Whoever killed him would have been risking a lot to get the body out of the pub and away safely, while bricking the body up would have hidden it at least long enough to allow the killer to escape."

"But that doesn't make sense," she said, looking up. "He can't have been murdered twenty years ago."

"We're fairly sure he wasn't faking it," Caz replied.

"Eve," I said, trying to sound as sympathetic as I could, "he's definitely dead. We found his body. Two gunshots."

"But how do you know it's him?" she asked, her frown deepening. "How?"

I glanced at Caz, who was also frowning.

"The police?" she asked, and I shook my head.

"We only know it's Billy," I said, "because Jimmy Carter told us it was. And since he didn't see the body, he can't have known who it was."

"Unless," Caz pointed out, "he's the one who put the body behind the wall."

"But if he had the stones," I said, "why would he have come back?"

"Tell me more about these diamonds," Eve asked.

"Not much more to tell. Billy was supposed to stash them somewhere safe until the heat died down. Somewhere an eye could be kept on them, but where nobody would think to look. Except, someone killed him and took the stones."

"Or not," Caz murmured, gesturing to Eve Stewart, who was muttering to herself and counting backwards on her fingers.

"No, definitely," she said. "I met Frank in ninety-seven, we were married in ninety-eight and Billy sent me a letter in early ninety-nine."

"A what?"

"A letter, dear," Caz said, shushing me. "It's like an email only on paper. Do you still have the letter?" she asked Eve Stewart.

The other woman shook her head. "I binned it. No real reason to keep it. It was pretty much what you might expect it to be. Fury that I'd gone with another man, threats of what he would do to me if he ever got his hands on me, all the rest."

"Can you remember anything else about it?" I asked.

Her brow creased in concentration. "It had a foreign stamp on it," she said. "I think it was Columbian."

"Columbian? He went to South America?"

She lifted her cup and sipped her tea again, still racking her brain for answers, then shook her head. "It might have been Peru. But I'm fairly sure it was Columbia."

"But if Billy was alive in 1999, then whose body was down in the cellar at The Marq?"

"Well surely the police can tell," Eve said. "I mean, they must have – what do they call it – DNA? Fingerprints?"

Now it was my turn to shake my head. I dropped into the kitchen chair, running my fingers through my hair. "They can only compare DNA if they have some DNA to compare with, and they're still trying to get fingerprints off the body because of the decomposition."

And then a light went on.

"You know," I said, "there may be a reason why we've been unable to identify, let alone locate, Gary The Ghost."

Caz rolled her eyes back in her head. "And that would be…?" she asked.

"Because maybe," I offered, "Gary has actually been a ghost for twenty years, ever since he was shot and put behind the walls of The Marq."

THIRTY-ONE

I knocked again at the door and stepped back, keeping an eye on the curtains in the window beside it to see if they twitched.

They remained almost resolutely still.

The glass of the window had been cleaned lately with, I assumed, some industrial solvent, but the shape of the spray paint that had been daubed on it was still visible in the shape of a ghostly 'F'.

The door I was banging on – a solid metal one that looked more like the door of a safe than of a fifth-floor council flat – showed the ghostly 'AK' under the obviously recently-applied red gloss paint, and the brickwork between the two, to which someone had obviously taken a wire brush, now had a patina of white paint smeared across it, as the 'R' and the 'E' had been removed, even if not all trace of them had been obliterated.

I banged again and stepped back.

"Maybe she's out," Caz murmured behind me.

"Maybe," I said, "but I'm not entirely convinced."

"So," Caz said, "apropos of nothing, if Billy the Brick killed Gary the Ghost, and – in keeping with his nickname – bricked him up behind the walls of The Marq before running off to South America with his ill-gotten gains, who killed Jimmy Carter? And why?"

"That," I admitted, "is a perfectly god question. And one

which I have – at present – not a single clue how to answer."

I turned away from the door. "Not in," I said, pulling a notebook and pen from my pocket and scribbling a note and my contact details on it, before realising that there was no letterbox to post it through.

Dropping to my knees, I attempted to slide the note under the door but found that even this entrance to the property was blocked.

Sighing, I stood, shoved the note back into my pocket and stepped back, looking around. A curtain in the next flat twitched but, even as I watched, it stopped moving. I moved towards the front door, which was open and was just in time to see a sour-faced woman appear in the hallway, glare at me and slam the door shut.

"Perhaps," Caz suggested, "we should come back another time."

There seemed little alternative. But just to be sure, I pressed the doorbell one last time, waiting until the dim and distant tones had rung themselves away to nothing before turning and walking back along the landing, heading for the stairs.

We had descended from the fifth to the fourth floor and were walking down the next set of stairs when a woman, head down, two heavy shopping bags straining at her side, pushed past us on her way up the stairs.

I stopped.

"Tara?" I said.

The woman's back straightened but she said nothing until she reached the landing above us, at which point she stopped, turned and stared down on us.

"Are you Tara?" I asked again.

"What's it to you?" she asked.

I smiled, putting my hand out and introducing myself as I began to re-ascend the stairs.

The woman lowered the bag in her right hand to the landing, her hand darting into the pocket of her raincoat. "Stay right where you are," she said, steel in her voice.

"I don't think you'll need the taser with us," I said. "We just want to talk."

"So talk," she said, all emotion flattened from her voice.

"Look," I glanced behind me at Caz, held both hands up in a position of surrender and took another step forwards, "this is probably best if I at least come up on to the same level you're at."

"What do you want?" she asked again, her eyes moving slowly between the two of us, her hand never leaving her pocket.

"To talk," I said, fishing in the inside pocket of my coat and pulling out a printout from the security cameras. "About him."

Tara glanced at the photo I was holding out to her, frowned, stared harder and looked up at me again. "Why?"

"Because he's our friend," I said, "and he's in trouble. We think you might be able to help."

She glanced over my head at Caz then dropped the other shopping bag to the floor. "Bring the groceries," she said, turning on her heels and heading for her flat.

Caz and I – me carrying both heavy bags – scuttled after her, as she withdrew a large ring of keys from her pocket and began turning the first of four visible locks. At last, the door swung open and, without so much as glancing at us, she walked into the flat, saying, "Take your shoes off."

I walked behind Caz and, on an instruction from Tara, put the groceries in the small kitchen to the left of the front door. She carried on walking, shoeless now, her coat hung on a wooden peg behind the door, down the hall and into the living room.

"Put the kettle on, while you're in there," she called. "The tea's in the caddy on the side. Mine's black, no sugar."

Teas made, I placed the cups on a tray and walked the length of the hallway to find Caz and Tara sitting and chatting amiably in a couple of red leather clubman armchairs either side of an old-fashioned fireplace with a small gas fire inserted into the space.

"Cheers." Tara laconically reached a hand out to me to accept the proffered mug and, tea delivered to Caz, I took my own and sat on a matching red leather art deco sofa on the opposite side of the small sitting room.

"You'd make a good butler," Tara said, sipping her tea and looking at Caz. "Don't you think he'd make a good butler?"

Caz considered this momentarily, then shook her head. "Not got the temperament. Or the height. In my experience, the best butlers buttle from a height. Otherwise, they get mistaken for furniture," she said, sipping her tea. "Tara's been having some trouble with the local population," she said to me.

"*Some* of the local population," Tara corrected, sipping her tea. "Most of 'em don't care. Either way. They just want to live their lives. But some of them can't live their lives unless they're making other people's lives unhappy. They knew me when I was Tommy," she said, glancing across the living room to a framed picture of a woman in a hospital bed, crocheted bed jacket thrown across her shoulders, a tiny newborn baby cradled in her arms, "and they didn't much like me then, so I suppose I've made it easier for them to hate me now. Never mind," she said, "I've survived worse."

"So, this friend," she turned her attention to me, "what's he done?"

"Nothing," I said, reluctant to mention murder at this stage.

"Well there should be nothing to worry about," she said, rising from her armchair. "I'll show you out. Only I like to make sure the door's locked behind any visitors."

"He's confessed to a murder. But he didn't do it."

"He's covering for someone," Caz explained, as Tara dropped back into the seat.

"Only she didn't do it either," I added, before finishing, somewhat lamely, with, "it's complicated."

"Jimmy," Tara said.

"You know him?" I asked, and she shook her head.

"He – Carlton– spoke about him a lot, that night. About how he wanted to kill this Jimmy. About how Jimmy had ruined his life, ruined his mum's life, ruined any happiness they ever had. He called him the devil."

"So how long did Carlton stay here?" I asked quietly, and Tara's guard descended again.

"What's that to you?"

"Look," I pressed on, "we're trying to prove he's innocent. So far we've managed to follow him from when he left my pub to when he ended up meeting you. And then he left with you. Jimmy was still alive at that stage, and dead – according to the coroner – by early the next morning, so we need to know how much of that time we can fill in."

Tara flicked her hair from her eyes, stared suspiciously at me, at Caz.

"We came back here," she said at length. "Look," she said, "it's not what you think."

"I don't think anything," I said quietly, "and even if I did, what business would it be of mine what it was what some might think?"

She stared at me for a moment, then glanced at Caz. "Does he always talk like Yoda?"

Caz chuckled. "He's not a bad guy," she said, "but prone to caring a bit too much. Give him a break," she smiled, "he genuinely wants to help."

Now Tara sighed. "I'd never met him before," she said, "just stumbled on him that night getting the shit kicked out of him by those gorillas. But I'm usually good at reading people."

"You pulled a taser on me," I protested.

"Correction," she held a hand up, "I fumbled in my pocket where I usually keep my taser. I did not pull it on you. And anyways – how do you know I've got a taser?"

"We saw the security footage of what you did to the fat gorilla," Caz explained.

"Yeah, well, he had it coming," Tara said, her eyes flashing momentarily. "Bastard's always been a complete pig."

"So as a reader of people…" I prompted.

"I brought him back here," she finished. "But it—"

"Wasn't what I think," I finished for her. "You've said. So what was it?"

"He was shaking," she said. "I thought with anger. Then I realised it was with fear. Not a fighter, really. When we got back here some of my neighbours had," she nodded her head towards the front of the flat, "decided to redecorate my frontage with some new street art for me."

"I'm sorry about that," I said, and she waved my apology aside.

"It happens. Carlton was livid. I thought," her glance dropped to the carpet, "because of me, but he was cool. It was the graffiti that wound him up. We talked."

Her gaze came up and fixed, coolly, on me. "That's all we did. Sitting on that sofa, him telling me about bullies – well, one particular bully, to be honest, and I think you know which one – and me just listening, until he asked me why I didn't just pack up and leave here."

"Why don't you?" Caz asked, and Tara's eyes flashed.

"Cos this is my home. This was my mum's home before me and my Nan lived here when they built the block. I've as much right to be here as anyone, and I'm not gonna let those fuckers push me away from my place."

"So, that night…" I prompted.

"He cried," she said. "Not at first. Took a while, then it was like he'd been storing it up his whole life. God," she shook her head, "I've never met anyone so sad in my whole life. It was like he thought it was all his fault. All these bad things that had happened, he thought, were because he hadn't been able to stop them happening."

"He was just a kid," Caz murmured, and Tara smiled sadly at her.

"That's what I told him, but I don't know if it helped."

"So what time did he leave here?" I asked, and she came straight back with the answer.

"I don't know," she said, "but he was still here when I left at lunchtime the next day. He slept for a bit that night, then woke up and asked if I had any paint thinners, so at first light, he was out on the balcony with some old newspaper and a bottle of turps cleaning the window, then he got my wire brush and rubbed the graffiti off the wall as best he could.

"When B&Q opened at nine we were waiting outside, bought a couple of pots of paint, got back here, and he rubbed down the front door and put a coat of paint over the graffiti. He was waiting for it to dry when I left – I had an appointment at one thirty I couldn't afford to miss. He'd done another coat of paint, locked up and left by the time I got back about half three."

I glanced at Caz. "By which time Jimmy Carter's body had been found floating in the Thames."

"So he's innocent," she responded, with a raised eyebrow, "which can't come as a surprise to anyone, really."

"Tara," I said, "would you be willing to tell your story to the police?"

"The police?" She laughed mirthlessly. "Love, the police round here don't place much stock in the word of people like me."

"They will this time," I said. "I promise."

She considered the request and, at length, shrugged. "If it helps."

"Oh, it'll help." I stood, collecting my cup and Caz's. "And thank you."

Tara stood too, following us out of the living room and to the kitchen where we put the cups on the side.

"I hope it all works out okay," she said, shaking my hand and receiving, from Caz, a hug and air kiss.

"Likewise," Caz said, handing her a card. "And if those artistes should ever return, would you do me a favour and ring this number?"

Tara glanced at the card and smiled. "Why thank you, Your Ladyship. Listen," she turned serious again, "would you do me a favour?"

"Anything," I said.

"Tell Carlton thank you, for the paintwork. And tell him I said hello."

I nodded. "Done," I said, and she reached out a hand and laid it on my arm.

"And tell him, please, that none of it – *none of it*," she repeated the phrase, loaded with meaning, "was his fault. He's a sweet guy. I hope it works out for him."

THIRTY-TWO

We left Tara's flat and made our way to a grim and desolate high street, the rows of empty shop fronts broken up by charity shops, burger bars and betting shops.

Caz looked around her in search, I supposed, of a cab and sighed. "Lord, Danny, how did we get to this?"

"By taxi," I answered absent-mindedly as I also scanned the horizon for a cab.

"I was speaking metaphorically, you dolt. Never," she gestured at the shopfronts, "do I feel *so* old as when I stand in the average high street. I mean, look at it. And meanwhile, that sweet woman back there," she gestured behind her, in the direction of the housing estate we'd just left, "is carrying a taser around with her."

I moved closer, putting my arm around her shoulder and pulling her closer to me. "You know what?" I said. "I think the world has always been fucked, in one way, shape or another. Always. But our generation got suckered into thinking we could make it perfect. Only we can't, cos you can't fix the fucked.

"But there's always been brilliance and beauty."

I gestured across the road at a tall, skinny youth, the pustules on his cheeks visible even from this distance as he lugged two heavy bags and chatted, unsmilingly, to an old lady, her hair a halo of white curls. "I mean, I'm not saying look at that hoodie over there, helping that old woman with her shopping."

"He's probably going to mug her when he gets her alone," Caz muttered morosely.

"Either that, or she's just lifted half the gear he's carrying and he'll be the one who goes down when the coppers catch up with them," I joked, and realised she wasn't smiling.

"Look," I said, squeezing her shoulder again, "there is good. Tara's living proof of that. She could have left Carlton to his fate, but she didn't. We didn't get here," I said, gesturing broadly around, and squinting as a car parked a little further along the road caught my eye, "we've always been here. Our generation has just noticed it. Things have changed, they do. But people don't. Oh," I slumped in disbelief, "you have *got* to be fucking kidding me."

Caz frowned at me. "Daniel, what on earth?"

The car – a long, glossy black limousine – pulled away from its parking space and slowly, and inexorably, made its way towards us, before pulling up.

The chauffeur, his grey uniform and peaked cap looking as out of place on this high street as a pair of Manolos on a street hooker, leapt out, ran around the car and stood, momentarily, to attention, before saying, "Mr Falzone sends his compliments, Mr Bird, and requests your company."

He yanked the rear passenger door open and gestured for Caz to enter. She stood, open-mouthed, and looked a million questions at me.

My whole body slumped. "What does he want now?" I asked of the chauffeur, who smiled, gestured at Caz again in the manner of a pony and trap driver to a British tourist on the Corniche in Luxor in the 1930s – all obsequious determination, and I realised I was not going to get an answer beyond the slightly disturbing rictus grin.

"We might as well get in," I said, gesturing to Caz, who raised an eyebrow, stared me straight in the eye and – in plain hearing of the driver – asked me if I was really suggesting that she – a member of the aristocracy, whose ancestors and progenitors fought at Hastings, Culloden, Normandy and Goose Green – should simply acquiesce to the instructions of what she termed – if I'm recalling this correctly – 'An obvious thug in an ill-fitting, cheap suit and climb into the back seat of a *hideous transport that looks equal parts Co-op hearse, Hen-night conveyance and Council bin lorry.*'

"Listen, Caz," I said, leaning in as the rictus grin on driver set like concrete, "we've all got rellies who fought at Hastings. Or would have, if there hadn't been points failings at Tonbridge. Now, as you've just been pointing out, the world is not necessarily as we would like it, but here – in the middle of this total absence of cabs – is a nice man in, admittedly, a somewhat poorly fitting suit, who wants to drive us, at no cost, I assume," I said, glancing at the driver, who nodded eagerly as though this would encourage us to enter the vehicle, "to somewhere at least closer to home."

Again, the driver nodded, reaching a hand out in entreaty.

Caz harrumphed. "Tell him not to make eye contact with me," she said, "and if I see so much as a hint of this in the *Daily Mail* gossip pages I shall know where it came from and have him dealt with severely." And, without another word, she slid, effortlessly, into the car.

I stared at the chauffeur as he firmly closed the passenger door. The look we exchanged was, basically, the visual equivalent of 'What the Fuck Just Happened?'

He walked around to the driver's door, leaving me to scuttle around to the other passenger door, yank it open and let myself – already stressing about what Chopper wanted from me – into the back seat.

It wasn't until I was settled, the car had drifted out into traffic and the driver had, in a mad jabbing panic switched off the car radio just as *The Archers* (to which he'd clearly been listening) came to an end, that it dawned on me.

Caz, sitting next to me – picking non-existent lint from her lapels – had to be the only person in history who had refused to get into the back of one of Chopper's limos, not through her fear of death or disfigurement, but for aesthetic reasons.

"So do we have any idea what Mr Falzone wants me for this time?" I asked the driver, who shook his head slightly.

"Just phoned me and told me to bring you in. Nicely," he said.

"Wait," I said, "have you been following me since the last time?"

"Mr Bird," he said, slowing to a stop at a set of traffic lights, "I've been following you since Mr F found out you'd discovered a body in the basement of that pub. And I've had the same instructions since then – watch, report and protect."

I looked at Caz, who rolled her eyes at me, whilst tapping her head in a universally recognised signal, and said, "Like a Saint Bernard. Only without even the brandy."

"The bar's fully stocked," the driver said, as the lights changed and the car slowly slid forward.

"Bar?" Suddenly, Caz perked up. "You never said there was a bar," she shot at me in the sort of accusatory tone I imagine the younger Fritzl kids might have said, 'You mean there's an outside world with trees we didn't know about?'

I looked wildly around the interior, but Caz, using some sixth sense born either of her nobility or of her incipient alcoholism, had already discovered the button that activated an almost silent servo motor, opening a door to a backlit minibar stocked with a bottle of Stolichnaya, one of Tanqueray, a Lagavulin and a Remy Martin, along with a selection of glasses and a crystal ice bucket filled with cubed and chipped ice.

Caz reached for the Remy, her eyes lifting to the rear-view mirror and locking with those of the driver.

"Tell me," she said, "do you have a name?"

"It's Norman, miss," he said.

"Well, Norman," she said as she slopped a large measure of cognac into a glass, handed it to me and slopped an even bigger measure of the same into a glass for herself, "I must humbly apologise if I was rude to you. Anyone who drives around with such a well-stocked cellar can't be all bad."

"Very kind, I'm sure," Norman – now reduced to a bit part in an Ealing comedy – replied and I swear, if his hands hadn't been gripping the wheel, he would have doffed his cap.

THIRTY-THREE

A little over half an hour later, the limo pulled up outside a bakery on another dull street of bookies and British Heart Foundation shops.

Norman, by now a firm friend of Lady Caroline's, rushed to open the door and assist her exit, even turning a blind eye as she deposited the hugely expensive bottle of cognac in her bag, "For later," whilst studiously ignoring me.

"Oh, now," Caz, pausing mid-flow on some anecdote about the time her maiden aunt had accidentally performed *Giselle* at the Bolshoi, dived back into her handbag and retrieved a card which she almost ceremonially relayed to the by now star-struck Norman. "I must, again, thank you so very much for your hospitality," she said, as though he were a genial host at some alpine ski lodge and not a rent-a-thug who had, basically, kidnapped us off the street, "and apologise, once more, for my unfortunate, not to say close to unforgiveable, remarks on our first meeting. I do so hope you'll forget them, even if you can't forgive."

"I don't even know what you're talking about, Lady Caroline," Norman responded, glancing down and moving his lips silently as he read the card she'd given him.

"That," Caz said, nodding at the small ivory-coloured item in his large hand, "is the number of my brother's tailor. Now I want you to pop in there tomorrow – or whenever you have a free few hours, Norman – and tell them I sent you.

"They'll fix you up with a new suit. Something suitable for a man of your obvious taste and talents. And you can tell them that I said they should send the bill to my brother care of his wife. Don't worry, I'll call Lady Priscilla myself and make sure that she pays up promptly." Caz glanced at me. "I think she owes me a couple of suits. Oh, and Norman," she added, as she clapped him chummily on the arm, "get yourself a few shirts as well. Right, where are we off to?"

I caught her elbow as she tottered slightly. "Rehab, my lady, if you don't lay off the brandy."

"Oh, Daniel," she patted my cheek, "I'll drink you under the table, my dear, and still have capability to put you to bed, clear the glasses into the dishwasher, read *Jude the Obscure* and decline proposals of marriage from two minor royals and an American arriviste before you even wake up. But it's kind of you to be concerned."

And, as much as it pained me to admit it, I knew that Caz was right.

We walked up to the door of a small patisserie and café, the name 'Chez Healey' etched into the glass door, which I pushed.

The door didn't move.

By now, Norman had climbed back into the car, and the limousine had pulled away and was slowly driving down the street. I pushed the door again, and again it remained solidly – not to say definitively – unmoving.

A cold sweat broke out on the back of my neck. Chopper had ordered us to be collected. What if Norman had brought us to the wrong place? What if Chopper was sitting somewhere else entirely while I was here trying to break into a closed bakery? Would he realise it wasn't my fault that I hadn't shown? Would he blame me if the bakery door was damaged?

At the moment my brain began spiralling off on disaster scenarios, Caz reached across me and pulled the door, which instantly opened.

"If at first you don't succeed," she murmured, as we entered a long, darkened room, filled with the scent of vanilla, caramelised sugar and baking bread. On our left, a long counter stretched off to the distance. To our right, two rows of small tables, each with a tiny flickering tea light in a coloured glass holder and two chairs facing each other, were lined up in regimental fashion, fading into the almost stygian darkness.

"Danny," a voice from the depths of that darkness called to me. "Down here. Shut the door – you're letting a draft in."

I glanced at Caz. Chopper in avuncular mood was a worrying concept, but one I'd have been ready to handle if I hadn't been accompanied by my best friend in a drunken mood. "Play nice," I whispered and, in the dim light filtering in from behind me, she gave me a look of deep sorrow and a little anger.

We made our way down the length of the room, until, right at the back, by a door which I assumed lead to the toilets, the diminutive shape of Martin 'Chopper' Falzone – his hair, a tightly-curled band of snow white around the glistening and deeply-tanned dome of his bald pate, shining almost luminescently in the light from the 'Fire Exit' sign above him – made itself known.

To his right, at a table pressed against the wall, sat a hulk of heavies, their silent, ominous bulk somewhat offset by the tiny espresso cups and half-demolished cinnamon rolls in front of them.

"Danny," Chopper gestured at the seat opposite him, and reached across and pulled another one closer, "and you've brought a friend." He smiled, nodding at Caz as he stood to his feet and reached a hand towards her.

"I'm Falzone," he said, his hand staying held out and unshaken.

"And I'm Holloway," Caz said, pointedly ignoring the proffered hand and dropping, not into the chair facing him, but into the chair to his left, "and I'd kill for an espresso."

Chopper's extended hand suddenly produced a finger-snap that echoed around the room and, from the other side of the bar, an espresso machine kicked in, the rich burnt caramel scents wafting across the room.

"You want a coffee, Danny?" he asked me, withdrawing his hand and pointing at the chair across from him.

I said I'd have a double espresso, eyeing the heavies and figuring, if this was going to be my last coffee, I should at least go out with a buzz on.

"You want a pastry? Have a pastry. Try the pastizzi," he said, like some sort of demented gangland Mary Berry. "It's a Maltese speciality."

I glanced at Caz.

"A pastizzi would be lovely," she purred, as she finished applying fresh lipstick and dropped the lippie and her compact back into her handbag, "if we've time."

"Time?" Chopper, confused, frowned.

"Before this place burns to the ground," she explained, smiling her thanks at the waitress as she placed the espressos and a plate of pastries on the table.

Chopper shot me a venomous look, as though I'd snitched on a big secret he'd deliberately told me to keep quiet about, and then smiled amiably at Caz. "Ah, this place is going nowhere, Miss Holloway."

"*Lady*," Caz corrected him immediately, lifting the espresso cup to her newly-refreshed lips and taking a sip. "Lady Caroline will suffice."

"Lady Caroline," he smiled, nodding, and picked up his own coffee.

"Lovely weather we're having," I said apropos of nothing as his hand crossed over, lifted a small pastry from the pile on the plate and shoved it, whole, into his mouth.

Chopper's eyes – two darkly malicious beads – squinted at me.

"Winter is coming," he intoned through a mouthful of pastry, in the manner of a short septuagenarian Maltese Ned Stark, "which means I'll be off to Malta for a few weeks.

Which'll be nice. You got any holiday plans, Danny?"

"Holiday plans?" I choked, wondering if the brandy in the car had been spiked and whether this conversation could get any more surreal. "Not really."

"Good," he smiled, picking up another pastizzi and nibbling at a corner. "Then you'll be around for a bit. Wonder if you could do me a favour?"

"Why are you following Danny around?" Caz interrupted and Chopper frowned, turning his big cow-like brown eyes on her.

"*Following Danny around*," he mimicked her, "makes it sound like something it's not."

"So what is it, exactly?"

I picked up my cup and sipped my espresso.

Chopper glanced at me, tilting his head in a way that seemed to say, 'Women, eh?' "I'd call it looking after someone I've grown quite fond of."

The espresso went down the wrong hole and I began to cough and splutter, while gasping like a beached whale.

"You okay, Danny?" Chopper glanced at me briefly before returning his attention to Caz.

"Fine. Fine," I gasped, but he'd already moved on.

"I'm not sure how much you know about the situation that Danny here finds himself in," Chopper began.

"Oh, I know about it," Caz answered, "we have no secrets from each other."

"Really?" Chopper raised an eyebrow, his eyes darting towards me before going back to Caz, as the eyebrow was righted and the benevolent old-man smile returned. "Well, then, you'll know that there appear to be some very dodgy geezers interested in recent events around Mr Bird here and The Marquess of Queensbury pub."

Caz nodded. "Dodgy geezers, indeed," she said pointedly, gesturing at the barista for another round of espressos.

The barista glanced at Chopper who, almost imperceptibly, nodded his head, and the familiar grinding hiss of the machine kicked off.

"I want to make sure that if anything were to kick off, Danny'd have some help at hand." Chopper finished off.

"So it's got nothing to do with wanting to make sure you're the first one to know when he finds out who got away with those missing diamonds?" Caz demanded.

Chopper chuckled, shrugging his palms up in a gesture that seemed to suggest he was either about to come totally clean or perform a card trick. "Be nice to know who had them all this time," he admitted. "I was… intrigued when that job went off all those years ago. Had my suspicions about who'd been involved.

"And yes, I had some wounded pride too. If anyone from my manor was going to work a job like that, I'd have expected them, at the very least, to let me know in case I wanted in.

"But I assumed that it had all been done by some gang from elsewhere in town. The robbery was on the other side of the river, miles from here. What was there to suggest it had been done by blokes from my neck of the woods, or that the cheeky bastards had used my pub to hide out in?"

"And then Billy the Brick went missing," Caz surmised, as our espressos arrived at the table. Chopper nodded.

"First I heard of it – any of it – was when suddenly the zookeeper wasn't around no more and the fucking chimps went mental. Literally. They were trashing this area trying to find him, threatening people, menacing my friends."

"And menacing was your area of responsibility, I assume." Caz idly selected a pastizzi from a fresh plate that had accompanied the coffees.

Chopper bridled. "I don't menace people, love. Not unless I need to. This lot were like monkeys flinging shit around with no fucking idea why, or where, they needed to fling it."

"So you stepped in?" she asked.

He selected a pastizzi for himself. "Don't tell the missus how many of these I've had," he said, smiling conspiratorially at me, as though Mrs Chopper and I regularly met up for manicures and gossip. "Let's just say," he said, smiling at Caz, "that I got the chimps together and reminded them of how unpleasant I could make it for them if they didn't turn their little disagreement down to an," he waved a hand in the air as though seeking the right phrase, "acceptable level of noise."

"Disagreement?" I asked, perking up.

"They'd turned on each other," he said simply. "Once they'd come to the conclusion that Billy the Brick had done a runner with their money, they spent a while trying to find him with no joy, then started blaming each other for the mess. I was worried they'd start popping each other off on my manor."

"And you couldn't have that," Caz murmured.

"No," he glared at her, "I couldn't. Look, Your Highness, I know what you think of me, but get one thing straight – I don't stand for collateral damage."

Caz sipped her coffee and put the tiny cup back in its saucer. "Go on."

"In business, you don't, shall we say, make an omelette without breaking eggs. But unless you want a kitchen that looks like a fucking war zone, you break only the eggs you need for the omelette, and you break them into the bowl.

"You don't go flinging eggs at the walls and hoping that some of the yokes will splash back into the bowl. Which is basically what these fuckwits were in danger of doing. Till I had a word, put them straight and things settled down."

Caz sipped her coffee again.

I wondered how far the cuisine metaphors were likely to go, lifted my cup and realised I'd drained it already and that my heart was racing.

"Oh don't get me wrong," Chopper clarified, "I don't believe for a second that they all stopped looking. But they went on to doing so quietly. Discretely. Until this bloody corpse showed up in your—" here, he glared an accusation at me, as though I had been responsible for putting the stiff where it was found, "basement."

"And now they're getting noisy again?" Caz asked.

Chopper laughed. "Darlin,' most of 'em are dead or locked up. Which makes the Chisel thing even weirder."

"The Chisel thing?" I perked up further.

"Oh yeah," he smiled wolfishly, "that's why I asked you to pop round."

"To be clear," Caz interjected, "you basically kidnapped us off the street." But she canned it at a glance from me.

"Talking of which," Chopper responded, "a friend of yours, Danny – one Charlie Chisel – has been reaching out on the grapevine to anyone he knows from the old days."

Caz frowned, leaning in to the conversation as Chopper dropped his voice.

"Seems someone very close to him hasn't come home in a couple of days."

"Alex," I guessed, remembering how Chisel's wife was no longer on the scene.

Chopper nodded. "Chisel's let it be known that if the boy's immediately returned – unharmed – there'll be no repercussions on anyone. But, if so much as a hair on his head is damaged, Chisel will burn the city to the ground."

"Shit," I whispered.

"Shit, indeed," Chopper nodded.

"Has he been in touch with the police?" I asked, realising, as I did so, how unlikely that act would be.

"Obviously," Chopper deadpanned. "He's also been in touch with the Battersea Dogs Home, Claire Rayner, Saint Anthony and Doris fucking Stokes. Of course he hasn't called the filth. He hasn't even been contacted by the kidnappers."

"So how does he even know that Alex's been kidnapped?" Caz asked.

"The kid's a bit of a loudmouth, but he's a proper daddy's boy. And Chisel's been everywhere, asked everyone. None of his mates have a clue where he is. And he had no reason to go missing, so…"

"So we still haven't explained," I said, "why he hasn't

gone to the police."

Chopper sighed deeply, in a more-in-sorrow-than-anger fashion, and shook his head. "Danny, I'm not entirely sure what Charlie Chatham told you about his business."

"Demolition," I said. "Sold it and made a packet."

Chopper nodded. "'Bout right," he said, "except it doesn't explain the nickname."

A light went on.

"Put it this way, son," Chopper's eyes glistened menacingly, "he weren't no fucking stone mason. Charlie was importing grade 'A' Columbian when half of London was on the stuff. Used the profits to build a nice little legit business and then sold it all off at a massive profit."

"Which left him," I guessed, "with time on his hands and a lot of ready cash."

"He's bright, your mate," Chopper smiled at Caz. "*Lots* of ready cash," he stressed to me.

"So he's gone back into his old business," I surmised, and Chopper nodded.

"Only, from what I hear, this time it's more of a hobby than a business. Now don't get me wrong," he held a hand up in silent display of his discomfort, "I ain't got a lot of time for drugs, but everyone's got something, I suppose, and he ain't pissing into my chips, so I live and let live."

"But now his son's been kidnapped," I offered.

"Well it's like this," Chopper admitted, "if it was me – if one of mine went missing, and I called Chisel – I'd like to think he'd offer whatever assistance he could."

"So, to be clear," Caz interrupted again, "you'd like Danny to look around for some possibly furious, probably heavily-armed drug gangsters that have kidnapped Chisel's son cos Chisel *Pere* has urinated on their French fries?"

This time I shook my head, my gaze never leaving Chopper's face. "That's not it, is it?" I asked.

"Then what?" Caz began, and only Chopper's sardonic little smile stopped her.

"Chopper," I said to Caz, "knows people. Hell, he

probably knows *everybody*."

"Kind of you," he smiled opposite me.

"The possible involvement of dodgy drug gangsters wasn't even mentioned by Chopper," I said, watching as the smile deepened. "And that, I'm guessing, is because you've already reached out to every psycho drug lord in greater London and discovered that none of them know what's happened to young Chatham."

"Went as far as Greater Manchester," Chopper admitted, "just in case. And not a fucking dicky bird."

"Which must be driving Chisel insane," I surmised.

"So if Alex hasn't been kidnapped because of the drugs connection," Caz – the light beginning to dawn for her too – offered, "he must have been kidnapped for some other reason."

"And the most obvious other reason right now," I offered, "and one which we think has already had two men murdered, is the mysterious theft and double-cross of a few millions in diamonds, which have never been seen again."

"So, what are we saying?" Caz asked. "That Chisel had a hand in the double-cross?"

"Or that someone thinks he had," I suggested.

"The chimps," Chopper muttered, "seem to be throwing their shit around. Again."

I shook my head. "Billy the Brick is dead. As is Johnny Ho and Jimmy Carter. Tim Boyle's got God – not that that guarantees he's not a murderer and kidnapper, I suppose, but that doesn't leave much of the original gang around to go kidnapping spoiled brats off the street."

"Wait," Caz interjected. "Billy was killed to get the stones, right?"

We nodded.

"And Jimmy cos he was nosing around and, it seems, might have found out who'd pinched them."

Again, we nodded.

"Johnny Ho," I noted, "choked on a crispy prawn. So what's your point?"

"Well, one was killed to get the stones and one to stop him asking where they'd gone to. What if this thing – this kidnapping – was because someone thinks Chisel actually has the stones and that someone wants them."

Chopper turned his smile on Caz. "What indeed?"

"So, what exactly do you want us to do?" I asked. "Find the boy? Or find the stones?"

"Either or," Chopper replied. "It's up to you."

I thought for a moment. "I guess we need to figure out who's got the boy first," I said.

"Well who's left?" Caz asked.

"From the original gang? Tiny Tim – God-botherer or not, he might be viewing this as a matter of honour. Chisel, though he'd hardly kidnap his own kid. Gary the Ghost—"

"Who the what?" Chopper asked.

"Gary the Ghost," I said, realising that this was a new name to him. "Some bloke – mate of a mate – who turned off the power in the vault during the robbery. None of the others ever saw him, he dealt only with Billy, so if he's been cut out of his share he would be a tricky one to track."

"And the only one left is Al Halliwell," Caz said, and Chopper threw his head back and laughed out loud.

"Well he ain't gonna be hard to track," he laughed. "He's been banged up for a couple of years, and, from what I hear about his behaviour inside, ain't gonna be getting out any time soon."

"Well," I said, unable to hide my disappointment, "I guess he's out of the equation."

I should have known better. "You've never met Mo Halliwell, have you?" Chopper asked, in much the same way Caz was wont to enquire if I'd ever made the acquaintance of one of the Astors, or Lady Hermione Fortescue-Fuckaduck.

I shook my head.

Chopper snorted. "So," he said, "you know the way the Pope is, like, God's voice on earth?"

I nodded.

"Well Mo Halliwell is her boy's voice, hands, legs and sodding fists on earth. They could bury Al Halliwell six feet under in a lead-lined box, and so long as Mo could get to a Ouija board, she'd still do his bidding."

I did not like the sound of this. "So where do we find Mo Halliwell?" I asked, hoping that Chopper would tell me she'd gone to her winter place in the Caribbean.

No such luck.

Caz wrote the address down in her tiny Mulberry notebook, slid the notebook and the pen back into the bag – ignoring the audible *chink* as the pen knocked against the bottle of cognac nestled therein – and pinned Chopper with a smile.

"So we'll go and see Mrs Halliwell," she confirmed, as though she were my own personal Moneypenny.

"Love," Chopper growled, "I only need Danny for this."

"Ah, but," she replied before I could say a word, "we come as a pair, you see. Where Danny goes, I go."

"No secrets," Chopper smiled, glancing surreptitiously at me.

"Something like that. So, here's what you can do for us," Caz, suddenly all business, answered him.

"I'm doing something for you?" Chopper came the closest I'd ever seen him to flustered.

"Fair's fair," Caz smiled coldly. "I would suggest that, whilst Danny and I," she glanced pointedly over her shoulder, "have something that your current staffing structure lacks, you, in turn, may have something we could use."

"Those two things," Chopper asked, "being what, exactly?"

"Brains and muscle," Caz responded without clarifying which was which. "Put bluntly, we've just met the most lovely young lady, who – for reasons we don't need to go into here – finds herself in need of a guardian angel or two."

"Caz." I could see where this was going. Caz ignored my attempt to interrupt.

"I'll give you her address, and you'll have someone keep an eye on her place for the next few weeks. Anyone attempts to harass, disturb or annoy her, I'd like your," her smile deepened, "associates, to make it clear to the young lady's harassers that such behaviour is severely frowned upon."

Chopper, the glisten back in his beady eyes, smiled a shark-smile at her. "How severely."

"Hospital severe," Caz answered, the smile gone from her face, "as opposed to mortuary. But severe enough to ensure the lady has a quiet life in the future."

Chopper considered the demand for a moment, then nodded. "Let me have the address," he said to Caz, before turning to me. "You wanna watch this one," he said, "she'll be doing you out of a job soon."

THIRTY-FOUR

"Well," Caz announced, as though she were observing a newly-acquired Titian at a country house party, "how utterly charming is this? And to think it's just a short walk from my flat. I mean, if I ever need my roots doing, my phone unlocking, my parts waxing or my person bronzing, I shall know *exactly* where to come."

The sign above the door of a shop on North End Road read: 'Mo/Reen Maison de Beauty,' and underneath, in smaller letters, announced, as if the primary sign were insufficient, that the services on offer within were those of a 'Hair Salon, Nail Bar, Tanning Boutique and Intimate Beautifier,' before – in even smaller and clearly more recent lettering – adding 'Mobile Phones unlocked.'

The street, despite a constant, slow drizzle, was buzzing, shoppers passing by with bags laden with purchases from the market, the Polish deli on one side, and the West African green grocer on the other doing a roaring trade in exotic meats and gourds, as traffic – trapped in the narrow channel created by the market stalls that began a little further along the street – crawled like treacle along the road.

From our vantage point under an awning outside a shop on the opposite side of the street, we watched the windows of Mo/Reen, which were so densely steamed up that the listed services might have been occurring, at this minute, just on the other side of the plate glass and nobody would have been any the wiser.

"I'm not sure," I murmured, imagining Caz's usual hairdresser, "that this lot would offer you a glass of Veuve with your trim and roots."

Caz smiled, dodging as a sudden breeze made a fluorescent orange plastic bucket and spade set – hanging from the awning we were sheltering under – swing dangerously close to her sleek coiffeur. "A shot of tetanus," she purred, "would be welcomed with open arms, if I'd been unlucky enough to be anywhere near sharp objects in there. Speaking of which," she nodded at the door, "oughtn't we go within?"

"Yeah," I said, yet I held back.

"Something up?" Caz looked sideways at me.

I frowned. "Something. I just can't put my finger on it yet."

Caz tutted, swatting idly at a bright plastic colander which had now joined the bucket and spade in a wind-powered aerial battle above her head. "Well we're not getting any younger, dear heart, and the merchandise in this store is becoming decidedly more aggressive. Not to mention," she added, eyeing a short dark figure who stood glowering at us from the doorway of the shop, "the proprietor himself."

I turned and grinned at the shopkeeper, who scowled back at me. "Okay," I said, zipping my jacket up and putting my head down against the rain, "in for a penny." And we both – Caz holding a hand above her head as though a set of splayed fingers would prevent her hair from frizzing – dodged between almost stationary vehicles and crossed the road.

The door, when we pushed it open, triggered a bell above it that didn't so much jingle as toll. Menacingly.

The space before us was a large open square, with the walls to the left and right basically made up of two vast mirrors. In front of the mirrors were four vast, almost sculptural, barber's chairs and at the back of the room – on either side of a doorway that lead, I presumed, to the rooms where tanning, manicures and intimate beautifying went on – were two more chairs, each with a space-age-looking overhead hair dryer hovering above.

In the middle of the floor stood two free-standing wash basins, the chairs beside these, in common with almost all the chairs in the room, completely bereft of customers.

The single obvious punter in the space was an almost unnaturally skinny woman who was managing the difficult trick of looking simultaneously vulnerable and hatchet-faced as a tall, younger female applied highlights; wrapping bunches of the customer's hair in tin foil, before listlessly shoving the most recent bunch to one side, grabbing another hank of hair, slapping it on another sheet of foil, and, with supreme boredom, dabbing more gunk – the floral scent which reached me across the room not quite masking the reek of ammonia – onto the hair.

To our right was a free-standing reception desk. The woman behind it, having glanced up on our arrival, now returned to studiously flicking through a magazine. On the counter top, a high-domed cage held a small black bird, its nervous, jerky motions the most energetic thing in the entire room.

Caz closed the door behind her, the movement triggering the bell once again.

"Nice tits!" A high, reedy voice cackled, before launching into hysterical laughter.

It was a moment before I realised that the sound was coming from the bird and not the receptionist, who slammed a hand onto the desk, silencing the avian harasser and glaring accusatorily at us. "We're fully booked," she growled. "Unless you want a sunbed."

I stepped forward, my smile – the one that I always assumed was 'little boy lost,' but which Caz insisted was more 'psychotic on day release, with chronic IBS' – in place, and was about to make some vague enquiry about times for appointments when Caz, dipping into her handbag, withdrew and held out an ancient Nokia and asked, "Can you unlock this?"

I glanced at the phone, the phrase 'The Rosetta Stone couldn't unlock that fossil,' in my head but kept my mouth shut.

The woman behind the counter – her face redolent of those shrunken heads you sometimes see in museums and tanned a colour redolent of something from a Cuprinol sample chart – glanced at the phone, her pinched mouth tightening even further as every fibre of her being telegraphed her feelings about Caz's ancient telephony.

"It'll cost you," the woman said, beckoning Caz forward and bending over the phone, her blonde hair – cut in a style that suggested someone believed the pudding bowl coiffeur was on the way back into fashion – dropping forward to hide her face.

"How much?" Caz asked and a figure was announced, in a way and with a tone that suggested haggling was not only expected, but would be appreciated.

Caz, of course, agreed the figure immediately, which caused the raisin-faced old dear to squint suspiciously at her and scrutinise the phone more closely.

"'Ere," she said, "it's out of charge." Which, since it had probably been in Caz's bag since the late noughties, wasn't entirely surprising.

"Yes," Caz purred. "Any chance you could charge it too?"

Now, the squint deepened, the mouth tightening so much that the whole face looked in danger of caving in on itself. "Cost you a bit more," the shopkeeper said. At which point the bird in the cage sprang back to life and shrieked, "She's got a shooter, Frank! Get down!"

Again, a hand – the size and colour of a cola-baked ham – was slapped on the counter.

"What you want it unlocked for? What's on it?" The questions were thick with the suggestion that we were up to something, she knew we were up to something and – even if she didn't know exactly what we were up to – as soon as she figured out what it was, she'd nail us to the floor.

"My granny's recipe for gazpacho," Caz deadpanned, and the battle-axe softened momentarily.

"Put him in the boot," the bird cawed, adding, "and bring the quicklime," before the hand slapped the countertop again. The words, "Shut it, Naomi," were growled and the woman, glancing over her shoulder, called out, "You nearly finished there, 'Reen?"

The other woman – tall and slender where this one was short and squat, and possessed of a head of wildly-permed curled ringlets all of which were pulled together by a huge red silk bow – peered at the silver-foiled head of the hatchet-faced woman in the seat, patted her on the shoulder, murmured something soothing to the customer and sashayed her way over to the counter, a welcoming smile on her face.

"Ooh," she said, "customers. New customers. Now that's a rarity." She looked pointedly at the older woman as she spoke, before turning her smile on us and holding her hand out. "I'm Rene – Reen – Halliwell. This here," she gestured at the other woman, "is my mother-in-law, Maureen. She does her own hair so have no fear – I'm not responsible for any of that."

This was accompanied by a swiping gesture as though the entirety of Mo Halliwell's being, body, make-up styling and hair were being judged, found severely wanting, and – for the record – being recorded as nothing to do with the daughter-in-law.

Mo stared daggers at her daughter-in-law and held up the phone. "They only want unlocking," she said, a hint of mockery in her tone, "so I just need you to watch the shop while I go," and she jerked her head towards the door at the rear of the shop.

Reen sighed. "That's a shame," she eyed Caz, "cos I'd have loved to get my hands on your barnet."

"Sorry," Caz smiled back, "but the barnet is taken. By Louis Khanze." She namechecked the latest tonsorial IT boy.

"Oooh," Reen mimed, impressed, and glanced over her shoulder at the hatchet-faced woman, who now seemed to be completely unconscious in the chair. "Well, if you ever fancy swapping Brompton Cross and the glamour of Maison Louis for this joint and a shared session with Ethel over there, you know where we are."

"Watch them," Mo said to her. Her voice had dropped enough to allow her to pretend discretion but loud enough for us to hear and be well aware of just what she thought of us.

"Like a hawk, mein obergruppenführer," Reen muttered as her mother-in-law stomped off across the shop, through the door to the rear space and out of view.

"Sorry about her," Reen said to us. "She wasn't really made for customer service. Oh I love your nails," she suddenly cried, spotting Caz's manicure and taking Caz's proffered hand, the better to inspect the work.

Caz smiled beatifically as the other woman – older, now we were close up, than she had at first appeared – cooed over the work. "I was gonna do nails," she said with the same sad tone with which Marlon Brando once mentioned he could have been a contender.

"I started going to school to learn it an' all. Only she," she jerked her head in the direction Mo had recently gone, "said I'd take too long to learn, so she hired in this Chinese woman. Or was she Pilipino? Anyways, she come from somewhere east. Every day."

"She commuted from South East Asia?" I asked and Reen, still clutching Caz's hand, blinked at me as though I had just spoken in tongues.

"Nah," she shook her head, "Dagenham, I think. For the pittance that that old bitch was payin' her. So, of course, Mei Ling told her, after about a month of fucking commutes from hell and getting treated like shit by the old cow, to shove her fucking manicures up her arse, and walked.

"Only by that stage she'd got 'nail bar' on the sign, so I

says again, 'Can I 'ave a go at learning it,' and she says—"

"Stupid cow Reen!" the bird shrieked and Reen glared daggers at it.

"Fucking thing," she muttered.

"You could go to evening classes," I suggested, as Caz, her beatific look now turning somewhat rictus-y, attempted politely but firmly to reclaim her hand.

Reen shook her head. "She'd never let me. Watches me like a fucking hawk. Afraid if I got a bit of training I might make a go of this place and show her and her son what for."

Mention of Mo's son gave me an opportunity to open a new line of discussion. "How's Al doing?" I asked and Reen dropped Caz's hand like a hot brick.

"How d'you know Al?" she demanded, suspicion shadowing her eyes almost as obviously as the powder-blue glitter eyeshadow she'd liberally applied some time, it looked like, in the previous century.

"I grew up in his old neighbourhood. Some of my uncles," I lied, "used to know him. Odd that your shop's all the way over here in West London."

She continued to stare suspiciously at me. "We moved, about fifteen, twenty years ago. There was nothing for us over the river. Al said we might as well see if we could make a go of it up West.

"Except we haven't really. Made a go of it," she clarified. "Al wasn't really cut out for business. He was a plumber for a while, till all his customers started getting burgled after he'd installed their showers and such. Well, burgled or flooded. He wasn't a very good plumber.

"Wasn't much of a burglar neither," she added, a faraway look in her eyes. "Got pinched letting hisself into someone's place in Chiswick. Did a year, by which time the plumbing business had gone tits up."

"I'm sorry to hear that," I said.

"I'm not," she said. "Neither of them," again, she nodded towards the door that Mo had vanished through, "could organise a piss-up if they had a busload of fucking alcoholics and the keys to a brewery. But they're good at telling me how useless I am."

"I hear Al's inside again," I said, fishing.

She laughed mirthlessly, glancing with disgust at the myna bird as it suddenly cried out, "Shut it, you slag!"

"Al's usually either on his way to, or just out of, the nick."

"What's he in for this time?" Caz asked as the hatchet-faced old dear in the corner began to snore with a noise like a chainsaw going at a breeze block.

Reen laughed. "Always used to think he was Al Capone. Only, you know how they finally got Al Capone for tax evasion? Yeah, well they finally got my old man for beating the living shit out of some poor kid in Hammersmith. Cos he laughed at his fucking bird," she cast a disgusted look at the cage. The myna bird, as though sensing it was being discussed, twisted its head and blinked at her. "All over a football game," Reen added. "Arsenal scored against Chelsea. A fucking football match."

"I didn't think he even liked Chelsea. Well," she shook her head, "the kid he attacked won't walk again."

"Reen," the woman in front of me visibly shrank as the stern voice of Mo Halliwell rang out across the salon, waking the sleeping pensioner, who snuffled, started and plaintively enquired whether she'd had her tea and biscuits yet.

"See to your customer," Mo ordered, crossing to us and sliding the phone across the counter.

"There's nothing on this," she snapped.

"Nothing?" Caz enquired, reaching for it.

"What's your game?" Mo asked, her eyes flashing angrily as she slammed her hand down on the device to prevent Caz removing it.

Caz paused, dived into her handbag, withdrew two bank notes and placed them on the counter. "Well I guess I'll just have to try to make granny's gazpacho from memory."

"What was she saying?" Mo jerked her head at Reen, who was busying herself removing tin foil from her pensioner's hair as the old dear noisily slurped a mug of tea.

"We were asking after your son," I said, wondering whether I could get the irascible Mo on to a nostalgia trip.

No such luck.

"Well now you've had your phone unlocked," she shot another furious stare at Caz, "you can be on your way."

I persevered: "You ever see any of the old crowd, Mrs Halliwell?"

She took a step back from the counter, the better to peer up at me as a look of utter fury settled on her face.

Even the bird, who had seemed ready to gear up to another round of foul-mouthed tweeting, silenced itself.

"I don't know who you are," Mo said, her arms crossed over her defiantly-immobile bosom, "or what your game is but you've had your twenty-quid's worth of my time, so now you can piss off."

I held up my hands in a placatory gesture, but she was having none of it.

"Piss off!" Naomi echoed and, for once, Mo didn't slam her hand on the counter top to silence the bird.

"Look," I said, "I know times are probably hard, what with Al being back inside."

"You don't know nothing," she spat, the fury mixing with something tragic. "My boy's been cursed his whole life by the likes of you."

"Us?" I asked, wondering what, exactly, 'the likes of us' was. I didn't have to wonder for long.

"Snitches, sniffers, middle-class ponces poking around in his business."

"And what, exactly, is his business?" I asked.

"He's a businessman," she blazed, "an entrepreneur. He," she flailed around for the phrase, "he sets up businesses, only some bastard always comes along and ruins it."

"Like the plumbing job that masked a burglary scam?" I asked, figuring if I could rattle her a little more she'd start to say something interesting.

"My Al had nothing to do with that shit. He was a

plumber. A proper one. Had his City and Guilds and all. It was that toerag apprentice he had who was the robber. It was all his fault.

"Al couldn't see it. I told him, I said, 'that toerag's gonna get you in bother,' and my Al'd be all 'No Ma, Alex is a good kid. He's a good learner. Plus, he knows the punters.'" She sucked her teeth.

"Putting on airs and graces and making out like he didn't come from the same stock as the rest of us. You mark my words – it was his fault that Al got done for them burglaries. My boy was as innocent as a baby on that charge."

I doubted this fact, but kept my mouth shut.

"But don't worry," she said, a cold look coming into her eyes, "I've got my eye on him. He'll pay. Toerag."

"So you haven't seen Jimmy Carter lately, then?" I asked, and the fury in her face blinked off momentarily in confusion, then – redoubled – came back on.

"I don't know what you're talking about," she announced unconvincingly. "I never heard that name in my life."

"Jimmy," I said, my tone avuncular as though trying to convince her that we were all friends here. "He was a mate of Al's, wasn't he?"

"I. Don't. Know. What. You. Are. Talking. About," Mo said, enunciating each word as though she were talking to someone who was slow-witted or hard of hearing. Or both.

"I heard he'd been around," I punted, fishing to see if she'd go for the bait.

She did. "Reen, you stupid cow – what you been saying?"

Reen, halfway through uncovering a set of – even from my vantage point – frankly alarming highlights, began to squawk and protest her innocence but it was too late.

"Whatever she said," Mo snapped into my face, "was a lie. Stupid bitch is backward. Got no idea what my son ever saw in her beyond her tits."

I was about to expand on my gambit – let Mo know just how Jimmy had ended up, gauge her reaction, see if it pushed her to any more involuntary admissions – only, at that exact moment, she dipped down below the counter, the myna bird cawed, "Bugger," and Mo reappeared holding a very large cricket bat, the blade of which was stained with some rather worrying dark red patches.

"Get the fuck out of my salon," she said and, in the best tradition of tabloid journalists everywhere, I made my excuses and left, hearing, above the jangling bell as the door closed behind me, Mo berating Rene in a string of profanities.

THIRTY-FIVE

"Well," Caz muttered next to me, "that was productive. Or something."

I took her arm and steered her away from the shop. "Maybe more productive than you think," I said, an idea forming in the back of my head.

"Where are we going?" Caz demanded as I walked her across the street, threading through the barely moving traffic and heading for a dubious-looking pub. "Daniel, why are we going to the pub when you have a perfectly good one at home?"

"Cos I want to talk some more with Rene," I said, "and I'm hoping Mo will leave her unattended for a bit."

We entered the pub and if there'd been a piano playing, it would have stopped. Likewise, if there'd been a general hubbub, it would have stilled to notice our arrival.

Instead, we got two young barmaids clad in too-tight black t-shirts at the far end of the bar.

Either of them could have noticed us and strolled up to serve us. Neither of them did, so deeply were they engrossed in rifling through a selection of underwear, security tags still clearly visibly attached, which had been piled up on the bar by a pensioner in a flat cap and a mac.

We waited a moment as the blowsier of the two blondes considered the merits of what looked like a black lace thong and bra set, before putting it to one side and diving back into the pile.

I coughed, and the trio jumped.

At the pensioner's side stood a shopping trolley and with one sweep of his arm he knocked the pile of panties into it, nodded at the ladies and toddled out of the bar, pulling the trolley of hot knickers behind him.

The (marginally) less blousy of the two sauntered up to us, a look of insolence and anger on her face, and looked us up and down as though we were a couple of narcs who had just cost her the deal of a lifetime.

"Awwwlllriiiiight?" she drawled, pulling a cloth from her back pocket and polishing the bar in front of us. "Get you anything?"

"A gin martini, straight up, with a twist," Caz deadpanned, and it took a moment before the shock registered on the face.

"We got no cocktails," the marginally less blousy barmaid responded, despite the fact I could see the gin and vermouth within touching distance on the shelf behind her.

"Well, then," Caz smiled, "let's just make it two double gin and tonics. Hold the tonics and give me a large glass of Martini Bianco on the side. Danny, what do you fancy?"

Drinks served, cash taken, and the barmaid having sullenly slouched back to the far end of the bar to pick her teeth and discuss Belgian literature with her colleague, Caz and I took a seat in the bay-fronted window of what could have been a pretty little pub, if they'd had any customers, or any staff, and began watching the front door of 'Mo/Reen' opposite.

"Pace those drinks," I said, nodding at the glasses on the table. "We could be here a while."

"Under the table, Mr Bird," Caz murmured, downing the first gin in one gulp. "Now, you said an idea was forming. Let's hear it."

"What if Jimmy went to Chisel, and Chisel sent him away with a flea in his ear? But what if Alex overheard the conversation?"

"What if the moon was made of cheese and little green men climbed all over it?" Caz responded, and I wondered how strong the bathtub juice was.

"I mean," I said, "the missing boy. Chisel's son. General consensus is that he's been kidnapped. But what if he hasn't been? What if he's just absented himself?"

"You think he might have killed Jimmy?"

"Well I've been assuming that Billy's killer and Jimmy's are one and the same, but what if Alex overheard the conversation and one of two things happened – he either knew his dad had done Billy and whacked Jimmy to keep that from getting out, or he decided to do his own searching for them stones."

"Those stones," Caz corrected me. "Really Danny, if you're going to insist on spending time with the likes of the fragrant Mo and her delightful avian friend, I'm going to have to insist on regular elocution lessons lest you turn into an Artful Dodger tribute act."

She swigged her second gin. "Now, back to those stones," she prompted.

"Well, if Chisel's kid was also looking for the stones, he might have come a cropper with Jimmy, offed him and gone on the lamb. Either way, I think I know where he might be hiding out."

Caz reached over and relieved me of my untouched second gin. "Is there a reason you're talking like something out of a Jimmy Cagney B Movie? And if Chisel *fils* had committed murder, don't you think he'd have informed his father rather than just going on the run? I mean, the papa is hardly the Dalai Lama."

"True," I admitted, "but what if he freaked, and before he could tell Chisel – who doubtless would have dealt with any unpleasantness – the father himself panics and puts out an APB."

"You're still doing it," she muttered, her eyes straying to the window as the daylight faded quickly. "But how does all this bring you to the idea that you know where Chisel junior is?"

"Al Halliwell had a plumbing business," I said, my own eyes fixing on the door of the salon opposite, "and in that plumbing business he had an apprentice."

"Ee-i-ee-i-o," Caz sang. "Get on with it."

"And the apprentice was just named," I nodded across the road, "by the fragrant Mo—"

Realisation dawned on Caz's face. "As Alex. The toerag apprentice." She frowned. "But hang on a minute, there are a million Alex's in London and there have to be at least a third of them in the Royal Borough of Kensington and Chelsea. It's stretching belief to imagine that the son of one of our villains, none of whom seem to have had anything to do with each other in over a decade, would end up working for another."

"That assumes one thing," I said as, across the road, the door of the salon opened and the hatchet-faced pensioner, a plastic cowl delicately tied over her new 'do' emerged, grimaced at the drizzle that was beginning to fall, shrunk deeper into her overcoat like a tortoise into her shell and tottered off up the street.

"It assumes that none of them have had anything to do with each other in over a decade."

"You think, maybe, some of them kept in touch?"

"Well," I watched as the bright shop lights opposite were extinguished, leaving only a trace light bleeding from somewhere in the back of the store, "the idea hadn't even crossed my mind but then Alex's name popped up and Eve Stewart turned up at Tiny Tim's when her fortunes dipped, and I begin to wonder just how tightly-knit the relationships actually were."

Across the road, the figure of Mo – bundled up against the drizzle and holding the bloody bird cage up like some badly-put-together Florence Nightingale – exited the shop and, her body language exuding belligerence, she stomped off in the direction of her only customer.

"But Jimmy didn't seem to have a relationship with any

of them," Caz murmured, sipping her DIY martini and intently watching the door opposite.

"No," I admitted, "but then he was a complete lunatic and more than likely a total fucking liability."

"Oh good," she brightened up, "we've moved from Cagney, James to Ritchie, Guy. I look forward to the Tarantino section next. So you think they – what? – cut him out?"

"I think it's odd that the rest of them got on with their lives while Jimmy simply vanished."

"And then he returned," she murmured.

"Oh shit." The hairs on the back of my arms rose. A cold chill went down my spine and I seriously questioned what was in the gin. "I've just remembered something."

Caz glanced at me. "Well if you're waiting for me to drag it out of you, you'll wait a long time. Get on with it," she said, not for the first time.

"When we met Alex, he was going off to – his dad said – his club."

Caz nodded. "Athletic gear. Running club? Gym?"

"They live in Twickenham. It's by the bloody river. His top had a little blue 'X' embroidered on it."

"Did it? I was far too busy checking out the rest of his Lycra-clad form. What of it?"

"It wasn't an 'X'," I said, "it was two crossed oars."

"A rowing club," Caz exclaimed, the light dawning. "So your guess—"

"Deduction," I attempted to correct her, but she waved my objection away.

"Guess, might have been correct. He had access to a boathouse where he could probably have held Jimmy underwater without being disturbed. Then, all he would have had to do would be to open the doors and let the body float away and off downstream.

"She's on her way." Caz nodded across the road, where the final faint light had just been extinguished.

We necked what was left of our drinks and hurried out of

the pub.

THIRTY-SIX

"Rene," I called the woman's name as she was squatting down turning the key in what looked like the ninth lock on the door, and she looked up, a bare smile testifying to the fact that she recognised my voice.

"Oh," the smile that had been bubbling up was stillborn as she stood to her feet and stretched up for a security shutter that was just beyond the reach of her fingertips.

"Here," I said, "let me help," and realised, as I said so and stretched upwards, that I was actually shorter than she was.

Caz, stepping forward, gently moved me out of the way, reached up easily, grasped the shutter and, in one swooping motion, slammed it down to the ground.

"I'm not supposed to talk to you two," Rene muttered, bending down to lock the shutter in place.

"Let me guess," Caz said, "Mo wouldn't like it."

Rene chuckled bitterly. "He's in solitary confinement and he's still running my fucking life."

"Al?" I guessed.

She nodded. "He's been in solitary for the past month. Stabbed some poor bloke with a knife he made out of paperclips. But Mo'll be straight up there as soon as he's out to give him the scoop on everything that's happened here and on everyone who's badmouthed him, or looked funny at her, or said so much as a 'Good morning' to me. He's fucking obsessed that I might cheat on him. I mean," she waved a hand at herself, "look at me. I'm clearly so fucking gorgeous the men round here are falling over themselves to shag me."

"You look great," Caz said.

"I look like what I am," Rene responded sadly, "a middle-aged old-before-her-time bird with a bully for a husband, a bitch for a mother-in-law and no fucking chance of escape in this life."

"Well the hair and nails are good," Caz smiled, and Rene chuckled.

"Look," she said, "I really can't be seen hanging round here with you two. Word gets round. What d'you want?"

"A coffee," I said. "Ten minutes of your time. No more."

She considered this, and seemed about to reject the advance out of hand, then a smile alighted on her face. "Right," she said. "Head to Hammersmith. There's a caff round the back by the Hammersmith and City line. I'll be there in half an hour. Forty minutes tops. I'm not waiting, so be there." And so saying, she turned and walked away from us, vanishing, quickly, amongst the throng of people leaving the market.

I glanced at Caz. "Suddenly, we're in a Le Carre," I said, but she didn't smile.

We turned, walking the opposite way to the one that Rene had, and made our way down North End Road until Caz spotted a passing cab, hailed it and instructed the driver to head towards Hammersmith.

We got to the café early and sat nursing an Americano for me and an Irish for Caz. Admittedly, the café didn't actually do Irish coffee but, since Caz had a small bottle of Jameson's in her bag, that oversight had been swiftly resolved.

Half an hour came and went, as did forty minutes, and I was beginning to think that Rene had had cold feet and stood us up, when the door opened and she entered the café, dropping into a chair opposite me and calling to the man behind the bar for a breakfast tea, two sugars, in a proper mug.

"Sorry," she said. "Couldn't get parked. And we'll need to keep this quick, cos Mo will be calling me at home soon. She does every night. Just to check I'm alright, she says. So I don't get lonely."

"She's checking up on you," Caz suggested.

"Of course she's fucking checking up on me," Rene flared. "I'd probably care less if she actually said, 'I think you're a skank and I'm checking up on you for my boy.' It's the fact she thinks I'm a skank who's so fucking stupid she can't see what's going on that pisses me off. Ta, love," this last said to the barista, who placed a huge mug of tea before her. "Oh, I need this," she lifted it and slurped noisily from the mug.

"So, yeah," she said, "I haven't got much time. Cos if I'm not there when she calls, she'll want to know where I went after the salon. So what d'you want?"

"You know you could leave," Caz suggested, a concerned frown on her face.

Rene snorted disdainfully. "And go where? I ain't got much, to be honest, but every penny I do have is stuck in that stupid fucking salon. Which I could make such a go of, if I didn't have to deal with my stupid fucking husband – who wouldn't know a business deal from an armed fucking robbery if it hit him in the mush – and his bitch of a mother, who can't decide whether she wants to be Vidal Sassoon or Alan fucking Sugar.

"I mean, there was a time I had dreams of owning a nice little hairdresser's. Maybe a little nail bar on the side. Now look at us. By Christmas, she'll have us offering hand jobs while you get your phone unlocked. Anyways, you know what people like Al do to women who walk out on them? There was this bird once, I heard, walked out on one of the Massive, and got a face full of acid for her efforts. 'If I can't have you, nobody will,' you know? No," she shook her head, "my days for going anywhere are almost over."

"Almost," Caz said, and Rene tilted her head.

"Look, what d'you want?"

I dived straight in: "Just a few things. First – was the apprentice that your husband had working with him Alex Chatham?"

Rene frowned. "How'd you know that?" she asked, answering the question. "He knew the kid's dad back in the day and, apparently, the kid was getting a bit big for his boots. Was a time when someone like Chisel would have had the little bugger taken out and taught a lesson. Only Chisel lost his wife – Alex's mum – a few years ago, and it sent him – Mo and Al reckon – a bit soft.

"So rather than have the kid hospitalised to teach him a lesson, Chisel cut off his money and told him to go find a job."

"And he ended up at Al Halliwell's?" I asked disbelievingly.

Rene nodded, agreeing with my cynicism. "I reckon Chisel was still not able to be totally hard to the kid, so he made some calls, found a mate – Al – who needed someone to work for them, and bob's your mother's brother. Only Chisel ended that relationship when he found out that Al was using the kid to get jobs in nice houses round Richmond and Twickenham that he'd burgle shortly after."

"So it was Al who was the brains there?" I asked and received a pitying glance for my question.

"No," she said sarcastically, "the kid led him – a man who's spent more time in the nick than out of it in the past twenty years, and who has convictions for armed robbery, burglary, GBH, ABH and shoplifting on his record – into breaking the habit of a lifetime and lifting other people's stuff. Jesus," she shook her head, "you didn't actually believe Mo's sermon about her little saint did you?"

"Not much," I admitted, and she chuckled disbelievingly

"Worst thing that little bugger did was try his luck with me. Said he liked a more mature woman and could show me a good time. All the usual guff about how he was at his sexual peak and I was too."

She laughed. "Al would have cut his bollocks off if I'd even mentioned the conversation. But no," she shook her head," Chisel junior was a decent kid. Just a bit cocky."

I considered this for a moment, then asked "Did Al have a yard?"

"Yeah," she nodded, puzzled at the question. "Out East. As far away from here as he could get it."

"Does he still have it," I asked, "or did it lapse when the plumbers went kaput?"

"No," she sipped her tea, "he still has it. It wasn't ever just for the plumbing. It's a place he can use whenever he has a bit of business that needs doing away from prying eyes. I think you can imagine what I mean," she finished.

"Have you got the address?" I asked, and she gave it to me, still frowning.

"I don't understand why you want to take a look at a shitty lock-up."

So I told her about Alex Chatham going missing.

"And you think he's hiding out there?"

"It's as good a place as any to start," I said. "His dad's tried everywhere he can think of."

Rene sighed. "Charlie's probably the better of them," she admitted. "Wasn't always, but I think losing his missus put him in a place where he suddenly realised how much the people he'd taken for granted meant to him."

"I need to know something else," I said, leaning in to the table. "Did Jimmy Carter make contact with you or Mo?"

"Contact?" Now, she actually threw her head back and laughed aloud. "Love, he didn't make contact, he fucking moved in. He turned up one day while I was out getting a cheese roll for my lunch. I get back to the salon and Mother Courage is dancing around like the sugarplum fucking fairy. Twittering around him like one of her own's come back to the fucking nest. Not even the bird had a bad word for him."

"And he moved in?"

She nodded. "For a few days. She made me do his hair – horrible naff cut and the cheapest dye job you could want, but he insisted on it. Said it was his trademark. The old bitch was all over him like a cheap suit. 'Specially when she hears that he's going to get hold of them stones."

"He knew where they were?"

"Not at first, but a few days later he announces he's on to something, which was when Mother Courage insists on his having 'a treatment.' While I was doing his hair, she was pumping him for info, only he kept it close to his chest. 'Got it narrowed down to two people,' was all she got out of him."

"But if he knew where they were, why was he still pushing Ali to dig up details on the suspects?"

"Aw, love, you ever met Jimmy Carter? Man was the biggest bastard on the planet. He could have had them stones in his sodding pocket and he'd still have taken pleasure in torturing that poor cow of a wife of his."

"Did he go visit your husband?" I asked, and she shook her head.

"Like I said, Al's been in solitary since before Jimmy came back. Not even the Archbishop of Canterbury's gettin' in to see him."

"So what happened?" I asked.

"He left. Day after the dye-job. Said he'd found better digs. 'I'm off,' he said. 'Got somewhere much fancier.' And that was it."

Somewhere much fancier? I glanced at Caz. Gethsemane Gardens was much fancier. "And did you see him again?" I asked.

Rene smirked. "Love, if I never see that scumbag again, it'll be too soon. Now," she emptied the mug of tea in one gannet-sized gulp, gathered her coat around her and stood, "I got to be on my way before Big Brother's Ugly Sister gets on the blower, but…" she paused, dipped into her pocket, a frown deepening on her face and extracted the bunch of keys as the frown blossomed into a smile, "here." She fiddled with the jangling keys, finally removing one from the ring. "For what good it'll do you, that's the key to Al's lockup and yard. I hope you find Chisel's kid. Tell him, if he did do for Jimmy Carter, he did the world a favour, and he should go home so his old man can help him out."

And, placing the key on the tabletop, she turned and bustled out of the café.

THIRTY-SEVEN

We found Alex Chatham at about eight fifteen that night in a builder's yard off the East India Road; in an area towered over, in the distant, by the monolithic temples to Mammon in Canary Wharf and, in the foreground, by tower blocks where dim bulbs burned behind curtains drawn against the world.

The taxi dropped us at the end of the street, the driver peering dubiously around him as Caz dived into her bag, withdrew a fuchsia-coloured purse and extracted his payment from it.

"I'd keep that out of sight round here, darling," he said, nodding at the brightly-coloured leather. "They'll take your arm just for the Gucci logo on it, let alone what's inside."

Caz slipped the purse back into her capacious handbag, zipped that, too, up, hooked it over her arm and smiled kindly at the cabbie; the steel in her eyes flashing as she thanked him for his concern, but advised him that she was sure she'd be fine, thank you.

"You want me to wait?" he asked, gesturing at the darkened road, the yellow glow of the street lights and the remaining Victorian brickwork casting deep dark shadows.

Caz shook her head, the smile remaining in place, and – the cabbie having muttered something about how he was sure she could have got whatever she was looking for couriered over to Fulham if she'd only just planned ahead –

turned to me.

"Why," she asked, "do some people always assume that just because an area looks less than pristine, the inhabitants will be either thieves or drug dealers? And why do they always assume that anyone who ventures into such places is either in search of drugs or kinky sex?"

"Well you *are* a bit out of place," I noted, taking in her designer jeans, wedgie shoes, the black nylon mac and flash of silk blouse underneath it. "Your manicure alone probably cost more than the average weekly wage round here."

"Which makes me lucky and profligate. I fail to see how it makes them thieves and pushers."

"People make assumptions," I said, "for better or worse."

"Usually, for worse," she groused. "And why aren't we using your father's cab these days?"

"Cos he's on holiday," I said, taking out my phone and opening the Map app on it. "Him and mum have gone to Marrakesh for a month."

"A month?" She squawked in disbelief. "How on earth is a cabbie affording a month in Marrakesh?"

"Now who's making assumptions?" I answered. "Mum paid for it. She's making good money now with the cleaning company she set up."

"Well I hope they have a lovely time," Caz said, as we set off down the street looking for a turnoff to Larchmont Lane. "And that they hurry back soon so I don't have to have too many more judgemental cab drivers."

I stopped at a junction and looked to the right.

This was Larchmont Lane and someone in the council, in their infinite wisdom, had decided not to bother switching on the street lights here. Well, either that or some gang of thieving crack-peddlers had deliberately smashed all the bulbs so they could lay in wait for unsuspecting passers-by.

The street, according to my map, was mostly builder's yards, lock-ups and small factory spaces, so I thought the fact that most of the employees would be long gone had actually decided the local authority not to bother illuminating the space. Still, it didn't make it easy in the dim glow cast by a half-moon, the clouds scudding across it as the wind picked up, to find number twelve.

Eventually, we stopped outside the door of a small industrial unit, the window to the left covered in a mesh screen for security, the door itself held fast by a padlock the size of my head. No nameplate or logo announced it as belonging to any commercial venture and the peeling paint, along with the fistfuls of pizza and kebab takeaway menus mashed into the overfilled letterbox on the door, spoke of the ages that had passed since anyone had let themselves in.

"Doesn't look like he's been here," I muttered, then realised the stupidity of my statement. "Mind you, he'd hardly be likely to tidy up the junk mail." I slipped the key from my pocket and slid it into the padlock.

Or tried to, because, as soon as I slid the tiny key into the lock, I realised that it didn't fit.

This padlock would have had a key the size of my hand, not the size of this smaller one I was actually holding.

"Fuck it," I whispered, "she's given us the wrong key."

"Are you sure?" Caz, keeping her voice low, peered over my shoulder. "Here, let me have a go."

I stepped to one side, surrendering the key and Caz, leaning over the padlock, fiddled with the security arrangements for a few moments before she, too, admitted failure and straightened up.

"Well this doesn't make sense," she said, stepping back to the edge of the pavement and staring upwards as a deep bank of clouds blocked out what little moonlight we had.

"If you're looking for inspiration," I muttered, "I think someone just turned out the lights."

Caz stepped into the street, her head turning left and right. "I wonder…" she muttered and crossed to the two huge wooden gates on the right of the office building as the clouds cleared and the moon, catching the wood in an oblique angle, showed, under the flaking paint, the phantom of an ancient identifier: 'Mayerlings Horsefeed.' Caz stepped up to the gates, inspected them and, after a moment of fiddling around, let loose a single, whispered, "Aha," and stepped aside as one of the two gates moved slowly inwards.

"The key for the yard," she said *sotto voce*, as she stood to one side and gestured for me to pass through the opening she'd created, "not the office."

I stepped through the gates. To my left and right, the walls of the buildings on either side created a long narrow corridor.

"That office looked pretty solidly locked," Caz said quietly, following me through the gate as a familiar shape appeared at the end of the corridor, the flitting clouds managing to make it obvious yet only semi-visible.

I held a hand up. "I think," I said, "he's been living in his car."

Which was when the smell hit me.

It was metallic, but sharper, more acrid. And then, like a second wave behind it, there was a waft of scorching and a sweet undercurrent of petrol and toast.

The clouds broke and the moon shone down on the scene as I walked forward into the yard at the back of the building. The pale blue light disclosed the car, the beautiful shiny paintwork – glossy and scarlet as a posh manicure last time I'd seen it – was now blackened and blistered down to the scorched bodywork. The front windscreen – whether from the heat of the conflagration that had incinerated the vehicle or from furious blows with a blunt object – had vanished and sparkling shards of glass were scattered all over the ground, their facets reflecting the moonlight.

The fire had obviously blazed furiously, but it had clearly burnt itself out some time ago because not so much as a wisp of smoke came from the blackened bonnet, the scorched roof or the tires; which were exploded and partially melted so that Dali-esque pools of melted and reformed rubber spread across the yard.

And, sitting in the driver's seat, as though staring out at us with the youthful arrogance we'd seen when we'd met him what seemed a lifetime ago – as his curly dark hair had shone in the autumnal sunlight and his long, slim tanned limbs had sung with vigour and life – was what was left of Alex Chatham.

I jerked my phone from my pocket and, with shaking hands, dialled 999.

THIRTY-EIGHT

A thunderous banging echoed around my head and it took a few moments to realise that it was actually echoing around my bedroom as I slowly swam towards consciousness.

I'd gotten home in the early hours of the morning, after being interviewed several times by numerous different East London coppers, all of whom had wanted to know what Caz and I were doing in the disused yard that night.

That we'd already decided to tell almost the whole truth hadn't really helped, because the fact was that the truth was so bizarre as to be almost unbelievable. Still, Alex's dad hadn't heard from him in a few days and had been worried. We'd managed to trace the fact that he used to work for Al Halliwell, who had – we believed – previously used this yard, we and came round just on the off chance that the missing young man might be hiding out here.

"Why would he be 'hiding out'?" One of them had asked, and I'd lied that I suspected the whole thing was just a spoiled kid trying to wind up his dad.

I don't know why I did that; it just seemed like anything else – the full unvarnished truth encompassing missing diamonds, dead bodies and a rapidly dwindling gang of crooks – would take too much explaining.

After the 999-phone call and before cops had arrived – before the scene of crime gang had erected a couple of arc lights, ushered us away, taped the place off and begun a fingertip search of the entire area – I'd summoned my courage up, crept forward and peered at the horrifying figure in the driver seat of the destroyed vehicle.

And clearly, unavoidably, seen the hole in the skull where a bullet had either entered or exited.

Which explained why poor Alex had simply sat still as his Ferrari burned around him.

The cops finally let us go sometime after 4:00 a.m. We'd come back to The Marq and crashed, exhaustion meaning we hadn't even had the time to discuss the events of the night, and now it sounded like someone was using a sledgehammer to demolish the four walls of my bedroom.

"Door," Caz moaned from somewhere under the duvet. "Back door." And she resumed snoring.

I staggered from bed in my t-shirt and boxers, and squinted at the time on my phone.

"Jesus," I said, "it's half eleven."

The banging continued.

Caz, still snoring, snuggled across to the warm spot I had just vacated and pulled the duvet over her head.

I walked to the window and lifted a tiny corner of the curtain to be greeted by yet another grey drizzly day, the light dim enough that it didn't offend my eyeballs.

The banging continued.

"Whoever they are," Caz sleep-muttered from under the duvet, "I don't think they're going away."

I glanced back over her, then, with a sense of impending doom, pulled on a pair of jeans, threw my feet into a pair of trainers and jogged – the laces flapping dangerously around me – down the stairs.

I opened the back door and Carlton, his hair and shirt soaked from the drizzle, fell into the hallway.

"What have you done?" he cried plaintively, grabbing on to my shoulders. "What the fuck have you done? And what did you think you were doing?"

"Nice to see you too," I replied. "You're looking well. Have you been at a health spa?"

"Don't fucking joke with me, Danny," he snarled. "What have you done?"

"Pointed the police to security camera footage and a living breathing witness that proves you couldn't be guilty." I hooked an arm around and lead him into the kitchen.

When we had entered the kitchen and I had closed the door firmly behind us, I turned to him.

"And before we start," I said, "you're welcome. For, y'know, your freedom and all that."

"Where's my mum?" he demanded, his eyes blazing.

"She's still inside," I explained, holding my hand up to stave off the verbal assault I feared was coming.

But no assault came. Instead, Carlton looked wildly around the kitchen as though searching for something.

Then, the smell hit me too.

"Mate," he choked, "this kitchen stinks. You got another body in here?"

I held up a hand to silence him and listened to the sounds in the room. "Shit," I hissed, charging over to the giant chest freezer in the corner. "Shit, shit, shit."

And then, stupidly, I lifted the lid and, as the smell of thawed and slowly rotting meat wafted out of the water-filled box, I gagged, staggered back and dropped the lid from my grasp.

My freezer, it seemed, had finally given up the ghost, although – from the state of what was left of the contents – the ghost had been given up some days previously.

"Any more?" I demanded, casting my eyes heavenward.

Carlton collapsed into one of the kitchen chairs, his long slim legs stretched out before him.

"This is all my fault," he said, despair filling every syllable.

"Oh mate," I sighed, "it was an old freezer. God knows how long it's been here, but everyone knew it was on its last legs."

"Not the fucking freezer," he snapped. "My mum. Jimmy. All of it."

I crossed to him. "Carlton – enough with the Jesus

complex. You're not here to take on the sins of the world. Or to be responsible for everyone in it. You didn't kill Jimmy Carter. We've proven that, otherwise you wouldn't be here now."

He looked at me wildly. "Are you really that stupid?" he asked, then choked back a sob and folded into himself.

"Carlton," I crossed to him and hunkered down, trying to look into his eyes, "this is not your fault."

"He threatened me," Carlton said, his eyes still downcast. "Do you have any idea how frightened I was when he turned up? I barely remembered him – I was just a baby when he left – but I just knew who he was, and I was so fucking scared."

"He's gone now," I said, putting a hand on his arm.

Carlton looked up at me. "Exactly," he said. "Because he attacked me, and he threatened me, and my mum dealt with it. Cos that's what mums do, innit?"

I straightened up. "Wait, you think Ali killed him? What am I saying?" I asked, shaking my head, and moving myself into another chair, which I pulled alongside Carlton. "Obviously you think Ali killed Jimmy, why else would you have confessed to a crime you clearly couldn't have committed?"

"Exactly," he said, looking back up at me. "She did this for me, and I was trying to take one for her."

"Oh Carlton, mate," I shook my head, "a couple of points on your licence, an evening babysitting instead of partying with your pals, even letting your mate cop off with the one person in the club that you fancied – those are all taking one for the team.

"But spending twenty years in prison for a crime you didn't commit is insanity."

"It's all my fault." He choked back a sob.

"It's not," I said. "And it's not your mum's fault either. Jimmy Carter was a nasty, worthless piece of shit, and he upset and offended a lot of people," I said, "and any one of those people could have killed him."

Carlton frowned, a light of sorts coming on behind his eyes.

I nodded. "Ali didn't kill him either. I saw her when he first turned up and she was terrified too. And I'm not saying that Ali would never have killed him. You're right, if she had no other way out, I'm not ruling out her doing something silly. But she's not a murderer, Carlton. You know that.

"Your mum is bluster and fire and pride and determination. She's ripped me off a strip once or twice, and I've seen her put nasty drunks in a headlock and sling them bodily out the door in that bar.

"But she's not a murderer."

"But she's still in prison," he said, his voice cracking on the last word.

"For now," I said, patting him on the shoulder. "But she didn't do it, and you confessing to having done it just muddied the water. So I had to clear you. Besides, your mum would have crucified me if I'd left you inside whilst Tara was out there with a full alibi for you."

At the name Tara, he looked up. "You met her?" he said and when I nodded, he smiled softly. "How's she doing?"

"She's doing okay," I said, "but worrying about you."

He nodded. "She's okay. You know—"

He broke off, and I nodded. "I know," I said. "Life's rarely perfect, but there are still good people in it. She's one of the good ones."

"You think my mum would like her?"

"I think if you like her, your mum would like her too," I said and he cracked again, a single sob escaping him.

"Can you get my mum out too?"

I shook my head. "Not yet. You had an alibi, and one that the police were able to independently verify. But Ali's not got one right now."

"So what are we going to do?"

"We're going to find out who the real murderer is," I said, as someone knocked on the kitchen door. "Come in," I called, turning back to Carlton. "And when we do, your mum will be back behind the bar here and all will be well again."

"How am I gonna look my mum in the eyes when we know she's in prison cos she was trying to protect me?" Carlton said morosely.

"You'll do it," I said, "because you know she's innocent, and you know we're going to find out who did this and get her out. Okay?" I asked, repeating the question, when he made no response, until he smiled sadly and nodded.

"Okay," he said, glancing over my shoulder and frowning.

I turned. A fill-in barmaid stood in the doorway. "A man is asking for you," she said. "Looks posh."

I squeezed his shoulder. "I'll be back in a bit," I said, following the barmaid down the hallway, wondering what posh bloke would be looking for me, and why.

The bar was quiet for the time of day. Only one or two lunchtime lushes sat in the far corners nursing pints as they fingered, idly, their iPads or newspapers.

A tall man, his upper half encased in a smart grey cashmere overcoat, leant against the bar, his back to me, and a quiver of tension ran though my body as, even from behind, I recognised him.

"Mr Lowe," I stepped forward and he turned slowly to me, a friendly smile on his face.

"Danny," he said, his eyes sparkling pleasantly, "nice to see you again. How have you been keeping?"

"I'm well," I said, wondering what the pleasantries were for. Balthazar Lowe, I was now sure, was a piranha and his presence in my bar was a source of real concern to me. Still, "How are you?" issued from my lips as I complied with the expectations of the scene.

"I," the smile altered, almost imperceptibly, "am as well as can be expected. Is there somewhere we could have some privacy?"

I glanced around the bar. There was no way he was coming back to the kitchen or the parlour. I didn't trust him and wanted at least the witness of the blonde, who was now polishing the optics with a duster and surreptitiously eyeing the two of us up whilst earwigging on our conversation.

"Sure," I said, affecting nonchalance, "we can sit over there." I nodded at a round table in the corner with two low stools beside it. "Can I get you anything to drink?"

He paused, smiled once again that slightly feral half-smile at me and shook his head. "Very kind," he said, "but no. Thank you."

I came out from behind the bar and followed him over to the table.

"So," I said, trying to keep my nervousness from showing in my voice, "what brings you here?"

"Here?" He looked around him, like a man who's just woken up and realised where he is. "Why our arrangement, of course. I did try Lady Caroline first, but she didn't seem to be at home so I thought I would pop round here and see if you had any updates for me. Re the," he paused, the smile appearing once again, "donation we discussed, when last we met."

"The donation?" I stammered, what I hoped was a friendly smile plastered on my face. "Well," I mentally scrambled for something – anything – to say, and failed, "um, you'll have to talk to Caz – Lady Caroline, that is – about that."

"Indeed," he murmured, his eyes boring into me. "Now, if only we knew where she was."

"Well," I began, wondering whether to tell him that she was upstairs in my bed, "she can't have gone far."

"Well that's comforting," Lowe said, dipping a hand into the pocket of his cashmere overcoat and extracting a brown envelope. "Mind you," he carried on, "we do know where she was on Sunday night, don't we?"

"Do we?" I asked, a cold sweat beginning to creep up my spine.

"Well, she was here, wasn't she?" Lowe said, peering into the envelope, selecting a photograph and placing it flat on the table facing me.

I looked down, though I really didn't need to.

There we were; Caz, me, Phoenix and Ray, caught with mouths open, eyes wide and looks of shock and horror on our faces.

"That lighting," said a voice behind me, "is criminal."

I turned. Caz pulled a stool from another table and seated herself beside me.

"Ah," Lowe smiled his shark-like smile again, "Lady Caroline. How nice to see you again."

Caz fixed him with her no-nonsense stare, anything that might even hint at warmth sucked from it, and stared unblinking at him for a few moments before glancing down at the photo and then back up at him. "What do you want?"

"To discuss the donation you promised," he answered.

"Donation?" She laughed dryly. "Blackmail money. Nothing more or less."

"As you wish," he answered, the steel in his voice being dialled up substantially. "I made a deal with you, agreed to give you time to make the necessary arrangements. I was completely unaware that the necessary arrangements would include attempting to hack into my system."

"Well that shows a singular lack of imagination, wouldn't you say?" she smiled at him, and I wondered whether, perhaps, she had been at the sauce already.

"That," he smiled back and, oh, that smile worried me, "or a sadly misplaced amount of trust."

"Oh, listen," Caz said, her voice firm, her gaze steady, "I spent most of last night being interrogated by the police about the incinerated remains of a young man. I hardly closed my eyes when I got back here because every time I did, all I could see was him as he was a week ago, and as he was last night, and you know what, Balthazar, old thing? I'm past caring."

"Caz," I reached a hand out to stop her, as the smile – the shark under the surface smile – on Lowe's face remained steady, but it was no use. She was off and running.

"Yes, we tried to hack you. People who have been given no alternative way out tend to do stupid things. But guess what? It didn't work. And guess what else? I still don't have the money."

"Yup," she ran a hand through her glossy bob, "I had hopes that we'd sort this out without needing to pay you a sou, you vile little man but, since that hasn't worked, I'm going to have to contact the folks and tell them to start liquidating assets."

At first, I thought she was lying: We'd already ascertained that the figure being asked was beyond Prissy's appetite, but then I looked at her face – the set jaw and the blush on her cheeks – and I knew that she'd simply had enough of the game and was willing to settle just to be rid of Lowe.

Despite the fact that it would give Prissy a failure to hold over her forever.

Lowe's smile widened as he dived, again, into the envelope.

"The price," he said, "has gone up. Considerably."

And he placed another picture on the table.

I glanced at it.

The planet, it seemed, stopped turning. The jukebox in the corner stopped tinnily kicking out Bananarama's greatest hits and suddenly only the sound of my own heartbeat pounding in my head filled the world.

Caz, reaching for the photo, frowned. "That's—" she said, and I finished the sentence for her.

"Me. And Nick."

She peered at the shot. "I didn't know he had a tattoo. Mind you," she smirked at me, "when would I have seen that part of his anatomy. My, my," she put the photo back down on the table, "but you are a pair of lucky boys. And you," she turned to Lowe, "are a really nasty little peeping Tom, aren't you?"

"Caz—" I tried, again, to stop her. And again, I failed.

"Why on earth would I pay a penny for these?" Caz asked as Lowe spread a sheaf of photos – more of the same, but also of Nick and I embracing in a lift, shaking hands in the street, me entering a doorway at night and him exiting what was clearly the same doorway in the early light of morning.

"Unless you've been in a coma, you moron, the Sexual Offences Act 1967 made what's going on in these pictures legal. And made you – as my dear friend here noted – a nasty little peeping Tom."

"Actually," I said, my voice a tiny mouse-like squeak, "you said that. Not me."

Caz stopped and looked at me for the first time in a while, and something – perhaps the squeak in my voice, or the fact that she saw the terror in my eyes – made her stop.

I remembered Chopper's comment, when I'd challenged him about following me around. Something about having to rough up some other geezer that had also been tailing me.

I'd put that down to either Chopper's paranoia or one of the Old Kent Road Massive wanting to keep an eye on me. Only now, I knew who it had been.

"Nick Fisher," Lowe indicated a picture, his forefinger tapping perfectly on Nick's left buttock, "a Detective Constable, who, I'm reliably informed, is currently studying for his Sergeant's exam. Likely to get it too, which will please his superiors, and his wife."

Caz stopped speaking. She turned to me.

"His lovely, fragile, Albanian wife, who he met on a business trip, who he married in something of a rush and who resides, now, in the United Kingdom, the only thing preventing her being returned to – I'm lead to understand – a very unpleasant reception in Tirana being the marriage to a British citizen which would, of course, be rather difficult to maintain if it were to be shown that said British citizen is not only gay, but – having married the lovely lady for no other purpose than to get her into the UK – guilty of a number of offences impacting section 143 of the Nationality, Immigration and Asylum Act 2002. I can quote it if you'd like."

"I'll bet you can," Caz snarled, turning back to me. "How could you?" she asked.

"I'm sorry," I said. "I should have told you."

"Oh for Christ's sake, Danny, I knew. I mean, how could you have been so careless?"

"You knew?"

"I've known you forever," she said. "I knew you were still seeing Nick. Danny, you've been known to mourn for a month when characters are killed off in soap operas. Did you not think I'd notice that you were getting on with life, just days after you and Nick had supposedly broken up?"

"But if you knew, why didn't you say anything?" I asked. "Why did you keep pushing me to get back with him?"

"Because I didn't want you to know I knew, of course. It would have embarrassed you, and I just wanted you to be happy."

"An admirable hope," Lowe smarmed, and Caz turned on him.

"I don't care what you've got," she growled. "Keep out of this."

"What am I going to do?" I whined at Caz.

"You're going to find a lot of money," Lowe – clearly ignoring Caz's instruction – stated. "Or these shots, along with several others, various items of security footage, details of registrations at various hotels, oh, and the string of texts you sent to each other and which my software acquired in a Biter Bit way, will all make their way to the Home Office, DC Fisher's superiors, a certain family in Albania and the *Daily Mail.*"

"Look," Caz turned to him, her natural sangfroid back in place, and attempted a placatory smile, "this is not Danny's war. You wanted Bobby, and you got him. You wanted money from my family, and you'll get it. Nick and he are," she glanced at me, and blushed slightly, "nobody's. They have no money. They can't pay you. Why do this when there's no profit in it?"

"Because there will be profit in it," he responded coldly.

"Lady Caroline, you either invited or allowed Mr Bird here and his various assorted misfits to join you in attempting to destroy what evidence I held over your brother.

"Yes," he nodded, "Mr Bird was foolishly careless in his actions but you, I would suggest, were almost criminally negligent in yours, and so – like any employer whose workforce have breached an agreement – you're going to have to pay compensation. To me."

He stood, waving at the pictures. "You can keep those. I have copies. And you have until midnight tomorrow night to arrive at my office with, shall we say five million?" he said, ending my life as he buttoned up his cashmere coat.

"Otherwise," he smiled his shark smirk, "these, along with everything I have on your dear brother, will be displayed where they can cause most discomfort to everyone involved."

He checked his watch. "That's just under thirty-six hours. I look forward to concluding this business then," he said, moving away from the table. "Oh, and," he turned back, briefly, to us, "please don't try any more silly stunts. One more, and I'll press send on everything I've got.

"Till tomorrow night." He nodded at us and left the pub.

THIRTY-NINE

We sat in stunned silence for a few moments, the sounds of the world around us seeping in as the realisation that we were doomed settled.

When I looked up at Caz, there were tears in her eyes. "I'm so sorry," she said, her voice breaking. "I'm so, so sorry. If I hadn't dragged you into this—"

"You've never dragged me anywhere, Caz. And none of this is your fault." I stood up, holding out a hand to help her to her feet. "What are you wearing?" I asked in surprise, as I finally registered the ensemble she had on.

"Jeans and a – I believe it's called a sweatshirt," she said, posing so that the 'I heart Unicorns' on my sweatshirt was fully displayed.

"I'm horrified," I said, "that it looks better on you than it does on me."

"That, my dear boy, is because no grown man on earth – no matter how gay he is – should ever wear an article of clothing with a unicorn on it," she said, pulling me close and hugging me tightly. "Now, what I think we should do is have a nice breakfast somewhere lovely, my treat. I always say that a good breakfast will help kick the cobwebs away and set you up for the day."

"Caz," I frowned, "I don't think I've ever seen you eat breakfast as long as I've known you. Besides, it's half one. I don't know anywhere round here that still serves this late."

"Who said anything about eating? Bloody Marys are a recognised breakfast food. I'll go get myself beautified. Who was at the door earlier?" she asked, as though suddenly recalling the racket that woke her.

I told her, nodding towards the kitchen. "He's sitting in there with a freezer full of rancid meat."

"I hope that's not a euphemism," she murmured, frowning. "Well invite him too. We shall have a hearty breakfast, and then I shall telephone Prissy and tell her to start liquidating every asset she can get her hands on.

"No," she held up a hand to silence my protests. "*Pas un mot*, Daniel. We made a good stab at it, but when you've run out of options, it is, I feel, time to pay the piper."

We walked through the bar and Caz went off upstairs to shower and change.

Carlton was just leaving the kitchen as I entered. "Mate, I can't stay in there," he said. "That freezer's totally kaput and the stuff in it stinks."

"Well Caz and I are going for breakfast in a bit if you want to come," I said, and he smiled but shook his head.

"I think I might go and see if they'll let me have a word with my mum. I mean, I don't know the rules or anything, but surely…" and he rambled off, his mind still not quite catching up with the rest of him.

Carlton was right about the stench. As soon as I walked into the kitchen the smell washed over me like a wave of vinegary sweet decay. I gagged then realised that, if I didn't get the freezer emptied, the smell was only going to get worse, and with my luck I'd get a visit from Tavistock while I had a trunk full of rotten meat in my kitchen.

"Right," I muttered, diving under the sink and pulling out a roll of industrial-weight black bin bags, "it's now or never," and, having put on a pair of long yellow rubber gloves and shaken one of the bags open, I approached the chest freezer and hurled open the lid.

Oddly, the stink didn't really worsen. I'd half expected the plastic sacks of chicken and beef to have revivified and attack as soon as the lid was opened, but it quickly dawned on me that the seals on the lid had degraded so much that the stench was leaking from the box and out into the room, rather than being restrained within the enclosed space.

Holding one of the bags open, I dived into the chest freezer and lifted out the first sack of putrescent meat, watching as the cloudy water below – defrosted ice that might, from the age of the freezer, have contained mammoth DNA – slushed around in the bottom of the box.

"You'd be amazed," I heard Chopper's voice in my head, "what people will do out of fear. Or for love," and I dug into the cold greasy soup and yanked out a bag of half-thawed chicken thighs, shuddering as they wriggled in my hand like slimy, nightmarish creatures attempting to escape my grip.

The thighs, too, went into the bag, as did various sacks of mince, a grim grey pallor replacing their once vibrant red. Within a few minutes, knowing I would definitely need to shower and change before I went anywhere, I was into a rhythm; yanking bags from the box and dropping them into the bag, which was now so weighty it stood, of its own volition, beside me. This freed up my right hand so that I could go at the contents of the freezer double-fisted, so to speak.

And go at it, I did, until, at length, there was nothing but the slopping, slushy water at the bottom of the chest.

I ran my hand through it one last time to make sure I hadn't missed anything, and frowned.

Most of the ice had dissolved but here and there were still small, rapidly-dwindling shards. And then my rubber-gloved fingers hit something bigger than the usual shards.

Something that didn't dissolve at my touch but actually moved away from me.

I put my other hand into the soup and surrounded the ice block in a pincer movement, squeezing it and realising that it still wasn't cracking up as I pulled it from its dingy prison and looked down on the package in my hand.

It shifted a little, catching the light.

And suddenly, the pieces fit together.

FORTY

"Okay," I looked around the table, "are we all clear?"

Next to me, Caz, still sulking at being denied her cocktail brunch, noisily slurped a triple gin and tonic through a straw. "I'll get on to them all and make sure that they're at the funeral. Then I'll get on to him and make sure he'll accept the new terms. And then, perhaps," she said pointedly, "I'll have time for breakfast."

"Ray? Dash?" I asked, and the twins looked at each other and frowned.

"I'm not exactly sure about this, Dan," Ray said. "I mean, the public records are okay, but the other thing... I mean, we don't know where it is, to begin with"

"Ah," I said, "but it's bound to be on the internet, which is – slightly – where you," I turned to Phoenix, "come in. You can help them locate the necessary."

"Listen," Phoenix, clearly over the shock of having been bitten by Balthazar Lowe's watchdog, had resumed his world-weary act and was exuding an air of being here under sufferance, "I'm not entirely sure what you think my skillset is, but Googling is not on the list, dude."

"Phoenix, mate," I said, "your talents aren't in question, but you're not here just to help the boys here locate a needle in a haystack. I've got something more," I glanced at Caz, "challenging for you."

This perked him up, and he was suddenly paying a lot

more attention. "Go on," he said, "I'm listening."

I held up a USB stick and told him what I needed him to do.

"Dude," his eyes bulged, "that's insane. I still don't know who you're facing off against but if this goes wrong…"

"Dude," I smiled calmly (I hoped) at him, "this won't go wrong. You're a genius. You told me so yourself."

"But I don't see *how* you're going to get it to work. The executable has to be kicked off *inside* the network and, last I checked, you were having trouble getting in."

"Don't worry about that," I said, "I – along with Caz – will get us inside the network. All I need from you is the code on here."

He considered this for a moment. "Not easy," he finally admitted, "but I think I can hide it in the basic docs so it doesn't take up any obvious space. It's gonna take some time, mind…"

I checked my watch. "You've got a little over twenty hours."

Phoenix laughed. "I won't need much more than two."

"Good," I nodded, happily crossing off another item on my mental 'to do' list. "Carlton, you good with your job?"

"She'll be there," he said, smiling. "But are you sure about this?"

I nodded. "Absolutely. I know who murdered Billy Bryant, Jimmy Carter and Alex Chatham. So long as you boys," I nodded here at the twins, "do your part, I'll be able to prove it."

"So what you got on your list?" Phoenix asked, already pulling his laptop out of his rucksack and setting it up.

"Me?" I glanced at Caz. "I've got to call a certain police officer, apologise for dropping him in the shit and ask for his help tomorrow to make sure we can nab a murderer. Easy-peasy. Right," I stood, pushing my chair back from the table, "let's get to work. Check in here at closing time."

The assembly, with the exception of Phoenix, who was already tapping furiously on his keyboard, stood and began to disperse.

"And folks," I called, and Caz, Carlton, Ray and Dash looked back at me, "thanks. And good luck."

FORTY-ONE

"He looks almost alive, doesn't he?" Eve Stewart leaned over the coffin, staring at the prone figure of Jimmy Carter as though she expected him, at any moment, to open his eyes and snarl threateningly.

"You on crack, Eve?" Lilly Ho's diminutive figure was swathed head to toe in black taffeta. Her hat – resembling a Victorian stovepipe that had been covered in tiny black silk roses, then sat on, hard, by an elephant – had a gauzy black veil hanging down in front of her face. Her every move left clouds of Joy by Patou into her wake and she had the air of someone who had looked up, 'What to wear to a funeral of someone you loathed,' and got the ensemble spot on.

Eve – the picture of home countries propriety in a belted black mac, well-pressed black trousers and black court shoes, the only colour being a dark red scarf tied rakishly around her neck – turned, a simulacrum of 'Aghast' on her face, and, seeing the other woman, stiffened perceptibly.

"Lilly," she said coldly.

"Jimmy Carter," Lilly announced, adjusting the midnight black Hermes clutch purse under her arm and lifting her veil, the better to see the figure in the box, "looked half dead when he was alive. He looks worse than shit now. Who did his make-up? Abu Hamza?"

"Lilly!" This time, Eve's tone was one of genuine shock. "The man's dead."

"He took his time," Lilly snapped back. "And he was a nasty violent piece of shit to the end. Which, you know, Eve, I can forgive. But he was cheap too, and that, I can never forgive. I mean look at that fucking barnet. Looks like he cut it blindfold."

"I did that fucking cut!" Mo Halliwell, who had arrived, unnoticed, behind the two women, thundered, and all eyes turned. "You got a word to say about that cut, you take it outside."

"Jesus," Lilly rolled her eyes, "its Scarface's mother. Alright, Maureen. You still running that ghastly barbershop?" She glanced at me and dropped her voice. "You do know that they're all just here for one thing," she said.

"To see if whoever has the stones turns up?" I suggested.

Lilly inclined her head, "That and for a good old bellow of *Jerusalem.* They love a sing-song, this lot."

Mo – unaccompanied, I noted, by the put-upon Rene – shoved the two women out of the way, and leaned over the coffin, tears welling up in her eyes.

"G'night, Jimmy," she murmured, choking on his name and reaching a hand out to stroke the corpse's cheek. "And don't you worry, we'll get the fucker what did this to you."

"Oh, please," Lilly muttered as Eve gasped, shocked, seemingly, by the profanity.

"You," Mo whipped up, her eyes flaring and, rather than turning on either of the women she turned on me, "and me," she said, punctuating each word with a jabbed finger, "is gonna have words after this. I don't know what you and that stuck-up bitch said to Rene, but I'm gonna fucking deal with both of you after this is done." Then her eyes suddenly widened, her mouth stopped working and her face went, first grey, then a colour I can really only describe as puce, as she focussed over my shoulder.

"Well, well, well," Caz, coming up behind me, muttered in my ear, "now *that's* an interesting development."

Through the door of the crematorium had walked a

visibly-shrunken Charlie Chatham, his eyes sunk in his head, his walk shuffling. Supporting him, tall and straight, was Rene Halliwell, her slim form wearing a pair of black skinny jeans; a long black silk shirt, hanging almost to her knees; and a pair of shiny black heels, the toes of which were open, exposing her nails painted glaring scarlet.

Rene, like Lilly, had opted for a hat, though this one was a wide brimmed black affair that spoke less of gipsy gloom and more of matador mourning.

She looked a million dollars. Chisel Chatham, next to her, looked half dead.

"The fuck is going on here?" Mo hissed, storming across the crematorium.

"There ought to be popcorn," Lilly murmured, in tones of pure delight. "If you'd warned me," she said, nudging me, "I'd have done a finger buffet."

I looked around the church. Apart from the deceased; the vicar, who was busy on his iPhone while he waited for the full audience to turn up; Caz; Lilly; Eve and the trio currently engaged in a sotto voce argument in the doorway, not one other person had turned up for the funeral.

And then, as I watched, Chopper Falzone, accompanied by the shade-wearing Cyril, entered the crematorium, unnoticed by the others, who were all, by now, either engaged in an argument or eagerly observing said argument.

Chopper nodded politely to me and gestured at Cyril, who removed the shades and stepped to one side, ushering Chopper into the rear pew and following him in with the air of a secret service agent who's been told the floral tributes are full of ninjas.

Mo's body language, meanwhile, was – unsurprisingly – aggression incarnate, while Rene, for once, seemed to be fronting her nicely; smiling condescendingly at the older woman, refusing to be drawn into a verbal argument and simply waiting until her mother-in-law stopped talking before opening her mouth.

Most times, she got a few words out before Mo went off

again and Rene would simply smile beatifically, adopting the air of the Mona Lisa in stretch jeans, and accept the onslaught.

Charlie Chatham looked as though he'd been fed a selection of pharmaceuticals, his awareness of the unfolding argument clear but his engagement, his ability to calm either the close-to-raving Mo, or to defend the woman by his side, limited.

Mo's voice rose, suddenly, "Al's gonna cut your fucking face off with a Stanley blade, you dappy tart."

Lilly chuckled. "Always classy, Mo."

"I think," I said, moving towards the trio, Caz by my side, "we might want to shut this down before it gets out of hand."

But there was no need to shut it down because as we approached the trio Rene leaned forward, her eyes glittering fiercely; put her lips close to Mo's ears, but not so close as to completely obscure the words she uttered; and, with one sentence, shut Mo Halliwell down.

"You say one fucking word, Mo, and I'm gonna tell Al all about Jimmy and what you did with him."

Mo's face blazed furiously, her jaw working desperately as though a torrent of words was still being generated, but something – some sense of self-preservation, some knowledge of the danger inherent in saying any more – was muting the volume.

"Slag!" she spat, her face freezing as, behind Rene and Charlie, a couple of uniformed Bobbies appeared, one of them handcuffed to an arm of Ali.

"Lord," Caz gasped, "I know she's feisty, but she's hardly Hannibal Lecter."

Mo turned, like a vampire who'd just spotted a couple of garlic salesmen framing a purveyor of fine crucifixes, and fled to the far side of the room, shoving herself into a pew so fast that it rocked.

This caused the vicar to look up from his Candy Crush, and lose a level. I clearly saw his lips mouth a word I never expected to see a vicar mouth at a funeral, before I turned back to a clearly exhausted Ali.

"How are you doing?" I asked.

She smiled. "Have we met? Only I ain't seen you in so long…"

I reached out to hug her and the two coppers bristled, but I went for it anyways. "I've been busy," I whispered to her, "but I think I've got us to a good place."

I pulled away, and there were tears in her eyes and a sad smile on her lips. "Thanks for sorting Carlton," she said. "Silly bugger would have insisted he'd done it to cover me."

"There's a lot of it about," I said pointedly, as, behind Ali, Nick arrived, another uniform with him.

"Yeah, well," Ali sniffed, "I may not have killed him, but I wish I'd killed him. Years ago. I might have had a life if I had."

"Or done life," I said.

"Your Majesty," Ali nodded, offering a fond smile to Caz. "You been keeping an eye on this one?"

"Always," Caz smiled back. "I'm doing my best, but I can't keep his pub going like some people."

"Well," Ali smiled sardonically, "it's genetic, innit. Some of us is just born to serve."

I wandered over to Nick. "No Reid?" I asked, referring to Nick's superior, who was what some people might have described as an unreconstructed old-school copper. I preferred the phrase pig, in every sense of the word, though Nick continued to insist that – despite being a sexist, homophobic, aggressive twat – Reid was actually not all bad.

"He's got piles," my beautiful man said, his green eyes flashing as the light through the high up stained-glass windows caught them, a failed attempt to suppress the smile on his lips causing the dimples on his cheeks to flare briefly. "Excruciating, apparently."

I plastered what I hoped was a look of grave concern on my mug. "Oh dear," I sighed. "Please send my regrets. To the piles."

Nick shook his head. "You'll go to hell for that, you know."

"Oh, mate," I said, "if that's the worst thing I've ever done then I'll argue that judgement."

"How are we doing?" Nick jerked his chin at the assembled – Mo on one side of the crematorium, pressed up against the wall and staring fixedly at the box on the dais at the top; Chisel and Rene in the third row on the opposite side of the aisle; Lilly Ho and Eve Stewart in the row behind them, but at opposite ends of the bench, as though needing to be close, but dreading having to communicate with each other.

"We're nearly all here, I think. Listen, is that," I nodded at the cuff on Ali's wrist and at the two stern-faced coppers, "strictly necessary."

Nick frowned. "Honestly? I don't think so. But rules is rules and if DI Reid can't make it here in person, he's going to make sure that he's here in spirit," and he clapped me on the shoulder and nodded at Ali. "I'll get Mrs Carter settled," he said, "and hopefully we can sort this mess out soon enough and get her back to normality." He nodded at Ali's escort and they, Caz alongside, wandered up the aisle to the front pew.

The other copper seated himself quietly and firmly in the back row, nearest the door, and the piped music continued to play – someone using a pipe organ to do to *Hymns Ancient and Modern* what Jack the Ripper had done to his victims; because nothing says, 'Anglican funeral for someone nobody liked,' like a bunch of eviscerated devotionals performed in a perfunctory manner by someone who'd once dreamt of being the next Billy Joel.

And just as I was pondering on strange approaches to religious beliefs, the light was blotted by the gargantuan figure of Green. Tim Boyle's manservant, wheezing slightly, like a mammoth with incipient emphysema, filled the doorway, scanned every inch of the space and then stepped deferentially to one side to allow his master – all Saville Row tailoring and creepy sobriety – to enter the room.

"Danny." Tiny Tim approached me, clasping my right hand in both of his and giving me such a look of bottomless sorrow that I had to remind myself that I wasn't even remotely related to the deceased.

"Thank you for letting me know this was happening today. A chance to say a final farewell to a man who, whilst he wasn't always an easy man, was still a good friend of mine. In the old days."

The last sentence, clearly designed to make clear that Boyle was nothing like the dead man now, wasn't lost on me.

"Well," I said, apropos of laughing in his face, "I'm sure he'd appreciate your coming to say farewell to him."

Tim nodded. "Indeed," he intoned, his eyes scanning the space now to see who was present. At length, he jerked his head, indicating to Green that he had decided where to sit and the wraith-like figure and his giant one-man protection unit, processed slowly up the aisle to sit just behind Mo Halliwell, who turned, scowled at them both and refocussed on the coffin, until, a moment later, realising who the newcomer was, squawked, "Fuck me, it's Tiny Tim," and turned around to offer her hand to him.

Tim shrunk back momentarily and was finally forced to shake the proffered hand, murmuring some meaningless words and gaining, for his efforts, a whispered rant from Mo (including gestures towards Chisel and Rene that suggested Mo was describing plans she'd been formulating since taking her seat).

Boyle blanched, nodded and swooped into his pocket, extracting a mini bible, which he opened and began, pointedly, to focus on.

Carlton was almost last to arrive, coming into the space with a degree of timidity which was offset by the tall, confident stride of Tara, who stood alongside him.

He was wearing a dark pinstripe suit in a style which I had previously heard described as 'Defendant chic,' whilst Tara had plumped for a floor-length woollen coat; high-soled Doc Martens; her hair dyed, today, a deep plum and combed sleek and straight; and a pair of heavy horn-rimmed glasses. She looked like Doctor Zhivago meets Clark Kent via Tank Girl, and I hugged her, before turning to Carlton

"So," I said, nodding at Tara, "you two are hitting it off."

"Jesus," Tara rolled her eyes as Carlton blushed. "We're friends. Why does everyone your age have to imagine that any two people who are hanging out together are romantically attached?"

"Two things," I smiled back, through gritted teeth. "One, I'm thirty-five. And two, because everyone likes a happy ending."

"What's wrong with happy middles?" Tara asked, then nodded to the top of the room. "I assume that's your mum, Carlton."

Carlton had already spotted Ali and took Tara by the hand. "Come and meet her," he said and Tara hesitated, looking at me for a moment.

"She'll like you," I said, thinking, as they went up the aisle and Carlton embraced Ali – who had shot to her feet, yanking the two coppers with her – that I wasn't, perhaps, the only one around who wanted happy endings.

Dash ambled into the church, his brother a step or two behind, both of them wearing tight-fitting black t-shirts and jeans, making it even harder to tell them apart.

"Not in the property," Dash said, cryptically.

My face fell. "The other place?"

Ray smiled, and I beamed back. "Get in," I muttered, then remembered where I was.

"Okay," I said, clearing my throat, "I suppose it's time to get started.

FORTY-TWO

"Good afternoon," I began, the microphone causing a shriek of feedback that led the vicar to jerk his head again and leap to his feet.

"No, it's alright Reverend, you're not up yet. I'll give you a shout."

He slumped back into his seat, as Lilly Ho snorted, "Love, it's hardly Wembley Stadium. The mike's a bit overkill."

She was right; it was. And so was the fact that I was standing atop the dais like I was about to perform a panegyric over the corpse. So I switched the microphone back off and descended the steps.

"I thought," I said, "as we're all gathered here, that it would be a good time to talk about some of the things that have been happening ever since a corpse was discovered behind a false wall in the cellar of the pub I run."

My words generated a flicker of interest in the room: eyes shifting to look at other eyes; frowns becoming scowls; even the vicar glanced up from his phone, turning around in his seat and making eye contact with both the copper at the back and the bulky figure of Cyril, as if to say, 'Did one of you bastards shove a stiff behind this poor man's stud partition?'

"Things like what?" Lilly Ho – still loving the opportunity to stir shit up – shouted out.

"Two murders, for a start," I said, thanking her silently for the call-and-response. "Three, if you count the fact that the body behind the wall had a bullet in his head as well."

"I hope you're not including him as a murder," Lilly answered, nodding at Jimmy's coffin. "Cos whoever topped that scumbag was doing a social service."

"Why don't you shut your yappy mouth?" Mo Halliwell suddenly snarled from across the room.

Lilly Ho stood to her feet, stared pointedly across the room, removed, from her clutch purse, a Chanel lipstick and applied it smoothly and evenly, all the while staring daggers at Mo Halliwell. Recapping and dropping the lipstick into her bag, she responded, "I'll shut my yappy mouth when you shut your flabby thighs," before sitting down and gesturing, as though she were the dowager empress and I Marco Polo, for me to continue my dissertation.

I glanced nervously at Mo, half expecting her to produce a shiv from her boot and lunge at Lilly, but instead the older woman merely sat, her mouth continuing to move in impotent fury as her eyes blazed at me.

'This,' she seemed to be reminding me, 'is all your fault. And I never forget a slight.'

"Billy Bryant," I continued, "was, as I was saying, the first to be murdered. He was killed shortly after he and his gang – the Old Kent Road Massive – had carried out an audacious robbery in Hatton Garden.

"Audacious means cheeky," Caz exclaimed loudly, and several of the mourners sighed in relief at the translation.

"The gang had used a con artist known as Gary the Ghost to persuade a BT engineer to turn off the alarm systems at a certain diamond merchants. That done, they'd made off with several million in diamonds, none of which were ever seen again."

"This is all, of course, allegedly," Tiny Tim piped up in his best Uriah Heep impersonation. "I mean, nobody who might have been involved in the *Massive* has ever confessed any involvement to the police and nobody here is guilty of any such crime."

He stared pointedly at the back of Nick's head, and back at me.

I sighed. "Okay," I said, "whatever you say. But what is a cold, hard fact is that some time shortly after that robbery, Billy Bryant arrived at The Marquess of Queensbury public house in Southwark.

"The pub was in the middle of a refurb and had been closed to the public, but Bryant had – it's been suggested – acquired the keys to the place from Jimmy Carter, and had intended – we're lead to believe – to stash the takings of that robbery somewhere safe."

"Only someone killed him and made off with the stones," Lilly Ho piped up and Charlie Chisel, finally surfacing from his narcotic fug, turned in his seat to cast an accusatory eye across the assembled.

"Which of you did it?" he demanded plaintively. "And why Alex?"

"Oh, Charlie," Eve Stewart leaned forward and pressed a hand on Chisel's shoulder.

"Why?" Chisel demanded of the crowd, as he fully surfaced, his face twisting furiously.

He stood, genuine fury in his eyes, and turned on the gang assembled there for Jimmy's funeral. "Why? Why did you kill him?"

"Why, isn't entirely easy," I said, "but you'll understand. Soon."

"Understand?" He shook his head, as though I'd said a word he'd never heard before and dropped back into his seat.

"So, Billy's dead – the gang assume he's done a runner with all the proceeds of the robbery, a search is conducted but no sign of Billy can be found and so life, eventually, returns to normal.

"Jimmy himself ends up vanishing, and he only returns when Billy's body turns up and he surmises that, if Billy didn't take the stones, then whoever killed him must have."

"Genius," Lilly snarled.

"Jimmy was a good man," Mo shouted back, at which Rene threw back her head and laughed aloud.

"Mo, love," her daughter-in-law cackled, "you need help."

"Don't fucking speak to me you tart," Mo shot back.

"Look," Rene – despite instructions otherwise – responded, "I get that you've spent your life stuck with these bastards, but you got to stop making excuses for them. Jimmy was a lowlife, your son is a scumbag, his dad was a fucking mentalist, Tiny and his fuckin' gargantuan boyfriend there," she gestured at the duo, "are – despite the nice bit of schmutter – still fucking lowlife gangsters."

"And what about your boyfriend?" Mo shouted back. "You think he's a fucking saint?"

"No." Rene was on her feet now. "No, Mo. I don't. I know exactly what Charlie is, and what he was, and I'm not making any fucking excuses for him. You, on the other hand could have Adolf Hitler for dinner and still say he was always nice to his mum. You got to stop making excuses for them; they're all bastards. And you got to stop sleeping with the fuckers 'n' all. You were old enough to be Jimmy's mum."

There was an audible gasp from the entire congregation.

"Fuck you!" Mo shrieked.

"If only you'd had kids," Lilly sniggered at Rene, "he," she nodded at the coffin, "would have been *a grandmotherfucker.*"

Mo inhaled, as though sucking in fuel for her fury and stood to her feet.

I glanced at Caz, who had already dived into her handbag and extracted a hip flask. Silently toasting me, she slugged from it, offered it to me and, when I gently shook my head, shrugged, recapped it, dropped it back into her purse and gestured for me to proceed.

"Fascinating," she mouthed, her eyes glistening encouragingly. Or drunkenly; it was hard to tell. How many shots had she had already? And how many hip flasks were in the bag?

I coughed, but the catfight was, by now, in full swing.

"Fuck you, Lilly," Mo snarled. "Just cos you're a dried up old lychee."

"Have you *got* a fucking mirror?" Lilly snapped back, laughing openly at Mo.

"I've got sex appeal," Mo announced, seemingly forgetting that the last man she had exercised said appeal on was currently lying stiff and cold in an oak-effect box at the top of the room.

"What you've got, *Maureen*, is a pathological need to mother nasty bastards and a delusionary streak wider than your arse."

I sighed, grabbed the mike, switched it on and, before Mo could respond, said loudly and clearly into it: "Alex was killed because he was driving Billy Bryant's car."

That shut them up.

"And Jimmy was killed because he'd found out who killed Billy Bryant."

"Well after fucking Mo, it was probably a blessed relief," Rene shot back, clearly having been encouraged by Lilly's digs.

"Forget Al," Mo barked back, "I'll do you myself with a fucking cleaver. Just watch your back, Rene."

"Ladies, ladies," Tim sang in the voice I imagined he used when trying to persuade, say, Quakers, to chill the fuck out, "there's surely no need for so much anger."

As one, the trio turned on him. "Fuck off, Gandhi," Mo snarled, as Lilly cackled and Rene shot him her filthiest look.

"You don't get to talk anger, your holiness, when everyone and her dog knows you had that thing," she nodded at Green, "shove poor Roxanne in the Serpentine while you set yourself up with a lovely little alibi."

At this, Nick turned slowly in his seat and fixed, in turn, Green and then Tiny Tim – who, now, had gone a shade that I might have called frog-like but which I felt sure Caz, who was uncapping the hip flask once more, would have called crème de menthe – with a steely glare.

"Look," I said, "Jimmy came back as soon as he heard the news of Billy's discovery and tried putting either the charm or the frighteners on anyone and everyone he could find who had been associated with the OKRM."

"Billy didn't have the diamonds, cos someone had parked a couple of slugs in him."

"Slugs?" Caz mouthed, her face a mask of almost cartoon horror. She paused in the act of recapping the hip flask, uncapped it again, swigged deeply and shook her head in approbation at me.

"Yes," Chopper suddenly announced, "we've got it. What you haven't said is – which of these fucking loonies did Billy the Brick, and who's got the stones now."

At this they all turned to stare at him and it was Lilly Ho who recognised him first. "Jesus Christ," she choked. "Chopper Falzone. I heard you were dead."

"Not lately," Chopper shot back, pointing at me. "So who's got the fucking rocks, Danny?"

"I'm getting there," I answered. "But first we've got to go back to Jimmy. He returns, looking for the one who'd got rich in the intervening years, only to discover that most of you had done well. Some of you," I nodded at Charlie and Lilly, "from business. Some of you," I said, gesturing at Tim, "from luck."

"Praise Jesus," Tim crowed, throwing his arms in the air and receiving, for his troubles, another turn-around-and-glare from Nick.

"The only people who hadn't done well," I expanded, "were Al Halliwell and his women," I nodded at Mo and Rene, "who'd had a number of failed business ventures; and Eve Stewart, who was living in rented accommodation and selling off her belongings."

"Jimmy had been staying with Mo, and Mo had provided a nice haircut and highlights and was happily looking after him when he suddenly announced he'd been asked to move in with someone else and went off the radar.

"But the reason this 'someone else' welcomed him back was because they wanted him around. They wanted to keep an eye on him.

"Jimmy was looking for Billy's killer and, I believe, when he left you, Mo, he moved in with the person who killed Billy. The same person who later went on to kill Alex Chatham."

"Get. The fuck. On with it," Chopper simmered.

I gestured at the coffin. "When Jimmy was found, he had a blueish tinge about him."

"No shit," Ali said. "He'd been dead a day. Blue was kind, compared to how he could have looked."

I nodded. "Agreed. But death – whether by drowning or not – doesn't normally turn your hair blue."

"Turn your hair blue?" Mo Halliwell frowned, the phrase not making sense, but Rene suddenly sat up straight.

"I noticed it straight away," I said. "His hair had a blue-green tinge and it took me a while to realise why. Because Jimmy was drowned not, as we'd all assumed, in the Thames but in chlorinated water.

"Chlorine will have a chemical reaction with some hair, particularly if that hair has already been treated with other chemicals. In that case, chlorine – the chlorine that you get in a swimming pool – can turn the hair bluey-green."

"Cheap bleach," Rene said in an accusatory tone. Her glance at Mo might as well have been accompanied by the words 'porridge for mortar,' so deep was her professional loathing of the other woman's approach to colour and styling.

"It was Jimmy," Mo protested. "I didn't know he was gonna get fucking drowned."

"I'm guessing," I said, addressing Eve Stewart, "that he moved into the house you're renting and, at some point, followed you – or was taken by you – to the other house; your beautiful house with eight bedrooms, seven en suites, a heated indoor swimming pool and a four-car garage, and you had to act fast.

"And there, you brained him and shoved him into the pool."

There was a silence and all eyes turned to Eve who shot to her feet, a look of fury on her face.

"Bullshit!" she cried. "I had nothing to do with any of this"

I shook my head. "I'll be honest," I said, "I'm not sure whether he would ever have worked it out, but he drowned in your pool because you couldn't risk him figuring out that you'd killed Billy."

"You're wrong." She shook her head, moving along the pew towards the aisle. But her route was blocked by Lilly Ho, who stood and pushed Eve back onto her seat.

"Let him finish," Lilly growled.

"This wasn't about the diamonds," I said. "Well, not at first. This was about a woman who got horribly scarred for trying to walk away from one of the Old Kent Road Massive. Several of you told me that story – how the women were kept in line, made into not much more than property.

"You were kept in place," I said to Eve, "by bullying and violence, and you expected that to be your life. And then you met Frank Stewart. You and Billy weren't married, so you should have been young, free and single, but you knew you weren't; you knew you were Billy Bryant's property and always would be.

"But then Frank. Nice, well-to-do, upwardly-mobile Frank, proposed."

"Bull. Shit." she spat, her eyes blazing furiously.

"You told me that your son had to sell his car to pay his college fees. That car was the Mondial you'd kept ever since Billy vanished.

Now she laughed. "Why the hell would I have kept some manky old car for two decades? And even if I had, why would I give it to Frank's child?"

"I'll admit," I said, "I don't entirely know. Maybe because you were afraid that if any of the rest of the gang saw you selling off Billy's motor, they'd ask questions you didn't want to answer.

"Either way, eventually your son discovered it and you made out it was a gift you'd been keeping for him.

"So, instead of getting rid of the car, you gave it to him. Then Frank died, the money evaporated. and within a year or so, your son had to sell the car to pay his college fees.

"The records are public, Eve. You married Frank Stewart three months after Billy went missing. A bit odd for one of a group of women who lived in fear of what their men would do to them if it was even suspected that they were cheating.

"But you didn't need to worry about Billy hurting you for marrying Frank Stewart, because you knew he wasn't coming back."

"So *she* took the stones?" Chopper called from the back.

I shook my head. "Like I said – this was never about the stones."

"Well it fucking was for me," he growled.

I ignored Chopper and pressed on: "Eve and Frank had a little boy – Eric – who was born three months after their marriage. Which means that Eve was already at least two months pregnant when she shot Billy."

"Wait," Tim shook his head, "a two-month pregnant woman shot a big burly man and bricked his body up behind a wall? Seriously? I mean look at her – she wouldn't know one end of a brick from the other."

"Billy the Brick got his name," I said, "from the job he did for his girlfriend's father. That girlfriend was Eve. Eve grew up around builders and building sites. It was her father's company who was doing the refurb at The Marq, which was how Billy got the key. Not from Jimmy, as had been supposed. And as someone once said to me," I added, watching as Eve shook her head in denial, "you'd be amazed what people are capable of, for love. Or terror."

"Jesus," Eve shook her head. "This is ludicrous. I'm getting out of here," she said, but she didn't stand and nobody in the room seemed to agree with her opinion.

"I'm willing to bet that you didn't even know about the

robbery."

"Okay then, smartarse," Eve shouted, "go ahead – tell us all why I would have killed Jimmy and Alex."

"Jimmy, because he figured out that you had a reason, apart from the stones, for wanting Billy out of the way. And once he figured that out, you knew he had to go.

"And Alex, because you knew that when you killed Billy there were no diamonds on him. Then, once everyone started quacking about how Billy had been the last one with the stones, you figured that meant that he'd already stashed them, and you assumed he'd stashed them in the one place they'd be safe and close to him."

"The car," Charlie Chatham said quietly. "The fucking car."

I nodded. "Billy's pride and joy was the car. He was – how was it described? – a real petrolhead. Alex was murdered after he'd been persuaded to drive to a deserted plumber's yard by someone he knew and trusted.

"You took him there, Eve, because you wanted to search that car. And once there, you shot him and tore the car apart."

"So *now* she has the stones?" Chopper called, a note of hope in his voice.

"I don't think so," I said, shaking my head. "I think, Eve, if you'd found those stones, you'd have gone as far away as fast as you could.

"No," I shook my head, "I think that, once you'd deconstructed the car and found there were no stones in it, you realised that the state of it would raise difficult questions, so you torched it to hide the search. But the police," I gestured at Nick, "have had forensics check and they can see that the inner door panels, the dashboard and even the seat covers had all been slashed, ripped and torn away before the fire started.

"You murdered Alex so you could search the car, and you burned what was left so the search wouldn't be discovered."

Rene Halliwell turned towards Eve, who was sitting silently in her seat. "Is this all true? Did you really do this?"

"You've got nothing on me," Eve Stewart shouted at me, ignoring Rene.

I shook my head in sorrow. "I might not have anything on you, Eve, but Jimmy never left home without his chain – the gold one with an ankh on it. And that chain hasn't been seen since he died."

"So. Fucking. What?" Eve demanded, her eyes blazing at me.

"So he might have lost it in the Thames when his body was dumped there. Or he might have lost it in your pool when you were using – what? – The pool cleaning net? A discarded curtain pole? To hold him under the water, in which case it'll be in the filter of the pool."

I knew this was not the case, because I had had Ray and Dash break into the empty house and check the pool, filter and all.

"But I'm willing to bet," I finished, knowing it was a rock-solid bet, "that it's in the boot of your car – the one that got all muddy when you drove Jimmy's body from your house to the river, where you could dump his body."

"There's nothing in my car," Eve said, a flicker of uncertainty crossing her face.

"Well," I said, knowing it was there, "the police will see. And then they'll test the mud spatters on your car against mud from areas where you could access the river relatively unseen, and they'll have enough circumstantial evidence to lock you up while they dig a bit deeper into dates of birth and marriage and so on."

"So wait," Chopper demanded, leaping to his feet in outrage, "there's still no sign of these fucking diamonds?"

"So they all died for nothing?" Lilly asked, turning towards Eve, a look of total horror on her face."

And that was when Eve snapped. "Nothing?" she spat. "Nothing?" She laughed bitterly. "They didn't die for nothing; they died because they *were* nothing. Billy was a vicious, greedy psychotic fuck, who terrorised me. So I did what I had to do. And you're right," she said, nodding at me, "I used to be a real Daddy's girl. I learned to lay bricks and make a wall as well as anyone on my old man's teams, so dragging the fucker into the alcove and bricking him up was a piece of piss.

"If Frank hadn't come along, I'd have been stuck with him forever and ended up like poor fucking Rene."

Rene visibly bristled at this but didn't say or do anything, though I noticed that Charlie had surfaced from his slumber and was staring fixedly at Eve.

"He would never have let me go, and he'd never have made me happy, and I didn't want to live my live as terrified and bitter as bloody Ali."

At this, I remembered my friend, the reason I'd been looking into this whole issue, and I glanced at her. Ali had turned her head and was looking at Eve in horror.

But Eve was, by now, on a roll. "*Nothing?* Jimmy Carter was as bad as Billy – a bully and an idiot, who knew only what he wanted. He never even met my son," she acknowledged, "but he turns up this evening, covered in bruises. He'd been in a fight and his head was all over the place. Then suddenly he's got the idea, 'You wouldn't have married that fucker if you didn't know Billy wasn't coming back.'"

She puffed her cheeks out; the adrenaline rush of her confession driving her on with righteous anger.

"I was so frightened. I didn't know what to do, so I told him they were at the house. Told him I'd never spent the diamonds and they were all there. Said I'd take him to them.

"Only you drowned him instead," I prompted and her outrage at the life she'd been given trumped any of her previous attempts to deny involvement.

"I told him the stones were hidden in the filter system," Eve said, "and he actually jumped into the sodding pool fully dressed. Which, of course, made him heavier and between that and the fact that I knew if he got out of that pool alive, I was dead, I had to make sure he didn't get out of the pool alive. So I called him over to me, hunkered down by the pool and whacked him on the head with one of Frank's Rotarian of the Year awards. Stunned him, then used the pool net to hold him under till he stopped moving."

"And Alex?" I asked. "Was he nothing as well?"

"Alex…"she stopped, as though trying to find the words to explain. "Alex was like you said. I've never had much luck with men. I mean, *I try*, but even Frank – even Frank, who I loved with all my heart – turned out not to have been worth the effort. He was a liar and a thief who ruined my life, just like Billy would have, just like Jimmy was threatening to. And I knew those diamonds were in that car. They *had* to be," she said, layers of disbelief at their absence still evident in her tone. "But I wasn't going to share them. I'd been through too much. Way too much," she said, glancing down at the floor momentarily.

And that was when Charlie Chatham moved.

I knew that Eve had a gun. She'd used it twice already. And I'd half expected her to pull it at some point during her explanation.

What I hadn't expected was that Charlie Chatham would not only have a gun, but would have brought it to a funeral. And now, having pulled the gun, he stood and pointed it at her.

"You killed my boy," he announced, somewhat unnecessarily as I slowly moved down the aisle so that I could be closer to the two of them.

"And how many people's boys did you and your lot kill, Charlie?" Eve snapped back. "Boys get killed. Men get killed. They kill each other and women have to stand by and watch it, and wait to see if they and theirs will escape untouched."

"He was all I had," Charlie half sobbed, the sound seeming to come from deep within him and echoing like something collapsing. "All I had."

"And now you know what it feels like," Eve spat back. "I did what you lot have been doing all your lives – all *my* life. I took what I wanted, I did what I needed to do to keep myself safe. I hurt whoever needed hurting. Don't fucking look at me like I'm a fucking monster, Charlie; I learned everything I know from people like you."

Charlie lifted the gun, his hand trembling slightly.

"Charlie," Lilly called, reaching a hand out to him. "Don't do this."

Rene Halliwell put her hand on his shoulder and Charlie, his eyes never leaving Eve's face, simply reached a hand across his shoulder and solidly, firmly, shoved her as hard as he could, sending her sprawling, a look of confused hurt on her face.

Nick and the other copper had moved from the front and back of the crematorium in a pincer movement and were steps away, each focussing intently on Charlie and Eve, while Ali's escort struggled to free himself from his silent and grim-faced prisoner.

A chorus of voices called out, beseeching Charlie to put the gun down, not to be stupid, to let the law handle it, and above it all came Eve's voice.

"Pull the fucking trigger, Charlie. Go on! If you're a man – if one of you stupid selfish bastards is a man – pull the fucking trigger."

I held my hands out to her, heard myself shushing her even as she spoke and realised that Eve and her ilk had been shushed for too long.

"Cos I tell you," she carried on, "I've had enough. I'm done. There's nothing left, and I'm not going back to living in a fucking hovel. I'm done with just surviving, so you might as well pull that fucking trigger!"

Charlie seemed to relax, his shoulders slumped, his breathing slowed and, "he was all I had left," he said, as the gun went off, one of the stained-glass windows shattered and Charlie dropped to the floor screaming in agony, his whole body spasming desperately.

Tara stood ten feet away, the small black box of the taser still held in her hand.

Eve sighed, her shoulder slumping. "*Typical*," she muttered. "Fucking useless, the lot of them."

"Right," Chopper grabbed my shoulder as the police descended on Eve and Charlie, "where are them fucking rocks?"

"Gone," I said simply, staring him in the face and realising that any trace of geniality had evaporated as his greed and fury at being thwarted fought with each other. "I suspect they went not long after the original robbery."

"Gone?" This did not compute, and he looked at me in confusion.

"Gary the Ghost," I said simply. "The con man you could find no trace of. The one who got the alarms turned off. I suspect he managed to nab them – probably told Billy he'd meet him at The Marq and while Billy was waiting, Eve turned up, and the story ended like this."

"So this," Chopper gestured at the chaos unfolding around us as Mo sobbed, clutching her chest; Tiny Tim and Mr Green were interviewed by one of the uniforms; Lilly and Rene huddled together, Rene sobbing onto Lilly's shoulder; and Charlie was dragged to his feet; whilst Eve, seemingly in shock, now that all of her secrets had been disgorged, was handcuffed and lead away, "was never about the diamonds? The money?"

"No," I shook my head, my eyes straying to where Ali, Carlton and Tara were together; Carlton sobbing as he hugged his mother and Ali kissing him on the top of his head, before reaching a hand out towards Tara who put her arms around the two of them and hugged.

"It was about something bigger than money, Mr F. It was about freedom. About happy endings. But it all went wrong. Maybe it went wrong because endings are never happy. Maybe Eve should have just asked for a happy middle."

Caz came up beside me and squeezed my shoulder.

"Yeah, well," Chopper nodded at Cyril, who came up behind him, "much as I love a bit of John Boy Walton, I got business elsewhere. Nice job, kid," Chopper patted my shoulder like a feudal lord praising his dog, nodded again at Cyril and the two of them left the crematorium.

We waited until they had left, and then I turned to Caz.

"Right," she said, "are you ready for act two?"

"Ready as I'll ever be," I said, and she kissed me on the cheek.

FORTY-THREE

"Are you sure about this?" Priscilla frowned at us, her lips pursed disapprovingly. "It seems rather flighty."

"Flighty?" Caz, dressed now in a Tiffany-blue Chanel skirt and jacket combo with an ivory silk blouse and pale-blue patent court shoes, reached a gloved hand out to Prissy and wiggled the fingers in a demanding style. "Coming from the woman whose stupid partying ways and inability to keep her mouth shut got us into this mess, that's rich. Have you brought my grandmother's brooch?"

I slipped on a pair of surgical gloves, dived into my bag and began setting up the disposable mobile that Phoenix had advised me to acquire. Checking that it was charged, the sim card functioning and the unit ready for use, I turned back to the ladies, as Prissy tutted, dug into her handbag and extracted a small black velvet box, which she opened.

The brooch was in the shape of a woman, her arms outstretched, her head lifted so that the throat – all delicately portrayed in almost creamy platinum, a corona of diamonds and rubies above her head, a field of emeralds and sapphires under her feet – stretched, the breasts pressed outwards, and the effect of someone captured as though in ecstasy or flight was complete.

"Gaudy little thing," Prissy said somewhat bitterly, as Caz – looking as though she had been born to wear it – pinned it almost rapturously to her lapel.

"Well if you didn't want it," Caz murmured, without lifting her eyes to Prissy, "you could have let me have it when I asked for it all those years ago."

"Did you ask for it?" Prissy frowned, her face doing a great impersonation of struggling-to-remember. "I really don't recall. Well," she shook her head dismissively, "no matter. It's yours now. I've never been very fond of diamonds."

"Speaking of which," I said, digging my own gloved hand into my rucksack, extracting the Ziploc bag that I'd found in the freezer at The Marq and slapping it onto the table, "you'd best put those into your purse, Caz."

The diamonds – a myriad of sparkling stars – glinted and glistened in the artificial light of the McDonald's where the three of us had met.

The presence, all these years, of the stones in the freezer – dropped there, no doubt, by Billy Bryant on his arrival at The Marq, perhaps as a temporary hiding place while he decided where best to actually secrete them – had been the key that had unlocked, for me, the entire mystery.

Eve had come to the pub and, in my imagination, Billy had let her in and taken her down to the basement where he was already busily preparing a hiding place for the loot.

He'd demanded to know what she was doing there, and she had pulled from her pocket the gun that she'd acquired, probably, from his own collection and shot him there and then.

And once she'd shot him, she'd simply entombed his body behind a fake wall.

The things, as Chopper Falzone had once said to me, *that people will do for love.*

And so Billy the Brick was bricked up in his own personal mausoleum, the freezer had been plugged in, the ice had formed, the meat and bags of petrified veg and frozen Yorkshire puddings had been dumped unceremoniously on top and the world had carried on until, one night, someone tried to torch The Marq, leading to the fire brigade dousing the hallway with water, which had seeped through the building, weakening the fake wall and, shortly afterwards, the freezer, already many years past its normal life expectancy, had finally given up the ghost and begun to defrost.

I'd looked at the bag of scintillating stones in my hand and realised, suddenly, that whoever had killed Billy hadn't done so for the jewels, which meant that I had to look at who else gained by having him out of the way, and why, if not financially.

And Eve – the 'Missus,' who wasn't his wife, the girlfriend, who was more like his property, was the most obvious first option.

Once I looked at Eve, and especially after I remembered noticing how discoloured Jimmy's dye job had been, everything else fell into place and I was left with a murderer and the bag of diamonds.

And I realised at once that Chopper and his ilk would never rest until they had found either the stones or the people who had taken them.

But I had a use for them. I had someone who was blackmailing my best friend and now me, and sitting in my hands was the means to pay him off.

"Gloves," I handed a pair to Prissy, who raised an eyebrow.

"How come you two have white cotton and I have yellow rubber?" she asked, a trace of a whine in her tone.

"Because we got to choose," Caz responded smartly, slipping the bag of jewels into her bag. "And I thought it would be a novel sensation for you."

"You know what to do?" I asked Prissy again; worried that she might mess up even the simplicity of this plan. In return, I got a look that suggested she was well aware I considered her a moronic aristo with less sense than a watermelon.

"I'll see you outside his office in an hour," she said, as Caz and I pushed ourselves off our plastic benches and, nodding sombrely to Prissy, made our way out of the restaurant, along Baker Street and turned off, heading for the square where Balthazar Lowe's office was located.

We got there in minutes. Caz, her hands still entombed in their white cotton gloves, pressed the doorbell and we reintroduced ourselves to the still sepulchral Miss Morgan, her tombstone teeth remaining, this time, tucked deeply inside her mouth, as though she'd been advised of the purpose behind our visit and found it *non-U* to grin at blackmail victims as they arrived to settle up.

Lowe was in his office – which we were shown directly up to – along with a small wizened old man who had the biggest, most pointy ears I had ever seen.

Basically, if Yoda had been Indian, and prone to wearing the most exquisite tailoring on the planet, he would have been Lowe's associate.

I kept my hands in my pockets and my jaw set firmly, as though simmering with rage. Which I sort of was, to an extent.

"Lady Caroline," Lowe smiled the smile of a victor, not bothering to extend a hand towards either of us but merely indicating the two seats on the opposite side of his desk and lowering his own bulk into a carved, high-backed chair opposite. "How lovely to see you again. This," he indicated Yoda, "is Mr Chatterjee, who has kindly agreed to assist us with this somewhat unusual transaction."

"Unusual?" Caz tilted her head in mimed confusion.

"Most people," Lowe said, "donate in cash, securities, sometimes a direct bank transfer from another account – though often from an offshore account not in their own name. You'd be amazed how many people do that, thinking that disclosing to me the fact that they have a tax-dodging offshore account is a good – or indeed wise – thing to do."

Caz smiled at him, a smile so devoid of warmth as to be glacial, and unclipped her handbag. "I think, Mr Lowe, that saying 'Good morning' to you would be an unwise and highly unpleasant thing to do. But we're here and we're here because you gave my family, and Mr Bird here, a deadline."

"Ah yes," Lowe turned his eyes on me. "The pretty policeman with the heart of gold and the fake wife. Careers would be ruined, lives destroyed, if it were to get out that he'd deliberately married her for the purposes of getting her into the United Kingdom and cheating the standard immigration processes."

"It's hardly international terrorism," I shot back.

"Doesn't have to be," Lowe smiled coldly back at me. "Just needs to be a big enough scandal, a serious enough breach for you, or people like you, to want to pay me to keep it quiet."

"Yes, well," Caz said, reaching into the handbag, "you gave us a deadline which made it impossible for me or anyone in my family to lay hands on sufficient cash or bonds, but these have been in the family since grandfather brought them back from out East after the war."

She, still wearing her white cotton gloves, laid the diamonds on the desk and sat back. Chatterjee leaned forward, opened the bag, lifted a jeweller's eyepiece from his pocket, inserted it into his eye socket and, choosing a diamond from the pile, eyed the stone.

"Which war?" Lowe asked and Caz frowned, confusion evident on her face.

"Does it matter?" she asked.

"Not really; just making small talk."

"I'd prefer," Caz said freezingly, "if you didn't."

Chatterjee grunted, dropped the stone back into the pile, selected another, holding it up to the light in a pair of tweezers and began, once again, the analysis. Three or four more and Lowe – impatience clear in his voice – demanded, "Well?"

"They're good," Chatterjee said. "Top quality, excellent facets."

"Good," Lowe said, "they'll cover the required donation. Thank you so much." He stood, opening his desk drawer and sweeping, with one hand, the stones into it whilst at the same time extending a hand towards Caz. "It's been a pleasure doing business with you, Lady Caroline. Mr Bird," he nodded at me, allowing his hand – unshaken by Caz – to drop.

"What happens," I said, "with the," I hesitated, as though searching for the right word, "evidence?"

"The evidence?" He paused, frowning, as though nobody had ever asked him that question before, then smiled, the shark glint back in place. "Oh, I destroy it. You have my word on that."

"Insufficient," Caz said flatly.

Lowe's smile flickered. "I beg your pardon."

"Not good enough," she said, to clarify her previous remark. "I want to watch you delete the necessary files. I know you've got them on computer. I want to see you delete everything from your system with my own eyes."

The smile came back, coldly. "I don't think," he said, "you're in any position to want anything, Lady Caroline."

"Really?" Caz dipped into her handbag, and extracted her mobile phone. "Only, I'm the woman who just gave you a fortune in diamonds, and I could easily call the police to ask them to come around here and ask you to explain what they're doing in your desk drawer."

"You wouldn't dare," he said, his eyes narrowing as Caz dialled the first nine on her phone. "If the police come here, all your brother's secrets – all Mr Bird's secrets – will be disclosed."

Chatterjee looked nervous, shoved his jeweller's eyepiece into the inside pocket of his Saville Row and eyed the door. "I really must be off, Balthazar. It's been a pleasure to see you again. Sir," he nodded to me, "Madam," a nod to Caz, and he shuffled out of the room as quickly as his little legs could take him.

"Nine," Caz said flatly, pressing the key on her phone again.

"Okay, alright," Lowe threw his hands in the air, pulled another desk drawer open and extracted an ultra-thin laptop from inside, opening it on the desk and tapping some keys.

"I just need to access my cloud account and find the right files. Ah yes," he paused, sighing deeply, as though disappointed that he was going to have to delete the contents, "here they are."

"Wait," I said, pulling from my trouser pocket a USB stick, "I want them,"

"You want what?" Lowe looked from me to the USB, to Caz, to her phone and his confusion mounted. "What the hell is wrong with you people?"

"I want you to delete the files," I said, "but first, I want the ones relating to Nick Fisher and I copied on here."

"Copied?" He goggled at me. "You want copies?"

"I want copies," I said coldly, holding the stick out to him.

"This isn't someone's holiday photos," he explained to me, as though I were an imbecile.

"I don't trust Nick Fisher," I said, "I've been messed around by men before, and I want some insurance to make sure he stays on side. Insurance which you have already collected for me. So I want those files copied to this USB."

"You're crazed," he said, his eyes still flicking back to Caz's phone.

"Just do it," she growled, and he snatched the USB from me, jammed it into the drive on the side of his laptop and commenced tapping at the keyboard.

A few moments later and having shown us the screen – filled with dozens upon dozens of folders stored in the cloud – as he deleted the two marked 'Bird' and 'Holloway,' he handed me back the USB, shook his head as though still marvelling at how I could be so untrusting as to want the blackmail evidence of a lowlife like him to keep my boyfriend in check and, all pretence at normality or formality gone, watched us leave the office.

As the door closed behind us, I heard the sound of his desk drawer slide open and the delicate click of diamonds as they ran through his fingers.

Back on the street and having been absolutely sure that I

had touched nothing with my un-gloved hands, we met Prissy on the far side of the square, the burner phone in my pocket vibrating slightly.

I removed it from my pocket and glanced at the screen. A text message had arrived. One word: 'INSTALLED.'

I handed the phone and an index card to Prissy, who read the text on the card and pursed her lips. "I'm not saying this," she said, vexedly.

"Neither of us can call," I said, "he knows both our voices."

"But this—"

"Just do it, Prissy," Caz snarled, and the other woman blushed, bit her lip and dialled the number and spoke, her cut-glass diction lending a wholly new slant to the somewhat vernacular script I'd written for her.

"Alright? This Detective Inspector Reid? How's the Chalfonts, mate?"

There was a tussle of noise from the other end, the sound, I imagined, of Reid spluttering, cursing and demanding to know who this was.

"Don't matter who I am," Prissy said, sliding a little further into character as a habitué of some demi-monde she'd doubtless seen once in a Dickens adaptation on the Beeb.

"I heard you're looking for *Gary the Ghost* and them missing diamonds from the Hatton Garden job… That's right… Don't matter how I know you're looking for him, Reid. What matters is I know where you can find him."

More squeaking from the other end of the phone and Prissy, further in character, nodded, picked some lint from her lapel, let him squawk some more, then interrupted him.

"Listen, this geezer's sitting in an office off Baker Street. You check your records, you'll find out he's been going all over the world scamming the rich, though nobody ever complains, cos he's such a good con artist half of 'em don't realise they've even been done.

"Only I know he's in his office, with those – I mean

323

them – stones. And I thought you ought to know he's about to do a runner."

After that, it was simple. Prissy gave him the address, Reid said he'd have a car around shortly and Prissy hung up.

We waited until we heard the sirens before I opened up the text with the word 'INSTALLED' on it, hit respond and entered – per Phoenix's instructions – the word 'EXECUTE,' and, as two police cars pulled up outside the offices of The Children's Protection Fund, the virus that Lowe had installed on his own system when he'd plugged the deliberately-corrupted USB into his laptop went to work, following – as his guard dog once had with me – the trail he'd left back to his cloud account, using the same password he'd entered to access said account and deleting every single piece of blackmail he had on his account.

Caz smiled at me.

"Not a bad job, Mr Bird. Are you going to stick around to see our *biter bit*?"

I considered this for a moment, then shook my head.

"I think," I said, holding up the USB stick, "I'm going to go find a certain green-eyed copper, and play him some home movie footage."

And that is exactly what I did.

THE END

Acknowledgements

Well, here we are again.

Whodathunk?

This one wasn't exactly an easy birth, and but for the love, support, encouragement, bullying, cajoling, and simple zen acceptance of a bunch of people, I might have given up on it.

So let me take a moment to thank, as always, my husband David, for his love and support and understanding. For chauffeuring, for accepting that dinner will be late, for cheering me on when I'm flying, and for geeing me up when I'm despondent.

My family and friends for reminding me that there is a real life out there too.

Lauren Milne Henderson / Julie Vince / Mark Hill for generosity, advice, books, laughs, and something to aspire to. Love you all very much.

Quentin Bates and Barbara Nadel for Icelandic Japes, and Bona Times. There's a gag in here specially for you two.

Paddy Magrane / Grant Nichol / Jo Perry / Charles Kriel and the Fahrenheit Press gang. Writers who make me want to write better stories, who make me laugh, LOL at all my jokes, and kick my arse when it needs kicking. I couldn't ask for better publishing siblings.

Bloggers, bibliophiles and boozers too many to name, but (I hope) you know who you are: You've chatted to me at festivals, featured me on your sites, said kind things about the Danny Birds to date, and made me feel so very welcome to this brilliant club. You are the lifeblood of this whole thing, and I salute you all.

Tara Benson for her boundless positivity and creativity; for smiles and for oysters, and for encouraging me to Dance a Great Dance, and to always remember that happiness is the end goal.

Suzanne Gray Cross, my one-woman West Country Sales team, for support and love and general cheer-leading.

The Karaoke Klan and all at the Scene of the Crime, for making me laugh so hard I thought I'd expire, for encouraging my Bowie delusions, and for making my dreams come true by letting me join the gang. I genuinely LOVE you all, and hope to be telling (drunken) stories and signing with you all for many years to come.

And – as always – Mr Fahrenheit, Chris McVeigh. Thanks for your patience, Chris. Now, there's a line I never thought I'd write.

Like someone once said, there's just not enough love in the world, and I'm truly blessed to be surrounded by so much of it, and if I have missed you out of this list, it's not because you are loved any less, or are any less important; it's simply because my coffee hasn't kicked in yet.

South Africa – London – New York - Montenegro
DF July/17 x

Other books by Derek Farrell

Death Of A Diva (Danny Bird 1)

Death Of A Nobody (Danny Bird 2)

If you enjoyed this book we're sure you'll love these other titles from Fahrenheit Press.

A Mint Condition Corpse by Duncan MacMaster

Hack by Duncan MacMaster

Sparkle Shot by Lina Chern

Jukebox by Saira Viola

All Things Violent by Nikki Dolson

23474519R00199

Printed in Great Britain
by Amazon